Praise for *New York Times* bestselling author

SAMANTHA YOUNG

'This is a really sexy book and I loved the heroine's journey to find herself and grow strong. Highly recommend this one'
—*USA Today*

'Will knock your socks off . . . [an] unforgettable love story'
—RT Book Reviews

'Humour, heartbreak, drama, and passion'
—The Reading Cafe

'Truly enjoyable . . . a really satisfying love story'
—Dear Author

'[Samantha Young's] enchanting couples and delicious romances make her books an autobuy'
—Smexy Books

'Hot, bittersweet, intense . . . sensual, with witty banter, angst, heartbreaking moments, and a love story you cannot help but embrace'
—Caffeinated Book Reviewer

'Filled with heart, passion, intensity, conflict and emotion'
—Literary Cravings

'[Young] is a goddess when it comes to writing hot scenes'
—Once Upon a Twilight

'Ms. Young dives deep into the psyche of what makes a person tick emotionally . . . [The] one thing you can count on from Ms. Young is some of the best steamy sexual chemistry'
—Fiction Vixen

Things We Never Said

SAMANTHA YOUNG

piatkus

PIATKUS

First published in Great Britain in 2019 by Piatkus

1 3 5 7 9 10 8 6 4 2

A CIP catalogue record for this book
is available from the British Library.

ISBN 978-0-349-42385-2

Typeset in Sabon by M Rules
Printed and bound in Great Britain by Clays Ltd, Elcograf S.p.A.

MIX
Paper from
responsible sources
FSC® C104740

Piatkus
An imprint of
Little, Brown Book Group
Carmelite House
50 Victoria Embankment
London EC4Y 0DZ

An Hachette UK Company
www.hachette.co.uk

www.littlebrown.co.uk

PART I

PROLOGUE

Dahlia

There was no way my parents could say I wasn't willing to do just about anything to make money *and* stay in my degree-related industry.

My father was a firefighter, my mother a nurse, and some of their five kids wanted to go to college. Cian and Sorcha McGuire had not been happy when I announced I was applying to art school. Except for Dermot, who jumped from one job to the next like he was afraid of catching herpes from it, and Dillon, the youngest, who had gone to beauty school, I was the third McGuire to go to college. That crap was expensive enough, my parents said. Why couldn't I choose something practical like Davina, who was studying business, or Darragh, who had studied journalism?

Yeah, so practical.

Okay, they were way more practical than art college but creating beautiful things was a huge part of who I was.

But even with a scholarship and financial aid, school was expensive, which meant I had to work several jobs throughout the year to help pay for it. I lived at home with my parents, which lowered costs, but it also made it harder to meet friends, so I tried to get jobs in the arts industry.

However, even I had to admit this job was above and beyond. The only reason I was standing there half-naked was that it paid a lot!

The exhibition in the small gallery in Allston was by the artist K. Lowinski. It was titled "More Than," and the paintings were abstract and made to look like they were ready to burst alive from the canvas. To draw people to the exhibition, the gallery hired me and two other girls and three guys to stand in the gallery like pieces of living art. We were supposed to stand completely still on a small round platform each and move now and then. What was so exciting about that, you ask?

That we looked naked.

We wore sheer body stockings that K. Lowinski had painted and decorated but only on very strategic parts.

Now I was a short, curvy twenty-year-old and there were pieces of the art that barely covered some stuff, if you know what I'm saying. In fact, when I first put the stocking on, I thought there was no way I could go out onto the gallery floor and be seen almost naked! Then I remembered the money and the fact that no one I knew would ever step foot inside an art gallery.

My parents would never find out about it.

More to the point, my macho-man boyfriend, Gary, would never find out. We'd only been dating two months, so it wasn't like he had a say anyway. Gary, however, was funny, hot, and the first guy who had succeeded in making me orgasm during sex. I was pretty excited about that, so I didn't want to mess that up.

Nope. No one would find out about this little stint as an exhibitionist in an exhibition.

See what I did there?

Trying not to smirk at my own joke, I ignored the slight pain in my lower back and tried not to move too much. When I took the job, I didn't realize how difficult it would be to stand for so long. I was not a person who stood in one place. Gary said he'd never met someone with so much energy. Not that he was complaining, wink wink, nudge nudge.

I let my thoughts turn to my project for college. This semester I'd taken a metalsmith class, and I was in love. Like, seriously, seriously in love. I think I'd found my calling. I was creating jewelry that my teacher raved over. I'd given a necklace I'd made to my mom for her birthday and even she, Sorcha "I can't believe a kid of mine is going to fuckin' art school" McGuire, thought it was beautiful. She ruined it by asking me how I expected to make real money out of jewelry-making. But whatever.

I was Dahlia McGuire, soon-to-be silversmith. How cool was that? As my brother Dermot would say, "Fuckin' A, Dahlia, fuckin' A!"

My musings were slowly brought to a halt as a burning sensation crept over my skin. Not literally burning. But you know that hot, tingly feeling that prickles your body when it feels like someone is watching you? Well, considering I was almost naked in an art gallery, people *were* watching me. I let my eyes move around the room and ...

There!

Leaning against the wall, next to one of the paintings was the reason for that hot, tingly feeling.

He grinned when our eyes met and wowzer. *Okay, speaking of hot, tingly feelings.*

I jerked my gaze away, flushing as his crooked, boyish smile flittered across my vision.

I got a distinct impression of broad shoulders and a narrow waist in the plain navy T-shirt he wore.

Thoughts off the hottie, Dahlia, I grumbled to myself. I had a job to do—and a boyfriend.

A boyfriend who knew his way around my clit.

I wouldn't jeopardize that for anything!

However, as I tried to remain as still as possible, I could feel the guy staring.

And staring.

And more staring.

He couldn't be. It had to be my imagination.

Ah, screw it. I snuck a peek and stiffened when I saw he was not only watching me, he'd moved closer.

This time I stared back.

Gary was taller but leaner, had dark hair with lovely blue eyes, and visible tattoos. He was from Southie but looked like a pretty-boy rock star.

This guy was rougher around the edges with his dark-blond hair and dark eyes. His face was hard hewn and at total odds with his beautifully shaped mouth.

He smirked as I looked my fill.

I narrowed my eyes.

This guy was not here for the art.

Perv!

Forgetting my job for a second, I grimaced, which seemed to amuse him.

Huffing inwardly, I decided the best thing to do was ignore the hot guy who came for a peep show. That negated the hotness. It really did.

There were other girls here.

Go peep at them!

To be fair, he only seemed to ogle my face ... but I knew when I wasn't looking, like now, he was studying me elsewhere.

That wasn't flattering. It was creepy and annoying.

I'm a living piece of art, dipshit, not window dressing in Amsterdam!

Oh, who was I kidding? Even the so-called "art enthusiasts" had come here to see the almost naked people. That's why the gallery did it.

Still, at least everyone else pretended to be interested in the art.

Growing increasingly irritated—and I didn't know if it was because my heart was inexplicably racing at his intense staring—I returned my attention to Mr. Hottie with the staring problem.

Yup. Still there. Still looking at me.

And now in this seriously smokin' smoldering way that made more than my heart beat fast. I felt a flip low in my belly as our eyes connected and shock floored me at the consequent heat between my legs.

What the hell!

Horrified that a stranger had elicited that kind of reaction in me (I mean, what was that?), I decided it was time to move and make a point. I raised my arm slowly, gracefully, as I bent my opposing knee, and as I brought my arm upwards, I watched the stranger's eyes flare with heat.

Shit.

Perv.

Bringing my hand up to my face, I curled it into a fist, except for my middle finger, which caressed my cheek with a pointed "fuck you" glare.

And what was his reaction to the sight of me flipping him off?

He threw his head back in laughter, drawing attention from everyone else. I lowered my hand in case my boss saw me flipping off a customer.

Dark eyes glittering, the stranger's laughter trailed off, and he gave me a weirdly affectionate smile before he turned and walked away. He disappeared around the corner, and I deflated with relief.

Or was that disappointment?

An hour later, I walked out of the small closet they'd given us to change in, wearing my own clothes and wishing for the money to get a massage. My back was all kinds of stiff from standing on my feet for four hours with only two fifteen minute breaks in between.

Later that night I had my first shift as a waitress in a bar in Malden, the neighboring town to my own, Everett. It was my sister Davina's old job, and when the college bar I'd been working at told me they were cutting my hours, I jumped ship. The pay was crappy, but you did what you had to do, am I right?

I tucked a piece of hair behind my ear as I passed a mirror in the back of the gallery. The gallery wanted our faces scrubbed clean except for mascara on the girls, so I looked very young. And boring. I'd been in my Dita Von Teese phase now for three years and loved vintage clothing, black-winged eyeliner, and red lips. Taking a quick glance at my makeup-free face, I decided I needed bangs. Bangs would look hot. Very vintage.

Altogether I wasn't my usual cute self as I walked out into the main gallery. I wore jeans, a T-shirt, and sneakers rather than a pencil skirt, blouse, and sandals combo. Sometimes I wore flattering dresses too. But being curvy, I loved the way a pencil skirt accentuated my small waist and fuller hips.

Jeans made me look ordinary.

My boss had said we could get a free coffee and a sandwich in the small café at the back of the gallery and I was definitely going to take advantage of the offer. After I got my food and drink, I sat down in the quiet café and almost groaned with pleasure at getting off my feet.

It was one of those quietly perfect moments of contentment. A seat and free food.

Until he ruined it.

The chair next to mine scraped back, and I jerked with surprise, only to tense when hottie with the dreamy eyes and lush mouth sat down at my table. Our eyes hooked and locked as he crossed his arms on the tabletop and leaned in.

"Hey."

I swallowed a bite of my sandwich, and my pulse skittered into takeoff. A flush spread over my skin and I hoped it wasn't visible. Attempting to ignore my body's inexplicable reaction to his proximity, I frowned. "Oh goodie, it's Perv Boy."

He flashed me a quick, crooked, boyish smile that did not give me butterflies.

Okay, it did. It totally did.

"People usually call me Michael or Mike." He had a thicker Bostonian accent than me. He sounded like Gary, and I suspected he too was from Southie.

"That's because they haven't witnessed you gaping like a prepubescent boy at a half-naked woman before."

Michael or Mike chuckled. "Was that how it came off?"

"You still have a little drool right there." I gestured to the corner of his mouth.

He didn't smile this time. Instead, he stared intensely at my face until I began to wonder if there was something on it. Flushing, I snapped, "You're doing it again."

Michael (I decided I'd always liked the name and hated it when people shortened it to Mike) shrugged. "I can't help it."

"Well, try." I bit into my sandwich and scowled at him as I chewed.

"Christ, anyone ever tell you that you're fuckin' adorable?"

"Anyone ever tell you that you're full on?"

"I never have been before."

"Oh, lucky me that you decided to give it a try today."

"You're a little smart-ass." He chuckled. "Your boss know you flip off customers when you're pretending to be art?"

"You're the first."

"I'm honored."

"You're also the first to blatantly come in to perv on the models."

"Not true." He settled back in his chair like he was getting ready for a long, comfortable chat with me.

I had to get rid of him. My heart was pounding way too fast, my belly was fluttering with butterflies. I was not supposed to react to any guy like this who wasn't Gary. At the thought of Michael getting up and leaving, however, an overwhelming sense of disappointment came over me. I was enjoying ribbing him, and he was . . . well, the way he made me feel was kind of exciting.

Oh boy.

"It is so true!" I guffawed. "You were absolutely perving."

"I was staring at one model. You. And I wasn't perving."

"Oh, so you're an art aficionado, are you?"

"No, I'm a rookie cop. This is my day off, and I told my friend I would drop him off at this catering gig he has going for tonight. That event is here. I was walking out of the kitchen to my car when I look over and yeah, I'm not going to lie, all I saw at first was a beautiful body. Then I looked at your face, and well," he shrugged, "I couldn't look away."

Maybe I was an idiot to hear the sincerity in his voice. But that's what I heard. No sleazy come-on. Just honesty. He looked like I'd caught him off guard, which made me feel better about my reaction to *him*.

I didn't know what to say.

"You gonna go all shy on me now?"

I narrowed my eyes. "I was formulating a response."

"Oh, were you?" He chuckled. "You go on, then, and you keep formulating. I've got time."

"I should think you're a creep."

He cocked his head. "The point of dressing you up like that was to make people stare, no?"

"Yes, I guess," I wrinkled my nose, "but other people are less obvious about it."

"Why you doin' it?" he nodded toward the gallery.

"It's not shameful," I said defensively.

"I didn't say it was."

"Well, you're making it all sexy when it's supposed to be about art."

Michael laughed. He looked good laughing. His laughter was deep and rumbly, and I felt that between my legs too.

Dear God.

"You make it sexy, and I think these people knew exactly what they were doing when they hired you."

I flushed at the compliment. "Whatever. It pays ludicrously well, and I'm an art student. I need the money."

"I'm not judging. Gotta say, though, if you were mine, I wouldn't be happy you were doing this."

Great, another Neanderthal like Gary. It was like they grew them on trees here. "Listen, Macho Man, no one tells me what to do."

"Oh, I got that sense when you flipped me off, dahlin'."

Ignoring the tingles his endearment elicited, I cocked my head in thought. "So, if you're a cop, you'll know that being a perv is frowned upon, right?"

He chuckled. "I can't believe I'm having this conversation. And yes, that is true. But I'm not a perv. I promise."

"All evidence to the contrary."

"Fuck, if I'd known you were this smart, I wouldn't have sat down," he teased.

"You're welcome to leave," I replied, though inwardly I thought, "Please don't."

"The seat is comfortable, and I'm finding your smart mouth extremely appealing right now." His dark eyes grew hooded as they fell to my lips.

My heart raced as this invisible rope seemed to lasso around us both, drawing us closer and closer. I didn't understand it. Every nerve ending tingled with life, my skin was hot, and my whole being was lit with awareness.

"I have a boyfriend," I blurted out.

Michael's disappointment was obvious. We looked at each other for a few seconds, and then he asked, "Serious?"

I shrugged. "We haven't been dating long, but it's good."

"How long is not long?"

"Two months."

His lips twitched. "That's not long at all."

I tried not to smile and failed. "You'd go after another guy's girl?"

"Never have before, but you're the exception to the rule."

"I am?" My heart was bursting.

Michael nodded. "You can't tell me you don't feel this?"

Biting my lip, I nodded slowly.

Something hungry flickered in his expression.

Wow.

I shook my head, as if to shake off the indescribable urge to jump him. This was insane. "I wouldn't cheat. Not ever."

"Neither would I," he promised. "Sit with me a while."

I wondered if that was a good idea.

"What are you thinking?"

"How much I shouldn't have liked that you were disappointed that I have a boyfriend."

"Speaking of, does he know you're working here?"

"No. And he doesn't need to. It's a temporary gig that pays a lot an hour, and it isn't causing anyone any harm."

"I beg to differ."

"How?"

"It's causing your boyfriend harm. If you hadn't been working here, I wouldn't have seen you, decided you're the most gorgeous fuckin' thing I've ever seen, and then sat my ass down to talk to you. Now I find out that not only are you gorgeous but you're smart and you're funny—which I already knew when you flipped me off—which means I'm not leaving until we exchange numbers. And I do this knowing if you feel half as attracted to me as I do to you, you'll put your not-so-serious boyfriend aside to call me and give me a shot. So yeah, I'd say this job caused your boyfriend some harm."

I gaped at him. "You're very cocky."

"No, but I am determined."

"My boyfriend is good in bed." I was exasperated by this sudden feeling of being torn in two. "That's difficult to find."

Michael smiled at my bluntness. "Dahlin', you've haven't seen anything yet. You're what, in your early twenties?"

I nodded. "Twenty. So?"

"So maybe you're mistaking okay sex for good sex." He leaned forward, so our noses were almost touching, and my breath caught in my throat as the spicy, dark scent he wore tickled my senses. "If I were lucky enough to have you in my bed, I'd make you feel things you never knew existed. If you were mine, you wouldn't flirt with other guys. You wouldn't want to, knowing no other guy would appreciate you the way I would. Trust me, dahlin', I appreciate the good things in life, and I'm more grateful than I can say when I come across special. Just never thought I'd come across goddamn extraordinary in my life, let alone find it in an art gallery."

Oh. My. God.

"What are you doing to me?" I snapped, sitting back in my chair to get some distance. "I'm Irish, okay. I grew up surrounded by Irish guys who know how to charm the panties off a girl. You, mister, you're like the freaking champion. And don't tell me you're not Irish. I know you're Irish."

"I am. But I'm not feeding you a line."

Flustered, I pushed my chair back from the table and grabbed my purse. I liked Gary. Things were going good! Like, great. And this guy scared me. I mean, I could be a pretty impulsive person, but I'd never wanted to launch myself across the table at a guy I didn't know and screw him six ways until Sunday. Sex until Gary had been about answering the calls of my hormonally charged body and being disappointed every time.

This pull with Michael was so much more than that. Yes, it was sexually charged, but there was something here. Some connection I didn't understand. It was freaking me out!

"I have to go."

"Don't." He stood, coming across unsure, which seemed out of character for him. But how would I know? We didn't know each other! "I'm sorry if I came on too strong. I've never ... " He shrugged, looking very young all of a sudden.

And I realized he was younger than I'd first thought—he had said he was a rookie cop. I put him at maybe my age or Gary's, who was two years older than me.

"Stay. Talk." He gestured to the table and then gave me a coaxing smile. "Tell me your name."

"I can't." I needed some distance from this guy, and I needed to see Gary so I could be reminded that what we had was pretty damn good.

But Michael's crestfallen expression tugged at my heart.

"Look, I'll be back here on Wednesday night and then on Saturday again. If you're sincere, then show up. We'll go from there."

His relief was visible.

"I like that too." I smiled at him, and his eyes zeroed in on the dimple in my left cheek. It was a gift from my dad.

"Like what?"

"No bullshit. You tell me what you feel without even saying it. And I like you're relieved. I take it you'll be here?"

"Dahlin', you smile at me like that, giving me that gorgeous little dimple, I'll do anything short of murdering someone for you. Maybe even then," he teased.

I grinned harder, and his expression turned tender. *My God*. "Then I'll see you soon."

"At least tell me your name," he called as I strolled away.

I turned, walking backward, "I tell you what. You show, I'll tell you my name."

"Tease."

I flipped him off with a playful grin, and his laughter followed me as I left. I was giddy with the kind of anticipation a girl with a boyfriend definitely should not feel.

"You doin' okay?" Ally asked me as I handed change over to a customer.

My shift at Wilde's Place had started two hours ago, and I'd worked my way around the bar pretty fast. I already had bartending experience, so it was no big deal, and the customers there were a lot more down-to-earth and fun to talk to than those at the college bar.

"Everything is going great." I threw her a smile.

"Your boyfriend gonna be here soon?"

The thought of Gary caused a prickle of guilt. I'd technically arranged some kind of date with another guy. It didn't seem like it at the time but giving myself distance from Michael made me realize how shitty what I'd done was. I'd flirted with another guy, and I'd arranged to see him again at my job. Yet, I couldn't forget those butterflies or how I still felt them when I thought about the stranger. I didn't have those with Gary, as much as I cared about him.

But was Michael worth ruining what I had with Gary? My boyfriend had called me before my shift to tell me that Sully had a Saturday night free, so he was bringing him to Wilde's Place to meet me. Sully was Gary's best friend, but he was a cop and hadn't had a lot of free time lately. He'd been with Boston PD for nearly two years so he was only now getting a regular shift pattern that would allow him to see his buddies more.

I was a little nervous about meeting him. Gary talked about him all the time. They'd grown up together, and while Gary screwed around a lot, Sully was always there to get him out of scrapes. From what I knew about my boyfriend, he'd definitely been the irresponsible one in that friendship. Until me, Gary had only been interested in casual sex, whereas he used to rib Sully for being a one-woman kind of guy. Sully had wanted to go to college to be a lawyer, but his family didn't have the money to send him, so he took his police exam at nineteen, was a cadet with the Boston PD before he could apply for the police academy at twenty-one, and he became a cop like his old man.

Gary, on the other hand, had flitted from one job to the next, getting fired right, left, and center, until his uncle took him on as a mechanic. Since then he'd settled down. Including with me.

If Gary and his best friend knew what I'd done today, they'd hate me.

But I didn't do anything, I argued with myself. *Not really.*

"Hey, gorgeous."

My boyfriend's familiar voice pulled me out of my guilt-ridden thoughts, and I handed over the beer to my customer. Gary leaned over the bar, grinning at me.

Smiling back, I leaned over to press a kiss to his lips. A couple of guys around the bar groaned in fake disappointment, and Gary smiled against my mouth before pulling back to shoot a grin their way. "That's right, fellas, she's mine, so back off."

I shook my head at his nonsense. "You doin' okay?"

"I'm supposed to be asking you that. How's it goin'?"

"Good."

He nodded and then turned to look over his shoulder. "I brought Sully. Told you he wasn't an imaginary friend."

I laughed because I'd teased him about that as more weeks passed without meeting this elusive Sully. Glancing past my boyfriend to smile at his friend as he stepped up to the bar, my smile stuck before it could widen my mouth.

Shock rooted me to the spot as I looked into familiar dark-brown eyes.

Michael?

Surprise momentarily flickered in his expression, but he was quicker at recovering than I was. He held out his hand and said pointedly, "Michael *Sullivan*, nice to meet you."

Oh my God.

Sullivan. Sully.

Duh.

Well, didn't this suck at the highest level? I swallowed my shock and disappointment and gingerly took his hand. My skin tingled at his touch, and his hand seemed to reflexively tighten around mine. "Dahlia." It was hard to get words out, so they came out soft and uncertain. "Nice to meet you too."

"Don't tell me you're going all shy on me," Gary huffed.

My smile was strained. "He's your best friend. I want him to like me."

Right. Only I hadn't expected to want him to *like me* like me.

"Of course he'll like you. Won't you, Sully? What's not to like?"

Michael gave us a flat smile. "You've talked about her so much, I feel like I already do."

Gary patted him on the back and then took a stool at the bar. Michael and I exchanged a loaded look before he slid in beside his friend.

Shaking inwardly and doing my best to hide it, I at once panicked that Michael would tell Gary I was flirting with him, and that Michael wouldn't turn up to see me again. Of course, he wouldn't! How messed up was that kind of thinking? We couldn't hurt Gary like that. It was ridiculous.

God, why was this happening? Why couldn't I have met Michael first?

And is that what I wanted? To have met him first? A guy I knew little about? I only knew what I'd heard from Gary (all of it good— FYI, my boyfriend hero-worshipped the guy) and what I'd felt today when we met.

But Gary was sweet, and he was good in bed, and he treated me well.

Oh hell.

I tried to be my funny, light, breezy self as I talked to my boyfriend and his best friend between serving customers. The horrible part of the evening came when Gary excused himself to the bathroom, and Michael called me over.

His dark eyes were no longer filled with laughter and desire. They were still warm but there was a polite distance in them, and I missed the way he'd looked at me that afternoon.

"I won't tell Gary about today."

I nodded. "I don't normally flirt with other guys."

He leaned over the bar and lowered his voice. "I know. I know today was unexpected for both of us."

I remembered then that Gary had told me Michael was twenty-three. Only three years older than me but he had this air of maturity about him that none of my other friends had. Not even Gary. It was very attractive.

Damn.

"It's against the code to tell you this, but Gary likes you. I've never seen him with a girl like he is with you." He gave me a sad smile. "And now I get why. But his life hasn't been easy and um … well, I won't fuck this up for him."

I found myself unable to meet his eyes as a swell of disappointment I didn't understand overwhelmed me.

"I won't be coming back to the gallery, Dahlia."

Nodding and swallowing past the lump in my throat, I replied, "I understand."

"He cares about you. Be good to him."

I gave him a weak smile. "I won't hurt him."

Walking down the bar to get away from Michael, I thought to myself, no, I won't hurt Gary because if it feels anything like this, I wouldn't want to sting someone that badly.

1

Dahlia

Years ago, during a short time in my life, I used alcohol to numb my feelings. Gin would soak through the giant, aching ball of grief in my chest and it eased its grip on my soul. It made getting through the next day and the one after easier. However, it numbed not only the grief, it stopped me from feeling much of anything. It almost killed me.

Once I gave up alcohol and let myself feel, I had to give myself over to time and patience. And, thankfully, time and distance (and therapy) did what the alcohol had attempted to do. Time dulled the pain. There were moments when not even time could do that, but for the most part, I lived my life relatively content.

So I guess I forgot.

I forgot that life doesn't let you have time and distance. You can't coast through your existence with nothing ever happening again to throw you back into that place.

Life doesn't work like that at all.

And that day was the day it decided to remind me of that fact.

It was nearing the end of summer, and I'd closed the gift shop/workshop that I owned on the boardwalk in the seaside city of

Hartwell, Delaware. It was technically a city, but it was small with a small-town mentality. The boardwalk was about a mile long, and the north end was made up of commercial buildings, including my gift shop where I sold unique items I not only sourced but jewelry I made and designed in my workshop.

We boardwalk owners were a tight-knit community. My best friend was Bailey Hartwell, and she owned Hart's Inn, which sat right next to my shop on the boards.

I'd closed up shop for an hour, and Bailey had left the running of the inn to her manager, Aydan, so we could grab a coffee with our friend Emery Saunders, who owned Emery's Bookstore and Coffeehouse.

Usually, our coffee breaks were an excuse to chat about everything and nothing, but that day we had a specific focus. Bailey. Not only was her little sister in town causing problems, but Bailey had started seeing Vaughn Tremaine. This was big news in our small town. Why? Well, mostly, because anything involving Bailey was big news. As a descendant of the founding family, she was well known. But more than that, she was liked and respected. When Vaughn Tremaine bought the old Hart's Boardwalk Hotel and ripped it down to build his contemporary five-star hotel, Paradise Sands, Bailey was not happy. She made sure the whole town *and* Tremaine were aware of how unhappy she was and in doing so caused a miniature war between her and the deliciously sexy Manhattan-born hotelier.

If that wasn't enough to keep tongues wagging, Bailey's boyfriend of ten years, Tom, shocked the hell out of everyone by cheating on her. After they broke up, the tension that had been simmering between Bailey and Tremaine sort of exploded and as I'd always suspected, they admitted they were attracted to each other.

After months of dancing around each other, they were finally dating.

I was happy for my best friend. No one deserved to get her happily-ever-after more than Bailey Hartwell.

"I never felt this way with Tom," Bailey said with a huff as we sat drinking our coffee. We were up in the raised section of the bookstore, sitting around the open fireplace. The light spilling in from the low, shallow windows behind us cast a copper halo around her auburn hair. "I actually liked the space from Tom, even in the beginning. But with Vaughn, I want to be with him all the time because every moment we spend together, I find out something new about him—his quirks, his sense of humor, his cockiness, his flaws. And do you know what? I like it *all*. *Flaws* and all! What is that?"

Emery beamed. "You're falling in love."

I grinned at the dreaminess of Emery's smile as Bailey denied such claims. To be honest, I'd kept to myself living in Hartwell these past nine years. Emery had moved to town a year after me, but she was so shy and socially awkward, no one really knew her. That is until Jessica Huntington came to Hartwell last year, befriended Bailey, and then Emery. Jessica was now Jessica Lawson. She'd married our friend Cooper who owned the bar next to Emery's bookstore. Jessica was one of the town doctors, and if she had time between appointments, she'd try to join us for coffee. However, she and Cooper were on their honeymoon in Canada.

And now all four of us were friends. Emery was coming out of her shell more and more, but the woman was still a mystery.

All I knew about her was that she inherited a lot of money from her grandmother, including property like the bookstore. I knew she was timid, especially around men, which made no sense considering she was one of the most beautiful women I'd ever met in real life. Seriously. She was tall, slender with curves in all the right places, had long white-blond hair that no grown woman should have naturally, and the delicate features of a Disney cartoon. Cooper's sister, Cat, often joked that Emery looked like Elsa from *Frozen*.

Aside from her resemblance to a Disney character, I also knew Emery was a total romantic. Anytime Bailey spoke about Vaughn, or Jess talked about Cooper, Emery got this sweet look of longing on her face.

"Shouldn't he want to spend all of his time with me?" Bailey pulled me out of my Emery thoughts.

"You need to talk to him about this. Now. Before it goes any further," I advised. There had been way too much miscommunication between Bailey and Vaughn already. "If Jess was here, she'd say the same."

Bailey wrinkled her nose. "I don't know ... "

Well, I did know, and I had no problems saying how I felt and doing so bluntly. Thankfully, Bailey appreciated that part of my personality. "Do you really want a husband and a father to your kids who is never there?"

"No." She shook her head and then straightened her shoulders with determination. "Fine. I'll talk to him. It'll probably scare him off, but I'll talk to him."

"After what he said to you, I don't think anything you do will scare him off," Emery offered, taking the words right out of my mouth. On the day of Jess's wedding, Vaughn had gotten into a fist fight with an old flame of Bailey's that turned out to be Vaughn's high school friend. The guy insulted Bailey and Vaughn decked him (you couldn't write this stuff!), and when the fighting was over, Vaughn gave her this amazing speech about all the reasons he loved her. When she'd told us what he'd said, I'd kind of fallen in love with him myself.

"Yeah, he certainly seems to get a kick out of your obnoxious honesty," I teased.

"*My* obnoxious honesty?" Bailey gestured to me. "Pot." And then to herself. "Meet Kettle."

I laughed. "Whatever. Just talk to him."

At the sound of the bell ringing through the bookstore, Emery got up to see if the customers needed her and I repeated to Bailey that she needed to talk to Vaughn. Seriously, my friend had to know by now that there was no chasing off Vaughn Tremaine. He looked at her like she was his whole reason for existing.

"They're just browsing the books, so I told them to come get me if they need me." Emery sat down with us again. "What were we saying?"

"We were discussing my possible relationship-ending talk with Vaughn. Oh, and the fact that my sister seems to have disappeared off the face of the planet. I swear to God, if I don't find her soon, my parents are going to get on a flight out here."

"And that would be a bad thing?" *I think not.* It wasn't my place to say anything, but Vanessa was a born troublemaker, and I didn't like the idea of her causing problems for Bailey as my friend was getting her life together. Maybe it would be a good thing if Stacy and Aaron Hartwell came back to take the responsibility of looking out for Vanessa off Bailey's shoulders.

"Right now?" Bailey said. "Yes. I'd like to get to know Vaughn without my dad breathing down my neck. I love the man, but he also is the only one in my family who knew about Oliver Spence."

Oliver Spence was the ex-flame Vaughn hit in the face. His wealthy family had vacationed in Hartwell for years when he was young, and when Bailey was nineteen, he told her he loved her and she fell in love right back. But at the end of the summer, he broke her heart and told her she wasn't good enough for his family. Bastard. If I'd been friends with Bailey back then, I would have found a way to take sweet revenge on the uppity asshole. Like filling his luxury sports car with piles and piles of cheese—so much cheese, he'd be clearing that stuff out for days, and he'd never get the smell out of the leather.

Unfortunately, I wasn't in Hartwell back then to execute such sophisticated revenge plans for my best friend.

"He might assume things about Vaughn, and I need to work out how I feel about Tremaine before I take into consideration anybody else's feelings about him."

I called bullshit. "Oh, please, you know how you feel about Vaughn."

"I'm going to smack you."

I grinned and turned my left cheek to her, tapping my finger against the dimple there. "Go ahead. Make my day."

Bailey's green eyes danced with amusement. "Ach, you're too damn cute for your own good."

I pretended to preen. "I know." The girls laughed.

"Miss," a guy's voice cut through our laughter. We all turned as a man walked up the stairs. There was something familiar about the way he moved as he led a short, pretty blonde up the steps with him. His gaze zeroed in on Emery. "We'd like to purchase a couple of books if that's okay," he said in a thick Boston accent.

That's when the familiarity made sense.

The shock that slammed through me I likened to how it must feel to step out onto the street, not see the car, and suddenly find yourself flying through the air with the unexpected impact.

No.

Jesus Christ, no.

What was *he* doing *here*?

My heart raced sickeningly in my chest. A flush of heat swept over my body so fast I could feel sweat gathering under my arms. The shock rendered my limbs useless, and I could only stare.

Michael Sullivan.

He was here.

In Hartwell.

In Emery's bookstore.

He had a short, scruffy beard and there were lines around his eyes that hadn't been there before, but it was him. I'd know him anywhere.

Tears welled in my throat as longing so painful gripped my chest. I hadn't seen him in years and all at once it was like breathing for the first time in a decade, only for that breath to painfully slip away, its momentary relief over all too soon.

He smiled at Bailey and then me.

As our eyes locked and surprise slackened his features, a weight pressed down on my chest. "Dahlia?"

How was he here?

Why was he here?

Go away, go away, go away!

"Michael," his name fell from my lips.

Michael. I loved his name. I loved ... I loved ... I ...

I was going to lose it.

Right there in front of him and the blonde whose hand he was holding.

I didn't want to see that.

I didn't want to see any of this.

But we couldn't stop staring at each other, drinking each other in. Michael's eyes were the same beautiful dark brown. The kind of eyes a girl could drown in. His blond hair was cut shorter than it had been when we were younger, so it appeared darker, and those broad shoulders of his seemed even wider. The T-shirt he wore clung to his body suggesting he worked out more than he used to. Not that he wasn't fit back then. There was just more muscle now. I realized it gave the illusion of him being taller than he was. He was five eleven, shorter than the men in my family, but he'd always had such a masculine, commanding presence.

He still had that presence.

Michael, what are you doing here? Please go away.

The blonde holding his hand (I refused to really look at her) tugged on it, and he looked away, freeing me from his stare. I sagged, the breath rushing back into my body. But as quickly as he'd looked away, his attention returned to me and demanded, "What are you doing here?"

What was *I* doing here?

Seriously?

Every part of me trembled, and I tucked my hands underneath the table so he couldn't see them shake. "What are you doing here?" I rejoined.

Seriously, what are you doing here? Leave, Michael. Leave, now!

I hoped he'd developed telepathic abilities over the last nine years.

"We're on vacation," the blonde spoke and pressed into his side like she belonged there. "Mike, who is this?"

Mike? My family called him Mike too, but I hated shortening such a beautiful name to something as ordinary as Mike.

"Uh, Kiersten, this is Dahlia. She's Dermot's little sister."

Dermot's little sister? Really? What a joke.

The blonde replied, "I thought she died."

Pain lashed through my chest, and Bailey grasped for my hand under the table. The words made me look at the blonde now. She was small, slender. Petite. And she would have been pretty if she wasn't wearing such a pinched expression on her face. My eyes flew to Michael. He'd told this person about Dillon. Who was she that she was important enough to know about Dillon but not important enough to know about me? Or was it that *I* was no longer important enough?

His grim expression caused the emotion in my throat to tighten. "That was Dillon."

The name cracked around the room like a gunshot, and I could feel my chest compress with panic. Little black dots covered my eyes, and I knew I was going to freak out in front of him.

No way.

I couldn't.

I might as well rip open my chest and ask everyone to look at all the little missing pieces of my heart.

"I need to go." I stood, leaving Bailey no choice but to release my hand. Eyes down, terrified to meet his, I marched by Michael Sullivan and his blonde faster than I'd ever moved in my life.

"Dahlia!" he called out as I hurried down the steps. The exit seemed so far away.

I heard Bailey's voice and then the deep rumble of Michael's, but I yanked open the door without paying too much attention to them.

I was out.

The salty ocean air filled my lungs as I hurried down the boards. Fear of him chasing after me made my heart pound and I ran. I ran through the light summer crowd of tourists, the soles of my tennis shoes gathering small granules of wayward sand that always made its way onto the boards from the beach.

The light, warm breeze blew through my long hair, and I ran as if the devil himself were chasing me all the way to my store.

That panic, that terror, didn't leave me until I'd locked the door behind me. I didn't flip the "Open" sign from "Closed for Lunch." I didn't turn on the lights. Instead, I scurried into the back of the store to my workshop where the demons of the past tried to overwhelm me for the first time in years.

The truth was they'd never left me.

Michael's sudden appearance had merely woken them up.

My hands shook as silent, dry sobs wracked my body. I looked around my workshop, searching for relief, for something that would dull the pain. Shaking, I fumbled for my apron and pulled it on. Then I connected my phone to the speaker in my workshop, hit Spotify, and The Vaccines blasted into the room.

Sitting down at my bench, I stared at the silver-and-amethyst earrings I was in the middle of making. They were elongated silver cats with amethysts for eyes. Bending over, I worked, trying to drown out my thoughts.

I could hide from Michael until he left Hartwell. Simple.

His reappearance had been a shock.

Life had kicked me in the gut that day, but I knew I'd be okay as soon as he was gone.

After all, time and distance had worked before. They would work again.

2

Dahlia

A fire crackled in the fireplace in Emery's bookstore, a delicious reprieve from the cold October day outside. By mid-October, the overcast days brought low temperatures to the boardwalk, and although we were open all year round, this was the beginning of our quiet season.

Thankfully, my shop brought in enough profit (as all of our businesses did) during the spring and summer to keep me going through the quiet season. I also made and sold my jewelry to boutiques around the country, so that supplemented my income. The good thing about the quiet season was more opportunities for my friends and me to grab coffees at Emery's and catch up on our lives. The bookstore/coffeehouse was empty except for me, Emery, Bailey, and Jessica.

Jess checked her watch.

Emery put a plate of cookies on the table in front of us, the many silver bangles on her wrist jingling with the action, and then settled in the armchair closest to the fire.

"Got somewhere to be?" I asked Jess.

"Ach, it's a habit." She sighed. "I'm constantly checking my watch during the week. I forget this is Sunday and I don't need to be at the practice."

"Well, I'm glad you're here," I said. "I need someone else willing to mock Bailey about her engagement to the man she once referred to as 'the devil himself.' And Emery's too sweet to mock."

Emery glanced over the rim of her teacup, her stunning pale-blue eyes wide. "Not true," she replied in her quiet voice. "I can mock as well as anyone. Only not about this." She smiled at Bailey. "I think this is amazing."

"Amazingly shocking," I added. "It's like Buffy hooking up with Spike. Unexpected but incredibly hot."

Bailey quirked an eyebrow at me. "Hilarious."

I shared a smirk with Jess. "I thought so."

"All you're doing is showing your age."

"What? The age that is younger than you?"

Bailey fought a smile. "I don't know why I put up with your smart mouth half the time."

"Hey, Vaughn may be smokin' hot, but we both know I'm your soul mate, Hartwell."

"Oh, it all makes sense." Jess grinned. "Dahlia's afraid Vaughn will take her bestie away from her."

"Not possible," I said on a nonchalant exhale. "I'm prettier and wittier than Vaughn Tremaine. What I provide to Bailey's life can't be replicated or replaced."

"He gives her multiple orgasms," Emery said, grinning. "I think he wins."

We were all shocked into silence by her comment before we promptly burst into laughter. It wasn't that funny. But coming from Emery, it was hilarious. "Aw, man, Jess, you should never have introduced Bails to Emery. She's ruining her."

"In the best way possible," Bailey argued.

"I'm only saying what I used to say to myself in my head. I

feel comfortable enough to say it out loud to you guys."
Emery shrugged.

My curiosity about Emery had been piqued seven years ago
when she showed up on the boardwalk and transformed Burger
Hut into a bookstore. She was so closed off and shy, however, that
Bailey and I gave up on trying to befriend her. Now that Jess had
paved the way for all of us to become friends, Bailey and I had
frequently discussed our growing curiosity. We knew nothing
about Emery, and we were afraid if we prodded, she'd slip back
into her shell.

However, I'd grown very fond of the soft-spoken, intelligent
bookstore owner. There was a sadness in her eyes that called to
the melancholy in my own. This woman had a story to tell, and
maybe she'd been waiting for people to trust enough to confide in.
I wanted to be one of those people.

"So, tell me, Emery," I tried my best to sound casual, "have
you ever had that? Someone like Vaughn in your life?"

Her cheeks flushed a becoming pink. "Uh... no."

"Who has?" Bailey snorted. "The man is one of a kind."

"Show-off," I teased.

"Just no?" Jess ignored us.

Emery gave an abrupt shake of her head. "Just no."

That was it?

Bailey wrinkled her nose. "No guy you cared about? A childhood sweetheart, maybe?"

"I lived with my grandmother, and she didn't allow me to date."

Jess, Bailey, and I shared a glance. We guessed that kind of
explained things. Well, some things. "Okay." I put my coffee mug
down and focused on Emery, my curiosity getting the better of
me. "You've got to tell us about this grandmother of yours and
how a smart, beautiful young woman of . . . "

"Twenty-eight," she offered.

"Of twenty-eight lives in a small town where almost everyone knows each other but is so shy, it takes her seven years to befriend anyone."

Emery's brows pinched together. "That's not true. I've been friends with Iris since I moved here."

"What?" Bailey huffed. "She didn't tell me that."

"That's because she knows how nosy you are." Emery winced. "I meant that nicer than it came out."

I laughed. "You meant it exactly how it came out."

Bailey stuck her tongue out at me.

"Children," Jess rolled her eyes, "back to Emery and her grandmother."

"Um ... there's not much to tell." She nibbled on her lower lip for a second, seemingly in contemplation, and then she put her tea down. Her lashes lowered over her eyes as she focused on the coffee table in front of us. "My parents were killed in the same airplane accident as my grandfather. He had a private jet. It crashed. I was in New York that summer, at a summer camp for musicians. I played the cello. I was twelve. After ... it was just my grandmother and me." Her gaze turned very direct. "This goes no further than this room."

We all nodded, and I realized we were all leaning forward in our chairs, genuinely intrigued. It didn't surprise me that Emery had lost her parents so young. There was an otherworldly air about her, a purity of heart, despite her surprisingly smart mouth. I trusted that Emery would never hurt anyone, but would, in fact, do all she could to help someone. That came from a well of empathy that was often born from adversity or grief.

"My grandfather was Peter Paxton, founder of the Paxton Group."

Who?

Seeing our cluelessness, she continued, "Paxton Group includes

American AirTravel and Invictus Airlines. Invictus Vacation Group. And Invictus Aeronautical."

Holy shit.

Those were some of the biggest companies in the US. The Paxton Group had to be a billion-dollar corporation. Jesus. Paxton, and thus Emery's dad, were billionaires.

Did that mean ...?

I gaped at Emery.

She did not look like a billionaire.

She did not act like a billionaire.

Not that I would know how they acted because until now, I'd never met one!

Seeing we understood, she flushed. "I was very privileged and until that point, not a very nice kid. I didn't know any different. We lived on an estate in upstate New York. We had staff that did everything for us, and I was spoiled. When they died, my grandmother took over their shares in the company. A board runs it with a chairman, CEO, et cetera, so my grandmother had her own ventures in real estate. She was ... " Emery paused, her eyes lowering to the floor, and mine narrowed at the way she seemed to wring her hands. "Very strict. Yes, she was very strict."

"What happened?" Bailey asked quietly, engrossed. "To your grandmother."

"Whole Lotta Love" by Led Zeppelin unexpectedly blasted out of my purse, and we all jumped about a foot.

Jess cut me a dirty look, and I bit back nervous laughter. "I'm sorry." Turning to Emery, I lost the smirk. "I really am." Fumbling through my bag, I intended to switch off my phone so we could get back to Emery's story, but the caller ID said it was my dad.

Two months ago, when Michael Sullivan had shown up at Emery's, I realized his appearance had been no coincidence.

The only person in my family who knew I lived in Hartwell was my dad.

When I called him to ask about Michael, he told me that Michael was going through a separation from his wife and Dad had suggested he take a vacation in Hartwell by himself. He didn't mention to Michael I happened to live there, and he didn't tell me Michael was on his way to obliterate my week. I knew what my dad had hoped that vacation would accomplish.

What he hadn't counted on was Michael giving his marriage another shot by going on a romantic vacation with his *wife*. It wasn't shocking to learn Michael was married. Of course, he was. He was a catch. However, it had been excruciatingly painful.

Suffice it to say I was pretty mad at my dad.

And I loved my dad.

I *adored* my father.

He was the only one in my family who truly understood me and I talked to him every other day. Yet since Michael's appearance in Hartwell, things between us had been awkward. So awkward, in fact, that I'd been toying with the idea of going home to Boston to settle the slight discord between us. I hadn't been back to Boston in nine years so that's how much I cared about my relationship with my father.

When my dad called, I answered.

Always.

"Sorry, guys, I need to take this." I hit the green button on my phone. "Hey, Dad, what's up?"

"Hey, Bluebell."

Usually, the sound of my dad's husky voice and his thick Boston accent was one of my favorite sounds in the world. I'd lost my Bostonian accent somewhere along the years and talking to Dad always reminded me of home.

Today, however, I tensed. Not at the nickname. My dad had

been calling me Bluebell since I was a toddler because my eyes were that exact shade of blue. My brothers and sisters all had my mom's hazel eyes. I was the only one with my dad's eye color and his dimple.

Yeah, so it wasn't the nickname that caused my heart to skip a beat. It was my dad's tone. A million scenarios ran through my head. "Is everyone okay?"

"Everyone's fine. But I have something to tell you, and I hate that I'm telling you this over the phone."

Trepidation froze me to the chair. "Dad . . . ?"

The girls' quiet murmur of chatter petered out as their worried gazes followed me.

"I know you're a grown-up and you'll handle this just fine but . . . um . . . well, Bluebell, your mom and I are getting a divorce. She moved out last week."

If it was possible, I thought my heart might have stopped. "Dad?" I didn't understand.

My relationship with my mother was in tatters, but no matter what was thrown at Sorcha and Cian McGuire, they handled it together. How could they possibly be getting a divorce?

My dad loved my mom.

He *loved* her.

"Did she leave you?"

"It was mutual, dahlin'. Things weren't working out."

"I don't get it."

"Love you, Dahlia, you know that. But like I said to your brothers and Davina, this isn't for you kids to get. It's between your mom and me."

He sounded exhausted.

And low.

And despondent.

The thought of my dad feeling that way without me there—the

idea of him going through this with my mother for who knows how long, and I wasn't there . . .

Guilt drenched me.

The words were out of my mouth before I could stop them. "I'm coming home."

He sighed. "Bluebell, you don't need to do that."

"No, I do." The thought was more than a little nauseating; however, I needed to see my dad. I needed to hug him. He visited me when he could but it was never enough, and I needed to hug my dad and make sure he was okay. "I'll get a flight out as soon as possible. I'm heading home to arrange it all now. I'll call you when I know my flight time."

"You know I'm not going to talk you out of this. I can't wait to see you, kiddo." Hearing how much his tone had lightened upon my declaration of homecoming put a pause on all my concerns. Whatever I felt, whatever I had to deal with in returning to Everett, it was worth it already.

"I love you, Dad."

"Love you too. You call me to let me know when your flight is coming in."

"We'll talk when I get there, yeah?"

"Of course."

We said goodbye and my throat clogged with emotion.

My dad had been hurting, and I hadn't been there. I blinked back tears and turned toward my concerned friends. "My parents are getting divorced. I need to go back to Boston to see my dad."

Emery and Jess hugged me, telling me they were sorry, but it was Bailey who grabbed my arm and told me she'd walk me out.

Because she was the only one who knew my story.

Arm in arm, we stepped out onto the boardwalk. The cold ocean breeze nipped at our cheeks as we strolled in silence.

Then . . . "Dahlia, do you need me to come with you?"

I gave my best friend a tremulous smile. "Thank you. I appreciate that offer more than you know, but my dad probably needs privacy right now."

"I get that. But what about what you need?"

I gazed into Bailey's anxious green eyes. "For nine years my dad has been putting what I needed before what he needs. Before probably even what my family needs. I not only owe him this, Bailey, but I need to be there for him. I can't believe he's been going through this and I haven't been there. I mean," I said on a shaky exhale, "he loves my mom. He loves her like you love Vaughn, like I love ... "

"Michael." Bailey pulled me into a hug. "And what about Michael, Dahlia? Can you deal with possibly seeing him? Seeing him with his wife?"

I curled my fingers into her shirt and forced back the tears her words caused, almost choking on them.

Her arms tightened around me as she felt the shudder roll through my body.

This was about my dad.

When my dad hurt, I hurt.

That's the way it was with the people you loved.

I'd put myself through the torture of seeing Michael again if it meant being there for my father when he needed me. That didn't mean I didn't want to cry over the prospect.

"I'm okay," I whispered. "I can do this."

My best friend gripped my upper arms and bent her head to peer into my face. "Yeah, you absolutely can. However, we're doing your makeup before you leave. You are not going back to Boston looking anything but your best, sexiest self."

I rolled my eyes and groaned. "I'm going back for my dad, not for anything else."

She followed me as I continued down the boardwalk. "It doesn't mean you can't look good. You would have said the same to me about Vaughn."

"Vaughn's not married. And considering the delicate reason I am returning to my hometown, I think your commentary is inappropriate."

We were quiet as we passed Antonio's, our friends Iris and Ira's Italian pizzeria.

And then as we neared my shop, Bailey asked, "You're going to pack the blue dress though, right?"

Knowing exactly what dress she was referring to, I threw her a dirty look. But on second thought . . . "Which shoes should I pack with that?"

Bailey grinned, and we argued all the way to my car, parked behind my store, about my reason for agreeing to pack the blue dress. Just like that, she momentarily took my mind off my dad's problems.

That right there was one of Bailey Hartwell's greatest gifts.

3

Dahlia

My childhood home seemed smaller than I remembered. It was a two-story in the northeast of Everett. The only reason my parents could afford the house was that it had belonged to my grandparents. My grandfather died when Dad was a kid, and he and my mom had moved in with my paternal grandmother when Darragh was born. Grandma passed away two months before I came into the world, so I never met her. She left the house to Dad in her will.

Concrete steps led up to our blue front door. Dad kept the white wooden shingles clean and painted fresh every few years, and he'd told me he'd replaced the gray slate roof tiles last year. Blue shutters decorated the front window and the two small windows on the second floor. There was a side entrance, like a miniature version of the front, that led into the kitchen, which was the largest room in the house.

The kitchen had been redone, and the living room had been redecorated. But it smelled the same. Categorizing the smell was hard—kind of a mix of scents the house had acquired over the years, ingrained into the walls. Furniture polish, Mom's roast dinner, and a unique aroma that was all McGuire.

Dad led me to Dermot and Darragh's old room. It used to smell like the boys' locker room, and you couldn't even put a foot inside without stepping on something, the floor was that badly littered with all their crap. Now it was a tidy guest room with two twin beds neatly made in plain gray bedding.

"I thought you might want to stay in this room." My dad's voice was gruff.

I glanced over my shoulder at the closed door behind us. It was the old room I'd shared with Davina and Dillon. We'd forever been arguing because we were so on top of each other. Then Davina went to college and Dillon and I had shared it.

Dad was right. I didn't want to sleep in that room.

"Thanks." I kissed his cheek and strolled into my brothers' old room.

Dad placed my suitcase on the farthest bed and turned to me. "Can't tell you how good it is to have you here."

I studied him. My dad was one of those men who grew more distinguished with age. Being a firefighter, he'd stayed in shape his whole life. He'd moved up the ranks to lieutenant to captain to deputy chief, and he was now chief of District Three and had been for nearly a decade. He was fifty-six and nearing retirement, but I couldn't imagine my dad ever retiring.

There was always, usually, a radiant cloud of energy around Cian McGuire. He'd done a hard, dangerous job his whole life and he'd seen a lot of tragedy in his time, but somehow it hadn't chipped away at his soul or his good humor.

Now that energy seemed to have drained from him. The only other time I'd seen my dad like this was when Dillon died. And even then, he'd been so distracted by the mess I was making of my life, he hadn't had time to entirely give into his heartsickness.

I was worried about him. "Are you depressed, Dad?"

He rolled his eyes. "I'm not a depressed person."

"But you're sad."

"Thirty-eight years I've been married, and it's ending, Bluebell."

God, this sucked. "I'm sorry."

His answer was to pull me into his arms. I sank into his embrace. Nowhere felt safer.

"Thanks for coming to see your old man. I know this is hard for you. But it's time, don't you think, to put the past to rest?"

I mumbled against his shoulder, "I don't know if I can."

"We'll do it together." Humor lightened his words. "Think of it as distracting your old man from this interesting turn his life has recently taken."

I laughed softly, despite my fears, glad to see he hadn't lost his sense of humor.

Before I could question him about the separation between him and Mom, the sound of the front door downstairs opening and slamming shut made me jerk away from my dad.

"Dad, you home?" I recognized my big sister's voice.

"Davina?" I whispered.

"Dad?" a male voice called.

"Darragh?"

Dad shrugged, looking only slightly sorry. "I told them you were coming and they both wanted to be here."

"Dad!" Davina yelled.

"Up here," he called out.

"Dahlia here?" I couldn't read Darragh's tone.

"Yeah."

Blood rushed in my ears. I was about to face my siblings for the first time in nine years.

Nine years.

How could it have been that long? It didn't feel that long.

"Fuck," I bit out.

Dad squeezed my shoulder. "Like a Band-Aid, Bluebell. Best to pull that thing off quick."

Over the years, Dad had sent me photos of my family and kept me up-to-date with their lives in our weekly phone calls. Darragh was thirty-seven and a sports writer for the *Boston Globe*. Lucky bastard had met the Pats, the Sox, the Celts, and the Bruins multiple times. In all seriousness, I was proud of him. Dad said Darragh and his wife Krista (I'd met her before everything went to shit and had liked her a lot) had bought a nice house in Everett a few streets over. They had two sons, Leo and Levi. I'd closed the shop when they were both born, heartbroken I couldn't be there. Devastated I'd never met them. When they were born, I sent gifts through Dad, and I did that for their Christmas and birthdays too. Same for all my siblings. Dad always passed along their thanks, but I didn't know if they said that. The gifts were never returned, as far as I was aware.

Davina was the second eldest at thirty-five. She had a busy and very successful career as a corporate investment banker. I didn't know what that was, but it meant Davina could afford a huge apartment in Bunker Hill. She'd gotten married during the nine years of our estrangement to a man I'd never met. They divorced two years in, and then three years ago, my big sister came out to my family.

She moved in with Astrid, a woman she'd been friends with since college. It hurt my heart that my sister had loved her friend for years but hadn't been able to admit it. Dad said Davina was happier than ever, but I had so much regret knowing I hadn't been there for my big sister when she needed me. One of the things I felt most contrition for was not breaking free of my self-imposed bubble to go to Davina when she came out.

I was remorseful for not being there for my family, but I experienced it particularly intensely over my two eldest siblings. Even though Dermot was older than me too, it was only by eighteen months, and he was definitely an annoying older brother, whereas Darragh and Davina had been more than that.

My parents' careers meant they worked a lot and therefore had depended on Darragh and Davina to look after us younger kids. My big brother and sister had helped raise me, and I adored them.

I was terrified to see them again. To see their disappointment and disgust.

Frozen, I stared at my feet. "Dad, I don't know if I can do this."

"Bluebell," he said, his tone coaxing, "they're not here to hang you from a cross. They're here because they haven't seen you in nine years. Now I'm not saying there isn't anger and hurt there, but it's time to work on that. It's time to heal the breach."

Dad didn't give me a chance to respond. He grabbed my hand and led me downstairs. My legs turned to jelly, and I wondered if they'd hear the shallow staccato sounds of my breathing.

When we walked downstairs, they weren't in the living room. My grip on Dad was probably painful.

I knew I was acting like a little girl, clinging to him, but I couldn't seem to let go as he led me into the kitchen.

Tears I'd held back for years flooded my eyes at the sight of my big brother and sister leaning against the kitchen counter with coffee mugs in hand. I knew from photos that Darragh had grown to look more and more like Dad. And Davina, except in style, looked a lot like Mom. It was rare to see Mom in anything but nurse scrubs. Davina's hair was similarly styled to mine, long, beachy waves but without the bangs, and she wore skinny jeans, a plain black T-shirt, and a stylish pinstripe blazer. She wore cute flats that looked like they cost a lot of money. In fact, everything about my sister, from her clothes to her makeup, although casual, hinted at quality and money.

Dad had gifted me his eye color and the dimple in my left cheek, and my paternal grandmother had gifted me her height and curves. Davina (like Dillon had been) was tall like Mom with slender curves. I'd cursed the fates for not giving me my mother's height and figure.

I took all this in, noting how well they both looked, and pride overwhelmed me. We came from a working-class, Irish-American family—my big brother was now a sports writer for the *Boston Globe* and my big sister worked in an office in the financial district. And, even better, they were both happy in their personal lives. All of that filled my chest with something that felt heavily bittersweet. I hadn't been a part of any of that, and it was my fault.

Darragh put his cup on the counter, and I braced myself as he strode purposefully across the kitchen.

Without a word, he pulled me into his arms, my face pressed to his warm chest.

He was hugging me.

Sobs that had stayed locked inside me for years burst out and I closed my arms around his broad back and bawled.

"Ssshh, baby sister," he tried to soothe, his arms tightening.

But I couldn't.

Hard, painful tears wracked me, and they held *everything* in them. All the pain of the past decade.

"Dahlia, please," he begged after a while, choking on the words.

I reached for some control, trying to squeeze the sobs back down. Slowly, shuddering, I managed until my tears were silently rolling down my face.

Darragh gently eased me away, and I let go of him to wipe at my face. He reached behind me and took tissues from Dad to hand to me. I wiped at my eyes, which I was sure were now giant panda eyes.

My brother's expression was strained, his hazel eyes bright with unshed tears.

Mortified by my reaction to his hug, I flicked a glance at Davina and froze. She was crying quietly, but her tears seemed to be uncontrollable too.

More tears slipped down my cheeks seeing her pain. "I'm so sorry."

"What are you sorry for?" She swiped at her face, clearly aggravated.

"For everything."

"Well, that's kind of the problem, isn't it? You blamed yourself for things that weren't your fault, and you took off. And I do blame you for that, Dahlia. I blame you for missing out on the last nine years of my life and for making me miss out on yours."

"Let's all sit down." Dad pressed a hand to my back.

The suggestion relieved my shaky legs. Dad took the seat beside me, and Darragh sat across from me beside Davina, but not before touching my shoulder in comfort.

God, I loved my big brother.

The ache of missing him swelled inside me.

"Where have you been?" Davina demanded first.

I opened my mouth to tell her, but to all of our surprise, Darragh beat her to it. "Hartwell, Delaware."

"How do you know that?" Dad was obviously put out by this information.

Darragh glowered at him. "You think I was going to take your word for it that she was okay? I love you, Dad, I respect you, you know it . . . but she's my baby sister. You should have known I needed to know for myself that she was okay." He turned to me. "I hired a PI. Found you in Hartwell, knew you were okay, and left it at that."

I was shocked. "Why didn't you say anything?"

"Because I was afraid if I told Dad I knew where you were that he'd tell you and you'd up and move."

Ashamed that he'd think that, I shook my head. "I wouldn't have done that, Darragh. Hartwell started out as a hiding place, but it became more than that. It's my home."

"This is your home." Davina's hazel eyes flickered with fire as she turned to our big brother. "You didn't think maybe I'd want to know where she was?"

"You would have gone there."

"Of course I would have." She turned to me. "I would have dragged your ass back home!"

"Davina," my dad warned.

"Stop protecting her," she hissed. "She's a grown woman, and she can speak for herself."

"Davi," I whispered in sorrow.

"Don't call me that."

That was like a punch to the gut.

Davi was my nickname for her. I was the only one who called her that.

"Christ, Davina," Darragh said. "We said we wouldn't do this to her."

"We should have done this a long time ago."

I needed them to understand something. "I couldn't come home."

"Of course you could have."

"I couldn't."

"Yes, you could have."

"No, I couldn't!" I yelled, losing my patience.

Davina sat back in her chair, her eyes wide.

I grimaced. "I'm sorry ... I ... you don't know ... " Not even my dad knew, which made how much he'd protected and cared for me over the years even more amazing.

But now that Mom wasn't here, now that my parents had separated, I could explain everything. I realized it was the real reason I had felt strong enough to come home now. It took me to get to this moment, to face my family, to truly understand.

I knew it didn't erase the years of cowardice, of hiding, but maybe it would answer some of their questions.

So, on a quiet Sunday afternoon in my childhood home, I told my family my story. It was painful, it was difficult, and I was ashamed to admit all of it, to tell them everything, but I did it because I wanted them back. I hadn't realized how much I wanted them back until I saw them again. And if I had to lay myself bare to get them back, I would.

I no longer needed to protect my mother.

When I was finished, Davina was wiping at silent tears, Darragh's face was pale and haggard, and my dad ... I couldn't look at my dad.

He pushed his chair back from the table and stormed out of the kitchen.

"Dad!" The word was garbled by my tears as I moved to chase him.

"Don't." Darragh reached across the table and grabbed my wrist. "Let him go."

"Why didn't you say anything?" Davina shook her head.

"Because she was wrong and she wasn't wrong. And her daughter had just died, and I didn't ... I didn't want you to hate her."

"Too late for that." Davina curled her lip.

Dread filled me. "Davina, she wasn't in her right mind."

"Oh? Is she still not? Because since I came out, she pretends like she's still my mother, like my being gay doesn't bother her, but she's never been to my apartment. She's never invited Astrid and me for suppa unless it was Thanksgiving and the whole family was here. And let's put aside her secret homophobia and remind ourselves that she erased you from her life. She doesn't talk about you, she doesn't let anyone else talk about you, and she acted like it was all your fuckin' fault!" She pushed away from the table.

"Davina," Darragh admonished.

"No!" She sobbed. "I hate her, Dar. I hate her."

"Come here." He stood up, and I watched as he pulled my sister into his arms as she cried. My poor brother. I wondered if he'd known he'd spend most of his day comforting his little sisters.

I knew that Davina wasn't merely crying about me. My heart

was already shredded by my mother, but Davina's confirmation that my mom had erased me was like a knife in my gut. The knife twisted as I realized she'd not only hurt me but she'd inflicted wounds on my big sister too. The depth of Davina's pain was about *her* relationship with Sorcha McGuire. I wasn't the only daughter my mom couldn't accept. It sounded like she hadn't fully come to terms with Davina being gay. I knew what it was like to feel the harsh chill of Mom's disapproval. You could be five, fifteen, or fifty, and feeling like one of your parents didn't love you or agree with who you'd become was one of the worst hurts in the world.

I wished I'd been there for Davina.

Seeing how close she and Darragh still were, however, soothed me. They had each other. I glanced over my shoulder at the doorway dad had stormed out of. I worried my bottom lip between my teeth. At once, the separation between Mom and Dad started to make sense. Cian McGuire loved his kids more than anything. We were his life. I had no doubt that Mom's treatment of two of their daughters had put a strain on their marriage.

And he hadn't even known the full of it.

Until now.

My concern grew.

Maybe I shouldn't have said anything after all if it had meant hurting Dad.

"Stop it."

Davina's harsh voice brought my attention back to her. She and my brother were no longer hugging. Instead, she was looking at me with a million things in her expression. "Don't sit there and worry that you shouldn't have told the truth because of Dad. It was long past due, and you did the right thing. He's not mad at you. He's mad at himself."

"I know what it's like to be mad at yourself and frankly, I'd prefer him to be mad at me."

She gave me a soft smile that made my heart race. "Some things never change. I'm still mad at you, Dahlia, but you didn't leave for selfish reasons. You left to protect him and to protect us from the truth."

"Don't make me sound noble. I was a drunk who ended up in therapy."

"Yeah." She walked around the table and held her hand out to me. "But now I get why. I'm still mad at you for not coming back sooner. But I guess I kind of understand that too now."

I took her hand and let her pull me up. My arms flew around her, and she gave a huff of laughter as I held on tight. "I missed you."

"I missed you too, baby sis."

"I'm sorry I wasn't here for you. For everything." I looked at Darragh. "I'm so sorry."

He nodded. "I know."

Pulling back, I sniffled. "We've got a lot of catching up to do."

"Yeah, we do," Darragh agreed. "Krista wants you to come for dinner this week. The boys are dying to meet their aunt Dahlia who gives them such cool presents every year."

My heart wanted to burst. "They know who I am?"

"Christ, Dahlia, of course they do."

Anticipation and trepidation filled me in equal measure. "I can't wait to see them. Dad sent me pictures. I hope you don't mind."

"I gave him the pictures to give to you."

This information caused an unexpected sob to burst forth.

For years I'd been so afraid to come home.

Now I couldn't think why.

My family was fuckin' awesome!

"If I"—I hiccupped—"if I don't ... if I don't stop crying ... I'm going to ... I'll be so ... dehydrated!"

My brother and sister burst out laughing, and I glared at their inappropriateness.

Davina threw her arm around my shoulders and hugged me to her side. "It's nice to know the old Dahlia is still under this bawling mess."

"I look like shit, don't I?"

"Pretty much."

That made me cry even harder, which only made my siblings laugh harder.

Bastards.

God, I loved them.

After a while, Dad came out of hiding, seeming to have gathered himself. We knew him well enough to know that you let Dad bring up a subject. He didn't want to talk about his feelings on what he learned, and as much as I wanted to discuss it with him, I let it be.

I'd like to say everything was hunky-dory with Darragh, Davina, and me, but that would be too easy. Darragh had forgiven me the moment he saw me. That was my big brother. He was so like Dad in nature that I shouldn't have been surprised by his reception.

And I knew Davina understood things better now and would try. But there were nine years of missing out on each other's lives, and as we sat around the table talking, awkwardness fell when we mentioned things about our past that left the other clueless.

"I can't believe you've had Aunt Cecilia's shop this whole time," Davina grumbled.

When I'd hit the bottle back in Boston after Dillon's death, Dad decided the only way to pull me out of that dark place was to get me out of the city. His little sister Cecilia inherited the shop on the boardwalk from her first husband. He'd left her a widow with a nice, hefty bank account. Dad knew Cecilia was thinking about selling the store and he convinced her to let me rent it instead.

She'd passed away two years ago while traveling across Europe, and that beautiful woman had gifted me the shop in her will. It was now all mine.

"You said Aunt Cecilia sold it." My sister narrowed her eyes on Dad.

"She rented it to Dahlia."

"And then she gave it to me in her will."

Davina's eyes widened. "Nice."

"She was kind. Really kind." Thoughts of Aunt Cecilia made me sad. She wrote me letters, sending me one every time she made it to a new city. Since I never knew when she would move on, I sent my replies via email. Still, Cecilia preferred the old-fashioned method. I'd loved that about her.

"I can't wait to see it," Darragh said. "Krista and I would love to vacation there with the kids this summer. Spend some time with you."

"Wait, you're going back?" Davina's brows pulled together.

Just like that, all the old hurt flared between us. Tentatively, I nodded. "I live there."

Before she could reply, the front door slammed and heavy foot-steps stomped inside. "Dad!"

Dermot.

Shit.

Growing up, it became apparent that Darragh, Davina, and I got a lot of character traits from Dad. Dermot and Dillon were a lot like Mom.

I braced.

"In here," Dad responded, and tension seemed to build around the table as Dermot's footsteps neared.

And then he was there.

His eyes drifted around the table and then stopped on me. Dermot may have had my mom's nature, but he looked like my dad and Darragh. His nostrils flared at the sight of me.

"Mom's only out of the fuckin' house five minutes, and that bitch is back."

My chest tightened with hurt.

Darragh flew out of his chair. "You watch your mouth."

"You all forgive her?" He glared at my family. "She took off, forgot we existed, and then turned Dad against Mom."

"Oh, that's right, Dermot, you let Mom's twisted lies poison you. You can't think for yourself. You have no idea what happened." My sister was livid.

"Mom's been here for the last nine years. *She* walks in and has obviously told you shit, and you believe that over Mom?"

"Well, yeah, because nine years does not negate the fact that I know *Mom* and I know *Dahlia* . . . so yeah, I know who *I* believe."

Dermot shook his head in disgust and then looked down at Dad. "This is Mom's house, and no matter what is happening between you two, it's a fuckin' disgrace you let that trash in here."

Instead of the tears that my brother's and sister's acceptance brought on, Dermot's vitriol turned me to ice. I numbed him out, unable to feel his words because they would hurt too much. Growing up, we'd been closer in age, and we used to hang out all the time. We shared the same friends. We'd *been* friends. Best of friends.

Now he hated me.

Dad rose slowly from his chair, and Dermot shifted back on his feet uncertainly. Our dad rarely got mad but when he did, it wasn't with a typical Irish temper of yelling and cursing.

He got real quiet.

"This is my house," he said, his voice all menacing softness, "and this is my daughter." He put a hand on my shoulder. "Now you either respect that this is my house and respect your sister's presence in it, or you can turn your ass back around and get the hell out."

Hurt saturated Dermot's features. He shook his head in disbelief. "Christ, you're all blind."

And on that, he stormed out.

An awful silence filled the kitchen as Dad sat wearily back down at the table.

I looked at my family who stared at me in concern.

I shrugged, needing to lighten the mood despite my inner turmoil. "That was not as bad as the time he rolled dog shit in a piece of newspaper and left it under my bed."

As I'd hoped, they all chuckled, thankful for the break in tension.

4

Dahlia

Seeming reluctant to leave me, Darragh and Davina both took calls from Krista and Astrid respectively and told them they wouldn't be home for dinner. Instead, they stayed, and we ordered Chinese takeout. I got the impression they were afraid that if they left, I'd disappear again. Along with some self-reproach came the reassurance that no matter how difficult it would be to move on from the past, my big brother and sister still loved me.

They caught me up on what was happening in their lives, and they asked about Hartwell. I had a lot of fun describing the characters who lived on the boardwalk, especially Bailey. Davina got quiet when I talked about Bailey, however, and I understood she was still upset with me. Bailey knew things about my life that no one else did.

After what I'd told them in the kitchen, it wasn't surprising that none of them asked about my romantic life. Maybe they were afraid it would set off another round of sobbing. It wouldn't. I know it hadn't sounded like it to them, but I'd moved on. If I hadn't before, I certainly had now, knowing Michael had a wife.

When my big brother and sister left, it was around ten o'clock. I didn't know about them, but I was emotionally exhausted. They hugged me goodbye after we swapped numbers, and Davina said she'd have me over to her and Astrid's place on Thursday for dinner when Dad was working so I wasn't alone in the house. Darragh already had me and Dad penciled in for dinner on Wednesday night.

The door closed behind them and silence fell between Dad and me.

I recognized his expression. "I know. You were right."

"But I didn't know what had set you running off and now it makes sense you'd come home when she wasn't here." My poor Dad seemed drained.

I didn't want to tell him he was right and make him feel worse. "Dad, I'd been toying with coming home for months. After I saw Michael, I realized I was stronger than I thought."

"So, you would have come home if your Mom was still here … after everything?"

"I would have come home for you. For them." I nodded at the door my siblings had walked out of. "Don't hate her, Dad."

He shook his head. "You should have told me."

"Dad—"

"I don't hate her. But I'm furious with her. I don't understand her." He dragged a hand down his face. "I'm tired, Bluebell. I'm going to catch up on the game before bed. You want to watch it with me?"

I strode across the room and got on my tiptoes to kiss his cheek. "I'm going to bed. Night, Dad. Love you."

"Love you too."

My heart twisted in my chest at the moroseness in his tone, and I gave him a reassuring smile. "I'm good. I promise."

He didn't seem to believe me, but something like determination hardened his expression. "I know you will be."

Squeezing his arm, I turned and made my way to the guest room. The sound of a football game filtered upstairs and a wave of nostalgia hit me. We'd been a sports family. I wasn't into it, but I'd loved how we all came together as a family during football season and the Super Bowl. I loved how Dad got us tickets to at least one game every year at Fenway to see the Red Sox play. There was nothing like the atmosphere at Fenway. The sound of laughter, the smell of beer, hotdogs, and popcorn. The music and sound of the announcer filling the stadium. The sounds of men and women with thick Bostonian accents running up and down the stands cradling goods shouting, "Beer! Get your beer!", "Hot dogs! Get your hotdogs!"

That pain in my heart twisted even tighter at the memories of all of us together.

My muscle memories automatically led me to the bedroom I'd shared with my sisters growing up. I'd already opened the door and was about to step inside when I remembered I wasn't sleeping in there.

My breath caught. Mom hadn't changed the room. Tears filled my eyes as a sick sensation took up residence in my gut. It wouldn't have surprised me if she'd kept Dillon's side of the room the same and emptied mine, but my side hadn't been touched either.

I could still see the photos pinned to the wall by my bed.

Unable to look at Dillon's space, I tentatively walked in, my heart thudding hard in my chest as I gravitated toward the photos. My walls were covered in them and pieces of paper with my old sketches and paintings. The dresser at the side of my bed was still littered with old perfume bottles and makeup. I sat slowly down on the bed, a lump forming in my throat, as I gazed at the photos.

Some were of my family and me. Davina and I at the kitchen table with Darragh standing at our backs with his arms around us. Dad and I outside Fenway. Dermot and I in his car after I'd gotten my driver's license. My heart squeezed at the sight of my head tucked against my big brother's chest and the bright, beaming smile he was giving the camera.

Then everything within me locked tight when I saw the picture of Mom and me. The photo was taken when I was sixteen, dressed for a formal dance. It looked like she was hugging me to death in the picture and we were both laughing into the camera.

Unable to bear it, I dragged my attention to the next lot of photos. Memories assaulted me. They were all of me, Gary, Michael, Dillon, Dermot, and our friends.

My eyes stopped on the lone photo I had of me and Michael. We were sitting in Angie's Diner off Main Street, and he had his arm sprawled along the back of the booth where I was sitting. Always drawn to him, without even realizing it, my body was curled in toward him. Someone had taken the photo—I think it was Dermot—when we weren't looking, and we were talking to each other. When I saw that photo, I'd kept it.

Because of the way Michael was looking at me. The way I was looking at him.

God, I closed my eyes. *Had we really been that obvious?*

When I forced my eyes back open, they shot to Dillon's side of the room. She had posters of the bands she'd loved on the walls, piles of romance books on her dresser, and makeup everywhere.

Suddenly I could see her, clear as day, as the memories flooded me ...

Following my little sister into our room, I didn't feel the happy exhaustion she seemed to feel after the party we were returning from.

"Ssshh," I hissed as her singing got a little louder. I closed the bedroom door behind us. "Do you want Mom to hear?"

Dillon shrugged and grinned as she sat down on the bed to take off her heels. "I'm nineteen, and I was out celebrating my big sister's twenty-first birthday. Not a crime!"

I laughed softly. "Shut up."

"What's up with you tonight? You act like you turned forty instead."

Slumping down on my bed, I stared at my bedroom ceiling and contemplated the disaster that was my birthday party. It had been an overcrowded gathering in one of Gary's friend's apartments in Southie, and my boyfriend was already drunk by the time we got there. First, he'd been all publicly handsy, and Michael had to pull him off me when he saw how uncomfortable I was getting. Then Gary had flirted with another girl for most of the night when he wasn't acting like a dipshit frat boy. I hated when Gary got drunk. He was like a different person.

I'd had a good time though. I'd spent most of the night in a corner with Michael laughing and talking. Dillon had hung out with us too, but there were times it was just the two of us and it had been great. In fact, I'd wanted the whole room to disappear and leave me alone with Michael.

He'd gotten the night off work especially to be there for my birthday.

I felt that low, deep flip in my belly whenever I thought about him. It occurred too whenever I was with him, and he gave me that focused, boyish smile of his.

Guilt swarmed me. Guilt I tried to rid myself of because I was pretty sure Gary, my boyfriend of eight months, was cheating on me.

There were secretive texts and phone calls, and he'd started "working late" at the garage a lot.

"Seriously, Dahlia, what's up?" Dillon asked. "I'm worried about you. You spent the whole of your birthday with Mike and me instead of Gary."

I groaned. "You saw how drunk Gary was." I sat up, needing to talk to someone so badly and since Davina was working crazy hours at some finance company, my little sister had become my closest confidante. "I think he's cheating on me."

Dillon wrinkled her cute little nose. "With that trashy girl he was flirting with tonight? No, he was just drunk."

"No, not her." Although who knew? *"He's been acting weird lately. Hiding his phone when he gets a text, working later and later at the garage when he's supposed to be hanging with me."*

"Oh." Dillon sighed. *"You should talk to him about it, then. Eight months is such a long time to be with someone without talking about it."*

I almost laughed at that. Eight months was nothing in the grand scheme of things. *"What about the way he was acting tonight? He sat on a guy's face tonight and farted."*

Dillon gave a bark of laughter. *"Okay, I admit, that was nasty."*

"Nasty? Dill, this is a twenty-two-, nearly-three-year-old man we're talking about."

"It sounds like you've already made up your mind."

I had.

Turning around I looked at the photos on my wall, my eyes drawn to the one of Michael and me at the diner. Dermot took it a couple of weeks ago. How could no one see what I felt for my boyfriend's best friend? It was blazing out of my eyes. And if that photo meant anything, if tonight—or any of the times Michael and I had found ourselves alone—meant anything, he felt the same way.

I knew he did.

I was totally and completely in love with my boyfriend's best friend.

Surely if Gary was cheating, then all bets were off, and Michael wouldn't feel bad about dating me then, right?

This longing inside of my chest was almost too much to bear. Tears filled my eyes at the thought of never getting to be with Michael, and I was not the crying type.

Oh God, I was so completely and utterly in love with him.

We'd connected from the moment we met in the gallery.

"You're going to dump him, aren't you?" Dillon asked.

Biting my lip, I turned back around to face her. "First, I'll prove he's cheating and then, yes, I'm going to break up with him."

"Good. You deserve better than him."

I smiled wearily at my sister, still feeling sick about the whole thing. I hated confrontation. I was good at it, especially with people I didn't really care about. However, confrontation with loved ones was hell on the heart.

"Speaking of deserving good things ... " Dillon gave me a wide-eyed, excited grin. "I'm going to ask Mike out."

What?

I shook my head, sure I'd heard wrong. "You're what?"

"I'm going to ask Michael out." She pulled on her pajama shorts and a tank, before getting into bed. So casual. Like she hadn't just rocked my entire world.

"Why?" I whispered.

Dillon chuckled. "Why? Uh ... because he's gorgeous and funny and nice. And I'm pretty sure he likes me back."

No. No. NO! NO WAY!

Michael didn't like Dillon.

No.

What the hell?

"Isn't ... Isn't he a little old for you?"

My sister huffed, "Dahlia, he's twenty-three."

"He'll be twenty-four in June." June 26 to be exact. "You've only turned nineteen."

"That's not a big age gap. And you know I'm mature for my age."

No, I knew she thought she was mature for her age.

Panic seized my chest, and I couldn't move.

"Don't worry, this won't affect you breaking up with Gary. In fact, I think Mike thinks you should break up with him. He was so pissed on your behalf tonight. I mean, Gary passed out on *your birthday night, and his best friend had to drive you home. So wrong."*

No, *what was so wrong was my little sister having a crush on the man I was in love with.*

As Dillon's snores abruptly filled the bedroom, I got up, feeling like a Mack Truck had hit me, and slowly changed into my pajamas. Once in bed, I stared at my ceiling for hours, desperately trying to fall asleep. Sleep only claimed me when I convinced myself that there was no way Michael Sullivan would date my sister.

No way.

"Bluebell, wake up."

I groaned, coming out of a deep sleep at the sound of my dad's voice. Blinking into the dim darkness, I turned my head and saw my dad standing over me.

"Daddy?"

Sadness filled his eyes. "What are you doing in here?"

"Huh?"

Realizing where I was, that I wasn't dreaming and that I'd fallen asleep in my old room, I sat up too fast, and the room spun.

"Come on, Bluebell. Let's get you to bed."

I hugged into my dad's side, still lost in that halfway place between sleep and consciousness, and I let him lead me into the boys' old room. He pulled back the duvet on Darragh's old bed and helped me in, drawing the covers up to my neck. He kissed my forehead and whispered good night.

I think I mumbled a reply before I gratefully let sleep draw me back under.

5

Michael

The computer screen blurred before his eyes and Michael pinched the bridge of his nose as if it would somehow relieve the ache in his sinuses. Why did he think switching to night shift was a good idea? It was now 6:00 a.m., well past the end of his shift, and he was only just finishing his report on the homicide he and his partner Davis had ended the night with.

It looked like it would be a rare open-and-shut case.

They'd been called to an apartment in West Roxbury where a seemingly normal twenty-eight-year-old woman had announced she'd shot her boyfriend in the kitchen.

Fuck, it had been a mess.

She'd shot him in the head.

Hours later in the interview room, she'd told Michael and his new partner on the night shift she'd suspected her boyfriend was cheating, he'd confessed when she interrogated him (her words), and she'd lost her temper and shot him in the head with her .380.

She'd been chillingly cool, and Michael didn't know if it was shock, if there was ultimately more to the story, or if she was a psychopath. He'd arrested her, written the report, and they'd wait to see if forensics corroborated her story.

"Mornin', Detective," a bright, cheery voice called.

He looked past his computer and saw the young redheaded

administrative assistant smiling at him from the coffee machine. He couldn't remember her name. Amber or Ashley or something. Giving her a fatigued nod, he turned back to his report and saved it.

"I think she likes you."

Michael glanced over his shoulder and up. Christ, he was so tired he hadn't heard anyone approach. Getting his body used to a new shift pattern was harder now than it used to be when he was younger.

Nick Bronson stood at his desk. He and Bronson had come through the academy together.

"You look too fuckin' awake," Michael groaned.

Bronson clapped him on the shoulder. "Maybe the redhead will wake you up."

Michael gave him a look. "She's too young."

His friend smirked. "She's twenty-three."

"You already checked?"

"She told me."

"Then you date her." Michael wanted to date like he wanted a bullet in *his* head. Sex, on the other hand, would be nice. Very nice, but not with young things working in his office.

Bronson lost his smirk. "Speaking of . . . can we talk?"

Michael wanted nothing more than to go home, but his friend sounded serious. Nodding, he grabbed his car keys and his jacket and followed Bronson through the office to an empty interview room.

"What's going on?"

Bronson looked weirdly uncomfortable. He exhaled heavily. "I don't know how to say this without getting punched in the face."

Just like that, the weariness started to slide off Michael. Alert, he leaned against the door and crossed his arms over his chest. "Spit it out, whatever it is."

"I'm dating Kiersten."

For a moment, Michael thought he'd misheard. "I'm really fuckin' tired this morning so you'll need to repeat that because I thought I heard you say you're dating my soon-to-be ex-wife."

Bronson winced. "That's what I said."

"Are you shittin' me?"

"Look, man, I didn't expect it to happen. Okay? We bumped into each other two months ago—you guys had decided to separate for good. It wasn't a date at first. We were just hanging out, talking about our divorces." His expression turned apologetic. "I care about her, Mike. And Kiersten feels the same way. But I wanted you to find out from me before we go public with it."

Jesus Christ. His wife was barely out of their bed, and she was already shacking up with someone new. And not just anyone, his goddamn friend. Michael knew his marriage was a mistake, and he'd known that for a long time, but that didn't mean this didn't sting.

"Guess the part where she told me my job was part of the reason our marriage didn't work was a lie, huh?"

Bronson frowned. "She said that?"

You bet she'd fuckin' said that. And that was when he worked the day shift. "Yeah, warning you now, Kiersten isn't the kind of woman who wants to know about your day."

"The shit I see? I wouldn't put that on her anyway."

Yeah, Michael hadn't either. But Kiersten didn't even ask him the simplest "How has your day been?"

Maybe that was just *their* relationship. Perhaps she'd be different with someone else.

And, truthfully, Michael wanted that for her. It was unexpected that she was trying to find it with a friend of his, and so soon, but Nick was a good guy.

He should be more upset than he was.

Part of him was almost relieved.

Did this mean he didn't have to feel so guilty anymore?

Exhaustion deflated him. He held out his hand to Bronson, who took it, relief relaxing his features. "Take care of her."

"Thanks, Mike. I appreciate it."

"Well, I appreciate you telling me."

They shared a nod and Michael left his friend, his tired brain now wired with this new information. As he drove home to his one-bedroom apartment in Chelsea, he thought of all the shit Kiersten had spewed at him during their many arguments. His job was depressing. He worked too many hours, and the pay wasn't even that great. They needed more money. They needed a bigger house, nicer things.

Their house had been in Everett, and despite all the crap she'd given him about money, Kiersten wasn't vindictive. She knew he couldn't afford to keep up mortgage payments *and* get an apartment near the city. Instead, she'd gone back to her parents' house in Southie, and they'd put the Everett house up for sale. Any equity would be split between them.

Michael sighed, feeling a weight compress his chest.

He'd never understood most of Kiersten's complaints but at the base of them was her foremost: that he was distant with her. That he kept putting off having kids with her.

At the time, Michael hadn't delved into it. He thought he was doing his best as a husband. After that ill-timed vacation in Hartwell to fix things between them, he realized all the crap Kiersten had been giving him over the years came from that belief—that he was distant with her.

That he didn't love her the way she loved him.

Seeing his reaction to Dahlia—finding out who she was—it was the straw that broke the camel's back.

They'd gone home the next morning, and Kiersten packed a suitcase and left.

The weight tightened like a vise around his ribs, and he squeezed his hands around the steering wheel. Of all the places to bump into Dahlia McGuire, it would be on fuckin' vacation.

Seeing her had messed with his head. He'd thought he'd get over it like he did her leaving in the first place, but the memory of seeing her in that bookshop lingered. The stricken look on her face kept replaying over and over in his head.

She had to be as beautiful as he remembered, didn't she? She couldn't have gotten bitter and old-looking. No, that would be too fair. His own bitterness twisted in his chest. Michael hadn't even known it was still there. He'd thought meeting Kiersten four years ago, settling down with her, meant he'd moved on.

Clearly, he hadn't.

But Michael would not make the same mistake twice.

The woman Michael had fallen in love with had died when Dillon died, and the person left behind in her body was a coward who'd proven she didn't love him the way he had loved her.

Michael pulled up to the triple-decker that had been converted into apartments and stared up at the second floor where his small one-bedroom was housed. Thirty-four years old and he was staying in a fuckin' bachelor pad, starting over again.

He thought of Bronson and Kiersten. His wife wasn't a stupid woman. She was strong and opinionated, and he'd always thought she was up-front about how she felt. But if she was now dating Nick after telling Michael for months that his job was the problem, then she'd been lying.

Michael rubbed a hand over his face, remembering their argument in their hotel room in Hartwell after he'd told her who Dahlia had been to him.

"All this time, Mike? All this time and I thought it was your preoccupation with your job. I hated your job. I blamed everything about it on why things between us weren't right. But it wasn't the

long hours or that look you'd get on your face that told me you'd just seen something awful again, or that we couldn't afford a bigger place on your salary. All of that was shit.

"I don't care about any of that. I didn't know what was keeping you from me. Now I do. It was her. I know it was her ... because you have never looked at me the way you looked at her. You have never sounded talking about me, not even at our wedding, the way you sound when you say *her name*."

Would Dahlia keep ruining things for him, then?

Would she haunt him for the rest of his fuckin' life, making it hard for him to connect with someone else?

Because that's what had happened, right?

He'd kept Kiersten at arm's length so she couldn't pull "a Dahlia" on him.

Sighing, he got out of his car, locked it up, and made his way into the building. Unlocking the door to his apartment, Michael stepped inside the airy space and tried not to process the emptiness. He hadn't done much to make it a home. There was a couch, armchair, table with a lamp, and a TV in the living room. A table and chairs in the kitchen. A bed and bedside tables in the bedroom. It had a built-in closet, so he didn't need anything else in there.

Their Everett house was filled with all the feminine things that seemed like nonsense to Michael. Now he realized Kiersten had made that place their home. She was right.

He slumped on his bed.

He'd checked out on her.

And she wasn't even trying to make their divorce hard to get her revenge, even though he deserved it.

He'd fucked over a good woman, the way Dahlia had fucked over him.

Lying back on the bed, Michael groaned, hating the way her

face invaded his mind. It was eleven years since they'd met. Eleven years.

Still feeling like this ... well, that shit wasn't right.

Jesus, his friend had told him he was dating his ex-wife, and still his thoughts went to Dahlia. It was her who caused this pain in his chest, like someone digging a small knife right above his heart and twisting it. He wished he had someone, anyone, even the redhead from the office who would normally be off limits, to fuck. To fuck until he'd stop thinking about her. Not Kiersten.

Apparently never Kiersten.

Always *her*.

"Why'd it have to be her?" he murmured into the room. "Go haunt someone else."

6

Dahlia

The next morning Dad made me a champion's breakfast of pancakes, eggs, and bacon, covered with a generous dollop of maple syrup. I couldn't finish it.

"You can eat more than that," he protested.

"Dad, I don't eat like this anymore. I don't know if you know this about women, but when we hit thirty, our metabolism decides 'fuck it,' puts its feet up, and decides it's done a lifetime duty in twenty-nine years."

He chuckled. "Who cares? Men like curves."

I rolled my eyes. "I don't care what men like, Dad. I care what *I* like."

Dad winked at me. "Good girl."

Shaking my head with a smile, I pushed my plate away. Then I snuck what had been on my mind since I'd woken up into the conversation. Okay, I didn't sneak it in. I threw it in like a wrecking ball. "So, how do you feel about this separation, Dad?"

His fork froze halfway to his mouth, and he cut me a dirty look.

I smiled sheepishly. "I'm worried about you."

"Don't be." His voice had gone all gruff in that way it did when he didn't want to talk about something.

"Dad?"

"What about you? You seeing anyone? What happened to that sheriff fella?"

I winced. Why did I tell my dad everything? "That was years ago. You know that."

"He sounded like a good guy. Never understood what happened there."

He was lying. He knew what happened there. And it was mean of him to mention it. So, of course, I was mean back. "The sex was too good. I couldn't take it."

Dad flicked me a dark look. "Dahlia."

Exasperated, I shrugged. "Why should I talk about my personal life if you won't talk about Mom?"

"Do you have a personal life?"

"Dad!"

"Well, do you?" He dropped his fork and looked me straight in the eye, which should have prepared me for what was coming but didn't. "Mike's getting divorced. He's just waiting on it finalizing."

Pain and longing crushed my chest, and I looked away.

"You've both been unhappy for a long time. You need to sit down with him and talk."

My dad: matchmaker. "Dad—"

"He's a good man, Bluebell. I care about him. I'd like knowing you had someone like him at your back."

Michael *was* a good man. But he wasn't my man. "He's not for me."

"I want you to be happy."

Staring at my plate, I smiled. "I am happy, Dad."

"And maybe if I hadn't known you your whole life, I'd believe that."

Getting up, I wandered over to the coffee machine, determined to change the subject. "What time is your shift today?"

"Two this afternoon. I finish at two in the morning. What are your plans?"

Relieved he was going with the subject change, I leaned against the counter and smiled for real. "I think I'll go into the city. I've missed it."

"Don't suppose you'll be going anywhere near Bova's?"

I chuckled. Bova's was my dad's favorite bakery. "I guess it's not far from Quincy Market. I think I can make the trip. Anything in particular you want?"

"You choose." He grinned boyishly at the prospect.

Laughing, I shook my head. "You know you'll have to hit the gym to work off a trip to Bova's."

"Worth it." He stood up. "You want to take a walk around town with your dad before I have to get ready for work?"

I couldn't think of anything better. "I'd like that."

And so we did walk around Everett, and wave after wave of nostalgia washed over me as we walked. We talked about the past, about almost everything and nothing. What we didn't talk about was Mom or Michael. I thought that meant Dad was letting it go. But I should have known that if I wasn't letting it go about Mom, Dad definitely wasn't letting it go about Michael.

Bailey had called that morning, a call I returned as soon as Dad departed for work. My friend was understandably worried about me, and I kept her on the phone for two hours while I caught her up on what had gone down with my brothers and sister. She spent a good fifteen minutes cursing and being pissed at Dermot for what he'd said.

I was trying to calm her down when a deep, cultured voice asked in the background, "What on earth is happening?"

It was Vaughn.

Bailey stopped yelling. "What are you doing here?"

"I wanted to see you," he answered dryly. "I see now that was a terrible idea."

"Ha." She sniffed haughtily. "I'm on the phone with Dahlia."

"And that constitutes using every curse word known to man? It's an odd friendship you have there."

I smirked at his sarcasm.

"You know, you're very pretty when you don't open your mouth," my best friend replied.

"I know for a fact that you prefer when my mouth is open and working."

"Okay, best friend can hear everything!" I yelled.

Bailey chuckled. "Dahlia can hear you."

His tone changed. "Is she all right?"

He sounded concerned. That was nice.

"She's fine. However, her brother Dermot makes Vanessa look like an angel."

"Not true," I disagreed, feeling the need to defend Dermot against that accusation despite his reaction to my reappearance. Vanessa was a demon hellhound in a woman's body.

"Would you like me to have him killed?" Vaughn sounded worryingly serious.

Bailey answered, "Let's see how the visit goes. I'll get back to you."

I rolled my eyes. "I'll let you go."

"You don't have to."

"No, I've had you on the phone for two hours, and it sounds like Prince Charming wants to work his mouth."

Bailey chuckled. "I wish he could hear you right now. On second thought, he likes a woman with a smart mouth. He might fall in love with you."

"Not possible," I replied. "I'll call you later."

"You better."

We hung up, and I found myself alone in the house.

Just like that, it felt like the walls were coming in on me. I couldn't get out of the house fast enough. Not only did I pick up a box of baked goodies from Bova's to take home, I spent hours in the city. I didn't get a bus home until ten o' clock, and I took myself to bed as soon as I got home.

The house was cold and lonely without Dad in it.

Thankfully, after hours of walking, sleep came quickly.

The next morning, Dad surprised me by getting up at nine, early considering he usually didn't get home until around three. I knew it was because he wanted to spend as much time as possible with me before I went back to Hartwell. No decision had been made yet about when that would be.

I guess when I was certain Dad was going to be okay.

What I didn't realize was that Dad was equally determined to make sure I was okay before I went back to Hartwell and as good as his intentions were, he went about it the wrong way.

That day we went to Angie's Diner, and Winnie, the sixty-year-old owner, and Angie's daughter greeted me like I'd never left. I thought that was nice. Part of my fear of coming home was how everyone else, not only my family, would react to me. Dad and I hung out there, and we talked more about life. He told me stories about Leo and Levi that made me laugh, and I grew more excited than nervous about meeting them at dinner the following day.

My time with Dad that day was peaceful, and I was lulled into a false sense of security.

Everything went to shit at seven o'clock.

"Dress nice, we're having steak," Dad had said later that afternoon.

I hadn't thought anything of his comment. Or the fact that he'd asked me to set the dining table, even though it was only him and me. It was kind of a tradition around here to dress nice and eat in the dining room when we were having steak to show our appreciation for Dad's favorite food and gratitude for being able to afford it.

When the doorbell rang at seven, I knew I'd been extremely naïve.

"I'll get it," Dad said before I could question him.

My stomach roiled slightly with unease when the doorbell rang. I think my body knew before I did.

The murmur of masculine voices sounded from the living room, and as they grew closer, I began to recognize the voice that didn't belong to my dad.

I'd recognize that voice anywhere.

Dad came through the kitchen doorway, his expression wary but stoic, and I braced myself.

Michael stepped inside behind him and jolted to a stop in shock. *Shit.*

Not only had my dad invited him for dinner, he hadn't told him I'd be there.

The whole world seemed to disappear, and it was like my body had abruptly awoken from a very long sleep. My heart was pounding, my fingertips tingled, and my blood pumped through me with restless, voracious energy. Michael was here. Michael was standing right there. Alive and vital and masculine and ... everything.

His dark eyes met mine and I saw the muscle jump in his cheek as he tried to figure out what the hell was going on. The beard he'd worn the last time I'd seen him had been shaved off and now the lower half of his cheeks and jaw were covered in a layer of sexy stubble.

The urge to cross the room and clasp his face in my hands so I could feel that stubble prickle my skin was overwhelming.

Thankfully, I managed to curb the urge.

"What's going on, Cian?" Michael's gaze never left mine.

I wondered if it was impossible for him to look away. It certainly was for me.

God, I'd missed him.

Longing crawled across my chest and dug its sharp fingernails in through my bone and flesh. An impossible, aching weight.

"Look—" My dad stepped between us, his expression determined. Still, I saw a flicker of wariness in his blue eyes when he turned to Michael. "Mike, I didn't tell Dahlia you were coming either. I thought we should have a meal together. I'm not suggesting we sit and hash things out. Let's sit, have steak, and catch up."

Michael shot him a look of disbelief.

Oh, Dad, this was a bad move.

And I feared it was only going to end in my tears.

"C'mon." Dad put an arm around Michael's shoulders and led him out of the kitchen, presumably to the dining table.

The air rushed out of me and I reached for a kitchen chair to steady my trembling legs.

Dad returned, trying to hide the fact that he was worried, but I knew him too well. I shook my head at him. "Dad."

"Take him a beer, and I'll get the stuff to set another place at the table." He reached into the refrigerator for a bottle. Then he paused, shooting me a look. "Shit, I didn't think."

Frowning, I didn't quite understand at first, and then it dawned on me. "Dad," I said, lowering my voice, "I haven't had a drink in nine years and I'm good with that. One of my closest friend's bar is our regular hangout spot." I smiled. "I can take a beer to someone."

He crossed the room, kissed my forehead, and handed me the Budweiser.

As soon as my hand curled around the chilled bottle, I began to tremble again.

"Maybe you should take it to him after all," I whispered.

"Get it over with, Bluebell. Like a Band-Aid, remember."

Reluctantly, I nodded and pulled my shoulders back. It was like I was preparing to march into war.

Little did I know.

At first, I strode out of the kitchen, but my strides slowed with my anxiety as I turned left into the dining room.

Michael wasn't sitting at the table. He had his back to me, staring at the framed photographs that covered the wall. I took the opportunity to drink him in. His broad back filled out the fitted dark-brown leather bomber jacket he wore. The fact that he hadn't taken his jacket off wasn't a good sign.

"Did you know you're not in any of these photos?" He made me jump a little with his abruptness.

Instead of answering, I walked toward him. I wanted to stand closer to him. Just a little closer. Catching me out of his peripheral, he turned his head from the photos to watch me approach. The chill in his eyes made me slow to a halt, and I gingerly held out the beer to him.

He flicked a disgusted look at it, not reaching for it.

I lowered my arm, bracing myself for what was coming.

"Well?" he asked.

Realizing he was still talking about the photos, I looked at the wall. The fact that my mother had erased me from the dining room wall was something I didn't like to think about. In fact, the deep-seated pain it caused was like a huge splinter under my skin. Some days it hurt for hours, the pain worsening the more I tried to work it out. The days I didn't think about it were the days it laid painlessly beneath layers of toughened skin.

"I know." I stared unseeing at the photos. "My mom kind of erased me."

"Do you blame her?" he bit out.

Fuck.

I was horrified that he'd think her erasing my existence was understandable.

Something flickered in Michael's expression, and he wrenched his eyes from mine. "Jesus fuck," he muttered under his breath.

"Everything okay?" Dad walked into the dining room carrying a plate and cutlery for Michael. It certainly took him long enough.

"I'm not staying, Cian," Michael announced, the words heavy with his fury. "If I stay, I'm going to say shit I can't take back."

Dad sighed heavily. "Mike—"

"No." He cut him off. "You cannot expect me to sit down and eat steak with the two of you like nothing ever happened." He turned to me again, imprisoning me in the dark ire of his gaze. "You didn't just leave, Dahlia, you fuckin' took off and wouldn't let me know where you went. For nine years!"

I flinched as he raised his voice, incensed. And rightly so. However, I'd thought, or I'd hoped, that him having married someone else meant he'd moved on. That he didn't care anymore. As much as that idea had ripped me apart, I realized it was better than this heaving lividity beneath his words. Michael had never been an angry person, even with all the issues between him and his dad.

God, had I changed him?

I guessed it was another crime to lay at my feet, huh.

"Where have you been and why are you back?" he spat.

"Mike, calm down."

"Dad, it's okay." I shook my head at him, and then, even though it was difficult, I forced myself to meet Michael's gaze. "I've been in Hartwell."

His nostrils flared. "Your friend said you were only there on vacation."

"She ... she knows who you are. She was covering for me."

"Jesus Christ," he said, disgust flattening his expression. Somehow it was worse than the anger. "I never met such a coward."

"That's enough," Dad cautioned.

"Yeah, it is." Michael curled his upper lip. "Yeah, it's definitely enough." He moved toward me and stopped. "Get out of my way."

Reaching for the numbness that had gotten me through the bad days this past decade, it eluded me as I sank back against the wall, trying to meld with it so Michael could walk past without touching me.

His expression was stony as he stormed by me and a few seconds later, we listened to the front door open and then slam shut.

Pain shuddered through me, and I gasped for breath.

All these years . . . all these years and he was still so mad at me. *"Do you blame her?"*

"Bluebell," Dad said. "I am so sorry."

I shook my head, staring at the floor. "He hates me."

"No, I don't believe that." My dad clasped my shoulders and then I was pulled against his chest.

I melted into him, clenching my fingers in his shirt as I shuddered harder in my attempt to hold back the tears. "Dad."

"No one stays that mad at someone for nine years for no reason. He still cares. He'll come around."

"I have to fix it," I decided. Not in the way Dad hoped I'd fix it. No. Michael and I were long over. But I found I couldn't stand his hatred almost as much as I couldn't stand him hurting. We would never have a relationship again, but before I left Boston, I wanted to mend what I could between us.

I added Michael Sullivan to my to-do list before I could leave for Hartwell:

Make sure Dad was happy.

Put my relationships with Darragh and Davina back together.

Talk to Dermot and hopefully get us back on the right path again.

Apologize to Michael and ask him to forgive me.

After the ugly confrontation with Michael, Dad and I tried to eat dinner, but my appetite was gone. I excused myself from the table and gave Dad a kiss on the cheek to reassure him. I hated the contrition in his expression. He was trying to do a good thing, and I wasn't mad at him.

Unfortunately, he'd underestimated the full extent of Michael's anger. I had too. When we'd seen each other for the first time in years last summer, I'd seen only shock and relief in his expression. But I guess me running away again was one too many acts of cowardice for him.

Was it cowardice? I asked myself as I walked upstairs.

I guessed it was. I'd never seen it in that light.

My past was awash with grief and Michael was inadvertently a part of that. Knowing I could never be with him, I'd cut our connection because seeing him every day, continuing our relationship, would have emotionally destroyed me. Distance helped numb my feelings for him. In fact, it had worked so well, it had shocked the hell out of me when I did see him again because the feelings overwhelmed me. They'd never gone away.

I'd merely put them on ice.

Michael, like always, didn't even have to speak to melt that ice. He just had to be in the same room. Breathing. Vital. Alive.

Electric.

The piece of me I'd never known had been missing until we met.

Glancing at the closed door of my old bedroom, I let myself into the guest room and slumped down on the bed.

Michael's angry voice filled my head, but soon the ghosts of the past drowned them out ...

Following Dillon into Angie's Diner, I grumbled, "I don't want to be here."

The evening crowds hadn't quite arrived, so Dillon managed to grab us a booth at the back. "We could sit at the counter instead of taking up all this room."

My little sister rolled her eyes. "Oh my God, if you don't stop moping and whining and complaining, I'm going to slap you."

I made a face. "I'm not that bad."

"You are that bad." She gave me a sympathetic look as we slid into the booth. "Maybe you underestimated how much you cared about Gary. Maybe he's worth a second chance."

Would it be wrong to squirt ketchup all over her nice white T-shirt? Trying not to glower at her, I snipped, "He's not worth a second chance."

The asshole had been cheating on me! I caught him!

"Well, this moping has to stop. I love you, and I'm sorry he was such a dick, but you are not the first girl to get cheated on."

Lowering my gaze so she couldn't see the fury in my eyes, I had to swallow a few times to stop the acrimony inside me from spilling out. I wasn't moping because Gary had cheated on me and we'd broken up.

I was heartbroken.

Not over Gary.

Nope.

Over Michael.

For a year we'd been friends. Good friends. Better friends than even Gary knew. Michael had been there for me, and we'd talked about everything. And I'd thought that my feelings for him were reciprocated.

But six weeks ago, days before I broke up with Gary, I'd found out that he had started dating Dillon. They'd been together for ten weeks. Ten weeks! I knew that because Dillon kept walking around on cloud nine saying, "I can't believe it's been ten weeks. This is the one, Dahlia. Definitely the one."

My little sister.

The fucker had started dating my little sister.

I hated him.

Because I loved him.

I really hated him.

I'd avoided his texts and phone calls since splitting up with Gary and was dreading the day he turned up as Dillon's date to some family event.

God, what an idiot I'd been. All that guilt I'd felt when I was with Gary because I wanted Michael instead.

Huh, what a joke.

"You're not yourself, and I don't know what to do about it."

"I'll be fine." I gave her a weak smile.

Honestly, I was trying hard not to be angry at Dillon too but I felt like she'd stolen something from me. And this wasn't like when we borrowed crap like makeup or jewelry that we'd told each other was off limits. This was like she'd punched a hole in my goddamn chest and ripped out a piece of me.

I didn't want to resent my sister.

"Hey, you made it!" Dillon cried happily.

I jerked in my seat as I followed her gaze.

Just like that, my heart thudded in my chest as I looked up at Michael standing by the table. What the hell was he doing here?

Our eyes met as Dillon got out of the booth. She broke our connection by pulling his face down to hers for a kiss, and I looked away.

Dillon wasn't to blame. Rationally I knew that. She had no idea how I felt about Michael. Had she? I personally thought we'd been a little obvious about it, but apparently, I was wrong.

As for Michael, although I'd never said the words out loud, he knew I had feelings for him.

He goddamn knew.

The Michael I'd known would never have hurt me like this. I thought that he'd felt the same but if he could date Dillon, if we were interchangeable, then that bastard had never felt about me the way I felt about him. Which meant the months of longing and agonizing over not being able to be with him was a waste of my emotions.

Dillon released him from her lip-lock and they slid onto the bench opposite me where I was forced to look at them. With Michael, I kind of looked in the direction of his face but refused to meet his gaze.

"How have you been?" he asked.

Screw you!

"Fine." I shrugged, staring at the menu. "Are we ordering food or . . . ?"

"I could eat some fries," Dillon answered.

"I, uh . . . Dahlia . . . " Michael leaned across the table.

I ignored him. "Do you want to share chili fries?"

"Dahlia, look at me."

Tension fell over the table, and I was so scared that Dillon would figure everything out.

"You've been ignoring my calls."

What are you doing? Putting that out there right in front of my sister?

I scrambled for a reason other than that I was in love with him, and he'd broken my heart by agreeing to date Dillon. Then it hit me. I glared at him. "Did you know?"

Uneasiness flickered in his expression. "Did I know what?"

"Did you know Gary was cheating on me?"

"You know what?" Dillon abruptly slid out of the booth. "I

forgot I have a client tomorrow who wants this complicated nail design that I need to practice, so I'm gonna go." She leaned down to peck Michael on the lips and then scooted out of there before I could scream after her that she was my ride.

My freaking car was in the garage!

"I didn't know," Michael replied. "Dahlia, of course, I didn't know."

I turned around from where I'd been staring in horror watching my sister flee because she thought she was doing a good thing, giving me and Michael, who she considered just one of my pals, time to iron out our Gary issues.

Everything I felt for him, all the betrayal, I knew it was on my face when I turned around because he flinched.

"I couldn't care less if you knew Gary was screwin' around on me," I said, voice lowered. "You know that's not why I'm ignoring your calls." I leaned in and hissed, "You know the reason."

Rage flooded me as I grabbed my purse and shot out of the booth.

If I sat there any longer, I might punch him!

His confusion filled my name as he called out to me.

Confusion? Seriously!

I stormed out of the diner, hoping to catch my sister but she was already gone.

Then a strong hand grabbed my arm, hauling me around and into him. Michael's heat and strength surrounded me, and I fought against it. "Let me go."

"Calm down," he bit out.

I lifted my eyes to meet his, all the heartbreak and pain flooding out of me. And I hated him for that too. "Let me go."

His expression fell, and his exhalation sounded painful as he whispered, "Dahlia."

"Why her?*"*

Michael's grip on me tightened, and he pulled me closer. "I didn't ... I didn't know about Gary. I didn't know or I wouldn't ... "

Anger flooded me. "Wouldn't have started dating my sister?" I ripped my arm away from his and pushed him away. "You should never have touched her in the first place!"

"What was I supposed to do?" he growled, his regret replaced quickly with his own anger. "Wait around and pine for something I couldn't have?"

"No! I never asked you to do that, and we both know you never have." I remembered all too well the girls he'd left parties with when Gary and I were dating. "But Dillon? Why would you do that? Why are you trying to hurt me?"

His eyes widened, and his features slackened. "Dahlia ... I was never ... I wouldn't." He ran a hand through his hair and shook his head. "I didn't think you'd care that *way and she reminds me of you, I guess."*

Well, fuck if that didn't hurt even worse. "So, she and I are interchangeable?"

Michael cut me a look. "You know that's not true."

"I don't understand this." I shook my head, angry at him and at the tears threatening to spill down my cheeks. How dare he make me cry! I hadn't even cried when Gary and I broke up! I retreated. "The Michael I knew would never have hurt me like this."

"I wasn't trying to hurt you." Michael reached for me, but I turned around and began walking away. There was nothing he could say that could change any of this.

I heard his footsteps behind me, but I didn't expect to find myself hauled behind the diner and pushed up against the wall. He loomed over me, his hands braced above my head as his chest rose and fell in shallow, agitated breaths.

My heart raced.

"If we're playing the blame game," he snapped, "how about you? One, you never made it clear that you and I were even an option. And two, Dillon tells me that you've suspected Gary for months and that you've been thinking of breaking up with him all that time!"

"Never made it clear? Seriously! And how does that even equate to what you've done?"

"I didn't know this would hurt you."

"Bullshit!" I yelled in his face.

"Calm down," he demanded, pressing his face so close, our noses almost touched. "Dahlin', calm down."

"Don't call me that." I pushed under his arm to leave, but he grabbed me by the waist. "Let go of me, Michael."

Instead of letting me go, he pressed his forehead to my temple, and I froze.

Longing so deep and painful overwhelmed me, and fresh tears filled my eyes.

"I'm an idiot. I'm a selfish idiot," he whispered. "And I'm so fuckin' sorry. You'll never know how sorry."

I shook my head. "Not as sorry as me. You should never have touched her."

He was silent a second. I should have taken that opportunity to break free of his hold. But it felt like the last time I'd ever feel his arms around me, and a pathetic part of me didn't want to lose that connection quite yet.

His breath was warm on my skin. It stuttered, like he was hesitating to say something, and then I knew why. "I haven't ... slept with her."

My insides twisted at the very thought. "What do you want me to say to that?"

"I could ... I could end things with her so you and me—"

I wrenched out of his arms, the spell broken. Backing away from him, I stared up at him in disbelief. "Don't you get it? You thought it would have been bad me breaking up with Gary to be with you? Can you imagine what this would do to my relationship with Dillon? She's serious about you, Michael. And she wouldn't see that she took something from me." My lips trembled, and I cursed the tears spilling down my cheeks. Tears were useless, and they made me seem weak. "She'll think that I stole you from her." I swiped at my tears. "I won't do that to her."

"What about us?"

"You fucked any chance we might have had."

He took a step toward me, and I lifted my hand to stop him.

"You wouldn't betray your friend, and I certainly won't betray my sister."

The full realization of what he'd done seemed to hit Michael at that moment, and something akin to grief filled his expression. "Dahlia," he said, sounding in pain.

My hatred for him melted. Michael was so together, so mature for his age that sometimes I forgot he was only a few years older than me. He was still a young guy, only human, stumbling through life making mistakes like the rest of us. I'd put him on a pedestal. That was my mistake.

His mistake just happened to be a big, painful, horrible one that affected me too.

"I'm sorry, but for the sake of my sanity, we have to be done, Michael. Don't text, don't call . . . just don't. I'll pretend whenever you're around with Dillon that we're okay, but we have to be done."

Twisting the knife in deeper, his eyes shone brightly with emotion. "I didn't . . . I hoped, but I always thought it was just me . . . that what I felt was only coming from me and that I needed to move on. You never said—we never said—"

"And we never will." I slumped and stepped out of the alley behind the diner. "I guess I'll see you around."

I walked away, proud of the tears I'd kept at bay as I said goodbye.

Thankfully, Dillon's car wasn't at home when I got there, and I snuck into the house before anyone could see what a mess Michael Sullivan had made of me.

Yanking myself out of that painful memory, I reached for my cell phone where I'd left it charging on the bedside table. I needed to talk with Bailey. She always gave it to me straight, and she'd tell me if I should try to fix the hurt between Michael and me. She knew our whole story.

She knew all the mistakes made on both sides.

The constant screw-ups that had kept us apart.

I knew I could never be with Michael again, have him fill that space in my life and my bed that no man had filled since. So trying to earn his forgiveness was inevitably going to hurt me, and I needed to tap into any selflessness I had to do it.

It would require me to be brave.

Ultimately, I knew Bailey would want me to be brave. She'd encourage me to, and I needed that push.

Because this was going to sting so very, very badly.

7

Dahlia

I met my dad's happy gaze across the room and grinned, giving him my dimple. This was so much better than last night.

"Did you see, Aunt Dahlia, did you see me rescue that Sprixie?" Leo yelled from two feet away.

"And that's Mom, Dad, Leo, Grandpa ... " Levi, my five-year-old nephew, pointed at the people in his drawing, "I could add you."

"Aunt Dahlia!" Leo cried.

I grinned at him. "I see." I did. And I couldn't believe they were still making *Super Mario Bros.* games. "You're awesome at this game."

"I know, right." His cocky grin reminded me so much of Darragh.

I glanced down at Levi, who was waiting patiently for my assessment of his drawing. It was amazing for a five-year-old. There were no stick people anywhere to be seen. That he might have inherited his artistic skills from me caused a flare of sweet aching in my chest. "Levi McGuire, you are an artist," I pronounced. "And I'd be honored if you added me."

He smiled shyly and took the paper out of my hand. Promptly, he ran over to his little table in the corner of the living room where all his crayons were and settled in to draw, looking over at me now and then.

I thought my heart was going to burst.

Leo was now deep in conversation with Dad, who was watching him play the video game on the television in the sitting room.

Mom and Dad bought the whole family a Nintendo one Christmas. It was agreed that it would be our combined main present that year. It was a big deal. The boys were the only ones with a TV in their room because Darragh had saved for one doing summer jobs. That meant they set the console up in their room and us girls hardly ever got a shot at it. I couldn't imagine Mom and Dad allowing us to set up that console in the family room. The family room was their domain.

But it seemed Krista and my brother had allowed my adorable nephews to take over their entire house.

"I think they like Aunt Dahlia," Krista murmured in my ear.

I turned around to see her leaning over the back of the armchair I was sitting in. Emotion bubbled in my throat, and I had to clear it to say, "They've been amazing. You all have."

She squeezed my shoulder and gave me a pretty smile. "It's so nice to have you back."

God, I'd forgotten how much I liked my brother's wife. Krista was one of those people who had a kind word for everybody. She hated confrontation, and my brother got frustrated sometimes that she was too soft-hearted with friends and colleagues who took advantage. But she also had this wicked sense of humor and, right now, I was particularly grateful for that and her ability to forgive and move on.

Dinner with my brother and his family was fantastic. In fact, I was kicking myself for allowing so many years to pass between us when it was clear Darragh never blamed me for any of what happened. I knew he blamed me for staying away and that underneath his attempts to move on, he was still a little sore with me. But he was trying, and it was wonderful.

My nephews were fantastic, and I was sad I'd missed so much time with them.

"I'll give you a shot in a second, Aunt Dahlia," Leo called over to me. He had a pair of lungs on him, and he wasn't afraid to use them. I'd discovered he liked to talk at a louder decibel than everyone else, as if he thought we all had hearing difficulties. "I want to get past this level, and then I'll show you how it's done."

My dad and I shared a grin.

Leo was full of confidence. I'd learned over dinner he was a pitcher in the junior baseball league. "I'm good too," he said around a mouthful of spaghetti. "Like, really good."

He was also in a taekwondo league and could "kick butt."

Levi was quieter, a little shy even. It could be his age, but I think he was more like his mom in nature. Physically the boys were the perfect mix of their parents. Krista had smooth umber skin, huge dark eyes, and long hair she wore in tight braids. The boys weren't as dark as Krista but had a beautiful tawny-beige skin tone, their dad's hazel eyes, and their mother's hair. Where Leo's was styled short in tight waves, Levi's was a wild, amazing Afro. I wasn't biased when I said my nephews were gorgeous little boys.

"Another coffee, Dahlia?" Darragh asked from the kitchen door. "Dad?"

"Not for me, I'm good," Dad answered.

I got up from my chair. "Let me help."

Krista stayed out in the sitting room, and I found myself alone in the kitchen with my brother for the first time. Immediately, I went to him and put my arms around him.

Darragh hugged me close, and we stood like that for a few seconds.

My hug said I was sorry for all the years I'd wasted.

His hug said he understood.

Pulling back, I gave him a soft smile. "The boys are amazing, Darragh."

My big brother grinned. "Yeah, we did all right there, huh?"

"You did." I leaned against the counter as he set about making us coffee.

"You going to Davina's tomorrow?"

"Yeah." I was still a little nervous about that. Despite the good night I'd had with her and Darragh at Dad's last Sunday, Darragh was definitely the more forgiving between my two eldest siblings.

"So ... uh ... Dad called me last night after what happened with Mike. He feels terrible."

I winced. "I told him not to. I know what he was trying to do. It unfortunately backfired."

"I take it Dad told you the reason Mike's still in our lives is because of Dermot?"

The thought of Dermot made my stomach roil. "Yeah." Dermot was a cop too. He and Michael worked from the same precinct. They'd become friendly when Michael and I were together, but they'd formed a little bromance after I left.

"I imagine the way Dermot feels about you has probably affected Mike's feelings too."

I shook my head. "No, Michael's feelings are all his own."

"Well, my point was going to be that Dermot has probably affected Mike, and Mom has definitely affected Dermot. And that point leads me to my next ... Are you thinking about seeing Mom while you're here?"

I looked back over my shoulder to make sure Dad was well and truly out of earshot. Then I leaned toward my brother and said in a low voice, "Dad won't talk about the divorce. I need to know he's okay and if he won't give me answers, maybe Mom will."

"Dahlia, the divorce is between those two."

"Is it, though?"

Anger darkened his countenance. "For fuck's sake, please do not tell me you're going to blame yourself for this too? Jesus Christ, Dahlia, do not let Mom's crap do this to you any longer. You let her, and you're a martyr."

I glowered. "Say it how you feel it, Dar."

"I know you're worried about Dad, but don't be. I think this is the best thing for him."

Shocked, I stared at him for a second. "How can you say that knowing how much they love each other?"

"Just because they love each other doesn't mean they're right for each other." Darragh studied me thoughtfully. "How . . . How can you want her to be happy after what she said to you?"

The memory burned but I shrugged it off. "She wasn't in her right mind."

"Yeah? Well, she hasn't been in her right mind for years. She pushed us all out after Dillon." He stared at the floor, and it was the first time I'd heard the hurt in my brother's voice. "She doesn't have time for Davina; she spends time with the boys but she holds herself back from them. The only person she's close to is Dermot, and she's filled his head with all her lies."

My first thought was for Dad. "All of this was going on, Dad was dealing with it, and he didn't say a word to me."

"Yeah. I'm sure it has a lot to do with the divorce. So stop blaming yourself and stop worrying. Dad will be fine." His gaze moved across the room out into the sitting room where Dad was laughing with Leo. "He'll be more than fine. Look at him. He looks great. He'll start dating soon, and it'll be a whole new chapter in his life."

Dating? I'd never even thought of that. "You would be okay with that?"

"Of course. Krista already wants to set him up with a colleague of her mom's."

The idea of my Dad with anyone but my mom was very strange. Then again, the only memories I had of my parents together were from before Dillon died. Darragh had been there the nine years I'd missed out on, clearly witnessing a deterioration I hadn't been around for.

I wondered how bad it could be that Darragh was so eager for Dad to move on.

"I still think I should face Mom. See what she has to say about all of it." The thought made me sick. Coming back to Boston, facing everyone, had been difficult, but I'd done it. And I was still breathing.

It occurred to me that maybe clearing the air with my mother might put to rest some very persistent demons from the past.

"I'm not going to stop you," Darragh said, sighing, "but I am noting my concern."

"Noted." I grinned at him. "God, it's good to have you back, big bro."

He slid his arm around my shoulders and walked me back out into the living room.

"Aunt Dahlia, just another level, I promise!" Leo shouted over at me.

"Aunt Dahlia, I drew you," Levi said quietly, coming toward his dad and me.

I sank into my brother's side, feeling so goddamn full I almost wanted to cry with the joy of it.

The next evening I found myself sitting at the dining table in the large, open-plan living space of my sister's gorgeous Bunker Hill apartment.

She must make serious money.

Seriously.

Wow.

I was so proud of her.

My effusive compliments on the apartment and her obvious success had seemed to go a long way to mollifying Davina's girlfriend, Astrid. When I'd first appeared at the apartment, she'd been quietly and intensely studying me, not giving much away.

Dad was working so he couldn't serve as a buffer.

This, and Astrid's cool appraisal, was making me jumpy, and I hated that feeling.

Silence fell over the table as we sat to eat. "Well, this isn't at all awkward."

Davina snorted. "You're making it awkward."

"How am I making it awkward?" I argued.

"Is it because we're gay?" Astrid raised an eyebrow at me.

I made a face, no longer caring about tiptoeing around her, after such an absurd question. "My sister could tell me she was thinking of transitioning into an orangutan and it wouldn't make me love her any less."

"Maybe more," Davina mused. "Orangutans are cute."

"Aren't they?" I leaned across the table. "The way they hug each other is so adorable. It's like a full-bodied 'I love you' hug. It's so open and cute. I wish people were like that."

"Seriously?" Astrid's eyes darted between Davina and me.

"Asking her if it's because we're gay was stupid." Davina shrugged.

Her girlfriend glared. "Well, not all of your family have been accepting."

My sister frowned at her plate. "I'm aware."

Not wanting an argument to break out between them, I changed the subject. "Have you thought about getting married? Because I make jewelry and I could make the rings. Something perfect and unique."

My big sister snorted. "You haven't changed. Still saying things you shouldn't say. What if marriage is a sore topic for Astrid and me?"

"Is it?"

"No," Astrid answered. "We've thought about it."

I grinned, happy for my sister. "Really?"

"Ugh," Astrid huffed, shooting my sister a look. "You were right. That dimple gets her out of everything. She's adorable." She turned back to me. "Annoyingly adorable."

I grinned harder as my sister laughed under her breath. "I've been told this. It's a problem, I know."

They laughed and the awkwardness melted.

As we ate, Astrid told me about her job as a publicist for Candlelight Press, a book publisher in Allston. Davina tried to explain her job for the hundredth time, but I couldn't get my head around it. Thankfully, neither could Astrid. And they asked about Hartwell, even though Davina seemed tentative.

"It's beautiful." I missed it. I'd already told Davina about it the other night, so I talked more about my friends. "Bailey got engaged to Vaughn, so that's been the latest excitement. Oh, and we sporadically have trouble from a family called the Devlins. Ian Devlin, the dad, he owns a hotel, some other businesses in town, the fun park, and he's a shady character, to say the least. He's been trying to buy property on the boardwalk for years and has these crass plans to turn it into a five-star resort that a tiny percentage of the population could afford to visit. His son broke into Bailey's inn and attacked her, trying to find confidential information he could use against her."

Davina and Astrid stared wide-eyed at me.

"What?"

"It sounds like the setting to my favorite soap opera," Astrid said.

I laughed. "It's not as dramatic as it sounds. That family is a menace. Every town has one."

Davina looked at her half-empty plate. "You're really going back there, aren't you?"

"I ... I live there. I love it there. But I won't *leave* again. You and Astrid could come vacation there in the summer, and I'll be back. I promise. Birthdays, Thanksgiving, Christmas ... whenever you want me, I'll come back."

My sister looked up, tears in her eyes. Astrid grabbed her hand tightly. "After Dillon died, I didn't only lose her. I lost you, and I lost Mom. It was like our whole family fell apart."

Grief clawed at my throat. "Da—"

"I'm not saying that to make you feel guilty. I think we both know you've lived with that emotion for too long. I just ... I need you to know how much it means to have you back."

"I need you to know how much it means that you would have me back."

"No more of that," she chided. "Deciding to forgive you means not bringing that up again."

Silence fell over the table and then Astrid piped up. "I bought a banoffee pie from Bova's."

I took a second to understand. "And you made me eat real food when you were sitting on banoffee pie from Bova's?"

Chortling, my sister's girlfriend got up to clear the table just as my cell blasted from my purse.

"I see your taste in music hasn't changed," Davina said.

Grinning, I reached into my purse to silence my cell. It was an unknown number. I showed it to Davina. She shrugged. "Answer it."

I did. "Hello?"

"Dahlia?" Dermot's voice filled my ear.

"Dermot?"

My sister's expression froze with alertness.

"I just got off the phone with Dar, and he said you're thinking about going to see Mom?"

"Ye—"

"Don't even think about it," he growled. "She wants to talk, she'll come to *you*. You go there, you corner her, and you'll have to deal with me." Silence followed his threat, and I realized he'd hung up.

That tight ugly knot filled my stomach as I lowered my phone.

Every time I took a step forward, there was someone to push me back.

8

Michael

The rain lashed against the windshield of their unmarked Ford Crown Victoria as Michael waited for Davis to come back with their coffees. Davis would also probably get himself a cinnamon pinwheel or two. Bastard. He knew Michael didn't eat that shit regularly.

It was one of the reasons Michael wouldn't let him stop at a Dunkees. He'd come out with a dozen fuckin' donuts otherwise.

The weather had been miserable all night, the rain chasing them around North Boston as they tried to nail down a suspect in an armed burglary. As soon as Davis pulled up outside the late-night bakery so they could grab a coffee, the rain had started pissin' down. The weather mirrored his mood.

Dahlia.

He squeezed his eyes closed and pinched the bridge of his nose. That woman had been messing with his head all week, and he hated being distracted on the job. It could be dangerous.

Dermot had called him to give him a heads-up that Dahlia was in town, and his friend was pissed to find out he was too late making that call.

"I don't know what my fuckin' family is thinkin', man. I'm sorry."

"I don't think your dad meant any harm."

"It wasn't Dad. Dahlia will have put him up to it. That bitch thinks she can walk right back into town and expect everyone to roll over. Mom is a mess. I don't know what to do."

Michael had flinched at Dermot calling Dahlia a bitch. Even now, after everything, it was his instinct to defend her. "She's still your sister, so watch your mouth. And it was definitely your dad's doing. She was just as shocked as I was."

Dermot had gone quiet. "Don't let her manipulate you, Mike. You just got out of a crappy marriage. You don't need my fuckin' sister messing with your head again."

Michael had gotten off the phone because Dermot's acridness toward Dahlia pissed him off. It wasn't fair, considering how angry he was with her and how he'd spoken to her when he saw her, but that was different. He could be mad as fuck at Dahlia and still not want anyone else to hurt her.

He'd hurt her.

The anguish had blazed out of her at his cutting remarks the other night. His consequent remorse made him even more pissed. What the fuck did he have to feel guilty for? *She* left *him.*

Jesus Christ.

An image of her from the other night popped into his head for the millionth time. She'd been wearing a blue dress, the same shade as her eyes. It was fitted and wrapped tight around her perfect body.

Dahlia had always had full hips, a tiny waist, and big boobs. It was the first thing he noticed about her.

He was a man. He loved her body.

No point pretending he didn't.

But from the moment he'd looked into her eyes in that art gallery all those years ago, he'd been a fuckin' goner. Michael had never met anyone so full of everything. Curiosity, humor, boredom, annoyance—it had all flashed in her eyes as she stood on that podium in that ridiculous body stocking that barely covered her.

And then she'd flipped him off more gracefully than anybody had ever flipped him off.

All that life, all that vibrant energy she gave off, she still had it. There was more sadness in her now, but she was still Dahlia after all.

That night, when he'd gotten home and eventually fallen asleep, he'd dreamed about her.

About fuckin' her. Angry hate sex.

The next night, he made love to her in his dreams.

And last night the dream had been a mixture of both.

A few hours later his alarm went off, and he woke up hard, frustrated and angrier than ever.

The passenger side door opened and Davis dived in, cursing under his breath, yanking Michael out of his thoughts. His partner's suit and hair were soaked. A warm coffee aroma filled the car as Davis passed him a cup. But that didn't appease Michael when he saw the brown paper bag in Davis's other hand.

"You fucker." He eyeballed what he knew were pinwheels.

His partner grinned. "Hey, *I* ain't watching what *I* eat."

Michael's looked at Davis's gut. The man was tall and lean everywhere except for his stomach, which had a small round swell to it. "Clearly."

"Fuck you, little pissant," Davis said congenially as he opened the brown paper bag with something akin to glee. "Come to Daddy."

Exhaling in frustration, Michael reached into the back of the car for his own brown paper bag. Inside was a little plastic container with homemade salmon teriyaki and rice. Kiersten used to cook healthy meals for him so now he was learning to do that stuff for himself. He didn't think he was half bad at it.

"Grow a pair and eat some real food, Mike." Davis sneered at the rice, salmon, and salad.

Michael ignored his ribbing. He ate well six days out of seven. There was no point hitting the gym before work every day if he was going to eat shit like pastries and burgers. Michael respected his body. He gave it the fuel it needed to be strong. Even if it was torture sometimes.

"No comeback?" Davis asked. "Something's definitely up with you. Is it Bronson? Word is out he's bangin' your ex."

Michael liked Davis. He did. But the man had no fuckin' filter or diplomacy. "I'm happy for them," he muttered around a mouthful.

"So, what is it?"

He shrugged, not ready to talk about Dahlia or the fact that every instinct in his body told him to go to her now she was in Boston. They were like magnets. Always had been. "Night shift. Not used to it yet."

His partner shrugged. "It takes time."

"It'd be easier if you wouldn't stop every five seconds for a pinwheel or a tonic." The man was addicted to goddamn Pepsi.

"You know, I think you'd benefit from a fuckin' pinwheel now and then. You moody little fucker."

Michael smirked.

"Where do you think this asshole is?" Davis asked after a few seconds of quiet eating.

"Back to the girlfriend in Chelsea. My bet is she called him after we dropped by. He might think her place has the all clear for the night."

Davis nodded.

They finished up as the rain calmed. "You're already wet." Michael shoved his garbage at Davis. "You can put this in the trash."

"I had to get a neat freak, healthy-eating, gym-going mother-fucker like you for a partner, huh," Davis muttered under his breath as he got out of the car with the garbage. Michael knew some cops let shit collect in the back and on the floor of their vehicles. He wasn't one of them. It sent a message you were a lazy cop, and Michael was anything but lazy.

"Bang a Uey," Davis advised as he got back in the car. "Road's quiet."

Michael attempted to shove everything else out of his head (and by everything else, he meant Dahlia) and pulled out onto the quiet street to do a U-turn. He needed her out of his head so he could do his job.

Then he'd go home and probably have another dream about her.

Thing of it was, there was a part of Michael, an element he despised, that anticipated the dream. A part of him that whispered from down deep inside that he looked forward to the fantasy.

9

Dahlia

During the next ten days, I not only attempted to cram as much family time in with Darragh, Krista and the kids, and Davina and Astrid, I shadowed my dad. Worrying about him distracted me from the fact that Dermot was nowhere near ready to forgive me. Dad still wouldn't talk about his divorce with Mom, and I knew him well enough to know he was inside his own head.

After all, I was my father's daughter. We shared a very similar nature, and I knew he was silently stewing. There was nothing I could do but spend time with him and hope he'd eventually open up. The one thing I knew was that I was not leaving Boston until I was one hundred percent certain Dad would be okay.

As for talking to my mom, Dermot had put a pin in that. I was already nervous about doing it, but after his phone call, I decided to be uncharacteristically cautious. It turned out, in the end, it wasn't me that forced our reunion.

It was Monday, late afternoon, Dad had left for work, and I was trying to keep my thoughts on the events of the day before, and not on anything else (say, Michael, who liked to intrude on my thoughts every five seconds!). Dad had invited Darragh, Krista, Leo and Levi, Davina and Astrid over for dinner and to watch the Sunday game.

We'd laughed a lot and ate a lot, and it had been a great time.

The boys always seemed to laugh when Darragh used a slang word, which led to us educating them in the language of our neighborhood growing up. There were words I'd forgotten, having lost them while I was living in Delaware. Like "bubbla" instead of a water fountain. That was adorable. How could I have forgotten that?

I'd also dared to ask about Dermot. Dad had kept me up to date on my siblings' lives throughout the years, but I didn't know much about Dermot's life at the moment.

Last I'd heard he'd been dating a girl Davina not so fondly referred to as a "Masshole"—a slang word Darragh did not want his kids picking up on. She apologized but not for the sentiment. Apparently, this girl came from money, kind of a blueblood, and Dermot tired of her trying to hide him from her family. After nine months together, he broke it off. He was single again, living in a shitty apartment (my sister's words) near Mom's new place, and screwing everything that moved when he wasn't working.

While Michael moved up the ranks, my brother, who had never been very ambitious, seemed content to remain a police officer. It sounded like my brother wasn't having the greatest time in his personal life. When we were younger, I was the one he came to talk to about girls and relationships. Once again, I hadn't been there when he needed me.

Music blared in the living room as I sat on the end of the couch near the lamp on the side table in the corner. I was working on a ring design for Davina and Astrid. They hadn't asked for it, but after taking a thorough inventory of their likes and dislikes as seen in their apartment, I had some ideas for the rings. Just in case.

Unfortunately, I liked my music loud, so I didn't hear the front door opening until Dermot and my mom strode inside.

Adrenaline flooded me when I saw my mother, and I fumbled for my phone to cut the music. I hurried to my feet, noting the intensity of my mom's expression.

Dermot closed the front door behind him.

Oh, shit.

My stomach flipped unpleasantly.

Apart from dark circles under her eyes, my mom looked good. She was tall and slender and looked young in her skinny jeans, *Blondie* T-shirt, and suede jacket. There was no gray in her dark, shoulder-length hair so I knew she dyed it because I'd started getting gray in mine when I was twenty-nine.

Her hazel eyes met my blue ones and fear held me frozen in place by the couch.

That look in her eyes, the one she'd had when she'd spoken to me last, was still there. All these years and it had never faded.

"What are you doing here?" My eyes flicked to Dermot.

"How dare you?" Mom seethed. "How dare you stand in *my* house and ask that?"

"Mom." Dermot put his hand on her shoulder. "You said it was time to talk to her. So let's talk."

"Your father came to see me the other day." Mom took a few steps farther into the room, her eyes shining with unshed tears. "You turned him against me."

"What?" I shook my head, confused. "What are you talking about?"

"Don't play stupid, Dahlia. You're the reason our marriage fell apart. You're the reason my life turned to shit!"

Suddenly, I was twenty-two again, hurtling back in time. "You still blame me for Dillon?"

"No one is saying that." Dermot stepped between us. "But you left when we needed to stick together, and it fucked us all up. You need to take responsibility for that."

I agreed. "I do. I have. That's why I'm here. But that's not why she's here." I looked past him to my mom. "Dad confronted you about what you said and did to me before I left, didn't he?"

That's what he'd been stewing over for days.

"What?" Dermot looked at Mom. "What did you say? What did you do?"

She didn't take her eyes off me. "The truth."

I flinched like she'd slapped me. Again. "I'm sorry that he's mad about that, but I needed them to know why I didn't just *leave*."

"You should have stayed gone."

"Wait ... I'm confused." Dermot frowned. "What is she talking about?"

Mom's gaze softened on him. "What we've always talked about. That's she to blame, and she's manipulative, and she should have stayed gone."

Dermot shook his head. "That's not what we talked about." He turned, glaring at me. "What the fuck are you talking about? What did you tell Dad? More lies?"

I narrowed my eyes on my gullible brother who ran to take Mom's side in every family argument growing up. Just like Dillon had. "I started to drink after Dillon ... after Dillon died."

He curled his lip. "We're fully aware of how badly you handled Dillon's death."

I glared at him. "I didn't start drinking just because of Dillon."

"Oh, here we go." Mom pushed past Dermot. "You're going to lay that fuckin' mistake at my feet too?"

Staring up at her in horror, I wondered how it was possible that this was my mother. How the woman who had given birth to me, raised me, comforted me when I was hurt, could hate me this much? Tears filled my eyes, and I despised myself for the weakness. "Everyone was out. It was just you and me in the house, and you found me in the bedroom. You attacked me." The memory flashed over me, and I could still feel the burn of her slaps. "You started slapping me."

Dermot pulled in a breath behind Mom.

"You kept telling me I was selfish. That it should have been me." The tears scalded my cheeks. "It should have been me, you said. Why did God take the wrong kid, you said."

"Jesus fuck," my brother whispered.

I swiped angrily at my tears as I saw my mother's eyes brighten with her own. "I didn't know how to deal with that . . . to have my mom hate me so much . . . So yeah, I drank to cope. I'm not proud of myself. I'm not proud that Dad had to send me away from everything that happened here. And I'm not proud that I stayed away because I was so afraid to face you again. Not because of you"—I shook my head at her as I realized I would never get the reassurance I needed from her—"but because I hurt *them*. The family that still loved me." I looked past her shoulder to Dermot, who had gone chalk white. "I'm sorry I abandoned you," I whispered. "I'm so sorry."

A deathly silence filled the room.

Dermot stared at Mom in accusation.

"Don't look at me like that," Mom whispered.

"Is it true?" he grunted, like he could hardly get the words out. "Did you do that to her?"

My mom was quiet for a while and then she whispered tearfully, "She ruined your sister's life."

"Mom, you know that's not true."

"You all can't see it, but it's true. And Dill—" Mom sobbed. "She was *my* little girl. God took my little girl."

"And what about Dahlia?" Dermot retorted. "She's your kid too, Mom."

"No. She was never mine. She was always *his*. God would take mine, wouldn't he? Story of my fuckin' life."

"I can't . . . "

I turned to see my brother glaring incredulously at her.

"I can't believe what I'm hearing. You made it seem like you were angry at her for leaving. Not for coming back!"

"Don't." Mom hurried over to him, cupping his face. "My whole life has fallen apart, and it's her fault. Don't let her take you too."

Dermot shook his head, yanking her hands from his face. "Mom," he said, "that's so fucked up. That's so fucked up. You need to see someone. You need to talk to someone about this because this is ... " His voice trailed off. My thirty-three-year-old brother looked like a lost little boy, and I wanted to comfort him.

"That's what Cian said." Mom stepped back, wiping at her tears.

"Then maybe you should listen to us."

Mom looked just as lost. "You don't understand."

He shook his head again. "It's not rational, Mom. It's fucked."

She choked on a sob and then rushed past him, dodging his hands as he tried to stop her. The front door slammed shut behind her.

Seeing her now, and not through the grief-shrouded fog of the messed-up young woman I'd been, I realized with a sick feeling in my gut that Sorcha McGuire was not mentally well. She'd twisted everything up inside her and saw what she wanted to see. As I'd gotten older, hitting my teens, I realized that was a part of my mom's personality. But it had been in smaller, less significant ways back then. If she didn't like an idea, like when I'd first said I wanted to go to art school, she pretended like it wasn't true. She would talk to me about law school and business school like I hadn't repeatedly told her they were a no-go.

However, what she'd convinced herself—that I'd ruined her life—had done nothing but *destroy* her life, like a self-fulfilling prophecy. No wonder Dad had gone to see her to tell her she needed therapy.

My mom *needed* therapy.

Knowing that didn't remove the ball of ugly that sat in my gut. My own mom hated me.

There weren't any magic words in the world that could take away that kind of pain.

"Dahlia," Dermot said my name quietly, drawing my attention from the door to his. His expression turned pleading. "I didn't know."

I nodded.

"She's..." His gaze darted to the door. "I've never seen her like that ... She's ... she's not ... that's fucked up."

My brother looked crushed. Alone, sad, and totally crushed.

Without thinking about it, I crossed the room and drew him into my arms.

Dermot didn't hesitate. He buried his head in my neck and held on for dear life.

10

Dahlia

Before he had to leave for work, Dermot asked me to tell him everything from my side of the story. When I was done, he'd looked at me in weary defeat. "I still think you should have come home. But I get it now why you didn't."

I'd hesitated over my own question. "She never … In all these years, she never talked about how she blamed me for Dillon's death? How she felt about it?"

Dermot had shaken his head. "She never talked about you at all. When we tried, she would walk out of the room. I thought it was because you left and would only tell Dad where you were. I didn't realize it was because she'd poisoned her own fuckin' mind against you."

"Maybe if I had come home sooner, it wouldn't have gotten this bad. She would have had to deal with her grief rather than letting it fester like this."

"Maybe." He'd agreed impatiently as he stood up to leave. "You don't actually blame yourself for Dillon's death, do you?"

"I changed the course of her future, Dermot. There's no getting around that fact."

"Jesus fuck," he'd sneered. "One's crazy, and the other's a martyr. I can't … I can't deal with this shit right now. I've got work."

He'd taken off without saying goodbye, and it left me unsure of where I stood with him.

For a while, I'd sat in silence going over the last hour in my head. Every part of me seemed to ache. "Well, this trip home has been super fun," I muttered.

The urge to pack my bags and leave was strong. Back home in Hartwell, I didn't have to deal with all this stuff. My life was simple and peaceful.

However, I couldn't leave Dad. Especially not now, knowing how bad Mom had gotten. Hands shaking, I crossed the room to where I'd left my phone on the side table and swiped left, bringing up my main contacts. My finger hovered over the B button. I didn't want to keep calling Bailey when I was feeling lousy because then she'd worry. However, she was my person now.

Before Hartwell, it had been Michael. I sighed, slumping down on the couch, remembering the first time I ever went to him because of my mom. It was before he dated Dillon. It was before I suspected Gary of cheating . . .

Stepping out of my bedroom, I caught sight of Dermot preening in the bathroom mirror as he reached for his bottle of cologne.

"Don't," I warned him.

He whipped around. "Don't what?"

"Put more cologne on."

Dermot gestured with the bottle. "Too much?"

"Yes. Unless you want to suffocate the poor girl."

He flashed me a wide grin. "I like this one so that would be a no."

"You like them all," I teased.

"But this one is spicy. I like her smart mouth." He stepped out of the bathroom. "She reminds me of you, without the icky sister factor."

"It's still icky," I grumbled, even though I thought it was kind of sweet. "Also, I think the police academy would frown on you

using the word icky at your age. You ever going to grow up, Derm?" I followed him downstairs.

Darragh and Davina had both moved out, but Dermot couldn't afford to yet. As a scholarship student at MassArt (Massachusetts College of Art & Design), I couldn't afford student housing, and as a student at a beauty academy in the city, my nineteen-year-old sister Dillon definitely still lived at home too.

"It's all relative," Dermot answered breezily. "I'll be mature as a cop."

I snickered. "But not out of the uniform?"

"Now where would the fun in that be?"

"In what?" Davina asked from the couch. She'd come over for dinner, and Dillon had talked her into being a guinea pig for the night. She had one eye entirely made up with makeup and the other not. It was very Clockwork Orange.

"Nothing." Dermot grabbed his jacket and keys. "Mom, I'm out!" he yelled through to the kitchen.

She called back to him to wait, but he darted out the door and was gone by the time she walked into the sitting room. Mom frowned. "Where did he go?"

"Date," I answered succinctly. "Speaking of . . . " I pulled my cell out of the back pocket of my jeans and checked it.

Nothing.

Gary was supposed to be picking me up in five minutes for date night, and he usually texted to let me know he was on his way.

"He owes your dad and me grocery money," Mom grumbled. "Who is he spending it on this time?"

"Abigail," Dillon answered. "I think."

"Addison," I corrected. "Her name is Addison."

Mom curled her lip. "She sounds stuck-up."

I grunted, used to her judging my brother's girlfriends before she'd even met them. Mom was the total cliché who believed no girl deserved her sons. My phone beeped, and I flipped it open, only for my heart to sink.

Sorry, doll. Gotta cancel. Workin' late. Call you later.

"Great." I sat down on the stairs with a heavy sigh.

"What is it?" Mom asked.

She was frowning down at me in concern, so I made the stupid mistake of giving her the truth. "Gary canceled our date for tonight."

She shook her head. "I told you he was a loser."

Indignation rushed through me. "He's working late."

"So he says."

"Mom," Davina warned from the couch.

Mom ignored her, glaring down at me. "What is this guy doing with his life, huh? A mechanic in his uncle's garage. Oh, there's a career."

"He's still young," I argued through gritted teeth. "He's got time to decide."

"In the meantime, he gets you knocked up, and your dad and I are lumbered with two kids raising a kid because one's a mechanic who doesn't make a lot of money, and the other is smart-assing around a fuckin' art college."

Oh, here we go.

"Mom . . . " Dillon sighed in frustration.

I stood up and glowered at my mother. "Why do you always do this when Dad isn't around to hear it?" Dad was working night shift.

Anger pinched my mom's pretty face. "Because he mollycoddles you. That's how you ended up at fuckin' art school in the first place. What are you going to do with that degree, huh? Because if you think you can waste a perfectly good scholarship on art school, come out with nothing for it, and end up staying with us, you've got another thing coming."

"I'll get a job," I seethed.

"Doing what?"

"A jewelry designer," I announced. I'd been loving my silver-smithing classes and was leaning more and more toward jewelry design. However, I hadn't wanted to admit that to my mom yet in case I failed. I was always blurting shit out around her I didn't mean to.

She scoffed. "A jewelry designer? Oh my God, your head is so far up your ass in dreamland. Do you know how many people succeed as jewelry designers?"

I clenched my fists at my sides. "I'll be one of them."

"Why? Because you're special? It takes more than a little creativity to make a career out of jewelry design, Dahlia."

"Jesus Christ, Mom," Davina snapped.

I narrowed my eyes. "I know you don't think much of me, but I'm good at this stuff. You don't get into MassArt if you're not, Mom. I know you didn't think it was a big deal I got in, but it is."

"A big deal? Getting into Harvard is a big deal. Getting into art school is a waste of your life. Why am I always the bad guy here? All I'm trying to do is talk some sense into you. You're wasting your life, Dahlia. On that guy and on this school. You need to—where are you going?"

"I'm not sticking around to listen to this shit." I grabbed my keys, my coat, and hauled open the front door.

"Don't talk to me like that and don't you—Dahlia!"

"Why do you do that to her?" I could hear Davina shout as I hurried down the porch stairs. "You're always on her back!"

"Always," I hissed, drawing back the tears that threatened to spill. Only my mom could make me feel like utter garbage.

Fingers trembling, I called Gary, but he didn't pick up, which made the tears spill over. Fuck, I hated crying! I ducked my head and hurried down the street. My thumb hovered over my contact list, wondering who I could call.

I knew who I wanted to call.

But he was probably working.

And I shouldn't call him.

Michael.

I'd been dating Gary for six months now, and in that time the feelings I had when I first met Michael hadn't gone away. If anything, they'd only gotten stronger. Michael was funny like Gary but more ... he was also mature, and I could talk to him. When we were at parties, when he wasn't chatting to some pretty girl, and Gary was off being an idiot with his friends, Michael and I would talk.

I felt this weird electric awareness around him, but I also felt like I could tell him anything.

There was something comforting about him.

Something safe.

I shouldn't call him for comfort.

I shouldn't.

Trying Gary again and getting nowhere, my thumb moved with a mind of its own and pressed Michael. The phone rang in my ear and with every ring my heart thudded harder and faster.

He picked up on the fifth ring, and I belatedly wondered if he was working.

"Dahlia, you okay?" he answered.

I hesitated, tears choking my throat. I never cried. I was not a crybaby. But after the altercation with my mom and the realization that the one person I wanted to talk to was my boyfriend's best friend, I was feeling pretty vulnerable.

I should not have called him.

"Dahlia?" Michael sounded worried.

"Hey," I choked out. It came out all croaky.

"Dahlia, what's wrong?"

"You working?"

"No. What's going on?"

"I shouldn't have called." Shit, I shouldn't have called.

"Where are you?"

"No, really, Michael, it's stupid. I'm being a baby."

"Dahlia, where are you?"

I told him where I was.

"I'll be there in five minutes."

He hung up before I could ask him how he intended to get here so fast from Southie.

As I waited, I tried to calm down, but I kept replaying the argument with my mom over and over again. It wasn't even an argument. It was a verbal beatdown.

I pushed off the tree I was leaning on when I saw Michael's old Ford turning the corner. He pulled up beside me and leaned over to push open the door. I scrambled to get in, and that electric awareness zinged through me when our eyes met.

"How did you get here so fast?"

"I was in Malden."

"Why?"

He shrugged, turning away. "Just hanging out."

Oh my God. He'd been on a date. I grimaced. "You were on a date, weren't you?"

"It wasn't a date. Put your seat belt on."

I did, but guilt consumed me. "Not a date" was guy speak for a hookup. When I first started dating Gary, he told me Michael wasn't a casual hookup kind of guy, but ever since I'd known Michael, that's all he did. He didn't seem to want to get serious with any girl. Ignoring my jealousy, I concentrated on the guilt. "Michael, I'm sorry. You should go back."

He flashed me a grin as he pulled the car back onto the road. "There is no going back. She wasn't exactly pleased I bailed on her."

I flushed. "Why did you? Bail on her?"

Michael's grin fell, and he gave me a quick, serious look.

"*Because you sounded like you were crying. And you look like you've been crying. What's going on?*"

Feelings I didn't even want to contemplate flooded me. Michael had ditched a girl for me because I'd sounded upset.

I felt that in an ache in my chest and, to my chagrin, an ache between my legs.

Heat rolled through me, and I did my best to ignore it. "Now I feel terrible. It was only a stupid argument with my mom."

"*Dahlia, I've never seen you cry so I'm guessing it wasn't stupid." He shot me another look. "Why didn't you call Gary?*"

"*I tried. He was supposed to be taking me out tonight, but he canceled. That's how the argument with my mom started.*"

"*So you called me? You don't have a girlfriend you can call?*"

Embarrassment prickled me, and I hated that feeling. Especially in front of him. "I'm sorry I called, okay? You can drop me off here."

"*Hey, I'm not mad that you called. I'm ... glad." He kept his eyes on the road, and I took the time to study his profile. Why was he so freaking handsome? His voice was a little hoarse when he continued, "I don't like the idea of you being sad."*

Why was he so freaking wonderful too?

To cover my rush of inappropriate feelings, I teased, "Even if it means being cockblocked?"

Michael chuckled. "I think you might have saved me. When I told her a friend needed me, she went off like a fuckin' shrew." He winced at the memory. "Not sexy."

"*Well then, I'm glad to have helped.*"

Michael shot me that boyish, crooked smile of his and I couldn't help but smile back. "That's better," he said quietly.

I bit my lip at the awareness that sprung between us and turned to look out my window. "Where are we going?"

"*Somewhere we can talk.*"

We were quiet a moment as he drove out of Everett.

"*Thank you,*" I said.

"*For* what?"

"*For dropping everything to come get me. I don't ... I'm not usually such a drama queen.*"

"*Dahlia, no one would ever accuse you of being a drama queen.*"

"*It's just you seem older than the rest of us. I don't want to seem immature in comparison.*"

"*Does older mean boring?*" he asked.

Surprised by the slight insecurity I detected in his voice, I reassured him. "*Absolutely not.*" *It was sexy. So, so sexy.*

I definitely should not have called him.

A few minutes later Michael pulled into a parking lot in South Wellington at the Mystic River Reservation. The lot was empty. "*We're not supposed to park here after dark.*"

He shrugged. "*We'll take off if we see a patrol car.*"

I gave a huff of laughter. "*Michael, you're a rookie. I don't think you should take this chance.*"

"*I'll say you got sick and I had to pull over somewhere.*"

I studied him a second as he parked the car. "*You would absolutely get away with that.*"

"*I have a sincere face.*"

"*You do.*" *I laughed.* "*You so do. I bet you got out of a lot of trouble growing up because of that face.*"

He took off his belt and turned a little in his seat to face me. "*Gary would have gotten into some serious shit if it weren't for this face.*"

"*I believe that too.*" *My eyes roamed over his features, and I tried to avoid his lips. His eyes always ensnared me, and it was hard to avoid them, but I had to avoid his lips. They were so beautifully formed. Almost a little pouty for a guy. The hard angles of the rest of his face stopped those lips from making him a pretty boy. However, it did not stop me thinking about his mouth more*

*than I should. When I drew Michael's face, I took extra time on
his lips, trying to get the curvature perfect.*

Oh damn, I was staring.

*I cleared my throat and looked out across the lot at the dark
park beyond.*

*"So . . . ," Michael prompted, "you going to tell me what hap-
pened with your mom?"*

*"Ah, Sorcha McGuire." I tried for breezy and snarky. "I'm
pretty sure she gives more than ten percent in her tithe in the hopes
that Jesus will set me on the right path."*

Michael stared at me until I squirmed.

"What?"

*"You don't have to be 'on' all the time with me. I get it. You're
a funny smart-ass, and I love that about you. But let's be real here,
Dahlia. Whatever happened tonight, you are not as cool about it
as you're trying to make out. Or you wouldn't have called me."*

Tears burned my eyes and I looked away.

*Seconds later his warm, calloused hand wrapped around mine
and I turned back to him. "Talk to me."*

*So I laid it out. Everything my mom had said tonight and
everything that had come before. I swiped angrily at a tear that
slipped by my defenses. "It wasn't so bad when I was a kid. At
least I didn't notice it so much. But the older I got, the more she
singled me out. I don't remember her coming down on Darragh,
Davina, or Dermot like this. I mean, as far as she's concerned,
Dar and Davi are the best. They both went to college, they're both
doing jobs that will eventually make them good money—hopefully. Dillon can do no wrong in my mom's eyes, so the fact that
my sister will probably struggle financially as a beautician for the
rest of her life doesn't even seem to register with Mom. It's apparently a practical skill set to have." I rolled my eyes. "And
Dermot . . . my God, my brother has moved from job to job, before*

settling on the police academy. And we're all holding our breaths on that one. But did my mom come down on him throughout all those years? No. It was all 'Don't worry about him, Cian, our boy will find his way.'

"While me . . . " I gave a snort of bitter laughter. "I'm wasting my life. MassArt is a waste of time. I'm not special enough to make a career out of my creativity."

"She said that?" He glared at me.

I nodded. "She's said that to me my whole life. When I wanted to try out for gymnastics, she told me there was no point, because I was too chubby as a kid. When I wanted to join the school choir, she laughed and told me I was tone deaf, so I didn't bother. When my art teacher put my portfolio forward for a regional award, and I won . . . " I bit back more tears as I remembered. "She, uh . . . she looked at the award and said, 'Wow, I guess they were short on talent this year.' I know she said it to dissuade me from art and not because she meant it, but it stung."

"Jesus fuck." Michael looked disgusted.

I wiped away another tear. "My dad lost his shit with her and wouldn't talk to her until she apologized. Which she did. But I knew underneath she was mad at me about that too."

"What she said isn't right, Dahlia."

I nodded. "One night we were arguing about my boyfriend at the time. I was sixteen, and I stupidly left condoms in my bedside table. She found them and went off about me having sex. That, I don't blame her for. I get it now, but I didn't then. So we had this huge argument, and I asked her if I was even her kid. If Dad had cheated on her and I was the result, and she hated me for it? I have never seen her so pissed. I thought she was going to hit me, she was so fuckin' mad. Instead, she grabbed my hairbrush and said she'd do a DNA test to prove that my worthless ass was unfortunately hers." I exhaled shakily, the old confusion rolling over me when I told him. "Later that night I overheard her crying in her bedroom. My dad was comforting her because she wasn't mad at me. She was mad at herself . . . that she had made me feel like I wasn't her kid.

"So she knows." *More salty tears rolled down my cheeks.* "She knows what she's doing, Michael. She can't seem to help herself, and I don't get it."

He'd not let go of my hand since he'd first taken it, and he squeezed it now. "Have you thought about asking your dad?"

"I'm afraid if I do, I'll cause problems between them. My parents love each other. Like, so much. I want what they have. And I adore my dad, Michael. He's the best guy ever. I don't want to put him in the position where he feels like he's in a war between his kid and his wife. I need to get out of there. I think once I have my own place, my relationship with her will get better."

Michael nodded. "You could be right. My life is better now I'm out of my parents' house."

I knew from Gary that Michael had followed in his dad's foot-steps to be a cop, but I'd picked up on little things Michael had said over the last few months and I suspected his family life hadn't been great. "You're not close with your dad, are you? Despite the cop connection?"

He shook his head. "My dad is a lot like your mom. He, uh . . . he tried to crush my confidence my whole life. I guess he saw something in me he didn't like very much, something that made him feel insecure. He tried to stop me from succeeding, but it only drove me to succeed at whatever I put my mind to. I worked hard at school, and I played ball. Gary's dad was a fuckin' nightmare, and he didn't deal with that very well. Gary pulled a lot of shit he shouldn't, and I was always there, trying to get him out of it. Dad liked that. He liked me in trouble." *The muscle in his jaw clenched, and I squeezed his hand.* "I wanted to go to law school, but we *couldn't afford it. I was trying for a scholarship, but Gary broke into a liquor store, and I got caught trying to stop him. Gary told the cops I was there to stop him—so did a couple of idiot guys who were with him. The police believed me, let me go. But Dad told my coach, who was a hardass. He benched me. My math teacher, who I respected, and who was a Boston U alum, found out why and withdrew his recommendation offer. There was no way I was getting that scholarship. So, I graduated, and I did the next best thing, which was to apply to the police academy.*

"That pleased my old man. 'See,' he said, 'you ain't no better than me.'"

"Michael," I said, hating that for him.

He shook his head, his dark eyes blazing with determination. "It's not going to stop me, Dahlia. One day I'll make lieutenant. Then detective. And if I want to, I'll go all the way to captain. Let him choke on that."

"You'll do it too." I knew he would. "Absolutely."

We shared a tender smile, and I watched the shadows lift from his eyes. "Gary said the same thing. At least I have him. He's the one person who has always had my back."

"I never realized when I called you that you'd understand so completely what I'm going through. I wish you didn't. I don't want that for you. Do you at least have a mom who's like my dad?"

Just like that, the shadows came back. "No. My mom is a timid woman. She's afraid of my dad."

"Does he hurt her?" I was almost afraid to ask.

"Not anymore. Not since I got big enough to take the hits instead. I was worried when I moved out, but I think he knows, me being a cop now, I'd fuckin' ruin him if he touched her again."

Without thinking about it, I reached across the center console and wrapped my arms around him. Michael hesitated for a second but then his strong arms enveloped me.

I rested my chin on his shoulder and tightened my embrace, soaking in his warm strength and hoping he was soaking in mine. I was kind of awkwardly sprawled across him, but I didn't care.

His voice was hoarse in my ear. "What's this for?"

I pulled back so I could look deep into his beautiful eyes. "Because you deserve so much better. I hope you know that."

Michael's breathing stuttered, and he looked so young all of a sudden. He loosened his right arm but only to cup my cheek. Heat flooded me, and I realized that my impulsiveness had once again gotten me in trouble. "So do you," he whispered. "You deserve everything."

His eyes had dropped to my mouth, and his thumb was caressing my skin, drawing closer and closer to my lips.

My own eyes, with a will of their own, lowered to his beautiful mouth.

At the hitch of my breath, I knew when we both became completely aware of every inch of each other. My breasts were crushed against his chest and if I swung my right leg over, I could straddle him in seconds, so every part of us was touching.

I was suddenly so hot, I was burning up.

His mouth was millimeters away from mine. All I had to do was move a tiny bit . . .

Our lips brushed, and Michael's arm tightened around me as we both let out a little gasp.

My lower belly flipped, deep, low, and there was a rush of slickness between my legs. I was desperate for his kiss, for his tongue against mine, but it was more. Never had I been so needful of someone. I wanted Michael inside me. I wanted to ride him while he touched me and kissed me.

I wanted that more than I'd ever wanted anything. The want became a red haze over my mind.

Our lips brushed again as I swayed into him.

"Dahlia," he panted.

We were out of breath, and we'd barely touched each other.

And then Michael's words from earlier whispered in the back of my mind. "Gary said the same thing. At least I have him. He's the one person who has always had my back."

I couldn't do this! Not to Michael. Not to Gary. But mostly not to Michael. He'd never forgive himself.

Pull back, Dahlia. Pull back before you can't ever go back.

With every ounce of will inside me, I wrenched myself away from Michael, falling against the passenger side door. "I'm sorry." *I panted hard.* "I can't."

Michael blinked rapidly as if he was coming out of some kind of spell. Realization dawned, and he squeezed his eyes closed and pinched the bridge of his nose. "Fuck, Dahlia, I'm sorry."

"No, don't." *I didn't want him to feel guilty about something that hadn't happened.* "We didn't do anything. We talked, we hugged. End of story."

He looked like he wanted to argue but whatever he saw in my face made him stop. Instead, he nodded and put on his seat belt. "I'll take you home."

I flushed from the memory of that night. Michael had driven me home, the atmosphere between us thick with sexual tension that refused to abate, and I dove out of the car to get away from it. It hadn't taken long for us to get back on track as friends. I think mostly because we were addicted to each other's company. Neither of us would admit it, so neither of us knew at the time how the other felt.

But he was my safe haven from the bad blood between my mom and me.

Bad blood I didn't understand then, and I still didn't understand now.

Dillon's death had been the end of whatever possibility my

mother and I had of finding our way together. I understood that. I just didn't understand everything that had come before.

Maybe if I could, I'd find a little bit of peace. And perhaps if I could mend the hurt between Michael and me, I'd get closer to that peace. Facing my mom was the scariest thing to happen to me since returning to Boston.

Facing Michael for the second time, knowing how much he despised me, was just as terrifying. However, I'd faced Mom and survived.

I could survive Michael.

I hoped.

11

Michael

Walking into the precinct at the start of his shift was better than walking into it at the end. It never used to be like that for him. Not until night shift. At this time in the evening, the precinct was busier, more alive, and that's what he was used to having worked day shift most of his career. He was worn down, but he couldn't remember if he'd felt that before or after his change in schedule.

"Hey, Mike!" Wilma, the precinct's main receptionist, called to him as he passed. "A friend of yours is here. I told her to wait at your desk."

Confused, he gave a vague nod, wondering who had turned up. It couldn't be Kiersten. She made it clear she didn't want to see him again when they'd filed for divorce.

He turned the corner, striding down the open-plan office space toward his area, and he almost stumbled mid-stride when he caught sight of the person sitting perched on his desk with her head bent toward the phone in her hand.

Dahlia.

Michael's heart felt like it had lurched up into his throat, and he hated she still could make that happen. Years ago when she was with Gary, he'd be waiting for them somewhere, a restaurant, a party, and as soon as he saw her, his heart would leap in his chest.

She could make him feel like a prepubescent teen with a crush.

When he was younger, that feeling made him pine for her. Fuckin' *pine*.

Now it pissed him off.

Michael picked up his pace, and as if sensing him, Dahlia's head jerked up, and she gave him those big, wounded blue eyes. "Michael," she said, slipping off the desk as he came to a stop.

Jesus Christ, he thought, taking in her attire. She did this to him deliberately. She wore a fitted T-shirt tucked into a tight skirt that was high at her waist, showing off how tiny it was, and tight around her thighs. He didn't want her to turn around. He'd never get the vision of her gorgeous ass out of his head.

"What are you doing here?" he bit out. Michael couldn't believe she'd ambushed him at work, for Christ's sake. How selfish could this woman get? He had to concentrate here. He couldn't allow her and all the garbage she brought back up to distract him.

She straightened her shoulders, her features hard with determination. "Can we talk? I'm sorry for coming here, but I didn't have your address."

He glared at her, hating the way his skin seemed to crackle with life around her. She was dangerous. He needed her gone. If that meant giving her this last chance to talk, then he'd do it to get rid of her.

"Follow me." He exhaled heavily and turned around, hearing her light footsteps behind him. Once he found a free interview room, he pushed open the door and gestured for her to go ahead. Manners were ingrained in him but, Jesus, as she strolled past him into the room, he wished he'd forgone them for her.

The skirt cupped her ass in a way that he knew if he stripped it off her, her ass would be round, pert, and goddamn luscious in his hands. And the shoes. Shit, he hadn't seen the shoes. They were high heels with a strap around the ankle. What the hell kind of shoes were those to be wearing in late October? At least she was carrying a coat in her hands.

Michael slammed the door shut behind him, making her jump. "Well?" He crossed his arms over his chest.

Her gaze danced nervously around the room before coming back to his. "I wanted to clear the air between us."

The anger that had seethed in his gut for nine years flooded upward out of him. Michael took a step toward her, and he knew all that ire was blazing out of his eyes. "Clear the air? Okay, let's start with you answering a few questions."

Dahlia gave him a wary nod. Everything about her current demeanor pissed him off. The Dahlia he knew would tell him to go fuck himself for his demanding attitude. "Okay."

"Why did you stay away all this time without at least letting me know where you were?"

"Michael, I didn't tell anyone," she said, her voice soft, placating, as she stepped toward him. "Only my dad."

"Why?" The torment she'd caused still resided in him. Like the fragment of a bullet that had never worked its way out of his body. Only his parents had ever hurt him like that, and it royally fucked him off that the one person he used to confide in about all that shit had caused an even worse affliction. "You used to tell me everything. Or was that a lie?"

"No." She was more forceful now, her annoyance obvious. "You know that's not true."

He liked seeing that fire. But at the same time, he thought maybe it would be easier to get rid of the Dahlia who acted like a whipped puppy around him because that wasn't the Dahlia he'd known and loved. "All I know is that I can't trust a word you say. Let's make this quick so I can get back to work."

She clenched her jaw and hugged her coat to her body. "Michael, I don't want to go back to Hartwell without making peace between us. I know we'll probably never be friends, but I don't want to leave here with you hating me."

The urge to rush her, to grab her and kiss her until her mouth was bruised with the imprint of his was overwhelming. His lust for her seemed to cloud his brain, but he wasn't a stupid kid anymore. The damage this woman could cause him ... fuck, she was still doing it. He never gave Kiersten a chance. Not a real one. Because he didn't want to be hurt the way he had been by Dahlia.

And now she was standing in front of him and, despite it all, he still wanted her more than he'd ever wanted any woman.

He pretty much despised her for it.

He needed her gone.

For good.

"I do hate you," he said with a calm he didn't feel, using his blank cop expression so she'd have no idea of the battle raging inside him.

As soon as the words were out of his mouth, he wanted to pull them back in. He might as well have backhanded her.

The color drained from her face, and she didn't hide the damage his words caused.

Her blue eyes were bright with agony.

Every instinct in him was to reach for her, pull her into his arms and reassure her he was lying, that he didn't mean it, that he was sorry.

And Michael *was* sorry, but he wasn't sure it was a lie. Because he didn't get it. He didn't understand how she could stay away from him all these years if she cared about him as much as her pain seemed to suggest.

Thankfully, before he could take it back, Dahlia lifted her chin and strode slowly past him with her head held high. But the tremor in her full mouth gave away her upset almost as much as the way she had to fumble with the door handle to get out of the room.

The sudden fear that something would happen to her while she was distracted by his words, by the apparent turmoil they'd caused, washed over him. Michael's feet moved before he could think about it too hard and he followed her out. However, she must have started to jog or something because she was already out of sight. Hurrying to catch up with her, he turned the corner, saw no sign of her in the office, and picked up the pace.

When he came out into the main reception, he pulled up short. Dahlia hurried down the steps to the precinct doors and a man in uniform rushed down the steps after her. He grabbed her arm, drawing her to a stop.

It was her brother. Dermot.

Whatever he saw in her face made Dermot's expression tighten. He asked her something, and she shook her head frantically and pulled at her arm.

Dermot held on and said something else.

His sister seemed to slump into him, and to Michael's relief, he watched as Dermot led her to the door. Her brother was taking care of her.

Good.

As Dermot held the door open for his sister, he turned, as if feeling Michael's gaze. His was questioning. Michael gave him nothing.

Yet he wasn't giving him nothing, was he? He was standing at the top of the steps watching her leave. That pretty much said it all. If he didn't give a fuck, he wouldn't care how she got home.

Dermot seemed to understand and gave him a nod before he took his sister by the arm and led her out.

The ache in Michael's chest flared worse than ever.

He thought getting rid of her would be like exorcising a ghost, but he was wrong.

Inflicting pain on her was worse than petty. It was revenge.

A hard knot formed in his gut.

"What was that all about?"

Michael jolted out of his thoughts. He cut a look to his left where Nina, a police sketch artist he'd known for years, stood staring at the now-empty entrance. "What?"

Nina gestured to the doors with her coffee cup. "Who was that gorgeous number McGuire led out of here? The one who seemed to be running away from you as if her sweet little ass was on fire?"

Michael flinched. "It's McGuire's sister."

"Yeah?" She shot Michael a look out of the corner of her eyes. "What she do to you?"

He realized Dahlia *was* a bullet fragment. One, it seemed likely now, that he'd never be able to work out. And she was slowly filling him with poison because Michael never thought he'd be the guy who would hurt Dahlia McGuire the way he'd hurt her. And he fuckin' hated *himself* for it.

"You ever been in love, Nina?" he asked.

Nina raised an eyebrow, but answered, "When I was eighteen. She was older. It didn't work out."

"Do you hate her now?"

"Not really."

"You still love her?"

Nina sighed. "Are heart-to-hearts going to become a regular thing between us? Because I'd like to prepare myself."

Not in the mood, Michael turned to leave, but Nina grabbed his shoulder.

"No, I don't love her anymore. You okay? This about McGuire's sister?"

"I used to love her," he bit out, feeling cold. So fuckin' cold.

"Ah, okay."

"She did something. Now I hate her."

Nina studied him, not saying a word, but it was the way she did it, like she could see what Michael wasn't saying.

He looked away, gutted. "But I still love her too. How fucked up is that?"

"Mike ... " Nina tightened her hand on his shoulder and squeezed. "That's when you know it's real."

He frowned in confusion.

"My mom always told me when you love someone, even on the days you hate them, that's when you know it's real."

That ugly knot in Michael's gut tightened because he didn't want it to be real with Dahlia. It hurt too much.

"Maybe you shouldn't be in tonight, Mike. Your head is somewhere else."

"I'm fine," he snapped.

"You're not. If I were you, I'd sort your head out. Say you're sick and come back to work tomorrow night."

That was the problem, wasn't it? Because it would take more than a goddamn night to sort his head out. It had been eleven years since he'd met Dahlia McGuire, and his head, his heart, had never been the same since.

12

Dahlia

Something broke inside me after my confrontation with Michael. With my mom, I'd always been able to convince myself that she was partly to blame for my behavior and that her vitriol was not my fault.

However, Michael was a different story. One of the reasons I'd fallen for him was because he was that guy who didn't judge—he understood that people made mistakes. And he forgave. He forgave Gary for a lot of stuff he'd pulled over the years because he knew that Gary hadn't had it easy growing up with an abusive single father.

He forgave his mom for never defending him against his dad because he knew it wasn't in her nature to be confrontational or . . . brave, really. It hadn't meant she didn't love him and so he'd forgiven her.

That he couldn't forgive me, that he *hated* me, made me realize the magnitude of what I'd done. How could everyone else forgive me? How could Darragh and Davina? Even Dermot, who had been kind to me when he saw how fucked up I was by the encounter with Michael? He'd taken me back to Dad's where I'd promptly locked myself in his old room.

Because I couldn't face Dad.

Out of everyone, my father should be the one who couldn't forgive me. I'd made him promise he wouldn't tell my family where

I was, and I'd put him in the middle of that. I'd driven a wedge between him and my mother.

I'd ... I was the catalyst in his youngest daughter's death.

Why didn't he hate me?

Like Michael.

"I do hate you."

During the car ride home, all I kept thinking was that if I could just hear the voice of someone who loved me, someone I hadn't hurt, I'd be okay. So I called Bailey. I couldn't remember much about the conversation, only that she said she wanted to come to Boston and I'd told her no. My selfish crap wouldn't disturb someone else's life. Again.

Yet as I laid on the bed in my brothers' old room, I felt like that twenty-two-year-old all over again. So goddamn lost, I could hardly breathe.

I didn't know how many times my dad knocked on the bedroom door. The only way I knew hours had passed was by the light that began to break through the curtains.

It had been quiet for a while as I laid in the shadowed room trying to pull all the pieces of myself back together again.

I was stronger than this.

I could do this on my own!

A knock sounded at the door. "Dahlia, someone is here to see you."

I turned my head, the whisper of my hair across the pillow sounding especially loud to my ears. "Tell them to come back later."

"Dahlia, it's me."

I blinked, wondering if I'd misheard.

"Dahlia?"

Bailey?

I lurched out of bed, dashed across the room, and yanked open the door. Bailey Hartwell stood in the doorway, my dad behind her.

Relief flooded me, and I threw my arms around her, drinking in her unconditional, unafflicted love.

She closed her arms tight around me. "It's okay," she promised. "I'm here now."

Bailey and I sat on the guest bed, the bedroom door wide open, but there was no Dad. I assumed he'd left to give us privacy.

Bailey's eyes were brimming over with concern. "I think I'd feel better if you were crying. This scary quiet you've got going on is somehow more disturbing."

I ignored that. "How did you get here?"

"Well, I have your keys, so I snooped in your apartment until I found a number for your dad. He gave me the address and told me I was welcome to stay here. Aydan and Vaughn are watching the inn for me, so I'm here as long as you need me."

I wanted to cry, but the tears had all dried up. "I love you."

"I love you too. And I'm seriously worried about you."

"Where's Dad?"

"He went downstairs. Do you want me to get him?"

"I can't face him." I shook my head. "Bailey, why does he forgive me? Why do any of them? If Michael and my mom can't, then maybe the rest of them shouldn't."

The flash of temper flared in her cat-shaped eyes. "Like hell! I cannot believe he said what he said to you. As for your mother, she's psychotic when it comes to you. I'm not saying that with bias. I am saying that as an emotionally mature human being. If Michael can't deal with the past and move on, that's his problem. You tried to mend the breach. You tried. That's all anyone can ask.

"And your dad and your brothers and sister forgive you for leaving because they love you. As for the other thing, there is nothing to forgive, and if you don't get that through that stubborn head of yours, I'm going to physically haul you back to therapy."

I smirked at her no-nonsense attitude. "Your bedside manner leaves a lot to be desired."

"You're not sick, Dahlia. You're sad. And you're loaded with guilt. Yes, you could have come home sooner, and yes, you made your family worry about you. That *is* your fault. You know that. You've explained, you've apologized, and everyone but Michael is moving on. But Dillon is not your fault. None of them believe that—and my guess is that not even Michael believes that. You have to let it go."

"My mom believes that, Bailey. Maybe she's right. Maybe I was born to hurt the people I love."

Frustration flashed in her eyes. "No. I won't hear it. And I won't let you do this to yourself. Not again. Christ Almighty, this isn't the Dahlia I know and love. You're stronger than this."

"Bailey."

We both jerked around, surprised to see my father standing in the doorway. We hadn't even heard him approach.

"Can I talk to my daughter alone, please?"

Bailey turned to me, silently asking what *I* wanted, and I loved her for that too. After I nodded, she got up and strode toward Dad. "I'll make some tea." And then she squeezed my dad's shoulder in comfort, treating him like she'd known him her whole life.

My dad gave her a fond smile, and I was not at all surprised that she'd endeared herself to him already.

Dad walked into the room, eyeing me in concern. I was getting sick of that look, but I guess if I didn't stop wallowing and buck up, they'd continue to look at me that way.

"We're all allowed to have weak moments, Bluebell." Dad sat next to me. "It's not a failure to admit that you can't cope with something. It's not a failure to admit that you need people to help you through."

"Bailey, you mean?" I dared to look at him.

"She's your family now too. It's okay that she can help you in a way that we can't."

"It's not that," I hurried to assure him. "She's not part of my mistakes. I don't feel guilt around her. I get to be sad around her. No judgments."

"And you feel like you can't be sad with me?"

"I don't deserve to."

"Oh, Bluebell ... " He put his arm around me, his voice cracking a little. "That breaks my heart, dahlin'."

We were silent as I burrowed into my dad's side.

"I overheard what you said to your friend, and I need to tell you something. I need to explain something that I probably should have explained a while ago."

I stiffened against him. "Okay?"

"You are not to blame for Dillon's death. I have never thought that. Your sister and brothers have never thought that. And Michael Sullivan has never thought that. I don't know what happened between you and him last night and Dermot couldn't tell me, but whatever it was, it wasn't about Dillon. As for your mother," he said, letting out a long exhale, "that goes way back. Way back before Dillon. Way back even before any of you kids came along. Deep down, your mother is a good person, but she has her problems. There is a reason we don't talk to her parents or her sister."

I pulled back to stare at him, surprised. My maternal grandparents were another thing my mom pretended didn't exist, along with her sister. The only reason I knew about them was because Davina had found a shoebox full of pictures and asked Mom about them. She'd told Davina a little about it and then proceeded to pretend they didn't exist again whenever Davi tried to mention them.

"Your mom's dad was physically abusive, but your grandmother was emotionally abusive."

I sucked in my breath. Despite everything she'd said and done to me, I hated that for my mom. "What did they do?"

"Her dad had a temper, and he was quick with his hands. As for her mother, well, her affection wasn't freely given. It had to be won. She would play off your mom against her sister. It was a competition to see who could do better that week and win their mom's love. Sometimes your mom won, and sometimes her sister won. It bred ugly competitiveness in your mom and jealousy like I've never experienced. That jealousy destroyed her relationship with her sister. I knew all about it, and I loved her so much I tried to understand when she acted a little nutty. She was always possessive and resentful whenever someone she cared about showed someone other than her more affection. It wrecked a lot of her friendships, and I had to be very careful about how I acted around other women."

"But you stayed with her."

"I loved her. When we were younger, your mom was hilarious and fuckin' cute. I loved making her laugh." He smiled tenderly at the memories. "No one needed laughter and unconditional love more than your mother. And we managed through it. The more she trusted me, the less jealous she seemed to get. Then we started to have kids, and our relationship got stronger. Until you."

My breath caught in my throat, my heart pounding. Had Mom lied? Was I not hers after all? "Dad?"

Seeing my fear, he understood and shook his head. "It's nothing that dramatic. No matter how bad things got, I never cheated on your mother. But when you were born, you and I formed this automatic bond that was a little different from the one I had with your brothers and sister. Don't get me wrong, I love all my kids, but from the moment you were born, you were definitely more mine than your mother's. It became more apparent why as you got older. You were my little mini-me, a McGuire, through and through."

He grinned down at me with so much love, it almost obliterated all the pain. Then his smile fell. "Your mom hated it. When you were little, you would come to me when you were hurt or cry for me when you'd had a nightmare. When you were sick, you didn't want anyone else. Only me. Your mom and I used to fight about it all the time. She said I was taking you away from her. And then when you got a little older, even though you were still just a kid who didn't know what she was doing, the hurt festered in your mom. I knew because she was harder on you about everything. She'd started to resent you because she thought she was losing out on the affection game."

Shocked, I stared at Dad with a feeling akin to horror. "But I didn't mean it."

"I know that." He tightened his hold on me. "And your mom should have known that, but what her mother did to her and her sister screwed her up in ways I couldn't fix. It concerned me so much over the years, I even asked her to go to therapy to talk to someone about it, see if it would help, but she refused. I hated the way she treated you, and I should have done something about it a long time ago. For that, I am to blame. No one else."

"Dad—"

"No, it's true. I'm your father, and it's my job to protect you. Even if that meant protecting you from your own mother. The friction between you two was a sore spot in our marriage for years."

"I'm sorry."

"Not your fault. Your mother is a piece of work." He exhaled heavily. "She set out to make Dillon hers when she was born. She wanted that bond with Dillon that I had with you. She blames you for Dillon's death, and that's not because it is true, and God, dahlin', you need to get that out of your head. Your little sister loved you. I know she was angry in the end but that little girl hero-worshipped you. If she's watching over us, her fuckin' heart is breaking knowing what this is doing to you. What your mother is doing to you.

"I love your mom. But she wouldn't talk to someone about what happened to her as a kid, how it affected her as an adult, as a parent, and now everything is so twisted up inside her she can't see straight. Losing Dillon broke something inside of her, and it was easier to blame you than to make peace with the fact that it was a tragic, senseless accident. This way she has somewhere to channel all her anger.

"And now she's lost everything," he whispered. "She lost me, and she's losing her kids. All of them. The only girl she had left was Davina, and she didn't turn out the way Dillon would have so she's pushed her away too. I love your mom, but I love my kids more, and I won't lose them because of her.

"Our marriage has been on the rocks for years, and we drifted too far apart. But there was a kernel of something left, until she confessed to hitting you and saying the toxic shit she said to you all those years that led to you drinking. Amazingly, finding that out gave me peace, knowing that leaving her was the right thing—that she was no longer the woman I married all those years ago. Our divorce is not on you. It's on her and me. You get that, right?"

Silent tears I didn't know I had left in me fell down my cheeks as I nodded.

"You've got to let whatever poison she put in you, out, Bluebell. Because I can't sit back and watch my baby girl live an empty life, punishing herself for something she did not do."

I fell against him, crying quietly, because his words, this history lesson about my mother, had a profound effect on me. For years, I'd thought there had to be something fundamentally wrong with me that my own mother could hate me. However, knowing there was a reason for the way she was freed something inside me. Not all the guilt, but some of it. The blame that didn't belong to me.

And just like that, I breathed a little easier.

13

Dahlia

Laughter filled Darragh's house as we sat around his dining table a few weeks after that life-changing discussion with Dad. And it *was* life-changing. Between the knowledge he'd given me and the support and love I got from my family over the subsequent weeks, I was slowly shedding the guilt that had crippled me emotionally for years.

It was almost Thanksgiving and Bailey had to return to Hartwell—Vaughn was threatening to come to Boston to bring her home. I was returning with her, content that my family and I would be okay.

There was still the thorn in my side that was my relationship with my mother.

And the hole in my heart that Michael put there when he told me hated me.

However, I'd decided I could live with it.

I had to.

"I wish you would stay for Thanksgiving," Krista said.

I smiled regretfully. "I have to go back. We have the annual Punkin' Chunkin festival next weekend, and it's one of the few weekends during the quiet season where I make a lot of money with the tourists."

It was true. I couldn't afford to lose out on that income.

"Well, maybe Bailey can stay, then." Dermot winked at my friend.

One of the nicest things about the past few weeks was getting Dermot back. It had been tense at first (and there were still moments of awkwardness), but he was smiling and joking with me more and more.

And, unfortunately, flirting shamelessly with Bailey.

Bailey rolled her eyes. "Once more, I am engaged."

My brother puffed up his chest. "Yeah, to some stuffy, New Yorker business guy who probably doesn't know his way around a woman's *feelings,* if you know what I mean."

While Darragh cut him a warning look because the boys listened to everything their uncle Dermot said, I almost choked on a bite of roast chicken.

Bailey grinned at me, a smug twinkle in her eyes.

"What?" Dermot frowned.

I cleared my throat, wondering how to say it in a way the boys wouldn't understand. "You couldn't be further from the truth. Not only does he, by Bailey's account, excel at women's *feelings,* Vaughn Tremaine is anything but stuffy and boring. Oh, and he looks like an underwear model to boot."

"He does," Krista agreed. "I Googled him. Well played, Bailey."

Bailey preened. "Thank you."

Dermot frowned. "*I'm* good-looking."

"You're very handsome," Bailey conceded. "But even if my fiancé weren't an annoyingly perfect physical male specimen, I'd still love him. So, unfortunately, I'm heading back to Hartwell with Dahlia."

"Well, all I can say is he must be special to have caught your eye."

Dad groaned. "Give it up, son. She's taken. Get over it."

"What? I'm not allowed to admire her? She's smart, and she's fuckin' gorgeous. It's physically impossible for me not to acknowledge that, I'm sorry."

While we laughed, Darragh smacked Dermot across the head. "For the fortieth time, watch your language."

Bailey bumped my shoulder with hers and whispered, "I love your family."

Warmth spread across my chest. I did too. And my family had, unsurprisingly, taken to Bailey. The only one who had been a little standoffish with Bails was Davina. Astrid cornered me and explained that it was hard for my big sister to see how close I was with Bailey when she'd missed out on so much of my life.

Thankfully, Davina warmed up a little more as the days wore on.

"I called Rosie's in Somerville. They've reserved a table for us tomorrow night," Davina said. Rosie's was a bar my dad and Darragh liked. It served pub grub and had big TVs all along the walls that continually played sports. It was relaxed, the food was good, they allowed the boys in, and we couldn't think of a better place for a family night out before I went back to Hartwell.

"And then Sunday Steak at mine on your last night." Dad smiled, but I could see the shadow of melancholy in his eyes. I knew it was because he didn't want me to leave. He and Dermot had gotten the entire weekend off work to spend it with me before I returned to Hartwell. It meant a lot to me.

I reached across the table and curled my hand over his. "I'll be back at Christmas."

He nodded and grinned, his dimple popping out. "I can't wait, Bluebell."

Later, after Davina and Astrid had gone home and Krista was putting the boys to bed, I helped Darragh load the dishwasher while Bailey, Dad, and Dermot stood around the kitchen drinking coffee and joking around.

"Hey, I don't want to spoil the mood or anything," Dermot

said, sounding serious, "but, um, you should know I convinced Mom to go see a therapist."

I whirled around from stacking the dishes. "Seriously?" I could feel Bailey's concerned gaze, but mine automatically went to my dad.

He stared at the floor, pensive.

"Yeah," Dermot replied. "I don't know what will come of it, but I thought you should know."

I nodded. Did I still care?

Yes, I did.

I didn't want my mom to lose everything, despite her feelings toward me. Especially now I understood where some of those feelings came from.

"Dad?" Dermot asked, and my dad's eyes flew to his. "I'm not trying to get in the middle of you two with this. It's just no one else is talkin' to her, and I get why. I do. But I don't want her to be alone."

Tears burned in the back of my throat and I looked to Darragh. A muscle ticked in his jaw, and I knew he was conflicted about the whole thing too.

Dad shook his head at Derm. "It's up to you kids what you decide to do regarding your mom. I understand either way, and I'm glad she's got you. Okay?"

My brother nodded, and I could see him struggling to hide his emotions.

Silence fell across the kitchen.

And then Bailey piped up, "Did I ever tell you guys about the time Dahlia accidentally flashed old Mr. Shickle, who owns the Ice Cream Shack?"

Horror filled me. "Don't you dare! This is my brothers and my dad."

Snorts of laughter came from all three, and that propelled

Bailey onward to my mortification. "It was a rare day off, we'd been on the beach in our bikinis—stop leering at me, Dermot—and we'd gone to the Ice Cream Shack. But Dahlia leaned against the wall as we waited for our ice cream and got the ties of her bikini caught in an old picture hook on Mr. Shickle's wall. Instead of patiently trying to untie it, she yanked it." Her laughter-filled eyes came to me. "Bikini top came off, and Mr. Shickle was rushed to the hospital with a suspected heart attack. In the end, it was only arrhythmia, and he survived, but there left no doubt in the minds of the people of Hartwell that the sight of Dahlia McGuire naked was too much for old Mr. Shickle to cope with."

My cheeks burned with mortification as my dad and brothers veered between horror that their daughter/sister had flashed her boobs in public, and hilarity that I had, indeed, sent an old man to the hospital.

"I cannot believe you told that story!"

"What story?" Krista asked as she wandered into the kitchen.

So I had to endure another retelling. Embarrassing! Krista nearly peed her pants laughing. And Bailey succeeded in doing what she'd set out to do.

To take our minds off my mom.

To make us laugh.

Even if it was at my expense.

The following night most of my family was gathered at Rosie's. Levi had woken up sick that morning, and although he'd gotten better throughout the day, Darragh and Krista didn't think it was a good idea for him to go out for dinner. Ultimately, they decided both boys should stay home since they'd have to leave after dinner with Krista anyway, so Darragh had come alone. I was disappointed Krista and my nephews weren't there and hoped Levi would be well enough to go to Dad's steak dinner tomorrow for my last night in Boston.

"I will miss the hell out of you," Davina said as we stood at the bar to order drinks. We'd already all eaten and were now moving onto the drinking portion of the evening. Well, *they* were. I was sticking to soda water and lime.

I leaned into her. "I'm going to miss you too. But I'll be back before you know it."

She seemed to hesitate before blurting out, "If Mom wanted to try to have a relationship with me again and I wanted to see if that could work, would you hate me?"

Of course not. "God, no, Davina. Look, I understand why things are the way they are between Mom and me, and as much as it hurts, I've found more peace about that than I could have hoped for a mere month ago. I know now she and I will probably never have a relationship and I'm coming to terms with that. But I wouldn't wish that on any of you. Or her. So if she makes steps to mend fences, I'd be happy for you, Davi. Honestly."

She gave me a tremulous smile. "I love you, kiddo."

I grinned. "I love you too."

Her smile widened, and she opened her mouth to say something else, but Bailey popped up by my side. "Sorry to interrupt but I need to tell you something."

"What are you doing?" Dermot appeared behind us.

We all turned. My brother glared at Bailey.

Bailey glowered back. "I'm not ambushing her."

"This was *your* idea."

"I didn't think it would work and you gave me very little notice."

"What the hell is going on?" Davina scowled at the two of them.

Bailey swallowed hard and gave me an apologetic look. "Michael is on his way here."

"What? Why?" Was the room spinning? Because I was all of a sudden very light-headed.

"*I do hate you.*"

I blinked away the sound of his voice ringing in my head as Bailey replied, "Dermot told me that Michael was there, watching you two leave the station that night and that he looked worried about you. Neither of us believes someone who didn't care about you would follow you out of the station. Also, *hate* isn't a bad thing in this case. The thing you have to worry about is indifference. And it's clear that Michael is definitely not indifferent to you. So, long story short, I asked Dermot if he thought Michael would turn up for drinks with the family. One last chance at trying to mend the breach, you know."

Ugh. How had I forgotten Bailey's second career as a matchmaker? She'd done this to Jessica and Cooper too. "Bailey ... "

"Thing is—"

"Thing is"—Dermot ran a hand through his hair, an apology in his hazel eyes—"I didn't exactly tell him you'd be here."

"But one would assume he'd know that you're here," Bailey interjected. She met my horrified gaze. "Still, I wanted to give you a heads-up."

I glared at my brother to cover the shipwreck of turmoil that was crashing and rolling in my stomach. "But *you* thought I should feel ambushed?"

"No, I was just worried you'd leave."

I wasn't going to lie—the instinct to leave was there.

However, I wasn't running anymore.

I looked over at the table where Dad, Astrid, and Darragh were laughing together. "I'm not leaving. If Michael is unhappy with me being here, then *he* can leave."

Then, right on cue, as if we really were magnets drawn to each other, I felt it when he stepped inside the bar. My eyes moved past Dermot toward the door.

There he was.

Michael wore the same leather jacket I'd seen him in at my dad's house, with dark jeans, a dark shirt, and black boots. The only thing different was that he'd shaved.

Either way, he was so goddamn handsome, it killed me.

Being at the station with him, in that interview room, so close I could smell his cologne, it had been the worst kind of torture. Until, of course, he'd opened his mouth and gutted me.

Realizing he wasn't walking into the bar alone, my already fast beating heart started pumping so hard, I thought it might knock itself out of my chest.

He'd brought a date.

She walked confidently at his side. A young, edgy blonde with pixie-short hair.

Why was it always a blonde?

"He brought a fuckin' date?" my sister snapped under her breath.

"She looks familiar." Dermot narrowed his eyes.

Michael's gaze landed on us at the bar, and when ours met, his didn't widen with surprise.

He knew I'd be here.

And he'd brought a date.

Bailey's hand slipped into mine and she squeezed, but her comfort did nothing to hold back the tide of memories. Of the last time he'd been with someone else instead of me. I doubt he regretted the blond the way he'd regretted it all back then. Memories flooded me, soaring me straight back into the past . . .

14

Dahlia

Massachusetts College of Art & Design
NINE AND A HALF YEARS AGO

The sound of hammering filled the workshop as me and my fellow metalsmiths worked on our projects for class. The room was warm from the blowtorches we used for the annealing process (heat treatment on the metals to soften them enough to make them workable), so despite the fall weather, I was in a summer dress and biker boots. Mom had given me a hard time about catching a cold, so I'd thrown my winter coat over the dress. Wearing tights while working for hours in a room where multiple blowtorches were in use might make me sweat to death, so I'd foregone them.

Thankfully. Otherwise, I'd be like my classmate, Shauna, who had stripped down to the tank top underneath her sweater because she'd been melting in her knit top and jeans. She still was, I noted, seeing the shimmer of sweat above her top lip.

The heat was worth it to see my jewelry come together. My favorite metal was silver, and I was using it to make a collection for a theater production of A Midsummer Night's Dream. *It was part of my final project.*

As I hammered the silver frame of the necklace that Titania would wear, I was careful around the inserts where I'd place my peridot gemstones. As a poor student, I couldn't afford emeralds. Even the much cheaper alternative of peridot was a lot out of my budget, but I was happy with how the stones were turning out for the fairy queen's jewelry.

Our teacher, Rita, was pretty relaxed. She wandered around the room giving advice, critique, and praise, but ultimately, we could work in our own space at our own pace.

Something made the hair on my neck stand on end like someone was watching me. Slowly, I lifted my head and turned toward the doorway.

The sight of Michael Sullivan standing there in his cop uniform caused a little flip in my belly.

He jerked his head in a "c'mere" motion.

Shit.

Since our confrontation at the diner, Michael had broken up with Dillon. She had been a moody, petulant mess about it, and I was feeling all kinds of contrition. I'd consequently been ignoring Michael's calls and texts for the last six weeks since their breakup.

"Can I help?" Rita asked from the front of the room, her eyes on Michael.

Michael stepped inside the doorway. "I need to speak with Dahlia McGuire."

"Oh. Dahlia?"

I glanced at her.

If Michael was tracking me down at school while he was clearly on the job, then I guessed he wouldn't stop hounding me until I spoke with him. As much as I wasn't ready for it, I knew I needed to get this over with. "Is that okay?"

"Sure."

I got off my stool. "I'll be back in a second."

Rita nodded and turned to another student.

My legs shaking a little, I ambled toward Michael. His intense regard made me flush.

Halting in front of him, I was more than a little annoyed about being ambushed. And about how hot he looked in his cop's uniform. "What are you doing here?" I hissed.

He scowled. "Is there somewhere we can talk in private?"

I nodded and brushed past him, hating the tingle of awareness that shot through me as I did. Leading him down the hall, we strode in silence until we came to the photography department. There was a row of lockable darkrooms here. A few were already locked but the second to last opened and although photographs were being processed, the room was empty. I ushered Michael in and closed the door, locking it behind me.

In the back of my mind, I knew it was a bad idea.

A horrible idea.

But it didn't stop me.

"A darkroom?" His handsome face was awash in the low red hues of the safelight.

"No one will disturb us in here. Now, what do you want? And why are you in uniform? Rita probably thinks I'm in trouble, thanks to that getup."

Michael's expression turned incredulous. "I'm in uniform because I'm working. I'm on break, I was in the area, and I thought to myself, 'I'm going to go see Dahlia to ask her why she's avoiding my texts and calls after I broke up with Dillon.' Six weeks, Dahlia. Six weeks. You want to tell me why you've left me hanging for six fuckin' weeks?"

I rubbed the back of my neck, unable to look at him. "Michael, you know why."

"No, I don't. I dated Dillon for less than three months, and we never had sex."

Jealousy and anger at the mere thought of him touching her curdled inside me. "I don't want to hear it."

"Dahlia ... " *He stepped toward me, and I stumbled against the door, trying to maintain distance. I heard his exasperated huff.* "I'm sorry. I don't know what I was thinking dating your little sister, and I'm sorry. Fuck, I'm sorrier than I can say."

That was all well and good, but he'd completely screwed us over. My sister would hate me if I dated him after this and it would be more ammunition for my mom. It would support her opinion that I was selfish and spoiled.

"Yeah. Me too." *I scrambled for the lock and the door handle.*

"Don't."

His hard body pinned me to the door, chest to chest, as his hand curled around mine to stop my escape. Heat flushed through me, and I forced my whimper of need back down my throat when he pressed his forehead to my temple.

"I can't bear it," *he said, his voice gruff.* "I can't bear it if I lose you. I've missed you so fuckin' much. It's like walking around without an arm."

Willing to say anything that would cease the touching, the torture, the temptation, I whispered, "I suppose we could try to be friends again."

"Is that why you're avoiding me? Because you want to be just friends?"

"Michael, that's not fair."

He turned his head so his cheek was pressed to my cheek, his lips touching my ear. "I love when you say my name. I dream about it. I dream about being with you as you whisper my name."

Every part of my body came alive in a flare of ardor like someone had struck several matches across my skin. My breasts seemed to swell against his chest, the nipples tightening into little buds that were probably obvious through my cotton dress.

And I couldn't even bear to acknowledge the slick, sudden heat between my legs.

Why did it have to be him?

"Michael . . . we can't. What about Gary?"

He lifted his head and our eyes connected. I knew that whatever was between us was more than physical. It was so much more, it hurt. And it had the torturous side effect of making our physical attraction feverish. "He cheated on you. He's my boy but . . . This is so much more than what I thought it was, Dahlia. Now he doesn't get a say in this. He fucked up. I want a chance to do better than him. So much better you'll never want to let me go."

He dipped his head, his lips hovering near mine as his hand traveled up my arm. "I miss you," *he repeated.* "You're all I think about."

My eyes burned with tears because I'd never dreamed that I'd feel this way about someone and have him feel the same way. Why did he have to screw it up before we even got a chance? "You hurt Dillon, and she's my sister."

"I'm sorry," *he groaned.* "Fuck, I've never been sorrier for anything in my whole life. But we're not talking about some quick fuck here. What we have is worth whatever shit we have to deal with to hold onto it."

I shook my head. "I can't do that to her."

Michael pushed off the door and away from me. He glowered, his face taut with frustration. "This isn't about upsetting Dillon. What she and I did hardly qualified as dating, and you know it. You're pissed at me for going there in the first place, and now you're punishing me!"

Rage flooded me. "Of course, I'm pissed! You pulled my kid sister into our shit!"

"Our shit? Our shit! This is our lives, our future, we're talking about, Dahlia."

"I just want to know why! Why her? When you knew how I felt about you?"

"Knew how you felt?" His voice got scarily soft.

I pressed further against the door, hoping I'd melt into it.

"That night you called me, and we nearly kissed in the parking lot, who was it that pulled away and said she couldn't do it? I didn't pull away and say I couldn't. I was seconds away from betraying my best friend, and at that moment I didn't fuckin' care, if it meant I got to be with you. I took it to mean that even if you were attracted to me, you wanted Gary more. I dated Dillon before I found out about your breakup. She reminded me of you a little. It was fucked up, I know that, but I've been fucked up over you for a long time."

That heat, the wet, between my legs increased and I could hear how short and shallow my breathing had gotten. "I pulled away that night because of you. Not because of me. I knew what your friendship with Gary meant to you, and I didn't want to come between you. I didn't want you to feel that guilt."

He was silent a moment. Brooding. Intense. Too sexy for his own good. "And that's why I feel how I feel for you. But you should know I've felt guilty from the moment I realized you were Gary's girlfriend. Guilty because I resented him for meeting you first. And I tried to make my feelings for you go away." He shrugged. "But they won't go away, Dahlia."

How was I supposed to resist that?

How?

But Dillon, my mom . . .

Jesus Christ.

"Do you want me or not?" he asked.

I should lie.

I should send him away.

But this mindless haze of longing and need was tormenting me past the point of being able to cope. "I've always wanted you."

A second later, he was on me, his lips crashing down on mine.

I gasped and lifted my hands to push him away but the taste and feel of him overwhelmed my senses, and I clung to him instead.

As our tongues touched, he groaned, the sound rumbling down my throat and straight between my legs. My fingers curled tight into his hair, pulling him closer, and his restraint fled. His hands were everywhere like he was frantic to touch every inch of me. When he cupped my breasts and kneaded them, I whimpered as pleasure swirled low in my belly. Michael ground his hips into mine. He was hard.

A moan of realization was lost in his throat as his kisses grew hungrier and wetter. My body shuddered with need as his hold on me became the only thing that mattered. My hands pulled at his shirt while his slid down my hips. It was the spine-tingling touch of his calloused fingertips on my inner thigh beneath my dress that jolted me. Enough to hear the voice in the back of my head screaming at me to stop him before it was too late. I wanted to push the voice back, desperate for the feel of him inside me but—

"Michael, stop," I panted, pushing against his chest.

He tensed. "Dahlia?"

All my nerve endings screamed to let him keep going, to let him slide his hand between my legs. I needed that more than I'd ever needed anything.

However, my sister's face kept flashing in my head and what she wanted had to supersede my need. It had to. And I wanted to be up-front and honest with my sister about Michael. If I had sex with him and she found out I'd done that before talking to her, I knew she wouldn't forgive me.

This way, at least if I were honest and honorable as I could be, maybe she and I would be able to figure things out.

"Fuck, Dahlia, don't tell me to stop," he pleaded.

I stroked his hair in comfort, maybe more for me than him.

Tears of sexual frustration burned in my eyes. I didn't know until then the horrible sting of unfulfilled lust. If Michael felt half as bad as I did, I was sorry. "We have to."

He braced his hands on the wall beside me, his face buried in my neck. Then he kissed me. A soft, sweet kiss to my throat. With a low grunt, he pushed off the wall and rolled away from me.

A shiver rippled through me as I turned to look at him. He was so handsome.

Feeling my regard, he looked toward me but without meeting my eyes. "I better go."

Hearing the bitterness in his voice, I realized he didn't know why I'd stopped. He thought I was pushing him away.

I moved to him, pressing my body against his, and cupped his cheek in my hand. I loved the way he automatically wrapped his arm around me to pull me close.

"I'm not sending you away," I explained. "I just ... if I'm going to date my kid sister's ex-boyfriend, I have to go about it the best way I can. That means not letting anything happen between us until I've had the chance to tell Dillon."

Michael's whole body relaxed. "You mean, you're giving us a shot?"

I nodded.

He broke out into a wide grin that was so wholly infectious, I laughed.

"Fuck, I want to kiss you again but apparently kissing you gets out of control pretty quickly."

Feeling cocky that a few kisses with me had turned him into a ravisher, I tilted my head and grinned. "You saying I'm the only woman who makes you lose your mind like that?"

He pressed his forehead to mine. "I nearly made love to you in public wearing my uniform. What do you think?"

Made love to me.

Gary always called it "screwing."

Michael turned serious. "I want to be there to tell Dillon. It's not fair to put it all on you."

I liked that too but ... "If we both do it, she'll feel ambushed. Humiliated, even. I think it's kinder if I do it."

Michael's hands flexed on my waist. "Okay. But I'm here if you need me."

"I know. Thank you."

He pressed a sweet kiss to my nose. "It'll all work out, dahlin'. We'll get through this."

15

Dahlia

To say the night took an awkward turn was a goddamn understatement. Michael wouldn't acknowledge me, but I didn't want to be rude to his date. Her name was Nina, and she looked a little younger than me.

That didn't hurt at all.

Nope.

My stomach roiled as we sat around the table with our drinks. My family and Bailey were great and chitchatted through the awkwardness, despite Michael's less than loquacious terseness. Nina seemed not at all concerned by his attitude and tried to make conversation with Bailey a lot.

It turned out she worked as a police sketch artist, and that's why she looked familiar to Dermot. Also, Bailey asked what age she was, and the chatty blonde declared she was twenty-five.

He'd brought a twenty-five-year-old as his date, and by the very little attention he was paying her, I knew it was deliberate.

Now and then, I'd feel his attention on me, but when I'd turn to look, he was glaring sullenly into his water like a teenager.

The longer we sat with his treating Nina like a ghost and not talking to my family, the more the ball of emotion tightened in my throat. This wasn't the Michael Sullivan I'd known and loved. This guy was bitter and selfish and needed to grow the fuck up.

The remorse I'd felt for leaving him eased a little every time I saw him. Or maybe it was the chat with my dad. Or years of therapy kicking in. All I knew was that, yes, I was at fault for leaving him, for not coming back. It was a big mistake, and I was sorry. However, he'd never given me a chance to fully explain. And he'd made mistakes too. Dating Dillon was the catalyst in everything changing so dramatically. I'd let that go because it was the right thing to do. Yet he was sitting there seething.

Who was this guy?

"I do hate you."

"Do you blame her?"

I wanted to confront him. I wanted to scream at him. Make him listen!

"Let *me* buy the next round." Nina's voice drew me out of my angry inner diatribe.

She was staring at Darragh, who was half standing from the table. I assumed that while I was lost in my thoughts, he'd offered to get another round of drinks.

"Oh, that's—"

"No, let me." She frowned at Michael. "Mike, another water or do you want a tonic or something?" He'd already told us he was driving so he was foregoing alcohol. That meant he didn't even have a depressant to blame his foul mood on.

He shook his head. "You're not paying. I'll pay."

That was the old Michael. Old-fashioned to the core. I curled my lip in annoyance.

Nina shrugged nonchalantly. "Not going to argue with that."

Either she was very laid-back, or there was something I was missing here because who acted like they didn't care if their date was behaving like a total asshole?

Giving a reluctant nod, Michael stood from the table as Nina asked everyone for their order. When she got to me, and I said I'd have another soda water and lime, she cocked her head and frowned at my glass. "Are you the designated driver tonight too?"

Usually, whenever anyone asked me why I wasn't drinking in a social situation, I told them I didn't drink alcohol. No explanation. It was nobody's business but mine.

The tension I felt from my friends and family, however, choked a response in my throat.

"Dahlia doesn't drink," Michael answered, his eyes cool and flat. "She can't handle her drink. Turns her into a lush who betrays everyone around her, isn't that right, dahlin'?"

His words prickled all over me like tiny, biting bugs. They were meant to wound, to eviscerate my emotions.

And just like that, I was determined to kill whatever feelings I had for him. His hateful words made that easier than it sounded. Maybe there was more of his father in him than he thought.

If I was done being my mother's punching bag, I was definitely done being his.

Outrage emanated around the table, and I sensed Bailey was going to be the first to speak, so I put my hand on her arm to stop her. Trembling with indignation, I got up out of my seat, grabbing my purse.

Michael watched me like a man defeated.

I was done with that too.

Just because he felt remorse for saying horrible things to me didn't mean it was okay.

The truth was I'd said worse over the years with my negative self-talk. But I was trying to be kinder to myself, which meant not allowing others to fill me up with their poison anymore.

I never thought Michael would be one of them.

"Thank you," I told him.

He flinched ever so slightly. "What?"

"For killing it." I nodded. "Yeah, for finally killing it. The way I feel about you. The guilt. All of it. The Michael I knew would never have treated me the way you've treated me since I came home, no matter what I'd done. You hate me?" I remembered Bailey's words earlier and shrugged with an ambivalence I wished I felt. "I don't hate you. I don't feel anything for you anymore."

The muscle in his jaw ticked as he glared at me.

Breaking eye contact, I looked down the table to my dad. "I'll call a cab and see you all at home."

Thankfully, no one protested. They let me walk out of there with dignity.

Michael

He watched her make her way out of the bar, and his knees shook.

"I don't feel anything for you anymore."

Fuck.

Cold sweat beaded under his arms and above his lip as he watched her leave. What he'd said . . .

What had he been thinking? As soon as the words were out of his mouth, he wanted to shove them back in. She made him crazy. He said shit he shouldn't. All because of the anger in the pit of his stomach. All because he'd assumed all these years he'd loved her more than she'd ever loved him, and he'd resented her for it.

But what if he'd been wrong?

"I don't feel anything for you anymore."

Panic suffused him, and he looked across the table at Cian. A man he respected. Cared about. A man who was looking at him in disappointment.

"I don't feel anything for you anymore."

That wasn't true. It couldn't be true. Not when he felt so fuckin' much.

They weren't done.

She couldn't walk away again.

We're not done.

He whipped his head around and looked down at Nina. What the hell had he been thinking bringing her here? Why did he keep screwin' up like this? "Thanks for coming but I'm sorry," he said. "I gotta go. One of the guys will see you home." He knew the McGuires would give her a ride. He knew it didn't make bailing on her after she'd done him a favor any less shitty, but right now all he could think about was getting to Dahlia.

None of them stopped him going after her.

They knew like he knew, they weren't done.

Apparently, they never had been.

Dahlia

Hurrying away from Rosie's, that momentary feeling of freedom, of saying out loud that I was done with Michael Sullivan, fled completely. I didn't feel free. Fury and hurt and resentment and hatred and love and longing and more resentment filled me until I was fit to bursting. I wanted to smack something.

I wanted to scream and scream until the feelings inside me exploded into dust.

Bracing myself against the bitter wind as I marched down Broadway, I remembered I'd told my dad I'd call a cab, but right then, I needed to walk it off.

Except I was walking in the wrong direction.

"Shit," I muttered, drawing to a halt and turning.

That's when I saw the black Honda Accord pull up beside me and Michael jumped out of the driver's side.

Anticipation and indignation were strange emotional bedfellows, but that's what I felt right then.

"Get in the car," he said, marching toward me.

My jaw dropped at his demand. "Are you crazy?"

"Get in the car, Dahlia." He glowered, bracing his hands on his hips. "We need to talk."

"I'm done talking with you. I don't particularly like what you have to say."

Michael practically bared his teeth. "Get in the fuckin' car."

I pushed my face into his, refusing to be intimidated. "Go fuck yourself."

"There she is," he bit out somewhat mysteriously, and then grabbed my upper arm. "Get in the car."

"Get your hands off me," I hissed, trying to pull out of his grip.

Instead, he hauled me up against him so I had no choice but to brace my hands against his chest or be crushed. The aforementioned very powerful chest heaved beneath my touch. "Don't make me pull out my badge or my blue light because I will."

My eyes flared. "That's an abuse of power."

"Yeah, well, you've been abusing your power over me for fuckin' years, so get in the car." He led me around to the passenger side, and I was so stunned by his words, I was in the car before I knew what was happening.

"What?" I huffed to myself as he got in. The car smelled of leather polish and Michael's cologne. The doors locked as he pulled on his seat belt, and the anticipation I'd felt earlier made my heart rocket into hyper speed. "This is kidnapping!"

He pulled into traffic, apparently ignoring me now.

"Michael!"

"You wanted to talk." He cut me a hard look. "We're going to talk."

"Too late."

"You run off again without having this conversation, I'm not going to think much of you anymore."

Disbelief boiled in my blood. "I thought you hated me anyway! I tried to talk! You turned it into a verbal gutting!"

"Lower your voice."

"Don't tell me what to do." I seethed beside him. As soon as we got to Dad's, I was going to let it rip. He thought he was the only victim here?

"For someone apparently so indifferent to me, you got a lot of anger in you."

I narrowed my eyes and stopped myself from opening my mouth to snap back at him. That would only support his point.

I kept my mouth shut as the minutes passed. Fifteen minutes was like an age. It wasn't until we reached the Sweetser Circle on the Parkway and Michael didn't come off onto Broadway in Everett that I opened my mouth. "Where are you going?"

He kept driving down the Parkway. "Chelsea."

"Why?"

Michael flicked me a look before staring straight ahead. He was surprisingly calm. "My apartment is in Chelsea."

My pulse skittered.

Alone with Michael. In his apartment.

Nope.

"Turn around and take me back to Dad's."

The bastard ignored me and kept driving. I stewed on this new indignation until he pulled to a stop outside a three-decker in Chelsea.

He'd parked with the passenger side to the sidewalk, and I looked up at the building, curious and fearful all at once.

"Let's go inside."

"I'm not going in there. This is kidnapping, Michael."

"Stop being so fuckin' melodramatic," he said without heat.

"Melodramatic?" I clenched my teeth. "You manhandled me into the car. As a cop, you know that's not right."

"I know you. If you didn't want to be here, there is no way I could have gotten you in the car. Now get out." He pushed open his door, slammed it shut, and came around the hood of the car to open mine.

Michael's dark gaze shuttered. "Will you get out of the car or do I need to bring out my cuffs?"

"You wouldn't dare," I growled as I launched myself out of the vehicle.

When he tried to retake hold of my arm, I yanked it away from him and hurried up the stoop to the front entrance.

In favor of the cold day, I'd donned the only pair of boot-cut jeans I owned and a pair of high-heeled boots. They were much more comfortable to run away from him in than the high heels I'd worn the last time I'd seen him. Only I didn't appear to be running away, did I?

I felt his attention as he opened the front door, but I refused to look at him. He muttered something under his breath.

"You do realize I've got whiplash?" I followed him upstairs to his apartment.

He frowned down over his shoulder at me. "What?"

"Emotional whiplash. You banged a mental Uey so fast, I can feel the burn of it up my goddamn neck." I could also hear my Boston accent getting thicker with every angry sentence out of my mouth.

Michael didn't answer as he led me to the door on the second floor and I took that to mean he knew I was right about the whiplash.

As soon as I walked inside his apartment, some of my ire died. Michael hit the lights, illuminating everything. Or, well, nothing actually. The place was almost unlived in. Bare walls, blinds at the windows but no curtains. No photos. Nothing personal at all.

It was depressing.

I hated that for him, even if I was angrier at him than I'd ever been in my life.

The apartment door slammed behind me, and I slowly turned inside the airy sitting room to face him. Michael dropped his keys on a side table that had a lamp with a dull beige shade on it. Then he met my gaze. "I shouldn't have said what I said."

I lifted my chin, ignoring the piercing hurt as I remembered *everything* he'd said. "Which part?"

He raised an eyebrow. "What do you mean?"

"Well, you've said a lot of horrible things. Something about my mom being right to blame me and erase me from her life. Oh, and that you hate me. And my favorite was the recent dig at my brief reliance on alcohol."

Michael exhaled and rubbed a hand over his head. "I'm sorry. You just ... turning up like this has brought a lot of crap back for me, and it's made me crazy. I'm saying and doing fucked-up things—"

"That's not an excuse," I cried softly. "You don't get to hurt me like that and say it's because I make you crazy. And don't blame me for your actions either. Your actions are your own, and I'm not taking responsibility for them."

"I know!" He threw his hands in the air. "Don't you think I fuckin' know that? I hate myself for what I've said. For what I've done. But it was never intentional. It just happened in the moment."

I scoffed. "Nina wasn't intentional? You knew I would be there and you took a stab in the dark and thought, 'Hey, I know what I'll do to kick her in the gut even more. I'll bring a younger model and show her I've moved on!' Well, news flash, Michael, I already knew that! I met your wife, remember?"

"Ex-wife," he bit out, taking a step toward me. His whole being bristled with contempt. "I'm not going to apologize for marrying Kiersten. You left! You fuckin' left, and you didn't come back! And don't even pretend you haven't been with other men."

I narrowed my eyes because he was avoiding the topic of Nina. "Well, a girl has needs too."

His features grew taut, and he took another somewhat menacing step toward me. Refusing to be intimidated, I stayed where I was. "Yeah? You fuck any of them without thinking about me?"

My skin flushed with outrage because he wasn't wrong. There had been only one man in the last nine years who made me temporarily forget the heat I had with Michael. But when we were out of bed, I couldn't forget. So I'd let that man go too.

He looked smug as he said, "I'm right, aren't I?"

Was I to assume he always thought of me when he was with his wife? With other women? I thought not. "There was someone," I whispered. "He made me forget."

That stopped Michael in his tracks. Distress he couldn't hide flashed across his face, and a flare of pain panged in my chest. "You still with him?"

"No."

"Did he leave you or did you leave him?"

I shrugged. "What does it matter? This isn't important."

"Did you leave him or did he leave you?"

"Michael—"

"Answer the question, Dahlia."

I could feel that familiar electricity zinging through me the nearer he got. "I left him."

His shoulders seemed to relax, but he whispered, "Seems you have that habit."

"Is that why you wanted me here? To get in a few more hits? Because you aren't perfect, Michael. You aren't blameless!"

"What the hell does that mean? Are you talking about Dillon?"

"You made a mistake then. I made a mistake too. But I let it go, and you didn't."

"*Your* mistake kept you away for nine fuckin' years!"

That was it. Something inside of me cracked. "You're a cop!" I screamed, my chest heaving and shuddering. I lowered my voice, the words hoarse from my shriek. "You're a fuckin' detective, and you're telling me you couldn't have found me even if you'd wanted to?"

He flinched like I'd slapped him, staring at me with those soulful eyes that made me want to die.

"Why did you bring Nina?" I repeated.

"Because I'm a dick. She's a friend. She's also gay. She was at the station when Dermot asked me out for drinks, and I knew by the shifty way he was acting that you'd be there. So I asked Nina to pretend to be my date. I was so busy trying to make sure I was okay going into that situation, I convinced myself you wouldn't care."

Relief I didn't want to acknowledge made me relax a little, knowing he hadn't screwed over Nina to get at me. Also, her focused interest in Bailey made more sense now.

As for Michael's reason for bringing Nina? I nodded reluctantly because I could understand that. Still, he hadn't answered my previous question. "Why didn't you try to find me?"

Something I *didn't* understand turned his gaze heavy. "I didn't want to."

I gasped, the words slicing through me.

Well, I'd asked, hadn't I?

Feeling numb, or rather wishing I'd feel numb, I moved to walk past him. To leave. To go home to Hartwell where I could lick my wounds in peace.

Before I could, Michael grabbed my upper arm, hauling me against him. His tortured expression was hard to take. "You left me." His words caught like stinging cuts on my lips. "You left me, and I was so in love with you. I didn't want to find you because you broke my heart, Dahlia. You broke my fuckin' heart."

Tears flooded my eyes as a tsunami of longing and pain filled me.

He'd never told me he loved me.

We both knew we felt it—or I hoped, at least—but there had never been a right time to confess it.

Until now, I guess.

"I blame you," he said, shaking me gently. "Do you get that? I blame you for this empty life you left me with."

"Stop," I demanded, trying to pull away. I didn't want to get sucked into another vortex of unrelenting guilt.

"Why should I stop?" he said, drawing me closer. "I don't want to stop until you're out of my blood. Why can't I get you out of me, huh? I want you out."

"Then let me go," I whispered.

His grip on me only tightened, his expression fierce with something else as he watched my tears fall. "There could be another way."

Seeing the heat in his dark eyes, understanding flooded me. A flush spread across my cheeks and neck, traveling lower. I wanted to shake my head, say no, but I also absolutely did not.

Hadn't I known this was what would happen if he brought me here?

I think, despite knowing how stupid it was, I'd anticipated this with a thrill I couldn't deny.

Michael curled his hand around the nape of my neck and drew me tight to him. The fever that crawled through me burned hotter, awakening my body inch by inch in a way only Michael Sullivan's touch could. His other hand slid down my back to cup my ass. His erection dug into my stomach, and a flush of wet slickened between my thighs. *Oh my God.* I trembled under his intense study.

"Think about it. We never got a chance to fuck. What if that's all this is? What if it's just physical goddamn frustration?"

I shivered in his arms. "You know that's not true."

"Yeah? Maybe, maybe not. But we could stand here all night,

yelling at each other, trying to find ways to dig out all the pain, or I could throw you on my bed, and we could fuck out all the anger and hurt."

I lowered my eyes because even though my mind was screaming what a bad idea it was, there was a part of me that wanted to know. To know what it would be like to have Michael inside of me.

If I looked at him, my body, my desire, would win over my good sense.

My breath hitched as Michael took my silence for acquiescence and flicked the button open on the top of my jeans. I froze at the abrupt sexual action as he slid the zipper down and gently slipped his hand beneath my underwear. Surprised and turned on, I made a guttural sound, my hands grabbing onto his upper arms for support as he pushed through my wet to touch my clit.

He grunted and pressed his forehead to my temple and continued to rub my clit. Now he knew that merely arguing with him got me as ready as goddamn foreplay.

I tried to stop undulating against his touch, but the pleasure was tightening between my legs. My fingers bit into his arms. "Mich—"

He covered my mouth with his, hungrily kissing the rest of my resistance out of me. Then I was up in his arms, my legs wrapped around his waist, and he carried me into the bedroom.

In my haze of lust, of need, I was ready to be thrown on the bed and screwed six ways till Sunday. Yet Michael surprised me.

He broke our kiss and lowered me to my feet at the foot of his bed.

His hands rested on my waist for a second before sliding down over my hips. We stared at each other in a mix of longing and defensiveness. I could see the wariness in his dark eyes just as I knew he saw that emotion mirrored in mine.

Why did he stop?

Stopping would only lead me to thinking, and I didn't want to think. I wanted to be impulsive and stupid. Even if it wrecked me.

"I should go."

Michael's answer was to tighten his grip on my waist. He gave me what felt like a reassuring squeeze before slipping his fingers under my sweater. I shivered at the soft caress of his rough fingertips.

"You're not wearing a coat," he said, his voice low. "You need to start wearing a coat." There was a dreamlike quality to his tone. Like he was in a daze. His touch was pulling me into that daze with him. When he caressed a little higher, across my ribs, goose bumps prickled over my breasts, and they felt heavy, desperate for his hands, his mouth.

"Michael . . . "

His hands came out from under my sweater to take hold of the opening of my jeans. He dug his thumbs into the waistband, expression determined and hot as our eyes stayed connected. And then he slowly tugged my pants down over my hips. The denim clung tightly to my generous hips, so he had to guide them down, lowering to his haunches to do so. I felt his hot breath on the cotton between my legs, and I shuddered with need. Bracing a hand on his strong shoulder, I lifted one foot after the other so he could unzip my boots and pull the jeans off.

A small part of me wondered if he was doing this deliberately, seducing me slowly so I could torment myself later with the knowledge that I'd had multiple opportunities to stop this. When he curled his big hands around my calves, looked up into my eyes, and caressed the back of my legs, I stopped questioning his motives. He didn't look like a man calculating every move. He looked like a man savoring me.

A tug deep in my womb caused another rush of wet to dampen the material between my legs, and as if he sensed it, Michael's gaze lowered there. His hands climbed higher around the back of my legs before smoothing around my upper thighs. Gliding his thumbs toward my inner thighs, he asked, voice hoarse, "Open your legs."

Excitement fizzled like champagne bubbles in my belly, and I moaned a little as I did as he asked. Gently, he pushed beneath my underwear, and I gasped as two thick fingers slid easily inside me.

"Oh, fuck." He groaned and rested his forehead against my right thigh. "You're so ready."

I flushed with embarrassment because a guy usually had to work a lot harder to get me to this point.

Easing his fingers from me, Michael pulled my underwear down my legs. I stepped out of them, my legs shaking a little. And then Michael lifted my right leg over his shoulder, and I gasped, resting my hand on his opposite shoulder for balance. He made a guttural noise of desire seconds before his tongue touched my clit.

Need slammed through me, and I undulated against his mouth. His fingers dug into my thigh, and his groan vibrated through me. *Oh my God!*

He suckled my clit, pulling on it hard, and I panted as beautiful tension built deep inside me. His tongue circled my clit and then slid down in a dirty voracious lick before pushing inside me.

"Michael!" I cried, thrusting against his mouth as I climbed higher and higher toward breaking apart completely.

Feeling my desperation, Michael returned to my clit and gently pushed two fingers inside of me.

It hit like an explosion of fiery, spine-tingling stars, release sliding deliciously through me as I shuddered against Michael's mouth.

He gently lowered my trembling leg, and I swayed against him as he stood. Rather than being languid with satisfaction, I was buzzing with longing. Like I was still on the precipice of orgasm. I needed more.

A thrilling feeling of power overwhelmed me as our eyes locked. His smoldered, and his jaw was set with a ferocious hunger. I did that to him.

Me.

I lifted my arms to help him raise my sweater over my head.

My chest heaved with my labored, excited breaths as Michael threw the sweater to the floor and brought his hands to my shoulders. His eyes followed his fingertips as they trailed with excruciating slowness across my collarbone and down toward the rise of my breasts. They were still full, large, but they didn't sit as perky as they once had when we were younger. I worried for a millisecond that when my bra came off, he'd notice, he'd care—

"Still so beautiful," he whispered, and goose bumps prickled in the wake of his touch. My nipples peaked against my bra with anticipation.

"Michael," I murmured.

In answer to my needy plea, he gripped my hips and pulled me against him so I could feel the steel of his erection against my bare stomach.

Gently, he cupped my face in his hands and kissed me so deeply, I could taste myself. But these kisses weren't like before. Not kisses of punishing hunger. Slow, sexy, and with tender reverence that brought tears to my eyes. My hands curled around his biceps, feeling his strength, his longing, and I didn't know what I wanted to do more: take him inside me or let him hold me while I cried.

The voice in the back of my head whispered that going any further was a bad idea.

However, before I could act either way, Michael's hands moved over my body. With light strokes, he learned every inch of me— my ribs, my waist, my stomach. Then his hands glided around to my ass, and his kiss deepened, grew hungrier, and he drew me against his arousal. I could feel the war inside him as his tongue caressed mine in deep, wet strokes. It was like he was determined to take his time, but another part of him wanted to ravage me.

I found that war inside him sexually thrilling, not knowing which way this would go.

As I stroked my hands down his arms, the touch seemed to calm him, and his kiss grew gentler. He nipped at my lower lip and then he eased away. But only to stare into my eyes as he glided his hands up my back to my bra strap. With a dexterity I remembered from the times we'd fooled around in his car, he unhooked my bra. Then he nudged the straps down my arms, and it fell to the floor. His gaze slowly disconnected from mine and I shivered as his eyes grew hooded. His hands tightened around my biceps while he feasted on the sight of my naked breasts. My nipples peaked under his perusal, tight, needy buds that begged for his mouth.

Any concerns I had about how he'd feel about the changes in my body dissipated at the taut, desire-filled expression on his face.

"Dahlia," he murmured as he reached up and cupped me.

I moaned and arched into his touch. Ripples of desire undulated low in my belly as he played with my breasts, sculpting and kneading them, stroking and pinching my nipples. All the time his eyes vacillated between my face and my breasts. I thrust into his touch, muttering my need for him.

The words had barely broken past my lips when his mouth found mine. This kiss was rough, hard, desperate, and his groan filled me as he pinched both my nipples between his forefingers and thumbs. I gasped, and his growl of satisfaction made me flush with pleasure. I was beyond more than ready. Feeling the fabric of his sweater beneath my hands, I curled my fists into it and jerked my lips from his. "Take it off."

Thankfully, Michael executed my order. He let go of me, stepped back, and yanked his sweater up and off. As he threw it behind him and then worked on his boots and jeans, I reveled in the sight of him. His chest, arms, and abs were definitely more powerful than they had been nine years ago. He'd worked out regularly then too and had a gorgeous body, but the tight rippled definition of his abs and the breadth of his shoulders confirmed that his workout routine had become more vigorous.

I wasn't complaining.

Uh-uh.

His thick thighs and muscular calves caused another hard flip in my lower belly, and I longed to see his ass. My God, I bet his ass was a thing of legend. I moaned when he had to peel his boxer briefs over his erection and when freed, he was so hard, it strained toward his abs.

Every part of my body swelled toward him as I watched him take a condom out of his wallet and roll it down his erection. No foreplay was necessary. I wanted and needed him inside me.

Whatever he saw in my countenance made him grasp me around the waist, but instead of guiding me down on the bed, he turned and sat on the edge. Then he guided me to straddle him, his arousal hot against my stomach.

Michael touched my chin, bringing my head up to lock gazes with him. My fingers curled into the back of his shoulders as I took in his expression. There was so much emotion in his eyes. Desire, need, yes. But also confusion, hurt, and something I didn't want to process. It looked like fear, and I couldn't bear that emotion in Michael.

Tears filled my eyes, and the visible emotion made his jaw clench. He slid his hand along the back of my neck, tangling in my hair to grab a handful. Then he gently tugged my head back, arched my chest, and covered my right nipple with his mouth.

I gasped as sensation slammed through me, my hips automatically undulating against him as he sucked, laved, and nipped at me. Tension coiled between my legs, tightening and tightening as he moved between my breasts, his hot mouth, his tongue—

"Michael!" I was going to come again with only this.

Then he stopped, and I lifted my head to beg, to plead for him to keep touching me, but halted when he gripped my hips. Guiding me, he lifted me up, and I stared down at him, waiting as he took his cock in hand and put it between my legs.

Taking his cue, I lowered myself onto him, feeling the hot tip of him against my slick opening. Electric tingles cascaded down my spine and around my belly, deep between my legs.

Michael.

I'm finally with Michael.

I'd never been so goddamn turned on in my life. Michael took hold of my hip with one hand and cupped my right breast with the other, and I gasped at the overwhelming thick sensation of him as I lowered.

The coiling tension left over from the orgasm he'd given me exploded with only the tip of him inside me.

I cried out and clung to his shoulders as my climax tore through me, my inner muscles rippling and tugging and drawing Michael in deeper. Shuddering, my hips jerking, my abs spasming, I wrapped my arms around Michael's neck to hold on through the storm. I rested my forehead against his.

As the last of the tremors passed through me, I became aware of Michael's bruising grip on my hips and the overwhelming fullness of him inside me. At some point during my orgasm, he'd plunged all the way into me.

Oh my God.

But before that . . . Well, that was . . .

Flushing, I lifted my head to see his reaction and the firestorm of desire in his eyes made my inner muscles pulse around him.

He grunted at the feeling and then said, voice hoarse, "Do you know how fuckin' hard it was to not come inside you right now? Fuck, you just came with me barely inside you." His hands slid up to grasp my upper waist, and he bared his teeth as he demanded, "That ever happen before?"

I knew what he was asking.

I knew what he wanted to hear.

And even though I shouldn't, I found that I couldn't deny him. I shook my head. "I've never wanted anyone the way I want you."

With an animalistic growl of satisfaction, Michael launched up off the bed, and turned around to drop us on it with me on my back. The motion made him drive so deep inside me, it took my breath away. I gasped to find it.

Michael muttered a hoarse expletive and then wrapped his hands around my wrists and pinned them to the bed at either side of my head.

The slow seduction from earlier was over.

He moved inside me with powerful thrusts of his hips, his eyes focused intensely on mine. Like he needed the eye contact. Like I needed it.

I wanted to feel him; I wanted to grip his ass in my hands and feel it clench and release with each stroke, but he held me down.

That only excited me more.

The tension built in me again with every thick drag of him in and out. His features strained taut with lust and with one more powerful glide in and out, I came again, shorter, sharper, but no less intense than the last. With just one hard tug of my climax, Michael swelled to impossible thickness. He pressed my hands hard to the bed as he tensed between my legs and then—

"Dahlia! Fuck!" His hips jerked and shuddered against mine.

Eventually, he released my wrists and slumped over me, his face in my neck, and I wrapped my arms and legs around him, caressing his warm, damp skin.

Slowly, however, as his breathing eased, and his whole body relaxed, the heaviness of his weight on me became too much. I couldn't breathe. And it wasn't because of his weight. I grew cold and panicked from the realization that I'd taken something I shouldn't have. I'd given something I shouldn't have.

Especially when I hadn't been sure of Michael's real motives for sleeping with me.

"We could stand here all night, yelling at each other, trying to find ways to dig out all the pain, or I could throw you on my bed, and we could fuck out all the anger and hurt."

I thought of all the pain and bitterness he felt toward me. All the horrible things he'd said. When I was younger, I thought what Michael and I had was special. Explosive and passionate. But maybe that wasn't a good thing. Especially if it could turn tender feelings to poison. If it could make a good man like Michael do and say toxic things ...

I wanted him to forgive me and to forget, but how could I when I wasn't ready to forgive him for trying to fill me up with all the hurt he'd carried for years?

Shivering from the sudden chill, I released him and stared at the ceiling. Pain, unimaginable pain, swamped me. My voice sounded flat, dead, even to my ears as I asked, "Is that what you wanted? Have you fucked me out of you yet?"

16

Dahlia

Michael braced his hands on the bed at either side of my head and glared at me. "Jesus fuck, Dahlia. I'm still inside you." With a huff of disbelief, he pulled out, and I shivered as he moved off me.

Lying on his back on the bed beside me, I waited for his response.

When none was forthcoming, I pushed up off the bed, and my upper thighs tremored a little from the thorough fucking. Because that's what it was, right?

Michael's face flashed in my mind as I swung my legs off the bed. The way he'd never broken eye contact as he moved inside me.

Was that fucking?

Heart heavy, I shook my head and put my feet to the cold floor. I'd been so hot with anger and lust when we'd come into his apartment, I hadn't realized that the place was freezing.

Hurrying around the bed, I grabbed my clothes off the floor.

I was aware of Michael in my peripheral vision as he sat up. "What are you doing?"

Not looking at him, I replied, "I have to go."

Hearing him getting out of bed, I looked at him. His dark eyes glittered under the bright glare of the overhead light. To my surprise, he bent down and snatched up my socks and boots. "I need to use the bathroom, so I'm keeping these," he said, lifting the boots, "as insurance you'll stay. We need to talk."

"Michael—"

"I'm not arguing about this."

I knew that resolute expression on his face so I didn't bother arguing, even though my heart was hammering at the pending conversation. With a huff of annoyance to cover my fear, I whipped around and began to dress.

"Dahlia."

I hesitated a second before I looked over my shoulder.

The man was staring at me like he was about to pounce and ravish me. Irritatingly my body awakened at the idea, tingles between my legs, breasts plumping.

Goddamn it.

"Next time I want you on your hands and knees so I can enjoy this view."

My lips parted on a gasp of excitement that I quickly swallowed. I narrowed my eyes. "There won't be a next time."

Michael smirked as if he knew something I didn't and then walked past me.

And his ass.

Oh my God, his ass.

It *was* the stuff of legend.

Regret filled me as I watched his rock-hard butt cheeks walk out the bedroom door, knowing I should have taken the chance to bite them. Too late now.

Forlorn, I quickly got dressed, flushing a little as I did, overcome with flashbacks of sex with Michael. It had blown past all my expectations, and they had been pretty high. My God, I'd had a hair trigger climax. Blushing harder, I shook my head as I put one shaky foot after another into my jeans. Wait until I told Bailey.

Oh shit.

Bailey. My dad. They were probably wondering where I was.

I needed to check my cell, and it was in my purse. Wherever it was. A vague recollection of dropping it when Michael swept me up into his arms came to me. It was in his sitting room.

Once I put myself back together (well, sort of), I made my way down the hall. I wasn't sure it was possible to ever be put back together the way I had been before sex with Michael. It had fundamentally changed me, and wasn't that a big kick to my metaphorical *cojones*?

The kitchen sat off the sitting room, and I stood in a daze, staring at the awful emptiness of the place. Why did it bother me so much that his apartment was filled only with the necessities? There was no warmth, no personality. It tugged at something deep in my chest. I stood there so long, lost in those thoughts, Michael wandered into the room. Thankfully, he was dressed in sweatpants and a T-shirt.

"Coffee?" He walked over to the coffee machine. "Sorry it's so cold in here. I have the heating on a timer. It's coming on now." He pulled two mugs out of a cupboard.

"I need to go. Can you give me my boots?"

In answer, he threw me my balled-up socks. "Your feet will be cold."

I glowered as I bent to put my socks on. "They'd be less so if you'd give me my boots back."

"Dahlia, stay and have a coffee with me."

"I need to check my cell." I ignored his placating tone, glancing around the place. Moving out of the kitchen into the sitting room, I saw my purse on the floor. My hands were shaking as I bent down to pick it up, and once I found my cell, it jumped out of my trembling fingers.

Suddenly Michael was there, bending down for the phone.

I opened my mouth to protest, but he took my hands, squeezed them in reassurance, and placed the cell in between them. His dark eyes held something like the tenderness they used to. "It's okay, dahlin'."

I bit my lip against the well of emotion that wanted to pour out of me and instead opened my cell phone case to distract myself. There were messages from my dad and Bailey.

Michael must have been looking because he said, "Tell them you're fine. That you're here."

"I'm telling them I'm on my way home."

His sigh was beleaguered. "Dahlia, I'm not going to say I'm not still fucked up about you. Sex didn't change that, no matter how amazing it was. I'm still angry with you. But maybe if you'd stay and talk to me, I could let that go. Please."

It was the please that did it.

Even though I imagined my heart was about to be bruised and pounded by whatever came out between us, I knew I had to have this conversation if either of us were to move on.

Flicking open my messages, I texted both my dad and Bailey to let them know I was at Michael's and I was okay. Done, I shoved my phone back into my purse and met Michael's wary gaze. "I'll need that coffee, then."

His features relaxed and he nodded, gesturing for me to go ahead of him back into the kitchen. Once there, he handed me a mug, and I settled down at the kitchen table. Michael took the seat next to me, and I tried not to look at anything but his face.

It was hard.

The T-shirt he wore did nothing to disguise his physique, and I wished we could hit a replay button on the scene in the bedroom, but this time add in way more of me exploring his body.

His hands curled around his coffee mug, and I unwittingly studied the movement. I'd always loved Michael's hands. Maybe it was the artist in me. I knew that they were large and masculine but at the same time long-fingered, big-knuckled, and graceful. It was a sexy combination, and I flushed remembering the feel of his hands all over my body.

"Why?" His voice was hard again. It drew my eyes from his hands to his face. There was so much turmoil in his expression. "Why did you leave and not come back?"

As difficult as it was to tell him, I knew I had to. He deserved to know that I hadn't just abandoned him. I released a shaky exhalation, feeling a wave of nausea in my stomach.

Wrapping both hands around my coffee mug, I drew from its comforting heat. "I pushed everyone away after Dillon died. Not only you. I don't know what might have happened if I'd been given more time. I like to think I would have let you in again, but we'll never know."

He opened his mouth to say something, but I cut him off.

"Before you argue about that ... " I couldn't look at him as the memories of my mom's behavior swept through me. Since I was twenty years old, I'd wanted Michael Sullivan to love me. As messed up as it might sound, I'd worried for a long time that if he knew that my own mother couldn't love me, he'd question why. Start to find reasons not to love me too. It was irrational and moronic considering his family issues, but I'd twisted a lot of things up inside me over the years. It was time to explain.

"Dahlia?" Michael's eyes narrowed in concern. "What am I missing here?"

"My mom," I blurted out. I could feel the emotion thickening in my throat, the tears burning in my eyes, and it made me so goddamn angry because I wanted to be past it. I wanted to make peace with the fact that my mom resented me and move on. "Not long after Dillon died, my dad was out. There was no one in the house but Mom and me. I was in my bedroom ... " Grief thickened my words. "Surrounded by Dillon's stuff. I was sitting on her bed, trying to make sense of it, you know. Like, how all of her things were sitting there waiting for her to pick them up, to use them, to put them on. And it would never happen. I had her brooch in my hand. You know how she loved roses, so a few months before everything went to hell, I'd made her a silver brooch. It was a single rose in bloom. She'd loved it. Wore it a lot."

I fought back the tears. "She wouldn't ever wear it again, and I couldn't make that make sense. It was driving me crazy. The agony of all her things sitting there was driving me nuts, so I started to put everything away." I looked up at him, and through the sheen of emotion in his eyes, I saw the vision of my mom's face when she caught me. "That's when Mom walked in. There was no buildup. No questions. She ... she just slapped me." I could still feel the brutal sting of those hits. "I was so stunned, all I could do was cower on the floor as she kept hitting me, open palm, on my head over and over, screaming that God took the wrong daughter. That it was my fault and she'd wished God had taken me instead." The last word broke out in a sob, and I heard the screech of a chair over the floor seconds before Michael's arms pulled me up out of mine. I burrowed into him, into his strength, as if I could somehow melt into him and in doing so, he'd draw out some of the pain and relieve me of it.

His arms banded tight around me and he pressed his lips to my hair as I shuddered and sobbed all the feelings I thought I'd cried out of me long ago.

Sometime later, with my head hurting a little, I sat on Michael's couch with a fresh cup of coffee and a used tissue crumpled in my hand.

I tried not to notice Michael's proximity on the couch or the way he kept looking at me like he was ready to take a bullet for me. It was beautiful and terrifying at the same time to see how my story had transformed him back into my old Michael.

"So that's when you started drinking?" His voice was soft, coaxing.

Nodding, I took a sip of coffee before responding. "That night I wanted to disappear. I was too ashamed to tell anyone, and I thought if I told my dad, I'd only make my mom hate me more. I convinced myself she was grieving, that she didn't mean it, but in truth what she said festered. So to get to sleep that night, I stole the gin in my parents' liquor cabinet. When I realized everything hurt less when I was numbed by alcohol, I kept drinking."

"I remember." He rubbed a hand over his face. "I was so fuckin' scared. Didn't know how to help you."

Flinching as I remembered everything I'd put him through, I turned away. "Dad was scared too. Like you, he thought it was only about Dillon. That's when his sister, who lived in Hartwell, reached out to him. She owned the gift shop on the boardwalk, and he convinced her to let me rent it. I said I'd go because I couldn't bear to be around my mother, but I made him promise he wouldn't tell anyone where I was."

"That's the part I don't get."

Meeting his gaze, seeing the betrayal in his eyes, was difficult. "I hated myself, Michael. I was responsible for my little sister's death, my mom hated me, I was drinking so I could sleep at night, and I'd pushed everyone I loved away. You deserved better."

"I deserved the truth."

I shook my head. "I wasn't in the right frame of mind. I thought leaving you was the best thing for you."

Seeing that I wasn't getting through to him, I realized I'd have to tell him everything. How low I'd gotten.

"I'd hoped the pain would stop once I was out of Boston. It didn't. It got worse, and so did my drinking. I wasn't there long when one night I was drunk and took a walk on the beach with my bottle of gin." Stray tears leaked out of my eyes. Annoyed that there could be any left in me, I swiped them angrily away. "My memories of that night are fuzzy. I vaguely remember walking into the ocean."

Michael stiffened.

"I . . . I remember the cold. I remember a momentary fear as I went under. But I also remember the relief." The tears fell faster, these ones with shame. "I don't remember Bailey pulling me out. I don't remember her giving me CPR. And I don't remember telling her she should have left me to die. But she told me all of it."

"Fuck." Tears brightened Michael's eyes, and he sat forward, his hands clasped on the back of his head as he glared at the floor.

"I'm sorry," I whispered.

He shook his head, his throat working to hold down his emotion.

"That's the place I was in, Michael. And no one, not you or my dad, could pull me out of it. The only thing that did was waking up the next morning in a hospital bed, sober and hurting, to a stranger telling me I was going to let myself drown and she'd saved my life."

Michael turned to me, dropping his hands. "Why didn't you come to me? I should have known all this shit, Dahlia. I should have known. And if you'd let me in, I would have poured so much fuckin' love into you, you'd never spend a day feeling as worthless as you had to have felt to walk into that water."

"Michael . . . " I shook my head, his words a balm and a wound in equal measure. "It wasn't that simple. You and I had never . . . and we never said we loved each other . . . and everything my mom said, and the shame of giving up on myself, all of it twisted everything. I truly believed that you would move on. Easily. That you were better off without my brand of fucked-up in your life.

"I gained a modicum of peace in Hartwell. Bailey became family, I made more friends because of her, and life there seemed simple. I was afraid that if I came back here and I faced my mom,

I would shatter again. So I stayed away, and the longer I stayed away, the harder it became to return. I felt so guilty for missing out on everyone's lives. I'm not proud of it, Michael, but it's the truth."

"So why did you come back now? Because you saw me?"

"Partly. Seeing you was shocking and scary, but I didn't die. I survived the encounter," I said, smiling sadly. "Seeing you with your wife was painful, but it also made me feel less guilty. That I'd been right. That you'd moved on. So when Dad called about the divorce, I knew I had to be there for him and after seeing you, I knew whatever happened, however bad it felt, I would survive it."

Michael seemed to stew on my words for a second or two, and then he pushed up off the couch. Outrage pulsated from him.

I watched him warily as he strode over to the window.

"Moved on?" he bit out, turning to face me. "Moved on! I didn't know any of this, Dahlia. When I wouldn't stop hounding your family to tell me where you'd gone, your mom told me you'd packed your shit and taken off. Without coming to me, without even a fuckin' goodbye. So I stopped hounding them. I got angry instead. Dermot eventually told me that your dad sent you away and that only he knew where you were. That fucked me off, so I went to Cian, and I tried to get him to tell me. But he said that if I loved you, I needed to let you go. That you'd come back on your own." He shook his head. "I didn't know what you were going through so all I could think was 'If she loved me, she'd be back already because if she felt half of what I felt, she couldn't stay away.'"

"Michael."

"I knew I could find you. If I wanted I could find you, but I didn't want to find someone who ultimately didn't want to be found. So I decided to move on for good. And I thought I had."

"Your wife."

Michael walked back across the room to sit down. He braced his elbows on his knees and stared at the floor. "My ex-wife. The divorce finalized a week ago. Her name is Kiersten."

Loving Michael meant I didn't want to know about her. I didn't want to know about the woman who had gotten to sleep by his side for years. To talk to him every day. To laugh with him. It cut me up inside so badly, I could hardly breathe. Yet, the masochist in me needed to know how much he'd loved her. "Why did it fall apart?"

He snorted, the sound derisive. "Why did it fall apart?" He turned his head to look at me. "Neither of us knew why it was falling apart. That's the honest truth. When we met, she was the first woman in ages who made me laugh. Kiersten is cute, and she's funny, and I liked that she could make me laugh. Over our four years together, we stopped making each other laugh, and I didn't know why. Until we took a vacation in Hartwell to try one last time to fix our marriage."

His gaze drifted over my face and down my body before he flinched and looked away. "After we met you, we got back to the hotel, and Kiersten lost it. She wanted to know who you were. So I told her. That I'd loved you. That you left without a word and I hadn't seen you in nine years. And you know what she told me?"

It was hard to breathe, let alone speak.

"That everything made sense now. That I'd kept her at a distance the entire four years we'd been together. That I never let her in. I never talked about my parents. I never talked about my past. I never talked about my work. Sure, I'd listen to her, but anytime she asked anything that was too personal, I avoided the question." He shook his head. "I didn't even realize I was doing it. But she was right."

"Because of me?" I was almost afraid to ask.

"I thought about it when I granted her the divorce. Decided

maybe I'd been a shit husband because I was afraid she'd hurt me like you had. But these last few weeks ... I know it wasn't only that. It was because she just. Wasn't. You."

Remorse filled me, and I hoped everything I couldn't say was in my eyes.

"I fucked over a good woman. I didn't mean it. But I did it." He rubbed a hand over his head and sighed. "Thankfully, she's moving on. Met someone new. A good guy."

We were quiet as I let all that sink in. I ached for him. I felt guilty that my leaving had caused him so much pain. Worse, there was an ugly part of me deep down that was glad he couldn't love his wife the way he'd loved me. Now wasn't that disgustingly selfish?

Attempting to push away those feelings, I thought about Michael's confession and how he wouldn't talk to Kiersten about his family. What did that mean? Had he completely lost touch with them? And what about Gary? I'd known they were drifting apart after Gary found out we were together, but there had been no mention of him at all since my return. "Do you still talk to your parents? To Gary?"

If he was surprised by my questions, he didn't show it. Instead, he relaxed against the couch. "I see Mom sometimes. I try to avoid Dad as much as possible. To say it fucked him off that I made detective and he retired as a plain old beat walker is an understatement," he told me. "Things between us went from bad to worse when I first made lieutenant. You know my dad. No matter what I do, I can't win. Last time I saw my mom was after Kiersten and I filed for divorce. My dad is usually out on a Sunday at a bar, but the bastard had deliberately stayed around so he could go on and on about how I might think I'm something with my detective badge, but a man isn't a man if he can't keep his woman happy."

Anger boiled in my blood. "Motherfucker."

Michael gave me a small grin. "Yeah."

"And Gary?"

He shook his head. "Gary left not long after you. Took a decent paying job in construction with a cousin in North Carolina. He never came back, and we lost touch over the years."

Goddamn it.

I left.

Gary left.

"I'm sorry."

"I had Dermot. Your dad." He shrugged. "They're like family."

The swelling feeling of love and heartbreak building in my chest was almost too much to bear. I knew we'd needed to have this discussion, to put it all out there, but it also became crushingly clear that I needed to let go of that little spark of hope I'd held onto all those years concerning Michael.

No matter what he'd discovered today, he would always feel abandoned by me. After his parents' abandonment came mine. Then Gary's. It didn't matter if he learned to let that go, *I* wouldn't.

I would live with all kinds of remorse, that feeling sharpening every time I looked at his handsome face.

The thought exhausted me.

I loved him.

God, did I love him.

But at some point, I had to start loving myself too.

My tangle of emotions wouldn't go away overnight, and I knew it was the same for Michael. "Do you blame me?"

Michael turned, studying me, and I wondered if he could hear my heart pounding. "I understand better now."

"That's not what I asked."

"I can get past it." He sat up, determination hardening his features. "To be with you, I can get past it."

Wrong answer.

Because while he was attempting to get past it, there would be more moments that would throw up our history, that might lead to arguments. And Michael had proven he could gut me worse than anyone.

I loved him. So much.

But as much as he blamed me for leaving, I knew there was a part of me that blamed him for not coming after me.

Too much blame.

Too much hurt.

And something more. Guilt I still kept buried deep that wouldn't release me from its grasp.

When Michael wasn't around, I didn't feel it. And I didn't want to feel it.

A ball of grief filled my throat as I realized I would have to say goodbye to Michael Sullivan for good. Pushing myself to my feet, my fingers clenched around the hem of my sweater as I attempted to keep myself together. Needing to be courageous because I hadn't been in the past, I bravely met his gaze and whatever he saw in mine caused him to snap to his feet and reach for me.

I retreated from his touch.

His vexation was obvious. "Don't do this to me again, Dahlia."

"I'm ... There's too much pain here, Michael." I gestured between us. "Aren't you tired of it? Of all the drama and pain?"

"It doesn't have to be that way. We can work through it."

"Can we?" I retorted, disbelieving. "I don't think you can work through that kind of bitterness and blame. I left. I'm sorrier than I can ever say for that. But the truth is"— I grabbed my purse and let out a shaky exhale— "as irrational as it may sound, I blame you too. I blame you for letting me go."

Michael was stunned. He looked like I'd slapped him. Hard. Or punched him in the gut. Either way, I caught him so off guard, he let me go again.

"Goodbye, Michael." I almost choked on the words.

He didn't respond.

He didn't come after me as I crossed the room to the front door.

Even as I stood out in the dark of the early morning, I didn't hear the door opening behind me.

A sob crawled up inside me, but I forced it down. My God, it hurt. I walked, huddled into myself, wondering how my life could be filled with so many regrets when I'd promised myself as a kid that I'd never have any.

I'd lied to Michael. To protect him. To protect me. Yes, there was an irrational part of me that blamed him for letting me go, but I'd lied when I'd used it as the main reason to leave him again. That reason was buried deep, a splinter that had never worked its way out.

Sometime later, I don't know how long afterward, I heard footsteps behind me and then a strong hand pulled me around and out of myself. I blinked stupidly up into my dad's face, confused and discombobulated.

"Dad?"

He put his arm around me and led me to his car that idled at the side of the road. I glanced around, wondering where I was.

"Michael called and told me to come get you."

"I'm sorry," I mumbled as he helped me into the car.

My teeth chattered.

I was freezing.

"It's okay." Dad shut the door and rounded the car. When he got in, he turned to me. "You'll be okay."

I nodded numbly. "Yeah."

I had to be.

17

Michael

Michael let himself back into his apartment and wearily moved into the kitchen to make a coffee to warm himself up. It had been freezing outside, and he'd chased after Dahlia in only sweats and a T-shirt. Keeping his distance as she walked down the street, hunched into herself, and seemingly wandering with no destination in mind, Michael had called Cian. He'd followed Dahlia and given Cian the directions he needed to pick her up.

It wasn't that he hadn't wanted to go to her himself. Of course, he did. However, her words kept going around and around in his head. They made sense, but they didn't, and Michael was left with the unnerving feeling that there was more to Dahlia's reasons for walking out on them again than what she'd admitted to.

Yet, he also knew she wasn't lying when she said she blamed him for letting her go.

He had, hadn't he?

He'd thrown away everything he knew to be true about the girl he loved when he decided she'd selfishly left him. The truth was, she hadn't. His fist clenched around the coffee pot handle as he remembered the scene with Dahlia earlier. What her mother had said and done to her that drove her away from them all.

"Do you blame her?" he'd said when she commented about her mother erasing her from her life.

Fuck. He rubbed at the ache of regret in his chest. Michael had assumed that Dahlia couldn't deal with Dillon's death and she'd started her life over somewhere else. It didn't mean she shouldn't have come back to him ... but would *he* have? If it had been him, and Dahlia hadn't bothered to go after him, to figure out what went wrong, would he have come home?

Michael knew the answer to that.

And for the first time in nine years, he acknowledged it was his fault too.

He let her go.

So he wasn't the one to put her in his car and take her home because he knew there was nothing he could *say* to change her mind.

Closing his eyes, she was there. He could hear her breathy gasps, feel her skin beneath his fingers. Being with her, moving inside her, feeling her all around him, it was the best moment of his life. It wasn't just fantastic sex. It was phenomenal because it was *her*. Because he had Dahlia.

And she wanted him to let her go again.

Michael's eyes snapped open, and he glared at the bare space around him. Circumstances with Dahlia had never been easy. It had been one long drama for eleven fuckin' years. Yet he couldn't say he ever felt more alive than when she was with him. She woke him up in ways difficult to explain.

He knew what his life without Dahlia looked like. Bare walls, a difficult job in a tough city, and more bare fuckin' walls. Life *with* Dahlia? Oh, he knew it wouldn't be easy at first, but he remembered what it was like between them before everything went to hell. A lot of laughter, a lot of affection. And never feeling alone. She'd made him feel like he wasn't alone anymore.

She'd felt like home.

Michael wanted that back.

Determination washed away any tiredness he'd been feeling.
It looked like he had some calls to make.

Because there was no way he was letting Dahlia McGuire slip
through his fingers a second time.

18

Dahlia

After a few hours of restless sleep, and by restless, I mean a sleep of Michael-filled dreams, I'd joined my family and Bailey in the sitting room that afternoon. My best friend was full of questions about what had happened, and I promised to tell her everything when we were traveling home.

"I'm sorry," Bailey said. "I thought we were doing a good thing."

"I think it was," I assured her.

"And just so you know, Nina is only an acquaintance. She's gay." A little hue of red crested Bailey's upper cheeks.

"Liked herself a little bit of cherry, did she?" I teased.

"Somehow she missed the gigantic rock on my finger and propositioned me." She shot me a round-eyed look. "I'm popular in Boston. Let's just say Nina doesn't beat around the bush."

I opened my mouth to pounce on that one.

She shook her head. "Don't."

Straining not to laugh, we settled in with the snacks that Dad had laid out before dinner. The TV was on in the background for the game later. We were sitting around, snacking and chatting. No one mentioned Michael or last night, and my nephews hopped from relative to relative for attention.

Davina was telling me, Bailey, Astrid, and Krista about this foul colleague at her work who constantly tried to undermine her, and I was vaguely aware of my dad and Dermot grilling Darragh about the tickets he'd be able to get for next year's baseball season.

It was Bailey's gasp, her eyes on the TV, that drew me out of our conversation. She launched across me for the clicker on the coffee table and jabbed it at the TV. The news story flooded the room, and I read the news banner along the screen: DIRECTOR OLIVER FROST FOUND DEAD.

"Sources say his fiancée screenwriter, Ivy Green, found his body early this morning," the newscaster relayed, and my heart sank. Worried, I looked at Bailey who was pale-faced watching the news. "Reports are circulating that Frost has died from a drug overdose, although authorities have not yet confirmed the cause of death."

"Isn't that the guy who made that film about the guys in Boston? You know, the one about the foster brothers who go after the guys who killed one of their kids?" Dermot asked the room.

"Yeah, that's him." Bailey turned to me. "We need to go home."

I laid a hand on her arm. "Our flight is early tomorrow. And there's nothing we can do right now anyway. I'm sorry, Bails."

"What am I missing?" Dad's brow creased in concern.

"Ivy is Bailey's friend," I said. "They were best friends growing up. You've heard me talking about Iris and Ira? Ivy's their daughter."

Dad nodded. "I remember you mentioned their kid was in Hollywood."

"Wait, what?" Davina asked.

"Iris and Ira Green own the pizzeria on the boardwalk," I explained. "They're good friends of ours. And Bailey grew up with their daughter, Ivy. Who is . . . *was* engaged to Oliver Frost."

"Oh, wow." Astrid patted Bailey on the shoulder. "I'm sorry."

Bailey gave her a pained smile, then turned it on me. "I'm going to call Vaughn for an update."

"Of course."

The news shadowed my last night in Boston. I could feel Bailey's concern even though she pasted on a smile and tried to make conversation at the dinner table. Vaughn didn't have much news for her; however, he promised to stop by Iris and Ira's place to find out more.

After dessert, Vaughn called and told Bailey that Iris and Ira were flying out to California to be with Ivy. He'd passed on Bailey's words of support, but I knew that wasn't enough for her. She wanted to be there for them in any way she could.

Her inner brooding was put on pause when my family departed. Levi and Leo were tired, and it was well past their bedtime.

My heart was full to bursting when I got hugs from them both, and Leo asked me if he could come to stay with me. Of course, I said he was welcome anytime, and I was excited for when Darragh and Krista would let my nephews stay with me. I'd spent only a few weeks with the boys, but it was amazing how quickly I'd fallen in love with them. I would miss them.

Krista hugged me, kissed my cheek, and whispered tearfully how glad she was to have me back and that she'd see me soon. However, it was Darragh who almost brought me to tears. Mostly because he didn't say anything. He hugged me, tight, his chin resting on the top of my head, and he wouldn't let go. Krista murmured to him about the kids, and he reluctantly pulled away.

"See you soon, baby girl." He gave me a little chuck under the chin like he used to when I was a kid.

I grinned, "giving him my dimple" as he called it.

Davina was pissed about my leaving. "You better come back

at Christmas," she'd ordered with a bite in her voice. Then she'd promptly enfolded me in a hug, and her breath hitched as I clutched her.

More swallowing of the tears for me.

I waved her and Astrid goodbye and then turned to Dermot.

His hug wasn't as long, but it was brutally tight. "I'll call you soon," he said. "Finally have you back for girl advice."

I smirked. "Dermot, if you're still dating *girls*, I'm going to guess that's part of your problem."

"Smart-ass." He punched my shoulder gently and then turned to Bailey. "As for you, let me know if you decide to get rid of your fancy businessman."

Bailey gave him a quick hug, but as she pulled back, she replied, "It's doubtful."

My brother laughed, bid my dad good night, and walked down the porch steps. I waited for him to get in his car and drive off before I closed the door.

Saying goodbye was emotionally draining. Yet it was good knowing that this time it wasn't permanent. Not at all. For the first time in many years, the pieces of me that had been missing slotted into place. They fitted differently than before, but they still plugged the hole in my chest.

There was still two missing pieces. Two wounds.

But for the sake of holding onto the peace that my family had brought me these last few weeks, I ignored those pieces. Time and distance. Maybe time and distance *would* heal all wounds.

At least this time.

Our flight was early the next morning and as was usual with early flights, I couldn't sleep through the night, knowing I had to get up in a mere few hours. Lying in bed, it was all too easy to fall into the memories of last night. To feel Michael's hands and lips. To remember what it was like as he pushed inside me. I flushed hot, writhing in my sheets with frustration. Being with him was a kind of ecstasy I wouldn't ever be able to explain or understand. It was also an addiction because as I laid there, I berated myself for not taking more from him while I had the chance.

Now I'd never feel that with him again.

An hour before my alarm was set to go off, I left Bailey sleeping in the other guest bed in my brothers' old room and went downstairs to have my first coffee of the day. As soon as I walked down the last few stairs, I knew my dad was awake. Light filtered through from the kitchen. My dad had always been particular about switching off lights as we moved from room to room and he always made sure all the lights were off at night.

When I walked into the kitchen, he was sitting at the table, reading a newspaper with his hand tight around a coffee mug.

"Couldn't sleep?"

Dad gave me a tired smile. "I knew we had to get up soon. My body clock woke me up."

"Thank you again for driving us to Logan. You know we could have called a cab." I puttered around the kitchen, making myself coffee and grabbing some Scottish shortbread Dad had bought yesterday. He'd been buying it from the British import section in the supermarket ever since I sent him some after my trip to Scotland a few years ago. Over the years, as business had gotten better, I'd been able to afford vacations. I usually took one a year, either just before or after the summer season. A few times Bailey and I had vacationed together, but being alone for so long had made me independent. I didn't mind traveling by myself, and I'd been to some wonderful places. I'd fallen in love with Scotland. And shortbread.

Now I knew Dad had too. We already had cookies like shortbread in Massachusetts but nothing as good as the imported stuff I munched on as I waited for the coffeemaker to beep.

"I want to take you to the airport."

"Have you got work tonight?"

"You know I do." He leaned back in his chair. "Who's picking you up from Philadelphia?"

Our flight was a little over an hour between Boston and Philadelphia. There were no commercial flights into the small airport in Wilmington, but Philadelphia was pretty close to Wilmington anyway. No matter what, we were looking at an almost two-hour drive to Hartwell from the airport.

"Vaughn."

Dad nodded. "He a good guy? Does he deserve Bailey?"

I smiled, pleased that my whole family seemed so taken with my best friend. "I'm not sure any guy deserves someone as special as Bailey. I can tell you that Vaughn is usually taciturn, sarcastic, and aloof, but as soon as she walks into the room, he changes." I shook my head in wonder. "He's charming and affectionate, and he looks at her like he's afraid she'll disappear. Moreover, he wouldn't drive two hours there and back for just anyone."

Grinning, Dad nodded. "I'm pleased to hear it. She's a good girl."

Coffee in hand, I sat down at the table and shoved the plate of shortbread toward him.

Dad raised an eyebrow. "That's not exactly a nutritional start to the morning."

I shrugged and took the piece he didn't want. He shook his head, but his smile was full of affection.

My prolonged study of him, however, caused him to frown. "What?"

Worry consumed me. It happened when you loved someone as much as I loved my dad. "I don't want to leave until I know you're okay. Bailey can go back. I could stay."

Dad shook his head. "You depend on the income from that

Thanksgiving festival, and I'm a grown man, Bluebell. I don't need a babysitter."

"I don't mean it like that, Dad."

"I know you don't. But it's not your job to worry about me. It's my job to worry about you." His stare was pointed.

I sucked in a shaky breath. "Are you talking about Mom or Michael?"

"Both."

Cupping my hands around my mug, I leaned forward, gazing straight into his eyes so he'd recognize my sincerity. "I've found more peace about Mom since coming home than I could have hoped for. Did we forgive each other? No. Is our relationship in tatters? Yes. It's not a perfect outcome, and I'm not pretending to be nonchalant about it. Of course, it hurts. But I understand her better now and having everyone else back has made it easier to let go of that relationship. Maybe I wouldn't be able to deal with it as well as I am if I didn't have you. If I hadn't always had you." A happy shimmer brightened my eyes. "Have I ever told you how much I adore you?"

Dad's own eyes shone. "You never have to. I feel it." He reached over and wrapped his hand around my wrist and gave it a little squeeze. "You know I love you more than life, Bluebell."

The tears splashed down my cheeks, and I gave an embarrassed laugh. "I swear the floodgates seemed to have opened and I can't shut them off."

Instead of smiling, Dad's brow furrowed. "I'm still worried about you."

I swiped at my tears with my free hand. "Because of Michael?"

"Because of the way I found you wandering the streets of Chelsea in the early hours of the morning where anything could have happened to you, and you seemed oblivious to your surroundings. Luckily for you, Michael was following you and called me to tell me where you were."

Shocked, I gaped at him. "He followed me?"

"Whatever is going on between you, he cares about you. He wouldn't let anything happen to you. Which doesn't change that what you did was stupid."

Hearing the bite in his tone, I realized my dad was kind of pissed about that and had been holding it in. It distracted me from the thought of Michael taking care of me from a distance. "Dad, I'm sorry. All I seem to do is worry you."

"I'm a parent." His eyes shadowed with grief. "Who's already lost one kid. Believe me, you could be living the safest, happiest life and I'd still worry about you."

My heart ached for him. He was always so strong that sometimes I forgot he dealt with Dillon's loss every day too. And it *was* every day. I knew that. The intense, suffocating pain of grief could lessen and dull over the years, but it never went away. Especially not for a parent. I knew Dillon was always with my mom and dad.

"Will you be okay?"

"I'll be fine," he promised, and I knew he meant it.

"Do you think . . . " I hesitated, hoping I wasn't out of line with my next question. "Do you think you might consider dating?" After Darragh mentioned it, I'd thought about it a lot. I'd decided it would be a travesty if Dad didn't date. My parents had us young, so my dad was only in his mid-fifties, and he could definitely pass for his mid-to-late forties. And he was amazing. "Maybe get yourself a hot, young thing?" I teased. "And by young, I mean a maximum of twenty years younger than you."

Dad gave a huff of laughter. "You think a woman Darragh's age is going to be interested in me?"

"Dad, don't be self-deprecating. You know you look good."

"And you're advocating that I date a younger woman?" he grinned.

"Yes! Why not? I have done the dating thing. After years of

terrible dates with guys my age or younger, I moved up ten years, and they're still morons. You'll be catnip to women Darragh's age, Dad. Trust me."

My father seemed amused by this, but I could also see the wheels turning in his head, and I smirked to myself. I wasn't trying to drive the wedge deeper between him and my mom. No, I only wanted him to be happy. Maybe dating someone with fewer issues than Sorcha McGuire would be a welcome change for him.

"Will you think about it?"

He gave me a small nod. "I'll think about it."

"Dermot can set you up on the dating apps but whatever you do, do not take any dating advice from him."

He snorted. "He's my son, Dahlia. I already know to switch off when he talks about women."

We shared a chuckle, and I almost thought I got away with changing the subject. Very naïve of me.

"So, Michael?" he asked abruptly.

"Oh, Dad."

"You don't want to talk about it?"

"There's nothing left to talk about. We got a lot off our chests last night." I studied my mug, trying not to blush at how much we'd "gotten off our chests." "Ultimately, although we both have a clearer picture of what happened, we decided there are too many issues between us to move forward. Plus, Michael lives here, and I live in Hartwell. The long-distance thing on top of our issues is a disaster waiting to happen."

Dad didn't bother to ask if I'd think about moving back to Boston. He knew I loved my family, but he also knew I was genuinely happy living in Hartwell, making and selling my jewelry.

"I'm sorry it didn't work out. You know I care about Michael. I would like you to have someone like him in your life. I'm not worried about you being alone anymore," he hurried to say. "You're strong and independent, and I couldn't be prouder of you. I just want you to find someone."

"I promise to try if you promise."

Dad grinned, his dimple indenting his left cheek. "I promise."

I got up and hugged him. He held onto my arm and leaned into me when I kissed his cheek.

"I can't wait for Christmas. It's so nice to be excited about coming home."

"It's so nice to know you'll be coming home."

Hearing the gruffness in his voice, I hugged my dad harder.

At that moment, I felt nothing but peace, and I breathed even easier than I had yesterday.

PART II

PART II

Dahlia

Hartwell, Delaware
THREE MONTHS LATER

It was still dark when I let myself into Hart's Inn, the large beautiful building next door to my gift shop. Architecturally, Bailey's inn was similar to my store. They were both clad in white-painted shingles, and each had a porch. However, Bailey's porch was a wraparound and mine was not. Bailey's inn also had two balconies off two of the guest rooms at the front over-looking the North Atlantic, and there was a widow's walk on the top floor. The inn was massive compared to my gift store, and my place wasn't tiny.

The days were short in February, and the weather was cold. We were at the beginning of the month and hadn't been able to break past forty-three degrees yet. Closing the stained glass door behind me, I shut out the smell of salty sea air I loved so much and wasn't surprised to find Bailey at reception to greet me. She only had two rooms rented, but she was an early riser and liked to be ready in case her guests were too.

"Guests are still abed," she said without preamble.

"The coffee's ready, though, right?" In truth, Emery made the best coffee in town, but her place wasn't open yet.

"And Nicky's in the kitchen this morning, so we have pastries, pastries, and more pastries."

While Mona was the main chef at the inn, Nicky was the sous/pastry chef, and her treats were to die for. I groaned. "You know I've been good since Christmas. Don't tempt me."

"You look great," she scoffed.

"Says the woman who never seems to gain a pound even though she's thirty-five this year. Your metabolism is supposed to slow down, you know."

"I'd say that bitterness sounds a lot like envy, but I know that can't be right considering I would kill for your figure."

I made a face as I sat at the table Bailey gestured to. We were total physical opposites, and I guessed it was true what they said: you always wanted what you didn't have. "Well, I put on ten pounds over Christmas. Dad feeds me like he's trying to fatten me up for the whole year."

"I thought you said you'd lost those ten pounds?"

"On a cleanse, yes. And I don't want to put them back on." It was a constant battle of balance for me. I'd always been curvy, but I'd never had a weight problem per se until I turned thirty and could no longer eat that extra candy bar without it ballooning out my ass! Now it was a case of not denying myself but watching that I didn't overindulge.

I glared balefully at the plate of mini-pastries Bailey put on the table. "This is just mean."

"Oh, shut up and eat." She sat down as she placed our coffee mugs on the table.

I took the one she offered and watched as she delved straight into the pastries.

Usually, my ear would be hot from my best friend trying to talk it off, but Bailey had been distracted for weeks. She was worried about Ivy.

"Spoken to Ivy lately?"

She grimaced. "Ivy's still doing the hermit thing at her mom and dad's."

After the police closed the case on Oliver Frost as a heroin overdose, Iris and Ira packed up an emotionally destroyed Ivy and brought her home to Hartwell. Bailey was convinced there was more to the story. Iris and Ira had aired their concerns over the last few years about how distant Ivy had grown with everyone. They'd never liked Oliver. I suspected *they* suspected some kind of abuse, but that was merely speculation on my part. I think Bailey had similar suspicions, but neither of us had said it out loud. You never knew who was listening in. I loved Hartwell, but it was a small town and rumors spread like wildfire.

Bailey scowled. "Did you know Ian Devlin asked the Greens if they were considering selling the pizzeria so they could concentrate on their daughter's needs? Direct quote!"

I made a noise of disgust. "That man is a vulture. Every time someone has something vaguely horrible happen to them, he swoops in to manipulate them when they're vulnerable."

"He's the devil," Bailey decided. "I'm convinced of it."

Maybe she wasn't far off the mark. Ian Devlin had four sons and a daughter. No one had seen or heard from Rebecca Devlin in a few years. She'd left town for reasons unknown and had not returned.

I didn't blame her. I hadn't known her well, but she seemed to be a sweet person, which would make her the complete opposite of her siblings. Well, the youngest Devlin, Jamie, was only eleven years old and hopefully played no part in the devious plans of his three older brothers and father.

We ate in silence for a while and then Bailey said, "That new restaurant couldn't be opening at a worse time for Iris and Ira."

Bailey was referring to George Beckwith's old tourist gift store.

He used to sell the traditional Hartwell tourist stuff I secretly considered junk. However, tourists wanted the mugs and rock candy, keyrings, postcards, and all that jazz. So when he sold his store to a fancy French chef who used to work in New York, I'd incorporated the traditional gifts into my store.

Iris and Ira were worried when they learned George's boardwalk property was being converted into a restaurant. Although I hadn't glimpsed the enigmatic owner and chef, Bailey had. She begrudgingly admitted he was a good-looking son of a bitch. His name was Sebastian Mercier. The sign had just gone up for the restaurant, and it was called The Boardwalk, which was decidedly unpretentious. We all thought it would be some fancy-ass place that wouldn't fit in, but apparently, Mercier was smarter than that.

"You said it will be a seafood restaurant, Lobster and all that stuff. That won't cut into Antonio's." Iris and Ira weren't Italian, but they did good Italian food in their pizzeria.

"It will." Bailey shrugged. "Any other restaurant opening on the boardwalk will cut into their profits no matter what style of food it is. People who don't want to wander off the boardwalk or want a meal with a view will have options now."

"I still don't think it'll impact them as badly as they think. Not everyone likes seafood. Almost everyone loves Italian."

"Hmm. Well, that may be true, but they're still worried. They're still stressed about it on top of worrying about Ivy. The last thing they need is Devlin harassing them."

I couldn't argue with that. I only wished there was more we could do to stop Ian Devlin from being such a pain in this town's backside.

Bailey groaned. "God, I'm such a bad friend. I've been so distracted for weeks I haven't even asked how you're doing?"

Bailey had been anxious about my return to Boston for Christmas considering the way I'd left things with my mom and Michael.

Thankfully, the trip home had been uneventful. I spent all my time with my family. We had a great Christmas together. I never heard from Mom or Michael. The former was a good thing. And I knew the latter was too. It was just harder to convince myself of that. I'd told him to let me go. He'd done it.

It was the right thing.

"I'm fine." I did not divulge that I still dreamed about Michael. Hot, sweaty dreams that were driving me crazy with frustration and longing.

"Jess and Emery said you're avoiding talking about it. You know I haven't said anything about all the stuff that's gone down with your family. I will, however, reiterate to you that if you don't want to tell Emery, please consider talking to Jess. I think you two will find you have a lot in common."

"Bailey, I'm moving on." I didn't intend to sound so short. I gave her an apologetic smile. "I'm moving on, and I'm happy. I don't want to keep emotionally and mentally going back to that place. I'm good. I promise."

If she wasn't convinced, that wasn't my issue and I was ignoring it.

After she'd fed me and given me coffee to start my day, I still had time before I opened the store. I kept different hours during the off-season because of the shorter days, which meant I had more time to myself. Bidding Bailey goodbye, I made her promise to call me if she needed me. These days she didn't need me so much. She had Vaughn, and I was happy for her. I was. Yet I couldn't help thinking maybe I should keep my promise to my dad and actively try to move on and find someone I could lean on too. Perhaps then I'd stop dreaming about the man I'd left behind.

Needing basics from the grocery store, I made the short walk to Main Street, bundled in my winter coat against the harsh wind off the ocean, and stopped in at Lanson's.

I was lost in my own musings as I walked the aisles with a basket in hand when I overheard someone mention the sheriff. Sheriff-related news made my ears prick up, alert to any mention of Jeff, so I turned my head slightly and saw Ellen Luther talking to Liv, the receptionist at the doctor's surgery where Jess worked.

"A detective?" Liv gawked. "You're sure?"

Ellen nodded, her eyes alight with the joy of spreading news someone else hadn't yet heard. "That's right. You know Bridget, the station receptionist, well, she and I do knit night once a week, and she was telling me last night that Sheriff King has hired some fancy police detective from Boston to run the county's Criminal Investigation Division."

"Is this about those rumors that there's something funny going on at the department?"

Ellen nodded eagerly. "No one's saying it, but it's got to be why they've hired this guy. Bridget says he is very handsome. *Very*. His name is Matthew or Michael something. Oh gosh, she told me his name. I'm getting so forgetful. I think it was Irish."

My ears buzzed with a rush of blood as I turned away from the biggest gossip in Hartwell and her eager audience of one. I shook my head, feeling my knees tremble.

No.

I dropped my basket, feeling my stomach roil. He wouldn't. It was merely a coincidence. He wouldn't.

He let me go.

Hurrying out of the grocery store, I sucked in a lungful of cold sea air.

It wasn't enough.

I needed to know.

Rummaging through my purse, I yanked my phone out with shaking fingers and scrolled through my contacts to Michael. Dermot had texted me his number not long after I left Boston at

Thanksgiving, and even though I told my brother I was deleting it, I never did. Hitting the call button, I felt nauseated waiting for Michael to pick up. I heard the click, and my breath caught.

"Hello?"

My eyes squeezed closed at the sound of his voice, the deep, beautiful rumble of it in my ear. Just that one word made my cheeks flush and my heart pound.

"Hello?" he repeated.

"Michael?"

He hesitated a second. "Dahlia?"

I stared up the street toward the ocean feeling stupid for calling him. Of course, he hadn't taken a job in Hartwell. Now he would think I was nuts!

"Did you call for a reason?" His question was broken by the wind whistling through our connection, but I caught the gist.

"What are you doing right now?" I blurted out.

He gave a huff of laughter like he couldn't believe I'd called him to randomly ask him what he was doing. And I didn't blame him for his disbelief. "I'm about to start work."

"I thought you were on night shift." That suspicion crept in again. "*Where* are you about to start work?"

He was quiet, and then I heard, clear as day, not through the phone, but from behind me, "Hartwell."

The breath expelled from my body, and for a moment I froze, afraid to turn around. I could feel him all around me. And like the magnets we were, I was forced to move, to turn, to face him.

He was as beautiful as I remembered.

The only difference was his unshaven face, his hair was slightly longer, and he wore a warmer coat than the one he'd worn in Boston. He kept it open, however, with a black scarf wrapped around his neck. I could see the police badge clipped to the belt threaded through his dark jeans.

Oh my God.

I took an involuntary step toward him. "Michael?"

His eyes were shadowed with a million emotions. "Sorry I took so long. Uprooting your life takes longer than you'd think."

I shook my head, completely discombobulated. "What are you talking about?"

A smile tugged at the corners of his mouth. "You left me again. But this time I'm not letting you go."

20

Dahlia

Fear, outrage, confusion, panic.

It all bristled through me as I stormed down Main Street toward the boardwalk. Michael's arm brushed mine as he fell into step beside me. It was frustrating that my quick steps were matched by his longer, slower ones.

"Dahlia, talk to me." His voice was as calm as his strides.

"I can't. I'm afraid I'll scream."

"Then scream."

I didn't. I sped up.

"Oh, for Christ's sake." He grabbed my arm, halting me by the bandstand at the top of the street. Dawn had well and truly broken, and people were making their way to work. We were not alone, and I did not want to cause a scene. "Talk to me."

Realizing if this man was determined enough to uproot his whole goddamn life (oh my God, I couldn't even think about it!), then he was stubborn enough to keep at me until I talked. "Not here." I yanked my hand out of his grasp. "And no touchy, no feely!"

A smirk curled the corners of his mouth, and I narrowed my eyes. Please tell me he did not find this amusing! If he found anything remotely funny about this, I would kill him.

With a growl of annoyance, I spun away and marched toward

the boardwalk path that would lead to my gift store. Michael fell easily into step beside me again.

I hated how alive I felt. The truth was I must have been sleep-walking through life all this time because whenever Michael appeared, I was suddenly wide awake. My skin tingled, my heart raced, and no matter how I felt toward him in the moment, there was always this hum of anticipation in the air.

Goddamn him!

Thankfully my hands didn't shake too much as I unlocked the front door to my shop. I flicked on the lights and locked the door behind Michael as he stepped inside. My wedged boot heels made a dull, soft sound across the blue-painted floorboards but Michael's footsteps echoed loudly as he wandered around the store. When his footsteps stopped, I turned in the doorway that led to my workshop. He was staring into one of my tall glass display cabinets where my jewelry sat nestled on black velvet trays.

When he leaned toward it to get a better look, my breath hitched. He stared for a while and then lifted his head in awe. "You made these?"

Pride caused a rush of hot blood to my cheeks. I nodded.

Michael's gaze turned tender. His expression was disarming. "They're beautiful, Dahlia."

Emotion thickened my throat, and I whispered my thank-you. Unnerved by his demeanor and my reaction to it, I turned away and disappeared into my workroom.

After switching on the bright overhead lights—necessary as hardly any natural light filtered in through the shallow windows along the top of the far wall—I shrugged out of my coat. I heard Michael approaching and felt him stop in the doorway to the room. Not even a few seconds passed before my gaze involuntarily swung to him. He stood, feet braced, arms casually at his sides as he took in my workspace.

There were two long benches in the middle of the room. One had my latest design sitting neatly on it along with my sketchpad and drawings. The other bench had the materials I needed for the current piece I was making. Along the far end wall were cabinets that held the plethora of tools I'd collected over the years. On the back wall were the safes that held my supply of metals and precious and semiprecious stones.

On the side of the room where I was standing were shelving units filled from top to bottom with stock. There was a door at the back that led to the toilet and a small kitchenette.

Michael wandered over to the bench closest to him and studied my work tools. "What are these?"

Seriously? He wanted to talk about my work?

I glared at him.

He shrugged. "Indulge me. I know nothing about how you do what you do."

Recognizing that little twinkle in his eyes, I surmised he was procrastinating for a reason. He thought if I took the time to show him my goddamn tools, I'd lose some of my agitation. I crossed the room and walked around the opposite side of the bench.

"Blowtorch," I snapped as I tapped it.

Michael grinned. "Used for?"

That grin caused a flutter low in my belly. "For the annealing process. I use the torch to soften the metal, so I can manipulate it."

"And you manipulate it with?"

"I know what you're doing."

"Dahlia." He gestured to the tools. "I'm genuinely interested. Your jewelry is amazing. I want to know how you do it."

Squirming at the compliment, I looked down at the tools. Why not indulge him? Draw him into a false sense of security. And then ream his ass for uprooting his life and following me to Hartwell!

Seething, I exhaled slowly, not wanting him to see how greatly he could upset me. I think he knew anyway. Bastard.

I tapped the bezel pusher and the bezel roller. They looked kind of like a doorknob before they were fitted into the door. "These help me push and roll the stones into their setting—bezel, prong, channel, bead, and burnish. Those are the different kind of settings." I picked up my burnisher, which almost looked like a surgical knife, except mine had an enamel handle. "The burnisher. It's like a peeler of sorts. When you insert the stone, sometimes there's this gap between it and the metal. The burnisher polishes and peels until there's no gap."

I checked to see if Michael was paying attention. He was. His eyes drifted between the tool and my face, and he nodded for me to go on. When our gazes locked, I was so close to him I could see the mahogany in his eyes. From a distance, Michael's irises appeared almost black. When he was angry, I swear they turned that color. But under the bright lights of my workroom, they were a dark reddish brown. A ring of brown so dark it looked black encircled the mahogany of his inner iris, while little flecks of dark brown created an inner circle around his pupil.

His lashes weren't long, but they were thick. If it weren't for his dark-blond hair, which he'd miraculously inherited from his mother instead of his dad's dark curls, those eyes and his natural tanned skin would have made him the spitting image of his father. But it wasn't just the hair that made the two men different. Michael had the warmest eyes I'd ever seen.

They were beautiful.

He was beautiful.

Feeling another flush heat my skin, I put down the burnisher and reached for the tweezers. "They are what they look like. Tweezers. For handling stones and manipulating the silver. I use mostly silver." I moved through the other tools. "Hammers for hammering the silver." I touched a shallow slab of square metal and the weirdly shaped piece of metal beside it. "Stakes. I use them to shape the metal." I gestured to the shelving unit above my cabinet of tools where I kept my stakes. "I have them in all shapes and sizes."

"And these?" Michael pointed to several long cylindrical pieces of metal. A few were round, and a few were oval, all different widths.

"Those are ring and bracelet mandrels. You choose the width you want depending on what size of ring or bracelet you're making, and you can work it into shape around the mandrel." I put down the mandrel I'd picked up and glared into Michael's face. "Now we're done with the tutorial ... you want to tell me what the hell you're doing here?"

He pushed off the bench and wandered around in a way he knew would piss me off. "Why does the whole place smell like coconut?"

I swear I growled.

"Well?"

"Because I sometimes oxidize metal and it smells like sulfur, so I use coconut diffusers," I replied through clenched teeth.

He nodded, trailing his fingers over my cabinets. "This is amazing, Dahlia."

Stop trying to soften me!

"Michael." I stepped toward him, hoping he'd hear the genuine alarm in my voice.

He did. Michael turned to me, his expression carefully neutral. "Dahlia."

"Please tell me you did not quit a job with Boston PD and come to 'nothing-ever-happens-here-Hartwell' because of me."

"I can't tell you that."

"Oh my God." I ran my hands through my hair, turning away in vexation. What was he thinking? With all the crap already between us, *now* he would end up resenting me even more. "This place may technically be a city, but it's tiny." I whipped around, wide-eyed, feeling frantic, desperate, panicked for him. "It has a small-town mentality, and nothing happens here. You cannot give up a career as a *detective* in Boston to be here for me. And not because it's crazy doing that for anyone but because *we* are a mess!"

Michael's face hardened, and he took a step toward me. "One: I'm working for the sheriff's department, so it covers the entire county, not just Hartwell. Two: three months. For three months, I've laid awake in bed at night missing every fuckin' inch of you."

I sucked in a breath, feeling a complicated mix of exultation and desolation.

"Our night together three months ago was the first time in nine years I have been truly happy. Until you walked away again."

"But you agreed. You didn't say anything, so I assumed you agreed there's too much hurt, too much history, between us."

"No. I realized there was nothing I could *say* to make you believe I wouldn't make the same mistakes I made all those years ago. I had to *do* something that would make you believe."

Shaking my head, I backed away from him. "You don't give up everything. That's insane."

"What was I giving up? Boston was wearing on me long before you came back, Dahlia. Working nights, coming home to that empty apartment, hardly ever seeing my mom now that my dad's retired. I'd lost most of the friends I had because most of them found themselves on the wrong side of the law and thought I was a sellout. My closest friends are your family. And I only got close to them because they were *your* family.

"When you left, I got in contact with the sheriff's office here, and I spoke with Jeff King. I considered it fate that he needed a detective with experience." He thankfully halted when there was still enough space between us to allow me to breathe. "I don't consider moving here giving up on something. For the first time, I am not giving up on what matters."

No, no, no! Him being here was ... no!

Every day Michael would tempt me with his mere goddamn presence. How could I fight my feelings for him when he was there all the time? And I had to fight my emotions. I had to.

"Tell me you love me," he said.

My eyes jerked up from the floor to stare into his. They were filled with love and desire and everything I'd ever wanted him to look at me with. When I was younger. Before everything turned to shit. Tears shone in my eyes because I couldn't say those words. Those words would change everything.

A muscle in his jaw ticked. "Fine." He bit out. "I'll leave. If you tell me you *don't* love me."

Horror filled me.

No.

I tried to coerce the words to materialize out of nothing. To let the lie trip off my tongue. However, even knowing what was at stake, I couldn't physically force out the words. They were like sandpaper against the inside of my throat.

The ire in Michael's eyes dissipated at whatever he saw in me. Confusion and affection replaced his disappointment, and I froze as he crossed the distance between us. Holding still, my breath caught and my belly fluttered as Michael bent his head toward mine. His heat and spicy dark cologne wrapped around me, and I closed my eyes against his impact.

A shiver caused the hairs on the back of my neck to rise as he whispered in my ear, "And that's why I'm staying."

Holding in a shudder of longing, I felt him pull away, and my eyes automatically opened to track his movements, hungry for the sight of him. He gave me a soft, knowing smile and retreated. "I've got to get to work. Can't be late for my first day on the job."

And then he was gone.

I listened to the sound of his footsteps moving across my floorboards, to the ring of the bell above my door as he opened it, and the soft click of it closing behind him.

Holy shit.

Oh, holy shit was I in big trouble.

Scrambling for my purse, I pulled out my cell and hit Bailey's number.

"What's up?" she answered after a few rings.

"Michael's here." I was breathless. "He took a job here. Fuck. Fuck, fuck, fuck, fuck ... Fuck!"

"I'll be right over." She hung up.

I was still standing, heaving in shallow breaths when I heard the front door to my shop open a few minutes later.

And then Bailey was there, standing in my doorway, her green eyes big with concern.

"Fuck," I whispered.

21

Michael

That Dahlia hadn't jumped into his arms as soon as she realized he'd moved to Hartwell for them didn't surprise Michael. Would it have been nice? Hell, yeah. Realistic? Not so much. Michael knew he needed to give Dahlia some time to adjust to the idea of him being in Hartwell before he determinedly pursued a relationship with her. Not a lot of time. But some.

And judging by the enigmatic comments his new boss, Sheriff Jeff King, had made when he'd accepted the job heading up the department's Criminal Investigations Division, Michael would have enough to distract him from his impatience.

Michael walked down Main Street from Dahlia's gift shop. He'd arrived in town on Friday, took a short meeting with the sheriff, and then gotten settled into his small apartment. He'd looked for a place before Jeff had even offered him the job and had been frustrated by the higher amount of short-term rentals versus long-term. It made sense with it being a popular beach resort, but no less concerning.

After he'd accepted the job with Hartwell SD, Michael was considering taking on a short-term rental until he could find something permanent, even though it would eat into his savings. However, thankfully, Jeff found him a condo in a private community called Atlantic Village on the outskirts of town. The lawns and trees around the three sets of buildings that housed the condos were immaculately cared for. Each unit had its own parking space, and there was a private gym, indoor swimming pool, a day care center, a convenience store, health food deli, and coffee shop. Apparently, there was a list of people waiting to rent there, but Jeff pulled some strings, and the co-op board was happy to have an experienced police detective living in the village.

So he got bumped up the list. The condo was a one-bedroom, and Michael begrudged paying the extortionate rental costs for it. He'd have to look elsewhere for a long-term solution, but for now it would have to do.

Yesterday he'd driven into town for some supplies. Having visited Hartwell with his ex-wife last summer, he'd seen most of the town center, so there was no reason to explore. But he'd wanted to familiarize himself with the town as quickly as possible. Despite it being off-season, the place was busy with tourists coming in for the weekend.

Michael had found a parking space at the top of Main Street and had gotten out at the boardwalk. He knew where Dahlia's shop was. It was highlighted on Google Maps, so he strolled along the familiar wooden planks. The building with its slightly weathered white-painted shingles and the porch was typical New England design. Hart's Inn sat next to it, a larger version of Dahlia's building, and Michael wondered about its owner. Bailey. He wanted to get to know the woman who had saved Dahlia's life in more ways than one. He wanted to thank her for being there when he wasn't.

That thought made his gut churn with self-reproach. He stared back at Dahlia's store. It was open. And she was inside.

The urge to go to her was overwhelming, but it wasn't the time. He'd find the right time. Instead, he drank in the sight of her place, wondering what it was like on the inside. A mammoth sign above the door of the building proclaimed Hart's Gift Shop in a feminine script. He'd wondered if Dahlia made the sign herself. Probably.

From where he'd been standing, he could see items in the window sparkling in the low February sun. Jewelry. Probably Dahlia's jewelry. Forcing his curiosity aside, Michael had turned back down the boardwalk. The ocean had been calm, and there had been plenty of people walking along the soft sand. Having found Dahlia, knowing she was within reach, Michael had relaxed enough to take in the rest of the boardwalk.

It hadn't changed much, except now he was really taking it in. When he'd been there with Kiersten, he'd been so uptight and stuck in his own head over their failing marriage, he hadn't opened his eyes to his surroundings.

Beside Dahlia's shop were a candy store and arcade, and from there the boards ran along the main thoroughfare. A large bandstand sat at the top of Main Street. Michael had remembered the bandstand—next to it was a plaque that told a town legend about one of the descendants of the founding family.

Michael had stopped to peer at the plaque. 1909. Eliza Hartwell. He'd realized then that Eliza Hartwell must have been Bailey's ancestor. The story went that she fell in love with a steelworker called Jonas Kellerman. He was considered beneath Eliza in social station, and they were forbidden to marry. Instead, Eliza was betrothed to the son of a wealthy businessman. On the eve of her wedding, a devastated Eliza walked into the ocean. By chance, Jonas was up on the boardwalk with friends, saw Eliza, and went after her. Legend said he reached her, but the waves took them under, and they were never seen again.

Michael thought it was a pretty fuckin' depressing tale, but Kiersten had gotten all moon-eyed over it. The plaque further said Jonas's sacrifice for his love created magic. For generations since the deaths of Eliza and Jonas, people born in Hartwell who met their husbands or wives on the boards stayed in love their whole lives. It told tourists that if they walked the boardwalk together and they were truly in love, it would last forever, no matter the odds.

Kiersten made them walk the boards hand in hand after that.

Of course, minutes later she'd discover Dahlia's existence and realized Michael had already met *the one* years before her.

Wincing at the memory, Michael had headed toward the boards. Main Street was wide enough for cars to park in the middle, which was where Michael had parked his Honda, and along either side were commercial buildings. Trees lined the street, where restaurants, gift shops, clothing stores, fast-food joints, spas, coffeehouses, pubs, and markets were neighbors in the kind of well-groomed tourist environment you'd expect from a popular vacation destination like Hartwell.

Michael had decided to get his supplies at the grocery store later and kept heading along the boards. He'd passed the small ice cream shack as well as a building beside it he didn't remember that seemed to be under refurbishment and had large classical signage along its roof that read The Boardwalk. A banner across the blacked-out windows told everyone COMING SOON. If Michael could guess, it was probably a restaurant.

Beside The Boardwalk was a surf shop, an Italian restaurant called Antonio's, and then the largest building on the boardwalk. It stood out from the New England seaside buildings around it with its stern, clean lines of whitewashed walls and lots of glass. There was no neon sign for this building. Huge gold metal letters three stories up spelled out its name— Paradise Sands Hotel.

Michael looked up at the huge building. He'd had dinner in the five-star hotel with Kiersten, and its interior was as modern as its exterior. It was more masculine on the outside, however, than it was on the inside and somehow added a quality to the boards that weirdly worked. At least Michael thought it did.

At the end of the boards, Michael had noted the traditional, earthy-looking bar called Cooper's. He and Kiersten had drinks there their first night in Hartwell, and it was his kind of place. Low-key and unpretentious. Next to the bar, a little farther down the boards, was the site of his infamous run-in with Dahlia last summer. Emery's Bookstore and Coffee House. Michael couldn't remember much about it—all he remembered was seeing Dahlia McGuire for the first time in nine years.

Distracted Michael had walked back to Main Street, bought necessities like coffee, milk, and bread from Lanson's Grocery, and took a walk farther down the street to Hartwell City Hall. The attractive sandstone building housed the sheriff's department at its rear. After he'd returned to his car, Michael hadn't gone directly home. Before leaving Boston, he'd done something he could have done years ago but hadn't. Deciding not to regret that or he'd never move on, Michael checked the DMV database for Dahlia's current address.

He'd already put the address into his GPS, and it took him out of town (but only a tantalizing seven minutes from his new place) to a small estate of condos off the coastal highway that led directly to Main Street. Dahlia was a fifteen-minute drive from the beach, and the apartment buildings seemed isolated. There were well maintained, and the area looked nice enough, surrounded by neat lawns and trees that offered some soundproofing from the highway.

However, Michael hadn't liked how far out of town she was. He did like how close she was to his condo, though.

As he'd sat outside her building, Michael had realized his behavior was almost bordering on stalking. So he'd left and made peace with the idea of approaching Dahlia once he had a speech ready.

Of course, he mused now as he walked toward the sheriff's department entrance, that had all been blown to hell. This town was smaller than he'd realized because it was clear someone had mentioned his arrival to Dahlia.

He'd parked his car at the station that morning and was heading to Main Street to grab a coffee before his shift when his cell rang. An unknown number. Then he'd heard Dahlia's voice in his ear and as he walked, heart pounding, listening to her demand where he was, he saw her.

Standing outside Lanson's in a blue wool coat with her back to him. He didn't need to see her face to know it was her. Michael would recognize Dahlia from a mile away.

It would be hard to take it slow with her. Especially when she looked at him the way she had when she was telling him about her silversmithing tools. No woman had ever looked at Michael the way Dahlia did. Like he was the sun, moon, and every fuckin' thing in between.

Something was holding her back. Something she wouldn't admit to.

With a heavy exhale, Michael strode into the station, coffee-less and prepared to accept the mulch usually provided in a police station instead. The middle-aged receptionist he'd met briefly on Friday gave him a broad smile as he walked in.

"Morning, Detective," she called brightly.

Bridget. Her name is Bridget, Michael remembered. "Morning, Bridget."

She beamed at him, her plump cheeks creasing with a pretty smile. "Sheriff asked to see you first thing."

He nodded and walked through the clean, open-plan station. There were a couple of officers who gave him the nod, which he returned before turning the corner down the hall toward Jeff's office. He'd introduce himself to the deputies and patrol officers later. Michael was the only detective in the sheriff's department. Considering it was a detective's job to follow up on criminal investigations, this information perturbed Michael. However, Hartwell was a quiet city in a small county. There had been serious crimes sporadically through the years, but the sheriff's department had usually joined forces with the FBI in many of those cases, as far as Michael could see from his research.

The last time Hartwell had detectives in its department was in the 1990s. Jeff had told him Jaclyn Rose, the mayor, and some of the wealthier businesspeople who made up Hartwell's city council would be eager to meet "the mysterious Bostonian detective" he'd hired to lead the Criminal Investigations Division.

Michael looked forward to that. Not.

He knocked on Jeff's door.

"Come in."

He strode inside. Michael liked to think he had good instincts about people, and he had warmed to Jeff King. He'd asked Michael why he wanted to work in Hartwell, and he'd been honest that he was moving here for his woman. Jeff hadn't grilled him about it or asked who she was, and Michael respected a man who respected another man's privacy.

Jeff stood from behind his desk as Michael walked in. Michael had done his research on Jeff King. He knew he was from Wilmington, had met his wife in Hartwell, moved here in his early twenties when they married, and taken a job as a deputy. Only a few years into their marriage, however, Jeff's wife was diagnosed with cancer, and she passed away. Michael knew he hadn't remarried but other than that, he knew little about the man's personal life.

Michael knew Jeff had first been elected to sheriff five years ago and had won another election since. He was up for reelection next year.

At six foot six, Jeff towered over Michael's five eleven as he rounded the desk to shake his hand. While the deputies and patrol officers wore tan shirts with the embroidered Hartwell Sheriff's Department insignia on either sleeve, along with khaki pants, Sheriff King's uniform was different. He wore a black shirt and black pants with his sheriff's badge clipped above the left shirt pocket on his chest.

Although Michael outweighed him in muscle, there was a lean, hard edge to Jeff's rangy physique. He possessed an aura of strength that Michael assumed went a long way to assure the people of Hartwell of his capability.

And Michael was a guy, but he wasn't a dumb guy.

Jeff King was a good-looking fucker, and Michael had no doubt that helped a little when it came to election time.

"Welcome to the first day on the job," Jeff greeted him.

He didn't comment on Michael's lack of uniform. On Friday night Jeff had brought the subject up and, thankfully, decided Michael wouldn't wear one.

"I don't have to wear a uniform," Jeff had said. "It's a small city, small county, people know me. I could clip on my badge and be done with it. But most days I wear the uniform because we have a lot of tourists here and you already know the psychological impact of the police uniform."

Michael had nodded, dreading the idea of putting on that hot, polyester crap after years of being a plainclothes officer.

"I don't want you to put on the uniform." Jeff had surprised him. "It'll spread fast around here who you are, and I want the fact you're plainclothes to make some people feel a little off-kilter. In your case, I'm hoping it elevates you. You're not one of my deputies. You're my *detective*. You get me?"

Michael had nodded, but he wasn't too clear on why Jeff needed to make such a statement about having an experienced city detective in the department.

Michael wanted to find out why now. "What's on the agenda?"

The sheriff pointed to the lamp on his desk. "I found a listening device in that lamp last year."

Oh fuck. Michael tensed. "Any leads?"

Jeff nodded and turned to him, his blue eyes hard. "I need you to catch a crooked cop."

Surprised, Michael rocked back on his heels.

And he thought his job would be the *least* dramatic part of his transition to Hartwell.

22

Dahlia

"Let's get this straight." Jessica peered at me over a mug of hot tea. "The new detective in town is an ex-boyfriend of yours. The ex-boyfriend you ran away from in this very shop last summer. He's newly divorced, you reconnected in Boston, and now he quit his job, took one in Hartwell, and uprooted his entire life to be with you?"

Seeing the inquisitiveness in her expression, hearing the incredulity in her voice combined with Emery's romantic puppy eyes, I groaned and turned to Bailey for help. "Tell them it's more complicated than that."

"It's more complicated than that."

I pulled a face. "Helpful."

She raised one eyebrow, which probably meant that if I wanted our friends to understand the situation completely, then I needed to stop being so secretive. However, I wasn't ready to put my tragic history out there. It had been four days since Michael had appeared and the town was abuzz with his arrival. I hadn't seen him since the day in my workshop, but I could not escape his name anywhere I went.

Instead, I shrugged at Jess. "Look, let's just say there is a lot of bad blood and painful history between Michael and me. I left Boston under the assumption that we would let each other go."

Emery cocked her head in thought. "But you don't really want that."

"Yes, I do." Her perceptive comment disturbed me.

"No, you don't." Her smile was apologetic. "Every time you say his name, your tone softens, and you get this look in your eyes, like how Bailey looks at Vaughn and Jess at Cooper."

I realized in all her quiet shyness, Emery had become a proficient observer.

Bailey's smug smile said, "I told you so."

"You don't have to tell us the details," Jess said, reaching for a cookie. "You know that. But you can be honest with us about how you feel. Michael gave up everything to pursue a relationship with you. How does that make you feel?"

"You sound like a therapist," I teased.

She was about to take a bite of her cookie but paused. "Do you see a therapist?"

"I used to. Anyway, that's not the point. The point is that this is crazy. No one gives up their entire career as a detective in Boston to move to nowhere Hartwell for a woman they've spent less than forty-eight hours with in the last nine years."

"Stop simplifying it." Bailey rolled her eyes. "You're absolutely simplifying it. If you don't want to talk about it, then don't. I love you, you know it. But I won't participate in you lying to yourself. It's not healthy."

Irritation niggled me, and the girls fell into awkward silence as Bailey and I launched into a staring contest. Part of me was annoyed by her curtness, and the other part knew it was born from her concern that I was burying my head in the sand. How irksome, because she wasn't wrong.

"I'm in a panic, okay?" I threw my hands up in defeat. "I have my reasons for not thinking Michael and I are a good idea. Leaving him in Boston, again, was one of the hardest things I've ever had to do. However, I was trying to move on! I would start dating again and this time give a relationship a real shot. Now he's back. And I can't deny that I want him. I want to climb him every time I see him. Extreme physical attraction versus what I know is best for me emotionally. That's what I'm dealing with here. So, yeah, I'm in a panic because I don't trust myself around him and he's made it clear that he's going to pursue me."

Bailey looked satisfied. "Was that so hard to admit?"

I snarled at her, and she threw her head back in delighted laughter.

"What's the plan?" Jess continued. "Do you need us to help keep you two apart?"

"No, I'm not dragging you guys into it. I'll just avoid him."

"Well, how are we supposed to act around him?" Emery asked. "Do we like Michael or do we not like Michael?"

I smiled at her loyalty. "Michael's a good guy. You act any way you want around him."

"So, blushing and stuttering, then?"

We chuckled at her self-deprecation.

"That reminds me about those man lessons." Bailey's eyes filled with excitement. "We need to start those."

Last year Bailey announced she intended to give Emery lessons in how to talk with men more easily. Both Jess and I could see the idea embarrassed Emery, but when Bailey got something in her head, she was hard to dissuade. Seeing Emery's panic, I cut in, "You have a wedding to plan. You have no time for man lessons."

The light dimmed in her eyes. "This wedding is killing me. Everyone has an opinion about it and a request. Being a descendant of the founding family is usually pretty cool. Not so much if you're planning your wedding."

"My point exactly. Weddings are stressful in normal situations. Yours will be the biggest event to hit Hartwell in years, so you have no time for extra stuff."

My friend nodded her head in reluctant agreement, and Emery shot me a grateful smile.

Jess began telling us a funny story about her and Cooper's dog, Louis, who, despite being almost two years old, was still in the puppy stage. He'd figured out a way to open drawers and was currently fascinated with Cooper's underwear.

As we were chatting, we heard the tinkle of the bell above the door, but before Emery could get up to check who had come into her bookstore, there was the sound of light footsteps hurtling up the stairs to where we were sitting.

It was Kell Summers. He was small, cute, blond, and a town councilman. He grinned when he saw us. "I heard you ladies had congregated in here. Where was my invite? You know I like a good gossip."

Bailey grinned up at him. "What brings you to our lady gathering?"

"Winter Carnival." He clapped his hands together with way too much enthusiasm for a Thursday afternoon.

Not only was Kell a councilman, but he was also the town's official event planner. That meant as much as we loved him, he drove us (and I had it on good authority, his partner Jake) nuts several times a year. I worked on costumes for the Winter Carnival parade depending on what theme had been chosen for the year. This year it was an homage to Disney for some reason only Kell understood.

While most people rented costumes, Kell liked the participants who rode on the two parade floats to wear original designs. Two locals handy with a sewing machine, Annie and Bryn, had started working on the costumes with me a few months ago. With only two weeks to go until the carnival, however, we got help from a few other people in town, including Kell's partner, Jake.

Jess's smile was questioning. "I thought we were all organized for that."

"Well, we were." Kell threw me a wide, sheepish grin.

I groaned. "Oh no, what now?"

"You know how hard it was to convince the sheriff to let a few of his deputies take part?"

"Uh-huh." I did know. Four of his deputies had told me Jeff had almost barred them from volunteering to be on one of the floats representing Hartwell's civil services. They'd done it anyway and were all now different Disney characters.

"Well, Deputy Rawlins is threatening to pull out unless we let her dress like her fellow deputies."

Annoyance itched under my skin at Wendy's demand. "Kell, her fellow deputies are all in different costumes. And I've spent weeks working on her Fairy Godmother costume."

"I know, I know." He winced. "But all the other deputies are male characters from Disney, like Wreck-It Ralph and Black Panther. Wendy is frustrated that we gave her, and this is a direct quote, 'a wimpy girly costume.'"

"And she couldn't have brought this up sooner?"

He rolled his eyes. "Do you not think I asked the same question?"

"Well, who does she want to be?"

"Katniss from *The Hunger Games.*"

"That's not a Disney movie, Kell," Bailey cut in.

"I'm aware it's not Disney, Bailey, but if it will stop the good deputy from cornering me every chance she gets, then I'm happy to let that one go."

I thought about it a second and heaved a sigh. "I can put together that costume from clothes we already have, and I'm pretty sure the props department at the Atlantic Theatre will have a bow and arrow we can borrow."

"Great! I knew you'd pull it off. Also"— Kell shot a look at Emery— "my Elsa from *Frozen* has come down with the flu. If she's not better by the day of the carnival, we'll need a replacement."

Emery seemed to sink further into her armchair, as if she could somehow disappear into it.

Feeling bad for her, I fibbed a little. "Emery is five ten and willowy. Janey is a five-foot-five, solidly built gymnast. I don't know if I can alter the costume."

Kell scoffed, "You can do it. Emery is the perfect Elsa."

She winced. "But don't you have Janey on the lead float this year?"

"Well, yes, but can you imagine how much more perfect it would be if it were you?" His eyes brightened at the idea. "Our ethereal bookstore owner gracefully leading the parade."

"And then upchucking on tourists as she passes them by," Bailey threw in. She shook her head at Kell. "Not happening."

He gave Emery a regretful look and seemed to decide to remain silent on the subject.

I smiled as the color returned to Emery's cheeks but then stopped smiling when Kell's eyes returned to me. I knew that expression. That was his "I have another favor to ask" expression.

"What?"

"I'm sure you've all heard about the delicious detective who has joined our sheriff's department. I've asked the sheriff to forward on my invitation to the good detective to take part in the parade."

My heart skipped a beat. "Detective Sullivan?"

"Yes!" Kell sat on the arm of Bailey's chair. "My God, have you seen him yet? Keeping my professionalism around him is hard. He's very masculine. Very, very, very ... " He sighed dreamily. "Of course, with that body of his, he'll make the perfect Mr. Incredible, and you know we've been struggling to find someone to take that part on. Fingers crossed he says yes, so be prepared to make the costume. Jake, Annie, and Bryn will take over the finishing of the rest of the costumes so you can work on Wendy's new costume and, obviously, if Detective Sullivan says yes, his costume."

Panicked at the thought of having to spend time with and *touch* Michael, I shook my head. "No. Two weeks is not enough time."

He frowned. "I've never known you to shy from a challenge before."

"A challenge? Kell, this isn't a challenge, this is impossible."

"You know that word is not in my vocabulary, Dahlia," he tutted with a shake of his finger.

Jess snorted beside me and I cut her a filthy look. She took a sip of her tea, but I heard her muffled bark of laughter.

"Kell," I said, trying to keep my impatience out of my voice, "Wendy is one thing. She's small, there's less fabric to work with. But Michael is five eleven and built like a brick shithouse. That's a lot of Lycra." As soon as the words were out of my mouth, I wondered what the hell I was panicking about. Michael would never agree to be in a parade as a cartoon character, let alone one who wore Lycra! I relaxed.

Kell's eyebrows rose to his forehead. "Your Boston accent is showing, along with your surprising familiarity with our good *Bostonian* detective."

Oh hell.

Bailey swallowed a smile and flicked her gaze to Emery whose mouth twitched suspiciously. She gave Jess a furtive look to find her shaking with quiet laughter.

Traitors.

All of them.

"I ... uh ... " Oh Jesus, whatever I told Kell would make it around town like wildfire, but if Michael was determined to pursue me, people would find out soon enough. "Yeah, we know each other. No big deal."

The councilman's eyes were alight with this newfound knowledge, but I stared at him stone-faced. He was getting no gossip from me!

"I see." He stood. "Well then, that'll make the fittings less awkward."

"Kell—"

"You're doing this, Dahlia. If you need help, all you have to do is ask."

"He won't do it." I shrugged. "There's no way he'll do this."

"Well," Kell gave me a mischievous smirk, "Dana Kellerman is playing Elastigirl."

The mention of Dana, Cooper's ex-wife, killed my friends' quiet amusement. Not only had Dana cheated on Cooper when they were married, she'd cheated on him with his best friend. Jack Devlin. Yes, the second youngest Devlin son. Once upon a time, Jack had been a good guy. A construction foreman who wanted nothing to do with his father or the family business. Jack and Cooper had been best friends their whole lives, more like brothers, until Jack mysteriously quit construction to work for his dad, and then committed the ultimate betrayal by sleeping with Dana. Both Jack and Dana became persona non grata with us all.

Unfortunately, in an effort to win back the hearts of Hartwell, the once-popular town beauty had started forcing her presence into events. First the Punkin' Chunkin' Festival last November. Dana held a charity raffle for a children's hospital. Now the parade. Her choosing to be Elastigirl over any of the other characters that would have allowed her to dress up as a princess had seemed weird at first. Then I realized she got to show off her rockin' body in a Lycra superhero suit. Plus, she would herd and look after three little Incredibles, and I suspected she thought the imagery of "playing mom" was good PR.

Fitting her had not been fun. She complained and whined constantly.

And I did not like Kell's insinuation that Michael would be tempted to play her cartoon husband.

I glowered.

Kell was smug. "Dana has promised to persuade Detective Sullivan to take part."

My heart lodged itself in my throat.

"Why?" Bailey snapped.

"Oh, surely you've heard she pounced on the man his first day on the job?"

"No, we have not heard that." Bailey leaned forward, her face pinched. "What is she doing?"

"My guess? Actively pursuing the only good-looking man left in town who doesn't have firsthand knowledge of her traitorous little ways." Kell looked directly at me. "I haven't seen such a gleam of determination in her admittedly beautiful eyes since she first decided to go after Cooper."

Jess gave a sharp intake of breath behind me, and her hand came to a rest on my arm.

"Not that it's anyone's concern here." He smirked knowingly at me. "Mind you, if you're friends with him, Dahlia, maybe you ought to warn him." With a wink and a "ta ta," he skipped out of the bookstore as if he hadn't just detonated a social bomb.

Dana Kellerman was pursuing Michael?

Oh, hell no!

Michael would never fall for her crap, right?

Then again, he and Cooper weren't that dissimilar, and Cooper had fallen for her crap before he knew better.

Dana was beautiful.

Like, on another planet level of beautiful.

I felt sick.

"Dahlia, Michael loves you," Bailey said, her voice soft, reassuring.

I lifted my eyes to meet hers. "And when he realizes he's made a mistake coming here for me, who will he turn to then?"

Her sigh was sad, almost weary. "If you're so determined not to be with Michael, then why do you care?"

"Because he deserves better." I snapped to my feet. "If I think he deserves better than me, then for sure he deserves better than the selfish, nasty cow that is Dana Kellerman."

The girls called after me as I rushed out of the bookstore, but I didn't want to be around anyone. I had to plan. Somehow, I had to make Michael see he and I were a bad idea while I kept him and Dana apart without him suspecting it was jealousy.

It wasn't jealousy.

It was friendship.

Okay.

It was jealousy too.

However, there had to be a way to do this without making it *seem* like it was jealousy.

23

Michael

It was Day Four, as Michael was calling it. Day four on the job in Hartwell and he was getting antsy not seeing Dahlia. Time was almost up on that. Striding into the station that morning, two coffees in hand, Michael said hello to Bridget and a couple of the deputies. As he turned down the corridor that led to Jeff's office, he saw Deputy Freddie Jackson coming toward him.

The deputy's eyes narrowed on Michael and as they neared each other, Freddie's gaze moved past him, determinedly not looking at him. Michael noted the way his hands clenched into fists at his sides. For a man who had been smart enough to cover his own ass for years, his reaction to Michael wasn't smart.

"Deputy," Michael acknowledged him.

Jackson's expression was full of loathing. He didn't return Michael's greeting.

Shaking his head, he continued toward Jeff's office.

Jeff believed Jackson was taking payoffs from the Devlin family in return for providing them with information he picked up at the station and city hall. Jeff suspected Jackson was the one who'd bugged his office. Moreover, he was concerned about complaints of trumped-up charges filed by Jackson over the last two and a half years. He'd pulled people over for speeding, had claimed to find drugs in a car in one situation, and charged another with drunk and disorderly. Things that were hard to prove either way without reliable witnesses, of which there were none in these cases.

The drugs could have been planted by Jackson, but there was no proof. The people he'd charged were people with businesses in Hartwell, people who had ended up either selling to Devlin or getting into bed with him in the business sense. Jeff believed Jackson was helping to intimidate and harass the people whose businesses were of particular interest to Devlin.

Moreover, Jeff suspected Jackson had been covering up crimes committed by the Devlins, including an attack on Bailey Hartwell last year. The eldest Devlin son, Stu, had broken into Bailey's inn wearing a ski mask and when Bailey caught him in her office, he attacked her. She was adamant it was Stu, but there was no evidence to prove it. The idea of someone attacking Dahlia's friend pissed Michael off. The fact that Jack Devlin started sleeping with Bailey's sister Vanessa, who owned a share in Hart's Inn, which led to Vanessa offering to sell her share of the inn to Ian Devlin, only substantiated Bailey's claim that it was a Devlin who attacked her that night. Jeff explained Vanessa had sold her share to Bailey's fiancée instead, thankfully cutting the Devlins out. Still, they were a shady family, and the idea they had a cop on the payroll didn't sound too farfetched.

Jackson's edgy behavior since Michael's appearance seemed to confirm Jeff's suspicions. Thankfully, making Jackson edgy was one of the goals of bringing Michael in. The deputy was a smarmy little shit but from what Michael could tell, he wasn't stupid. Merely arrogant.

He'd left no paper trail of his crimes. But that arrogance had tripped him up because he'd put himself on Jeff's radar. Still, they needed him to make mistakes. If he thought Michael was closing in on him, he just might.

Michael knocked and then strode in with a coffee for the sheriff. Morning coffee together had quickly become their ritual.

"Passed Jackson," Michael said as he sat down in the chair opposite Jeff's desk. "If looks could kill, I'd be fuckin' ash right about now. He's edgy around me."

"Good."

"You got an unmarked car Jackson won't recognize?"

Jeff lifted an eyebrow as he sipped his coffee. "You thinking of tailing him?"

"Think I need to. If he's as nervous about my sudden appearance as he seems to be, then he'll likely go to the Devlins in a panic. He'll want reassurance from them."

Jeff nodded. "I'll get you a car. In other business, Kell Summers just got off the phone. He's a councilman, and he does the events around here. The Winter Carnival is in two weeks, and the theme of the parade is Disney. Kell wants you to dress up as Mr. Incredible."

Not sure he'd heard right, Michael didn't respond.

The sheriff chuckled. "Do you even know who Mr. Incredible is?"

"I have pseudo-nephews," he said, thinking about Levi and Leo. "So, yeah. I'm also thinking you're not actually asking me to do this. Put on a fuckin' leotard?"

He scowled. "No. I think it's ridiculous Kell even suggested it and I told him no. It's hard to keep you under the radar in a small town, but we can do our best. Putting you in a fucking parade is the last thing we need or have time for right now. As it is, I had a hard time trying to dissuade my deputies from taking part, but if they want to, I can't stop them."

The thought made Michael's insides shrivel. "Yeah, there's no fuckin' way I'm doing it. That's not why I'm here."

"Kell knows that now. Heads-up, though. He told me Dana

Kellerman would try her best to persuade you because she's play-ing Mr. Incredible's wife." Jeff quirked an eyebrow. "What's that about? She sniffing around you?"

The blonde beauty who had introduced herself in the super-market had been getting in his face a lot these past few days. As stunning as she was, there was something hard about her. And something he couldn't quite put his finger on. Whatever it was, his gut told him to stay away. Not that he was interested anyway.

Michael nodded. "Yeah, she's been pretty obvious about that."

"I'm not one for gossip, but you should know she's not well liked around here. She's doing her best to ingratiate herself with everyone again, but she's not to be trusted."

"I got that impression. What did she do?"

"Well, other than being a spoiled brat ... You know Coo-per's? The bar."

"Yeah."

"Owned by Cooper Lawson. Good guy. Well respected and well liked. She was married to him, cheated on him. With his best friend. Jack Devlin." Jeff let that sink in. He'd filled Michael in on the dynamics of the Devlin family, and so he knew that until recently, Jack had nothing to do with his family business. "Then apparently, she tried to pull more shit when Cooper moved onto something better. He's married to one of the local doctors now."

None of that surprised or bothered Michael. "You don't need to warn me off Dana. I'm not interested."

Jeff nodded. "Your mystery woman?"

Michael smiled into his coffee, thinking about Dahlia. Four days was too long. He needed to drop by her shop. See where her head was at.

"Just be prepared for Dana. Kell said she's determined to have you by her side in the parade."

"No one is talking me into that. It's ludicrous to even suggest it."

Jeff rubbed a hand over his face. "I don't know what I was thinking letting the others do it."

"Community spirit," Michael offered. "It's not that bad. I think people will love seeing their officers do it. Just not me. And it's not like *you're* doing it."

"It's not that I don't enjoy town events." Jeff shrugged. "But there's no way I'm putting on a fucking costume and parading around town like an idiot. As for you, I'll tell Kell to back off. Dahlia will find another Mr. Incredible to suit up."

The mere mention of her caused Michael's heart to speed up. "Dahlia?"

"She owns the gift store on the boardwalk. A talented artist, makes her own jewelry. She also does the costumes for the Winter Carnival." He wore a small smile as he stared into his mug. "Everyone always looks great."

Something about Jeff's expression stirred an uneasy feeling in Michael. "Sounds like you know her quite well."

Jeff's smile wilted a little. "I used to know her quite well."

What the hell did that mean? "How well?"

Hearing the hint of accusation Michael couldn't hide, Jeff's gaze jerked to him and his eyes narrowed. "We dated."

Jealousy seized Michael. Vicious and ugly, twisting his gut. Was this the guy? Was this the guy who managed to make Dahlia forget about him? Yeah, he hadn't forgotten her admitting that there had been one guy who pushed Michael out of her thoughts for a while. She also admitted *she* broke up with *him*. "Dated? Past tense? Who broke up with who?"

Jeff sat up, his expression carefully blank. "She broke it off. Woman has commitment issues."

"You didn't want it to end?"

"This is feeling like an interrogation." Jeff scratched his stubbled jaw. "No, I didn't want it to end. Dahlia's pretty special."

Jesus fuck.

Michael looked away, his jaw clenched tight. He liked Jeff. Respected him. He did not want to fuckin' resent him.

"How did I not put two and two together?" Jeff sighed heavily. "You're both from Boston. Dahlia's your mystery woman. You two are a thing?"

Clearing his throat of the thick ball of emotion, Michael shook his head. "We were. I'm here because I want her back ... Tell me something. You over her?"

Jeff didn't answer. Instead, they shared a look filled with a lot of unspoken things and the easy camaraderie that had sprung up between them from the moment they met was altered. Tension shifted between them. Tension Michael hated.

It had never occurred to him that he and his new boss would be interested in the same fuckin' woman.

Michael threw back the rest of his coffee and stood up. "I better get back to work."

"This going to be a problem between us?" Jeff asked, straightforward as ever.

Michael decided he owed Jeff to be equally up-front. "I like you, Jeff, and I respect you as a man and as my boss. But I've let Dahlia McGuire slip through my fingers too many fuckin' times, and I won't let anyone, *anyone*, get in our way this time."

Jeff nodded, his blue eyes hard in a way Michael didn't like. "Got it. But if she doesn't want you in her way, I'll be there to make sure you stay out of it."

With a soft exhalation of frustration, Michael gave him an abrupt nod and strode out of his office.

24

Dahlia

When the gift store was quiet, I spent most of my time in the workshop. If the shop was closed, I blared my music and got to work. It was still open, however, so I needed to keep one ear out for the tinkle of the bell above my door. Which meant no music.

Hammering the final piece in the summer collection I was creating to put in the window display during high season, my brain didn't switch off like it usually did. Most of the time I got lost entirely in silversmithing, but not this time. Not after Kell's bomb about Dana and Michael over lunch. The only thing that had calmed me down was the fact that my dad called as I was letting myself into the shop.

After Michael first showed up, I called my dad to see if he knew Michael intended to come to Hartwell. He didn't. The only person who knew Michael had left his job was Dermot, but he hadn't known why. I was reassured that my family hadn't let me walk into that shock without a heads-up.

Dad had been calling every day to check on me. I wasn't sure if it was worry or if he wanted to see how Michael was progressing in his pursuit of me. My guess was it was the latter because he seemed awfully disappointed to learn that Michael had not approached me since Monday.

I was seconds off the phone with my dad when Davina gave me

a quick call to ask if I'd make a bracelet for Astrid's birthday. I had texts from Dermot and Darragh, and I'd been on the phone with Dermot for an hour last night talking about the redheaded administrative assistant he was interested in at the station. She sounded too young, and I told him so.

It was nice, though.

It was beyond nice.

My family was in contact with me all the time, and I couldn't be more grateful for how easy they'd made it. How quickly they had welcomed me back into the fold. Darragh even let me chat with Levi and Leo the other night, but since they're kids, talking on the phone was not one of their favorite things.

Still, it was awesome.

What wasn't awesome was the missed call from Bailey and the following text:

You think Michael deserves better than you? What's that about?

When I didn't respond, she sent another:

You're insufferable. But I love you. I'm here when you want to talk. xx

I text her back with a simple "I love you too."

I don't know why I said that about Michael and me. Or maybe I did know. Deep down, perhaps I did.

Rubbing my forehead, I glared at the ring I was working on. Why did Dana Kellerman have to shove her tiny ass into the equation?

"What did that ring ever do to you?"

"Ahhh!" I jumped out of my skin, dropping the mandrel and ring.

Michael stood in the doorway between the store and my workshop, grinning boyishly, mischief in his dark eyes.

As I tried to calm my racing heart, I ignored the anticipation that incited butterflies in my belly. He looked delicious. The stubble on his cheeks had turned into a short beard. In lieu of a jacket, he wore a thick, navy fisherman's sweater. His detective badge was clipped to the black belt he wore through a pair of dark-wash jeans. Why did he have to be so goddamn rugged and masculine? "How did you get in? I didn't hear the bell."

"The bell sounded," he said, strolling farther into the room. "You seemed lost in thought."

I watched him as he rounded the benches until he was standing opposite mine, looking down at me.

Michael's expression was assessing and tender at the same time. "Did I tell you I like your bangs?"

My fingers automatically touched the hair above my eyes. "Oh." I didn't know what else to say. I forgot that when we were younger, I didn't have bangs. Bailey said my bangs made me look like Zooey Deschanel.

"They're cute."

Cute was ... well, it wasn't beautiful or sexy.

As if he could read my mind his eyes dipped down what he could see of my body. I was wearing a floral tea dress that buttoned up the front. It had a low neckline. Michael seemed to more than appreciate my full cleavage. I shivered hotly even before his half-lidded gaze returned to mine. "Sexy and cute. Hard combination to beat."

He was trying to torture me. "What are you doing here?"

"I missed you."

"Michael—"

"I'm allowed to miss you. Plus I wanted to make sure the rumors were wrong."

I frowned. "What rumors?"

"That you and Kell Summers are trying to dress me up like a fuckin' cartoon and parade me through town."

Despite myself, I couldn't help the little smile curling the corners of my mouth. "Well, that rumor is partly true. Kell is trying to do that. Not me. I know you won't do it."

"Of course I won't. Jeff and I have made that clear."

The thought of Dana with Michael agitated the life out of me, and Michael turning up like this hadn't given me enough time to formulate a plan to approach the subject with him. "There's another rumor going around that Dana Kellerman is interested in you."

He studied me thoughtfully, looking for, I imagined, any sign of my distress over this. I kept my expression neutral.

"What about it?"

"Is it true?"

Michael sighed. "Do you care if it's true?"

"I care that Dana Kellerman is not a good person. Whatever goes on between us, Michael, I want the best for you. She is not it. She's far from it."

"People make mistakes, Dahlia."

"So, you know what she did?"

"I do."

"And you think that's okay?"

His dark eyes flashed. "I think people make mistakes."

I scoffed. "And the fact that she's beautiful probably makes it easier to forgive those mistakes."

"Well, I don't know. You're beautiful, and I've forgiven you. Is that why? Because you certainly haven't forgiven me and I have it on your authority I'm pretty fuckin' hot."

Any other time, his words would have made me smile. Not now. "What the hell does that mean?"

"You're holding shit against me, that's what it means." He cursed under his breath and turned away with his hands on his hips. "I didn't come here to argue."

"Why did you come here? To make me jealous about Dana?"

His eyes cut to me. "You brought her up. I didn't."

"She's not a nice person, Michael. And not just because of what she did to Cooper. She's selfish and hollow. You deserve better."

His expression turned hard. "What if I want what I want, deserved or otherwise?" He rounded the bench. I tried to slip off the stool, but he was on me before I could get away. I pushed my back against the bench as he towered over me, forcing his legs between mine. Pressing my hands to his chest, I tried not to think about how good he felt beneath them.

"Michael," I warned, but even I could hear how pitiful and lame it sounded.

His heated stare roamed my face before moving south. A muscle in his jaw flexed, and he trailed his fingertips over my left knee. My breath hitched as he pushed the hem of my dress up my thigh, his touch scattering shivers down my spine. "You need to wear warmer clothes," he muttered, as if to himself.

I curled my fingers into his shirt. "Michael." I wanted to tell him to stop. To go away. But I also didn't. I craved his touch.

His gaze returned to mine. "I'm not interested in Dana Kellerman. You know I'm not. So stop starting fights to push me away." His hand caressed upward, and my body moved of its own volition. My hips shifted so I could widen my legs. Michael's nostrils flared.

His other hand slid through the thick waves of my hair and curled tight around my nape so he could yank me hard against him. His mouth came down over mine as I clung to his shoulders. Our kisses were fierce and thorough, a hungry dance of our tongues and mouths that was so compelling, I wasn't aware of being lifted until I found myself atop my workbench. Michael kicked the stool out of his way and moved in between my legs.

As I lost myself in his voracious, desperate kisses, kisses so full of need, it was impossible to pull myself out of them, I felt his touch between my legs. His fingers slipped beneath my underwear. I jerked in surprise and then groaned as his thumb pressed down on my clit and started to rub.

The swelling sensation came over me so fast that my heart galloped while I struggled to breathe. Tearing my mouth from his, I looked up into his lust-hardened face, clinging to his shoulders in desperation as he pushed me toward climax.

It came for me almost as quickly as it had the last time, the tension he built inside me hitting its peak with sharp ferocity. I wanted to throw my head back and close my eyes, but Michael held me in place, forcing my eyes to stay connected to his. Something about the harsh depth of longing in his expression left me unsatisfied, despite my orgasm.

"Michael." My eyelids fluttered but never closed against him. He'd watched me come with dark satisfaction.

My inner muscles still pulsed as his mouth returned to mine. Impossibly, his kiss was deeper, more insistent, licking inside me, learning me, and I met him kiss for fervent kiss. It was with a jolt of awareness I felt him pull me almost all the way off the bench. I cried out as he broke the kiss and I had to grab onto him tighter for balance as he let me go to unbuckle his belt and unzip his jeans.

This was too far, that voice pounded at the back of my head. *You'll only confuse him.*

Yet the feel of his fingers pulling my underwear down my legs easily silenced that voice. Want, lust, need had overtaken me now. No guy ever made me lose my rational thought so completely as Michael Sullivan. I was a slave to my body when it came to him, and I didn't care. I lifted my legs to aid him.

God, I wanted him.

Seconds later, he was kissing me as he pushed inside me.

"Michael," I breathed, shuddering against him as he worked himself into me.

"Do you know how good you feel?" he panted, his fingers

biting into my thighs. "Nothing feels better than this. Eternity in fuckin' heaven would have nothing on a lifetime of being inside you."

My eyes dampened at his beautiful words, and I lifted my fingers to trace the mouth they'd come out of. His movements inside me should have been fast, furious, but they weren't. He took his time, he savored me.

"I love your mouth," I gasped, focused on the way his lower lip curved inward in the middle. I could nibble on that mouth forever.

"I love *you*," he panted. "So fuckin' much."

It was like a bucket of cold water. *Frigid* water.

The words cut through my rapture.

Oh my God, I was so selfish. What was I doing? I shook my head, tears filling my eyes. "Michael."

As if sensing my retreat, he growled, the sound vibrating down my throat as he crushed his mouth over mine and kissed me back under his spell. That's all it took. His heat surrounding me. His kisses drugging me.

Michael's glides became hard thrusts that pushed me quickly toward climax. Everything about his lovemaking turned frantic, desperate, needy. He left my mouth to trail warm kisses down my throat, his grip biting into my hip as his other hand moved over my body. His fingers plucked at the buttons on my dress so he could push his hand down inside my bra.

I gasped, arching into his touch as he rolled his thumb over my nipple and squeezed my breast in time with a hard thrust of his hips. It was too hard, almost painful, but a pleasure-pain that made me undulate faster against him.

I was mindless.

My body wanted his. It wanted to draw out every inch of pleasure from him and take and take and take.

I came with a guttural cry that echoed around the workshop,

my inner muscles clamping down hard around Michael. He swelled inside me and then throbbed, his hips shuddering against me in pulsing hot waves of wet release.

For a moment we clung to each other, quivering in the aftermath.

Then reality hit.

Cold. Hard. Reality.

What the hell had I done?

"Oh my God." I pushed against him, and Michael lifted his head from where it had been tucked into my neck.

His expression was guarded, wary as he eased off me.

I gasped as he pulled out and his eyes flared with renewed heat. "You on the pill?"

A bit goddamn late to ask that! I nodded. Flustered was an understatement.

"I'm clean, just so you know."

"Me too," I muttered.

Neither of us moved to fix our clothes.

"You're going to say that didn't mean anything," he said, his voice thick with unnamed emotion.

I shook my head, unbearably sad, guilty, and confused. "It will always mean something with you."

"Then don't push me away."

That ugly knot I felt whenever I gave into the idea of Michael and me returned. That ugliness would always be there, stopping me.

And hurting him.

"You shouldn't have come here, Michael."

Indignation flared in his eyes, and I watched helplessly as he put himself to rights. Even in his frustration, he didn't walk out. No, he found my underwear, and despite my protests, he insisted on putting them back on for me. Then he buttoned my dress.

His fingers lingered on the last button, and he looked from it to me. "What aren't you telling me, Dahlia?"

Scared that he might see the abhorrent truth inside me, I shook my head and tried to push him away, to slip off the bench.

But he held me there with the solid strength of his body. "There's something else here. Something I don't get. I'm not that stupid kid, afraid of rejection anymore. I can see past my own bullshit now. And I see you." He tapped a finger against my chest. "You're hiding something. Luckily for me," he leaned down to whisper across my lips, "I dig out people's secrets for a living." He kissed me. It was hard, irate ... until it wasn't. Until it was sweet, tender, and searching. Like he couldn't make himself stay irritated with me.

When Michael let me up for air, his breathing was shallow too. "I'm going to give you some time, some space to think." He retreated and exhaled. "That doesn't mean I'm going anywhere."

"I don't want to hurt you, Michael." I shook my head. "You cloud my emotions so I can't think when you touch me, but that doesn't mean I'll change my mind. And you are the last person I ever want to hurt."

My words did the opposite of what I'd intended—they didn't push him away.

He smiled. Boyish. Hopeful. "I love clouding your emotions. I intend to do it often and well. I'll see you around. Maybe at the Carnival." He winked and walked out of my place with an obvious jaunt to his step. He would be jaunty. He just got himself some in the middle of his working day.

He was also the most stubborn man I'd ever met.

I winced as I hopped off the bench, realizing I needed to clean up. As I walked toward the restroom, I glanced back at the bench and groaned. He'd tainted my workshop. It smelled of sex in here. My diffusers would mask it soon enough.

But no amount of coconut diffusers could scrub away the memory of Michael Sullivan making love to me on my workshop bench.

25

Dahlia

Clouds rolled in over Hartwell that morning. Fortunately, they didn't look heavy with rain. Overcast days were the norm in February, but as long as it stayed dry, we'd have no meltdowns from Kell.

Carrying my sewing kit in one hand, the cloak for Maleficent (I'd had last-minute sewing to do on the hem) in my other, plus my purse, car keys, and a bottle of water, I clattered down the stairwell of my apartment building already feeling flustered. Winter Carnival was a big day for me. The parade moved through town first before the festival kicked off, so I was on call as one of the seamstresses and walked behind the floats. That meant I also had to be in costume, so I dressed as Snow White. After the parade, I had to hurry to the top of Main Street, which we closed to set up a market. My stall was in that market. Thankfully, Bailey was helping me out this year, so she'd set up the stall for me while I was parade-bound.

I wondered if I'd see Michael today.

Nope.

Don't think about him!

Space, he'd said. He was giving me space.

Well, he certainly had done that. The only time I'd seen him in the last two weeks was the previous Friday at Cooper's. He'd been off duty and no surprise he and Cooper got along like a house on fire. Bailey, Jess, and Emery weren't much better. Once Michael decided to be charming, he was goddamn hard to resist. I'd never seen Emery stutter and stammer so much in my life.

And other than a few flirty comments my way, he'd left the bar around eleven o'clock. He'd said good night to everyone but stopped by my side. He'd looked at me a few seconds and then brushed his finger gently across my cheek before he said softly, "Good night, dahlin."

Unfair!

He might as well have kissed me for the way my body reacted to that simple touch.

Oh, and the girls swooned all over that.

Bailey was dying to interrogate me, I could tell. She wanted to know what was stopping me and I couldn't bring myself to explain.

I hadn't seen Michael since that night, but Cooper reminded me that working for the sheriff's department meant Michael wasn't only a cop in Hartwell. He was a cop in the whole county, and although the sheriff's department was based in Hartwell, there were much bigger towns on the west side of the county. Jeff had sent Michael to assist the police department in Georgetown in an investigation over a suspicious suicide.

I guessed that it was keeping him busy while he was giving me space.

The whole giving-me-space thing was making me jumpy. I didn't know when he was going to decide to *stop* giving me space.

Ugh.

Hurrying down the last flight to the first floor, I almost skidded to a stop at the sight of Ivy Green standing in the doorway of the apartment below mine. She grimaced when she saw me, and I would have been insulted if it wasn't for the fact that it seemed to be her reaction to everyone these days.

"I said I'd bring it in." Ira pushed through the door with a box in his hand.

"We need it before we need the box you've got," Iris said behind him.

And then they were both walking down the hall, bickering.

Iris saw me first and her face melted into a huge smile. I smiled in return.

The owners of Antonio's were the funniest, warmest couple I'd ever met. Iris and Ira bickered about everything, but everyone knew they adored each other.

I also knew from my brief chats with Iris that they were extremely worried about Ivy.

"Hey," I said, struggling to keep hold of all the items in my hands. I put my sewing kit box down. "What are you guys doing here?"

"We're moving Ivy in," Ira answered.

"Oh, we're neighbors?" I turned to Ivy. "That's great."

She gave me a listless nod.

I frowned, studying her.

Iris and Ira adopted Ivy when she was a baby. All they knew about her birth parents was that her mother was Filipino and her father was Caucasian. If they hadn't known it, it still would have been evident in their daughter. Ivy was stunning with large dark eyes that tilted slightly upwards and narrowed toward the outer corner. She had a perfect, light-bronze skin tone, high cheekbones, and a small but lush, full-lipped mouth. Anytime I'd met Ivy in the past, her poker-straight, jet-black hair was styled to perfection. Her nails were manicured and her light makeup professional in its application.

The most I'd seen of her in the last few years had been in glossy magazines and online tabloids. She'd met Oliver Frost when he came on board to direct her screenplay about a couple whose daughter had been abducted. It was a thriller. I'd seen it—it was clever.

Anyway, they both were nominated for an Oscar, and while Frost had lost out to another director, Ivy had won the Academy Award for Best Screenplay. I'd never seen Iris and Ira so proud as they were when she won.

So yeah, Ivy was the most stylish, glamorous person I knew.

Or she used to be.

Her dark hair was piled in a messy knot on top of her head. She wore no makeup and had dark circles under her eyes. Her cheeks were wan, she'd lost weight her slender figure couldn't afford to lose, and the sweater and sweatpants she wore were hanging off her.

There was also a ketchup stain on the sweater.

This was not good. No wonder Bailey was so worried about her. Yes, her fiancé had overdosed. It was tragic. Awful. Horrific, really. But this seemed like more than grief. This was like . . .

It was like she'd given up.

That was scary considering what I knew of Ivy, she was sassy, smart, talented, and ambitious. Bailey, who was the most energetic person I'd ever met, had found it hard to keep up with Ivy.

Iris and Ira watched their daughter with worried frowns.

"How are you?" I asked.

Ivy flicked me a dull look. "Fine." She turned to her parents. "I'll be inside unpacking."

I was ashamed to admit I relaxed as soon as she disappeared into the apartment.

"Sorry . . . " Iris's voice lowered. "She's still trying to pick herself up."

"Well . . . " I searched for something positive to say. "She's moving into her own apartment. That's progress."

"We wanted her to stay with us," Iris said, scowling. "She insisted on getting her own place."

"I still think it's a good thing."

"It's on the edge of town. It's a fifteen-minute drive."

"That's not too far."

"At least you're here, Dahlia." Ira pinned me with his concerned dad stare. "You'll watch out for her, won't you?"

"Of course," I responded, even though I was intimidated by the level of depressed Ivy seemed to have reached. It reminded me so much of how low I once got. However, Bailey would be ecstatic that her old friend was living in my apartment building, so I'd do what I could. For Iris, Ira, and for Bailey. "I'll watch out for her."

"Thanks, sweetheart." Ira gave me a genuine smile. "You off to the carnival?"

"Yes. Will I see you there?"

"If we talk the Walking Dead into coming with us," Iris quipped.

"Iris," Ira admonished.

His wife pulled a face and stepped into the apartment, calling goodbye over her shoulder.

"She's just worried," Ira said. "Honest."

"Ira, I've known Iris a long time. I know she's especially sarcastic when she's feeling something deep. It'll get better. Ivy will come out of this."

He nodded, but there was a bleakness in his eyes I hated to see. I sucked in a breath and released it shakily as I opted to share something I usually wouldn't. "A long time ago, I went through something. People who cared about me thought I'd never come out of it. But I did. It takes time."

He gave me a grateful nod. "Thank you, sweetheart."

Returning his nod, I walked away, hoping for their sake I was right.

*

The parade, thankfully, went off without any mishaps. I was needed only once to sew a tear in the shoulder of Cinderella's costume. I'd hurried to the market where Bailey was manning my stall only to find she wasn't alone. Vaughn, Cooper, Jess, and Emery were with her.

They whistled and catcalled as I strode up in my Snow White costume and I rolled my eyes. "Oh yeah, my puffy sleeves are so sexy." I slid in behind the stall and squeezed Bailey's shoulder. "Thanks, babe."

"Anytime. I sold a ring with peridot."

"Great." I glared up at our friends. "You guys will put people off hanging around like this. You're intimidating in a group."

"Gee, thanks." Jess snorted. "And here we came over to ask if you'd like anything to eat or drink."

"Hot chocolate," I said without hesitation. "And a churro would not go amiss."

"Ooh, ditto," Bailey added, reaching for her purse.

"No, I got it." I opened my cash box.

"Neither of you has it," Vaughn said. He followed Jess, Coop, and Emery, strolling off to get our order.

"Does he let you pay for anything?" I watched the tall, stupidly handsome hotelier walk away. He had a strong swimmer's build beneath his wool coat and suit pants. I had Bailey's description and a good imagination, so I knew he was drool-worthy model perfect beneath his expensive clothing.

"Are you ogling my fiancé?"

I released a weary exhale. "I'm sorry. I'm ... " *Sexually frustrated, horny, turned on all the time and have been since Michael Sullivan screwed me in my workshop.*

Not that I'd told Bailey about the incident. She would use it as an excuse to make me talk about my feelings.

"You're ...?"

"Exhausted," I lied. "I'll be glad when the carnival is over."

"Sacrilege!"

I jumped in my seat as Kell Summers appeared out of nowhere. He was dressed like a very short but handsome Prince Charming.

He glowered down at me. "Just for saying that, I am no longer asking you to do what I was about to ask you to do. I'm telling you."

Oh no. What was I about to get roped into now? "I'm afraid to ask."

"Speed dating. We're hosting it in Bailey's fiancé's hotel."

"His name is Vaughn," Bailey offered.

Kell grinned. "But calling him your fiancé sounds so much better, doesn't it?"

"Can't argue with that."

"Which reminds me"—he leaned on my stall—"I'd like to talk to you about letting me do a reading at your wedding. It's a little homage to your history here as a descendant of a founding family."

I could almost feel Bailey's need to scream, so I cut in, "Uh, Kell, speed dating?"

"Oh, right. We're trying it out. Next weekend. I'm roping all of our singles into it, and you do count as a single despite a rumor or two about you and a certain detective." He winked at me.

Oh, kill me now.

Goddamn small towns and their running mouths.

"Kell—"

"You're doing it, Dahlia. No arguments." With one last severe look, he flounced off in the costume I'd painstakingly helped put together.

I turned to my best friend and held up my hands. "Do you see these? I have cuts and scrapes and little needle holes all over them because I've helped Annie and Jake make over twenty-five costumes in the last few months. The majority of participants rent or buy their costumes for the parade, so why am I making this stuff? Why can't we all rent our costumes? It makes no sense! I spend a third of my year making costumes for that man. When will it ever be enough?"

Bailey was less than sympathetic. "When you say no."

I groaned and dropped my head to the table. "Life is not a fucking fairy tale."

A deep, throaty chuckle sounded above me and skated down my spine. Awareness rushed through me, and I slowly sat up to meet Michael's gaze. I wished he wouldn't keep popping up out of nowhere like that.

He was distracted from his intense focus on my face as Vaughn, Cooper, Jess, and Emery returned to the stall with our food.

"What are you doing here?" I noted he wasn't wearing his badge.

Michael's eyes drifted over me, taking in my costume. "Day off. Nice dress. Where'd ya leave the dwarves?"

"Speaking of trolls," Bailey interrupted as Vaughn handed her a hot chocolate. She smiled sweetly at Michael. "Word is that Dana Kellerman is on the prowl for you. Must be nice to receive such extreme attention from the town's ex-beauty queen."

Michael's lips spread into a slow grin and he shook his head. "I can see why you and Dahlia became friends."

"Why's that?"

"Because you're both full of shit," he teased.

Vaughn choked on a sip of coffee while Cooper gave a bark of laughter.

Bailey, for once, was speechless, which made me smile.

"You're right," Vaughn said to Cooper. "I like him."

"Watch it, pal." Bailey narrowed her eyes on her fiancé. "I'm the one who controls your access to certain activities." She turned from Vaughn to Michael. "How am I full of shit?"

He shrugged. "You want to know if I'm interested in someone

other than Dahlia, all you have to do is ask. If that's not what you're doing and you're trying to press Dahlia's buttons, then I'm going to have to ask you to stop." His dark gaze came to mine. "What's between us is between us and no one else."

"Ugh." Bailey shot me a look. "Blunt and up-front *and* handsome. He's ridiculously likable." I could almost hear her silent "What's wrong with you?" at the end of her speech.

"Okay, maybe I don't like him," Vaughn said.

Bailey chuckled but reached out to squeeze Vaughn's free hand. He curled his fingers around hers, and their eyes locked. They shared a look of such genuine connection and affection, it made me breathless with longing. And frustration. Because I could have that with Michael. If I could find a way to dissolve the knot of paralyzing fear in my stomach, I could be free to be with Michael.

"How are you liking Hartwell?" Jess asked Michael, snapping me out of my dismal thoughts.

"Good so far. I like the sea air more than I thought I would."

"Yeah, Cooper said you two have been running together on the beach."

They were? Since when?

I looked between Michael and Cooper, feeling slightly panicked that my ex was making such good friends with *my* friends.

"I used to run every morning back in Boston before hitting the gym. Sand adds extra resistance. It's good."

I took in Michael's body. He wore a dark cable-knit sweater with a row of three buttons at the neck he'd left open so you could see a sliver of the stark white shirt he wore beneath it. Again, he was in dark-wash jeans and boots. As long as I'd known Michael, he'd favored a lack of color in his wardrobe.

Jess patted Cooper's rock-hard stomach. "You guys gotta work off those burgers and beers, I guess," she teased.

Cooper smirked and shook his head. "Mike here is a health nut."

He was?

My gaze returned to Michael. He was studying me thoughtfully. I almost flushed under his intense regard.

"Really?" Jess asked.

Michael nodded and appeared reluctant to turn his head from me to her. "Body needs the right fuel."

Michael wasn't a health nut when we were younger, that was for sure, but it would explain his body. I'd seen Cooper running shirtless down the beach, and it was a sight to behold. The man had abs and muscles and all the yum. However, there was a rippling, steely hardness to Michael's body. His abs and his ass were ... ah, just thinking about them made me squirm in my seat.

Michael was a health nut.

It irritated me that Cooper knew that, and I did not.

It agitated me that Jess knew Michael was running down the beach every morning, and I did not.

What else didn't I know about him that other people knew?

That other *women* knew?

God, his ex-wife must know so much more about him than I did. Why did that hurt so much? It felt like someone had shoved a shaft of metal through my chest. Breathing was momentarily difficult.

"If you're looking for quality health food options, there's a deli on the outskirts of Atlantic Village," Jess said. "It's a luxury apartment block about four miles away."

"I'm renting a place there," Michael replied. "The deli is good."

Everyone, including myself, looked at him in surprise. Atlantic Village was not cheap. There was also a waiting list for those apartments. Considering the amount of gossip about Michael's appearance, I was surprised we hadn't heard about this from an outside source.

Michael's beautiful mouth curled at the corners. "Jeff pulled some strings, got me in past the waiting list. It's only temporary until I find somewhere more long term."

"So, you're staying, then?" Bailey piped up.

Instead of looking at her, he looked at me. "That's the hope."

Before I could die of discomfort, Jess intervened. "Emery, what are you staring at so hard?"

Emery blushed while Jess looked out into the crowded market. "Nothing," she mumbled, biting her lip.

Unfortunately, Jess's words made us all strain to look—even Michael stepped aside to turn around—and while the guys continued to look perturbed, Bailey, Jess, and I zeroed in on our suspected source of Emery's attention.

Jack Devlin.

Jack became kind of a leper in Hartwell society after betraying Cooper. No one trusted him, and he grew sullen. There was more to the story behind Jack's defection to the dark side. Even Cooper knew that, but any concern he had for his friend had been overwhelmed (quite rightly) by his betrayal. Coop had moved on.

Bailey and I weren't ready to. We both remembered who Jack used to be. We both had big imaginations, and we couldn't help but wonder if there was some sinister reason for his change in behavior. Bailey was even more forgiving than me because she thought she witnessed a spark between him and Emery and had all these romantic notions of Emery redeeming him.

I loved Emery.

Emery apparently had no experience with men.

I did not want her near Jack Devlin.

That would be like pushing a baby panda into a tiger cage. The thought brought out the hotheaded mama bear in me.

No Jack Devlin for Emery Saunders.

Nope!

Jack was standing in line at a temporary burger hut while a short, cute brunette who had to be a tourist stood by his side, chatting away. Only he wasn't paying attention to the brunette. Jack was around six four with a lean build and broad shoulders. He kept his dark-blond hair thick and slightly disheveled so he always looked like he'd just rolled out of bed. His broody, too-handsome-for-his-own-good, blue-gray gaze was locked on Emery.

That look was so intense, it made *me* hot.

This was not good.

Not good at all.

The woman with him pulled on his elbow, and he jerked out of his Emery daze to turn to his date.

"What are we looking at?" Vaughn asked.

"Nothing." Bailey was near squirming with excitement in her seat. I nudged her with my elbow, *hard*, and she glared at me. I glowered back.

"I ... uh ... I think I'm going to call it a day," Emery said. She refused to meet anyone's eyes.

"Oh, don't go," Bailey begged.

"She can go if she wants to," I said through gritted teeth.

My best friend narrowed her eyes on me. "I don't want her to go."

"It doesn't matter what you want, especially when your head is in cloud-cuckoo-land."

"I feel like we're missing something," Vaughn said to Cooper.

He nodded. "Agreed."

Bailey huffed. "You're making it sound like you don't want Emery here."

"I love Emery—of course I want her here—but I want *her* here. You want something else entirely." I leaned into her and hissed, "And it's insane."

"Uh ... ladies." Michael stepped closer to the stall, drawing our attention upward. "Your friend is already gone."

With a sigh of frustration, I noted the spot next to Jess was now empty, and Jess was staring at us like a disappointed schoolteacher.

"See what you did?" Bailey grumbled.

I leaned in and whispered in her ear, "If you don't back off Emery, I will tell Cooper and Vaughn about the madness swirling in your head, and they'll guard her ass so fast from Jack Devlin, your hopes will be crushed for good."

"Princess." I moved back to see Vaughn leaning over the stall table, his hands flat to it, his face inches from Bailey's. "What is going on?"

"Nothing." She gave him a bright smile, leaned forward, and pecked him on the lips. "All good."

"Then why does Dahlia, a woman who would usually throw herself in front of a bus for you, look like she wants to kill you? What are you up to and what does it have to do with Emery?"

Bailey crossed her arms defensively and narrowed her eyes. "Don't talk to me like that. Ever."

I gave my head a little shake. Bailey Hartwell was a master at deflection. Vaughn blinked in surprise at her snappish tone and she pushed back her chair. "I need a coffee."

Suspicion deepened in Vaughn's expression as he watched Bailey walk away. "Excuse me," he muttered before striding after her.

I lost them in the crowds and shot a look at Jessica.

"She's not genuinely annoyed at Vaughn?"

I rolled my eyes. "More like worried how well he knows her."

"Is this about who I think it's about?" Cooper was not amused.

Did Cooper know about Jack and Emery?

Oh boy.

"Why do I feel like I'm in high school?" Michael asked, perturbed.

Jess laughed. "Welcome to small-town life. Everyone is in everyone else's business."

"Speaking of . . . " Cooper frowned into the distance. "Who is that guy with my sister? And where's Joey?" He marched away, his hand tight in Jess's so she had no choice but to follow. She threw me a little wave, and I nodded back, feeling more than a flutter of butterflies at being left alone with Michael.

"Joey is Cooper's nephew, right?" Michael moved closer to the stall.

"Yeah." I nodded, straining back against my stool, even though there was a table between us. "He's almost ten, kind of a musical genius, and Cooper is more like a dad to him than an uncle."

"I get that impression."

I crossed my arms over my chest and studied him. "You seem to be making fast friends with him."

"He's a good guy."

"Michael, what are you doing?" I threw my hands up in exasperation. "Why are you doing this?"

"I've missed you. Have you missed me?" He avoided my question, leaning his hands on the table. "These past few weeks, have you missed me?"

More than anything.

Worse, despite not seeing him, I was becoming used to the idea of him living here, knowing he was in the same town, keeping everyone safe. Keeping *me* safe. I loved knowing that.

I loved it almost as much as the knot in my stomach resented it.

"Mike!"

I flinched at the voice.

I knew that voice.

I *hated* that voice.

Dana Kellerman's appearance followed on the heels of her voice. He pushed away from my table to turn to her. My eyes drifted down her tall body of toned curves, and I felt stupid and childish *and* plump in my Snow White costume. It was my own fault. I'd made the Lycra outfit for Dana, and it fitted her athletic body like a second skin. The Elastigirl costume should've looked stupid. It did not. The red looked great against her tanned complexion. She usually wore her long hair in beachy waves, but she'd tied it up into a high ponytail that accentuated and elongated her feline ice-blue eyes. She had a perfect little nose and perfect lips and perfect high cheekbones, and she was sans mask because why would she hide such a perfect face?

Dana Kellerman was one of the most beautiful women I'd ever met in real life, and I'd never hated her for it before. It wasn't in my nature to be jealous of other women's looks. However, seeing her in all her glory, smiling flirtatiously into Michael's eyes, I hated her.

She was so tall, she was almost the same height as him, and her legs went on forever in thigh-high black stiletto boots.

Hateful shrew.

"Mike, I'm glad I found you. I've got some kids from the parade at the ice cream shack, and they are desperate to meet a real-life, big-city detective. Will you come talk to them, please?"

Ugh.

Manipulative, hateful shrew!

She didn't care about kids. She didn't care about anything but getting into Michael's pants.

Dana placed a hand on his bicep and tilted her head to the side, pretty much fluttering her lashes at him. "Please."

Michael turned his head toward me. "You make all these costumes?"

Surprised by the question, I softened my scowl. "Dana's, and a few others. The rest are rentals."

He looked at me for a long, intense moment. "You're so talented, dahlin'. Everyone looks amazing."

That he had turned how fantastic Dana looked into something *I* had done was merely proof that Michael Sullivan was the best guy in the world. I couldn't help my smile. "Thank you."

He grinned at me.

"Oh." Dana looked at me, and I saw the flash of catty calculation in her icy eyes. "Yeah, Dahlia is great. So great, I know she won't mind if I steal you away. I know she's not exactly the maternal type, but even Dahlia wouldn't keep you from the kids."

Bitch.

I gave her a pinched smile. "Of course, I wouldn't. They're so very, very, very *desperate*, after all."

Michael coughed into his fist, and I grinned harder at him, making his dark eyes dance. He wasn't interested in Dana Kellerman. He wasn't interested in anyone but me, and that shouldn't make me as happy as it did. Was there ever a woman more complicated than me?

"You should go to the kids," I said. "They really will be excited to meet you. And thicken the accent. They'll love that."

His reticence was evident, but he nodded, and I watched as Dana threaded her arm through his and led him away through the crowds.

"What was that?" Bailey barked in my ear.

"Oh my God!" I nearly fell off my stool. I turned around to see her standing behind me with her hands on her slim hips. "Are you trying to give me a heart attack?"

"Did you just let Michael walk away with Dana Kellerman?"

"Did you just pretend to be upset with Vaughn to deflect from your devious matchmaking plans?"

We glared at each other.

Then Bailey rolled her eyes and slipped onto the stool next to mine. "It wasn't totally a pretense. Vaughn has a tendency toward high-handedness. I need to remind him who he's dealing with now and then."

"He knows you're up to something."

"Of course he does. He knows me too well. You didn't help by almost ratting me out." She blew a raspberry at me. "He sees everything in black and white when it comes to the people he cares for. He wouldn't understand Emery and Jack."

"There is no Emery and Jack." I grabbed her hand. "Bails, I adore you, you know that, but I don't get this. You hate Dana and Jack for what they did to Cooper. Why would you push Emery toward Jack Devlin?"

"Because she's stronger than you all think. You all want to coddle and protect her, but maybe what she needs is to be pushed outside her comfort zone. There are things she's not telling us. And there are things that Jack is not telling us. You forget I grew up with Jack Devlin. I hero-worshipped the guy. He is not a bad person, Dahlia." She shook her head. "He punched out Stu when he heard his brother attacked me, and he gave Jess a heads-up about his dad coming after Cooper's liquor license."

This was true. When Jess and Cooper first started dating, Ian Devlin had been harassing Cooper about buying his bar for months. Devlin had bribed someone on the city board of licenses so that Cooper's liquor license wouldn't be renewed, thus forcing him out of business. Cooper would never have found out until it was too late if Jack hadn't warned Jessica about it.

It was Jess's idea to make all of us who owned businesses on the boardwalk sign a petition stating we'd close our doors if Cooper's license wasn't renewed. Jess and Cooper took the petition to the city council, and the chairwoman saw it was in her best interest, and in the interest of our tourist economy, to investigate and renew his license.

"You know that I agree with you about Jack. That there's more to his story." I leaned toward my friend, hoping my words would sink in. "And I agree that Emery isn't telling us everything about her past. There's a reason she's so introverted and shy. And yes, that does make me want to handle her with care because I have this awful feeling that someone *didn't* handle her with care, Bailey."

Bailey sat back, her eyes darkening with worry.

"Jack is hiding something. That's a man riddled with issues. I know Emery has a crush on him. Anyone with eyes can see that. But speaking as a woman riddled with issues who has a good person interested in her . . . I don't want Emery to go through what Michael is going through. She needs someone gentle, who has his shit together. Don't push this. Please."

After a moment's study, Bailey nodded. "I'll leave them alone."

"Good." I heaved a sigh of relief.

"But I can't leave what you just said alone. You are not Jack Devlin, Dahlia. And Michael is not Emery. You *are* a good person. You *do* deserve Michael. And whatever demon is holding you hostage"—she squeezed my arm tight, her eyes blazing with sincerity and concern—"you have to let it go before you lose Michael forever."

"Bailey—"

"Have you thought about it? Really thought about it? What your life will look like again without him in it?"

I had.

It was hollow and empty and cold.

But it would be more than Dillon would ever get to have.

"These are for sale, right?" A female voice drew us out of our conversation. A tourist stood at the stall wearing a curious expression, glancing between us.

I forced a smile, pretending like I wasn't seconds away from falling apart, and gestured to my jewelry. "Yes. And it's all handmade."

26

Dahlia

Bailey was right. I needed to say *no* to Kell Summers. Maybe even *hell no*!

Gazing around the conference room in Vaughn's hotel, my stomach gave an unhappy lurch. It had been a week since the carnival, I'd avoided Michael and all the serious thoughts that came with him, but I had not avoided Kell Summers.

Kell had set up tables in two long rows with chairs opposite each other for the speed-dating event. The room was buzzing with familiar and not-so-familiar faces, so I surmised that the rumors were true. The event had attracted people from all over the county.

Dating was no big deal to me.

I'd started serial dating in my mid-twenties, and I'd used every app and online dating site available. Dating had led me all over our small state, and I'd gone on dates in Philadelphia, Maryland, and New Jersey. Very few of those dates had turned into anything resembling a relationship, and as soon as I realized that's what it was, I'd walked away.

The longest "relationship" I'd been in was with Jeff King. I'd considered it more a fling, but it had lasted three months. Subconsciously, I knew it was getting serious, but the sex was so good, I hadn't wanted to give him up. Plus, Jeff was great. He reminded me a little of Michael. However, he *wasn't* Michael, and when it became clear he was developing real feelings for me, I broke things off. It wasn't fair to Jeff, or to any man, to be with a woman who could never love him the way he deserved.

I'd returned to my serial dating, and it was a way to pass the time and deal with that pesky sexual frustration (although to be fair, my vibrator did a better job more often than not), so speed dating shouldn't have bothered me.

Yet, it bothered me.

It bothered me greatly.

Because Kell Summers hadn't only talked me into doing it.

Michael *and* Jeff were in the room.

Michael saw me as soon as I walked in, but he'd been cornered by Dana Kellerman. Surprise, surprise. He nodded at me, and I gave him a small wave in greeting. Jeff had also been talking to a woman, someone I didn't recognize, when he saw me. Nervousness shot through me as he excused himself and strode across the room.

Jeff was tall, and there was something about the way he walked that reminded me of the way cowboys swaggered in the old Hollywood movies. He had a rangy build, not thick muscle like Michael, but lean and hard. All of that was good. Very masculine, rugged, sexy goodness. And he knew what to do with it in the bedroom. I flushed and forced those memories away.

There was gladness in Jeff's blue eyes that told me he was happy to see me.

It wasn't that I wasn't happy to see Jeff. I was. I was always glad to see him. But my mind was whirring, wondering if Michael had worked out my history with his boss.

"You look beautiful." Jeff perused my outfit.

I was wearing a vintage red pencil dress that accentuated every generous curve of my body, matching red platform peep-toes with a delicate ankle strap, and I wore my long dark hair in waves down my back. Bright red lipstick finished my not-quite-but-almost fifties pinup look. "Thanks. You look good too." He did. He always did. "But who is manning the station with the sheriff and his detective here?"

He grinned at my teasing. "I was harassed into doing this and if I have to do it, why suffer alone?"

I bit my lip and peeked around his shoulder at Michael, who was glaring daggers at Jeff's back. Michael didn't throw out dirty looks willy-nilly.

Shit, he knew.

"He knows about us," Jeff confirmed.

I studied him. "What do you know about Michael and me?"

"Not a lot. He's pretty closemouthed. I know you know each other from Boston. That he's here because of you. He mentioned he let you slip through his fingers once before and he wasn't going to let it happen again."

He'd said that? To Jeff?

"Jeff, I—"

"Is he the reason, Dahlia?"

I knew what he was asking. Was Michael the reason I'd broken things off with him? "Yes."

"Then why are you here with me and he's over there with Dana?"

"It's complicated."

"Only if you make it complicated." He glanced over his shoulder before turning back to me with a playful smirk. "And it looks like Mike isn't trying hard enough." He bent his head to my ear, rested his hand on my hip, and whispered, "Maybe I should give him a little push."

My eyes flew to Michael. His features were taut as he watched Jeff and me. Then quite abruptly, he nudged Dana aside to make his way toward us. Jeff had already retreated. My heart raced like a jackhammer.

"Ladies and gentlemen!" Kell's voice boomed over the PA system and stopped Michael in his tracks. "Welcome to Hartwell's first-ever speed-dating event. I'll now ask the ladies to take a seat on this side of the room"—he gestured to the chairs that had their backs to the entrance—"and the gentlemen to take the seats opposite. When the bell sounds, you can commence flirting. When the bell sounds again, we'll ask the gentlemen to move one seat to their right."

I shot Jeff a worried look. "I don't think playing games with one of your employees is a particularly good idea, Jeff."

"Who says I'm playing games?" His expression was hot.

Oh, great. Just what I needed. More unwanted male attention. Why the hell had I let Kell talk me into this?

I avoided Michael as I crossed the room to take one of the last seats left. The men were already taking their seats, which meant Michael and Jeff were two of the last to do so as well. Jeff grabbed a chair four places to my left and Michael was three to my right.

My smile was pained as I scanned the guy across from me. He looked to be in his late to early forties, balding, skinny, and had a pinched, mouse-like countenance. His shirt was buttoned up to his throat, and I winced. Could he even breathe?

The bell rang, and Mousy Man spoke first. Loudly. "You're not my type."

My eyebrows rose. "Excuse me?"

"I thought I'd put that out there, so we don't waste any time here."

Unsurprisingly, this was not the rudest thing a guy had said to me on a date. "I gather you're only interested in women for their physical appearance?"

Mousy Man frowned. "No."

"You didn't even let me speak before you determined I wasn't your type, so I must politely disagree."

"Uh ... well ... " He shifted uncomfortably. "It's just ... I like my women thin."

"Did I hear you correctly?" Michael said from my right.

He was apparently not paying attention to the woman across from him but listening in on my "date."

"Michael," I warned.

"Do you have a problem?" Mousy Man asked Michael.

Michael leaned past the guys next to him to glare at my date. "You watch your manners."

Everyone on our side of the table grew quiet.

Then I heard Jeff pipe up. "Problem down there?"

Oh my God, kill me now.

"Michael, I can handle myself," I hissed.

He ignored me and called down to Jeff. "Sheriff, we got a guy here with no manners."

"Is that right? Well, I can see a couple guys in the room who didn't get a seat," Jeff said.

I didn't hear the rest of the conversation because I'd put my forehead to the table in mortification and was blocking the room out.

"I can't wait to get to him," the woman next to me whispered. "I love a man with good manners. And God, those arms. Yum."

I was officially in hell.

The scraping of chairs and the soft protests of Mousy Man brought my head up. Jace, a young bartender at Cooper's, slid into the seat in his place, while Kell manhandled Mousy Man out of the room. I turned back to Jace and his cocky grin. "Hey, Dahlia. Sorry I'm late." His eyes drifted over me. "You look hot."

I rolled my eyes because Jace was the biggest flirt on the planet. "What are you doing here? Like you need help to get a date."

"Like *you* need help to get a date," he countered, and then leaned across the table conspiratorially. "So, what's with the sheriff and the good detective ousting your last date?"

"He pretty much called me fat and was loud about it so they decided I'm a four-year-old who can't handle herself."

Jace nodded, his attention dipping downward. "Asshole. You're not fat. You're perfect."

"Eyes off my boobs, Jace."

His gaze drifted slowly upward. "Sorry. It's just they're right the—"

"I know. They're right there."

The bell rang before Jace could respond, and he winked at me before moving to the woman on his right, my left. The guy moving toward the vacant seat grinned at me, and I was about to return his open smile when Michael appeared and clamped a hand on his shoulder. "Sorry, this seat's taken."

He slid into the seat opposite me before the man could protest. We stared at each other like it was a contest while the guy floundered in our peripheral vision before eventually disappearing.

"That's not how this works," I said.

"She's right," the woman next to me piped in, a petulant tone to her voice. "You missed me entirely."

Michael flicked her an impatient look and then turned back to me. "What are you doing here?"

"What are you doing here?" I rebutted.

"Jeff coerced me into being his wingman. I didn't realize it meant being his wingman while he was all over you."

I cut him a dirty look. "I saw Dana keeping you company."

"I haven't touched her."

"I know." I sighed. "That's why she's still hounding you."

"Can't say the same for you and Jeff."

"Not here, Michael." I shook my head.

He leaned across the table, his voice low. "Just tell me one thing."

Caught in his eyes, I found it impossible to look away. "What?"

"Is he the guy? The one who made you temporarily forget me?"

I winced, sorry I'd admitted that and even sorrier that Michael hadn't forgotten. "That ... came out wrong."

"Well?"

"Michael ..."

"I'll take that as a yes."

Hearing the hardness in his voice, I impulsively reached for his hand to stop his withdrawal. "It's not what you think."

He covered my hand with his other, and I shivered under his smoldering attention. There was no other word for it. He *smoldered*. But I was the one catching fire. "Is this your idea of fun?"

"Speed dating?" I scoffed. "No, I'm in hell." I yanked my hand out of his, remembering his actions only minutes ago. "And for the record, I don't need you to protect me from dipshits. You embarrassed me."

"That little fucker is lucky I'm a police officer, or he'd have walked out of here with more than a red face. No one talks to you like that."

I hated how conflicted he made me feel. His actions annoyed me, but his sentiment did not. "I've been taking care of myself for a long time."

"Yeah, too long."

The bell rang, but Michael didn't move. He kept his focus on my face and without looking away said to the guy hovering beside him, "Move along."

After a moment of confusion, the man departed.

"Are you seriously going to stay here all night?"

He nodded, crossing his arms over his chest. He wore a dark Henley that showcased his superb physique. The muscles in his arms flexed with his movement and my mouth went dry. Why couldn't he be overly muscular and massive in a way I found off-putting? Why did he have to be that perfect amount of hard, delicious, well-maintained strength that suited his height and build? I wished he was naked so I could lick him.

Ugh. I scolded myself for the wayward thoughts.

"You're ogling." Amusement threaded his words.

I flushed at being caught and then narrowed my eyes in irritation. "You wore that shirt deliberately."

Laughter spilled from his lips. "Men wear clothes because it's the law. They don't wear clothes *deliberately*."

"Some men do."

His dark eyes dropped to my cleavage and then moved to my lips. "You chose that outfit deliberately."

"I didn't know you'd be here."

"Which makes it worse. You chose it for other guys."

"I chose it for myself. I dress for myself." I glowered. "If you remembered anything about me, you'd remember that."

He cocked his head in thought. "I distinctly remember a set of underwear you admitted to wearing just for me."

Heat spread through me at the memory. We'd been fooling around in his car, and I was wearing a satin emerald-green bra and underwear I'd bought for him. The lingerie had taken our making out from slow and delicious to hungry and determined. He was seconds from pushing inside me for the first time when we were interrupted.

I shrugged off the melancholy memory. "Lingerie is different."

"You buy lingerie for Jeff?"

Seeing the flash of jealousy in his eyes, I crossed my arms over my chest and countered, "Did your *wife* buy lingerie for you?"

The bell rang again.

Michael didn't budge. Again.

"Hey, man, you're supposed to move." A cute guy with a thick head of dark hair and glasses said to Michael. His eyes flicked to me with interest.

Cute.

Michael didn't think so. He turned to stare coolly up at the guy. Then he did the unthinkable and unclipped his badge from his belt and held it up. "Move. Along."

The guy scurried.

Actually scurried.

Amusement I didn't want to feel pushed at the corners of my mouth. "You didn't just flash your badge at that guy."

Michael recognized the laughter in my eyes and grinned. "I'll do what I must."

Kell appeared beside Michael. "Detective Sullivan ... you're supposed to move along every time the bell rings."

"I know how it works."

"Then why are you hogging Ms. McGuire? Do I need to ask the sheriff to intervene?"

Michael glanced around the room and found Jeff at the table behind us. "Jeff, it going to piss you off if I don't move from this seat?"

The room grew quiet as Jeff looked over, his gaze dancing between us, and if I wasn't mistaken, he found this funny! "Make you a deal—you let me switch seats with you at the next bell, I'll give you that seat back when the bell rings again, and I won't make you move."

Michael's shoulders tensed.

Jeff grinned. "I'd say that's a fair deal."

"But Sheriff," Kell whined, "that's not how this works."

"Well, Sullivan?" Jeff ignored the councilman.

My cheeks grew hotter as everyone turned to stare at me in curiosity as these two so-called professional cops (professional assholes more like it!) bartered over time with me.

"Let me make the decision easier." I pushed away from the table, not sure who I wanted to smack more. Snatching up my purse, I whirled and strode out, ignoring Kell's protests.

"Dahlia!" Michael called after me, but I pushed open the conference room doors and marched out of there as fast as my high heels would let me.

I was hurrying across the shiny tiled floor of the main reception when I was abruptly whirled around and hauled up against Michael's hard body. He gripped both my arms; I pushed against him.

"Let me go."

His expression was equal parts indignation and concern. "Dahlia, stop."

"No. You stop," I hissed, not wanting to make a scene. "Were you trying to humiliate me in there?"

His jaw clenched. "You know I wasn't."

"No." I jerked away with all my strength and stumbled out of his grasp. "You were just metaphorically peeing around me."

Jeff appeared beside us, the crest of his cheeks flushed. "Dahlia, are you okay?"

"I'm mad at you too," I announced.

He ran a hand through his hair and sighed. "I'm sorry, we didn't—"

"Didn't what? Mean to act like Neanderthal teenagers?" I scowled between them as both their faces darkened at my insult. "You're the sheriff, and you're a detective. And I'm a *person*. You are not two dogs fighting over a chew toy."

"Dahlia, you know that's not fair," Michael huffed.

"You know what's not fair? Being gossip fodder for this town. What did you two think would happen in there?" I gestured toward the room. "You think it's a joke? Michael maybe has an excuse, but Jeff, you've lived here long enough to know what happens when something like this gets out. Especially when a jealous Dana Kellerman is in the room. All of a sudden I'm the tramp who's stringing along the sheriff and his new detective."

"If anyone dares even say that . . . " Michael bristled.

But contrition softened Jeff's expression—he knew I was right. When I broke up with him a few years ago, people had gossiped about me, and a lot of it had been nasty. "I'm sorry, Dahlia."

Exhausted, irritated, dreading the consequences of their juvenile antics, I shook my head and was about to walk away when a commotion at the front of the hotel drew our attention. We turned to see Deputy Wendy Rawlins and Deputy Eddie Myers hurrying across the lobby toward Jeff.

"Sheriff." Wendy almost skidded to a halt.

Jeff and Michael grew alert at the deputies' drawn, pale expressions. "What's wrong?" Jeff asked.

"I know you're off duty but ... " Wendy glanced around and saw I was close enough to overhear. She turned to Jeff. "Sheriff, we need you and Detective Sullivan to come with us right away."

My heart raced at the grim seriousness in Wendy's tone and the deep concern that etched itself into Michael's and Jeff's faces.

"On our way," Jeff said. He looked down at me. "We'll talk later."

I nodded, my anger defused under the heavy, horrible vibe the deputies had brought into the hotel with them.

Jeff strode away with his officers, but Michael lingered. His expression softened at my concerned countenance.

"Be careful."

"Always am." There was so much in his eyes. So much I knew he wanted to say. He seemed to decide on an apology. "I'm sorry if I was a dick in there. I'm ... I'm terrified of losing you again."

Tears brightened my eyes as he lowered his head, rubbing the back of his neck in a way that made him seem vulnerable. I didn't like Michael vulnerable. I especially didn't like him vulnerable as he walked away from me into a possibly dangerous situation.

"What was that about?" Vaughn crossed the lobby toward me.

He watched the officers disappear. I heaved a sigh, my stomach roiling with anxiety. "I have no idea. Something bad, I think."

"So it would seem." His spectacular silver eyes focused on me. "Are you all right?"

"My life is one giant soap opera, Vaughn."

"That would be a no, then?"

"That would be a hell no."

27

Michael

Michael had come to learn a lot about the Devlin family in the last month since his arrival in Hartwell. He knew Ian Devlin along with his wife Rosalie, who was a bit of a hermit, and their youngest child Jamie all lived together in the Glades. It was a community of wealthy homes in the north of Hartwell. The Glades, despite their price tag, was not the prime real estate in town. There were several houses down the coast from the boardwalk, separated by land, that were worth millions. Vaughn Tremaine owned one of the sought-after beach houses that sat out over the water. Michael had garnered enough knowledge to know it would be a craw in Devlin's throat that he didn't own one of those homes.

Rebecca Devlin, the only daughter, left town four years ago for graduate school in England and had not returned since.

Kerr Devlin, the second-eldest son lived in a penthouse suite of the family's hotel, The Hartwell Grand.

As for his second-youngest son, Jack, his house was a nice but average home in South Hartwell.

The eldest, Stu, lived in a beautiful family-sized home on Johnson Creek. The creek fed into Hartwell Bay on the southern coast. If you didn't own a rare, spectacular oceanfront home, and you didn't mind trading in a mansion-sized home in the Glades for location, you bought a house on Johnson Creek. Stu Devlin's house was more than he needed. It was also on the bend of the creek with a private dock, and far enough away from its neighbors that someone could fire a gun and not be heard.

Which meant no one knew Stu Devlin was dead until the married woman he was screwing around with let herself into the house.

Michael stood in Stu's glossy white kitchen as Stu's body, now in a body bag, was loaded onto a gurney. There was blood splattered across the back window of the kitchen that faced the creek. Blood on the floor where Stu had died.

From what they'd surmised, and they'd know more once the coroner looked at the body, the two entry wounds were almost one hole, they were so close together. And they were on the chest, near the sternum.

The wounds were consistent with how a police officer was trained to shoot.

There had been an anonymous tip at the station that Freddie Jackson was involved in the selling and dealing of cocaine. No one had seen Freddie Jackson in hours. He didn't come into the station for his shift, and his car had been abandoned two miles from here on the side of the road.

"We got the emergency search warrant." Jeff strode into the kitchen. "Wendy called it in. They found four bags of coke and $10,000 in hundred-dollar bills in Jackson's apartment."

"Fuck," Michael bit out. Impotence and anger filled him.

By all accounts, Stu Devlin was a piece of shit but one that deserved to be behind bars, not fuckin' dead.

"Twelve years," Michael muttered.

"What?" Jeff asked, frowning.

"The last time there was a murder in Hartwell. It was twelve years ago." Michael had done his research before moving here. Although there had been a couple of murder cases in the county, the town of Hartwell had been spared for years. Possibly because the sheriff's department was based there, so Hartwell had more deputies patrolling the streets because of the number of tourists who poured in throughout the year. When it came to violent crime, there'd been physical and sexual assault cases in Hartwell, the highest percentage of which were committed by visitors.

But there hadn't been a murder case in Hartwell in twelve years. Not until Michael arrived.

"We wanted to spook him, Jeff." He rubbed a hand across the nape of his neck, agitated. "This wasn't supposed to happen. I've seen a lot of bad shit over the years. I've never played my part in the cause of it before."

Jeff glowered. "No. You don't get to do that. Because if you're to blame, then I'm to blame, and I'm not taking the blame for Freddie Jackson. All we can say is that we underestimated his brand of screwed up. My guess is he came to Stu Devlin for reassurance and instead Stu told him the police were raiding his place for coke."

A setup. Made sense. Michael nodded, exhaling slowly. "He was getting jumpy. Becoming a liability for them. They wanted him out of the way."

"It's only speculation at this point but my guess, yes," Jeff said.

"I need to find this fucker fast. A man this desperate ... who knows what he'll do next."

"First, we need to go break the news to the Devlins." Jeff shook his head. "Jesus Christ. I have to tell the man his son is dead and then ask him to come to the station for questioning."

It was going to be a long night. Following Jeff out of the house, Michael asked, "Is this your first homicide?"

"It's the first homicide where I knew the victim." Jeff gazed back up at what had been Stu Devlin's impressive home. "Looks like a Devlin finally tried to fuck over the wrong guy."

Maybe so, Michael thought, but Stu was a victim all the same. Michael wouldn't stop until he'd found the evidence he needed against Jackson. Then he'd bury him with it. Just as Ian and Rosalie Devlin would have to bury their goddamn son.

28

Dahlia

Murder.

It was in my thoughts almost constantly.

Murder had rocked our quiet seaside town.

No one much liked Stu Devlin. I detested him for attacking Bailey and getting away with it. But he'd deserved jail time—not two bullets in his chest.

As I worked away at a hammered silver bowl I was making for Old Archie to give to his woman Anita, I longed for music to drown out my morbid thoughts. Instead, I tried to concentrate on the bowl. Old Archie had been a regular at Cooper's for as long as I could remember. That was until almost two years ago when his "lady friend" Anita was diagnosed with a spinal tumor. He got sober for her and had been helping her through what we all assumed would be her final months.

To everyone's happy shock, Anita was in remission. She'd spend the rest of her life in a wheelchair, but she would live. Archie had seen Anita eyeing one of my handmade silver bowls a while back, and their anniversary was coming up, so he'd commissioned one for her.

I wished it would take my mind off Stu Devlin's death and Freddie Jackson's subsequent disappearance, but it couldn't.

Michael had called to tell me about Stu's murder, knowing it would be all over Hartwell soon enough. He'd been abrupt on the phone. I worried about him. While everyone huddled together in groups throughout the coming days, talking in whispers whenever they saw one of the Devlins out and about, Michael was hunting Freddie Jackson.

Two days after the news broke, I'd been working in my workshop when Michael stopped by to see me. My music had been blaring like it always was, and it was the first time I'd seen Michael truly angry at me since we'd left Boston.

"There's a suspected killer on the loose, and your shop door is open while you're blaring fuckin' rock music! Does that not seem a little careless to you?" he'd yelled.

It had taken everything within me not to argue back. But he looked like he hadn't slept in days, and he was only yelling because he was concerned. So I let it go. I promised I wouldn't listen to my music while I worked until Jackson was found.

To thank me, Michael had given me a quick, hard kiss on the forehead and told me he wouldn't be around much until he caught Freddie.

I understood that, but it troubled me. I remembered that even as a young cop, Michael had taken so much on himself. There was a whole sheriff's office out there looking for Freddie, but I knew Michael would feel responsible for catching him.

It had now been seven days since Stu's murder. Vaughn was shadowing Bailey wherever she went. Cooper hovered over Jess, his sister Cat, and his nephew Joey. No one believed Freddie would deliberately come after anyone, but the murder had freaked us all out. Rumors were flying about Freddie's connection to the Devlins. We'd all discussed it at Cooper's. Our favorite theory was that Freddie had done a lot of illegal things for Stu, whom he considered his best friend, and when he'd started getting shifty about Michael's presence in town, he'd turned to Stu for help. It was possible Stu, the sneaky ass that he had been, had made it clear the Devlins would let Freddie swing in the wind if anything ever came to light about his criminal activities.

But why kill Stu? That was the part that still didn't make sense.

My Led Zeppelin ringtone blared into the room; I jerked in fright.

Goddamn it.

I was so on edge.

Putting down my tools, I slid off the stool and crossed the room to where I'd left my cell on a cabinet. It was my dad.

"Hey," I answered. He'd been calling every day since the news of Stu's murder broke. "Everything okay?"

"I'm okay, Bluebell. I ... uh ... I wondered if you'd spoken to Mike lately?"

I frowned. "No. He's out looking for Freddie."

"Well, I ... uh ... look, I know things are complicated between the two of you but I just got off the phone with him, and he doesn't sound so great."

Surprised, I took a moment to process everything about that sentence. "You talked with Michael?"

"Yeah."

"How much do you talk to him?"

"Dahlia," he said, sighing. "We don't talk about you. Much. And when we do, it's never about whatever is going on with you two. I just ... he doesn't have a good dad to talk with. I'm here when he needs that."

Emotion clogged my throat. God, I loved my father. "I'm glad he has you."

"Yeah, well, I think he needs something a bit closer to home right now."

Concern filled me. "What's going on?"

"He's frustrated, and he's exhausted. I thought you might want to check on him."

I chewed my bottom lip, staring at the drawing of me that Levi had sent. I'd framed and hung it on my workshop wall. He'd put me in a superhero costume. Darragh said Levi had recently gotten into comics.

If Michael needed to talk to someone and I ignored that to protect myself, then what kind of a superhero did that make me? "A pretty shitastic one," I murmured.

"What?"

I blinked out of my thoughts. "Nothing. Sorry, Dad. Of course, I'll go check on him."

"Good. Now, how are *you* doing?"

"We're all a little tense around here. I guess we didn't expect things with the Devlins to escalate to murder."

"It made national news," Dad said. "Popular tourist town like Hartwell? Murder of one of its wealthy sons is newsworthy."

"Which can only add pressure on Michael and Jeff." I glanced at the clock. It was six o'clock and time for me to close up shop anyway. "When you called him, where was he?"

"At the station from what I could tell."

"Okay. I'll head over there now. Thanks for calling and giving me a heads-up."

"No problem, Bluebell. I'll check in later."

We said goodbye, and I quickly tidied my tools and locked up. It was early March and the days were still short. The sun had set as I hurried toward my old Mini. The drive to city hall was a short one, but it was long enough to get my heart pounding in anticipation of seeing Michael.

When would that feeling ever stop?

Parking in the lot at the side of the building, I took the side entrance that led to the main reception of the sheriff's department. There was no receptionist at the desk, so I walked up the stairs into the open-plan office. Jeff was standing talking to Wendy by the water cooler, and they both looked over at me. Jeff made his way over, and his blue eyes drank me in from head to toe. "Everything okay, Dahlia?"

I nodded, distracted by the busy office behind us. "Everyone's working long hours these days, huh?"

"We've got a killer to catch, and Ian Devlin and his press monkeys constantly on our fucking asses." Jeff's response was full of exasperation. He winced. "Sorry."

"Don't be. You're doing great."

He studied me carefully. "You're here for Mike."

Someone should have warned me how awkward it would be talking to an ex-lover about my ... well ... my other ex-lover. "I wanted to check on him."

"I sent him home," Jeff said. "He wasn't happy about it, but he's no good to me tired."

"Oh." I wasn't sure I should go to Michael's apartment under normal circumstances. I definitely shouldn't go when he was exhausted.

"As much as it kills me to say this ... " Jeff's lips flattened into a thin line. "You should go to him. He's taking this a little too personally for my liking."

I nodded, biting my lip in worry. "And we know it was Freddie who shot Stu?"

Jeff just gave me a look.

I pulled a face. "Right. Civilian. None of my business."

"You know where Mike lives?"

"I didn't say I'd go to him."

"We both know you're going to him." Then he relayed Michael's full address.

"Thanks, Jeff."

He nodded and then took a step toward me, bending his head to mine. "He's a good guy, Dahlia. I'm sorry it couldn't be me, sorrier than I can say, so if it has to be anyone, I'm glad it's Mike. You deserve that."

Too many feelings overwhelmed me. I didn't want Jeff's blessing, and that's what he was giving! I didn't want anyone's blessing. I wanted to check on Michael, make sure he was okay, and scurry into my cowardly hidey-hole again.

The cartons in my hand contained falafel wraps packed with hummus, salad, and spicy sauce. I had no idea if Michael liked falafel but the deli across from his apartment building sold them, and they smelled amazing.

If he was tired, he was probably hungry too.

I took a deep breath as I stared at his crisp, white-painted front door. "You can do this," I whispered to myself. "*Friends* check on each other." I knocked before I could talk myself out of it.

A few seconds later, I heard his footsteps as he approached the door. The chain sounded, then the lock, and he opened the door wearing a black T-shirt, jeans, no belt, no shoes or socks. Oh, and he was holding a gun casually at his side.

"Expecting someone else?" I nodded at the gun.

I didn't like guns.

My dad kept a gun in the house; Dermot and Michael both carried them for their jobs, so I was used to them.

I just didn't like them.

He squinted at me, and I noted the dark circles under his eyes and the pale pallor of his usually olive-toned skin. "What are you doing here?"

"I brought food." I pushed inside, taking in the modern, sleek surroundings. The apartment was open plan with a French window that led out onto a ground-floor balcony. Light spilled into the white room, showcasing the light gray, glossy kitchen cabinets and island along the back wall. Center of the room was the sitting area where Michael had a black leather couch, armchair, glass coffee table, matching glass TV cabinet, and a huge flat-screen TV. To my left, a doorway led to a narrow hall, which I presumed led to the bedroom and bathroom.

Like his place in Boston, it was devoid of the feminine touch.

His front door slammed shut, and I jumped, whirling around to face him. "Falafel?" I held up the takeout cartons.

"I already ate." He looked and sounded impatient as he crossed the room to put his gun on the kitchen counter.

"I went to the station, and Jeff said you'd be here." I felt nervous and awkward. Sighing, I put the cartons down on the coffee table and clasped my hands in front of me.

Michael dragged his eyes down my body and returned to my face. "That doesn't explain why you're here."

"I wanted to see if you were okay."

"Well, as you can see, I'm fine."

I flushed, unprepared for a snippy Michael. "Should I go?"

He rubbed both hands over his face and groaned. "No."

The need to reassure and comfort him superseded my uncertainty. I took a step toward him. "This isn't your fault, Michael. Freddie is not your fault. He always was a creepy little fucker, and if he was capable of killing Stu, then he was always capable of killing Stu."

Michael nodded, his dark eyes moving over my face. For a moment we stood in silence. When he eventually spoke, it wasn't what I expected to hear. "I used to come home after seeing some terrible things, and Kiersten didn't want to know." The thought of him going home to a wife, as always, was an unbearable sting I tried to hide from him. "I didn't want to give her the details—I wouldn't do that to her—but I wanted to talk. Get rid of it somehow, you know. I attempted a couple of times, sliding into bed beside her, reaching for her. She'd push me away. And I'd lie there, looking at the ceiling, and I'd think about you."

The air between us thickened. His confession hit my chest like a physical impact. "I'd lie there remembering all the times we sat in my car talking about everything. I'd tell you about my day at work, the good and the bad, and you'd listen. Really listen. And then you'd wrap your arms around my neck and kiss the bad right out of me." Pain slashed across his expression. "I never resented you so much as those nights I'd lie next to my wife wishing she were you so you could kiss the bad right out of me."

Tears flooded my eyes. Because I wished I'd been there too. So much. So much more than I could bear.

Michael took a hesitant step toward me. "If I asked you to lie with me right now—if I told you I wouldn't read too much into it, what would you say?"

Without hesitation, I crossed the room and reached for his hand. His warm strength curled around mine, the calluses on his fingertips rubbing gently across the soft palm of my hand. Without a word, I let him lead me to his bedroom, and for one perfect moment, I silenced all my fears, all my worries, so I could do the thing I needed to do most.

Take care of Michael.

29

Michael

Michael knew how he was feeling wasn't about Freddie Jackson. Yes, it was his job to find the dirty bastard, and he would. He was determined to. However, his need to find the guy had become wrapped up in all the ways he felt he was failing. With his family. With Dahlia. Since moving to Hartwell, he'd spoken to his mom only a couple of times, and any mention of his dad made her clam up. He worried that without him there in Boston, his dad would return to his old ways, taking all his drunken bitterness out on Michael's mom.

Then there was Dahlia.

He wanted to be patient. He'd promised himself he would be. Yet deep down, he thought the giant gesture of moving to Hartwell for her would've broken through all those solid defenses she'd surrounded her heart with over the years.

It wasn't working.

Michael was failing at the most important thing he'd ever faced.

He was just . . . failing.

Though as he led Dahlia by the hand into his spartan bedroom, he let go of all his miserable shortcomings. All he'd planned to do was lie down on the bed with her, feel her there in the dark, maybe pretend that everything was okay for a few hours so he could sleep.

He didn't expect her to stop at the edge of the bed, stare up at him with those soulful blue eyes, and whisper, "Let me take care of you."

Michael would never forget Dahlia's version of taking care of him for the rest of his life. If it was all he ever got from her, then he was sure it was more than most men had ever had from any woman. First, she undressed them both, and then she'd asked him to lie on the bed. She'd hovered over his body, a fantasy of smooth skin, big breasts, tiny waist, generous hips, gorgeous legs, and dark hair that cascaded down her back. Her full breasts, with their tight, erect nipples, were so tempting, he reached for them. Dahlia had allowed the touch for a second and then curled her hand around his and pressed it back to the bed.

"Let me," she whispered.

Michael would understand what that meant when she touched him. Her lips and hands were tender, slow explorers caressing their way around and down his body, learning every inch of him. She spent so long learning him, Michael's heart felt like it would explode from beating so fast. He panted in the dark, trying to catch his breath, his legs moving restlessly against the sheets, his hips pushing up toward her in need.

But he never lost his patience because there was a part of him that didn't want her to stop.

No woman had ever cherished—fuckin' *cherished*—him the way Dahlia McGuire was doing right then.

She took him into her mouth, and Michael felt like a boy again, helpless against his own passion. *This is heaven*, he thought, as the electricity licked at the back of his thighs and his lower spine. He could hear his hoarse grunts of her name, the loving words, the dirty words mingling, falling from his lips as he watched the woman he loved suck and lick and devour him.

Then it hit. Hard and explosive and so fuckin' phenomenal, he forgot where he was for a second.

Panting in the dark, his chest heaving as though he'd run a marathon, Michael could still hear his own shout of release ringing in his ears. His body melted into the mattress in utter satisfaction, his limbs tingling in the aftermath.

Dahlia.

Forcing his eyes open, he watched as she returned from his bathroom, her skin glowing in the moonlight filtering through his windows.

Christ, she was beautiful.

Not only beautiful on the outside. She was pieced together with layers of every kind of beauty there could be, so deep and full, it shone out of her.

Why couldn't she see that?

She crawled up onto the bed beside him, and he wanted to touch her, repay the favor, but he was tired. He hadn't slept more than an hour here and there in days. It seemed to take great effort, but he lifted his arm toward her.

"Ssshh," she whispered, pressing it back to the mattress. "Go to sleep, Michael. I'm here."

She rested her head on his chest and draped her arm over his stomach as she cuddled her soft body into his side. Cocooned by her, his eyes closed like they had a will of their own and the bliss of sleep took him into its dark.

30

Dahlia

For hours I laid awake, afraid to move in case it would disturb Michael. He was so exhausted; the weight of the world seemed to rest on his shoulders. And I knew his worries weren't only about Freddie. I knew *I* was probably more to blame than anyone for his burdens.

Which was why I'd given him the only thing I could. I loved him in the only way I could without ever saying it.

I'd never said it, I realized, tears burning in my eyes as I laid pressed into his side. I'd never told him I loved him. But he knew. He certainly knew after tonight.

My head rested on his chest, rising and falling with his even breaths. I glanced up at his face, but it was half turned away. Staring at his jaw, at his beard, I could still feel the prickle of it beneath my fingers and lips. I'd trailed sweet kisses all over his handsome face, learning every line and curve like a blind person, drawing him in my mind forever.

His skin was smooth and hot and hard beneath me. My lips and fingertips had moved over the slight hills and valleys where his muscle was tightly roped. For a while, I lost myself in exploring him. Everything else went away as I disappeared in the adventure of his body. I'd kissed the small scar on his right upper rib where a boy had swiped a fourteen-year-old Michael with a broken bottle. I trailed my fingers over a scar on his left leg above his knee

I'd never seen before. The question had hovered on my lips but the night wasn't for my curiosity. It was for Michael.

The memory of him coming in my mouth echoed in a low, deep ripple in my belly. I was slick and wanting between my legs, unable to sleep for the restless need buzzing beneath my skin.

However, panic was writhing over the buzz, overwhelming everything with the fear that despite him saying otherwise, Michael would take my lovemaking to mean something it didn't.

I wanted my giving to be altruistic, but somehow it was always turned selfish in the end.

Lifting my head slowly, afraid to wake him, I looked over at his bedside alarm clock, the red digits blinking in the dark. It was just past three in the morning. Wow. Hours had passed.

Good. It was good. Michael needed sleep.

However, I couldn't be here when he woke up in the morning.

Gently, I lifted the hand he had resting on my hip and scooted down until I could place his arm by his side on the bed. Breathing a sigh of relief he hadn't woken, I attempted to get off the bed without disturbing the mattress too much. I moved as silently as possible, picking up my dress, shoes, and underwear, and I tiptoed into the living room. I blinked against the lights Michael had left blazing and began to dress.

As I was pulling my underwear up, I heard the creak of the floorboards in his bedroom, and my stomach dropped. With a racing heart and trembling hands, I reached for my shoes and then stopped.

I wouldn't run out on him like a coward.

Michael was awake.

So I had to face him.

I straightened, barefoot but dressed at least, and then he was standing in the doorway. He'd taken the time to pull on a pair of sweatpants.

The sleep still shining in his dark eyes melted away when he realized I was leaving. His accusatory expression singed me.

"You were just going to slip out?" His voice was still hoarse with sleep. "Like a drunken one-night stand?"

I shook my head, hating that he would think that. "Never, Michael."

"But you were leaving?" He strode into the room, crossing his arms over his chest. I tried not to be distracted by all the beauty that was him, but it wasn't easy. My body was still strung taut with unfulfilled desire.

I took a step back, knocking over one of my shoes. I glanced down at them and back up at Michael to find him glaring at me in utter disappointment. "I ... I thought it would be better if I weren't here in the morning."

"Why?" he asked. "Because you know that I know now without a doubt you love me?"

Panic thickened my throat.

"Tell me you don't love me," Michael demanded again.

Shaking my head frantically, I wanted to escape. Bending down, I reached for my shoes, but Michael grabbed my arms. I cried out as he pulled me up, his face a mask of fury.

"Tell me," he said as he shook me gently. "Because if you run out of here without explaining this shit to me ... give me the truth, Dahlia." He let me go, and I could still feel the heat of his hands banded around my biceps. "I want the real reason we can't be together. If you don't give me that, then what I feel for you ... it'll turn. It'll twist, and it'll darken, and it won't be love anymore."

The thought of Michael not loving me was breath-stealing.

"Tell me," he begged.

"You won't understand ... "

"Then make me!"

I stumbled backward, falling rather than sitting down onto his couch. "Do you remember?" I whispered. "Do you remember that day with Dillon? I try not to ... but it's one of the most vivid memories I have ... "

Ugh, my palms were sweating, I was so goddamn nervous.

"Just do it," Michael urged beside me. We were sitting in his car outside my place, and we were about to execute our plan to tell Dillon the truth about our feelings for each other. That Michael and I were going to be together.

I'd decided I would be the one to tell my little sister, so the plan was to call her and tell her I needed to talk, ask her where she wanted to meet, and then Michael would discreetly drop me off.

While I was car-less after mine got relegated to the junkyard, my sister had a beat-up little banger she drove so I knew she could meet me anywhere.

Taking strength from Michael's reassuring expression, I dialed Dillon's number. "Christ, my heart is beating so fast, and I'm only calling to arrange a meet," I whispered.

He squeezed my hand, and I threaded my fingers through his. My sister and I would probably have a temporary falling-out over this, but once she realized how deeply I felt for Michael, we'd be fine.

This wasn't some stupid fling.

One day—and I knew it to be true—I'd be the mother of Michael Sullivan's kids.

"Hey!" Dillon picked up.

"H-hey," I stuttered, surprised because I'd been caught in my own Michael musings. "Where are you?"

"Driving home."

I sighed. "You're not supposed to answer your cell when you're driving."

"I am a multitasker. You know this."

Hearing the sweet cheerfulness in her voice, I hated myself for what I was about to do. "Listen, Dill, we need to talk. Do you want to meet somewhere?" I didn't want to do it at home where Mom could butt her nose in.

"You sound serious. What is it?"

"Let's meet up face to face."

"Okay." She drew the word out, and there was a bite to her tone. "Why do I have a feeling I'm not going to like whatever it is you have to say to me?"

"Dillon—"

"Is it bad news?"

"Um ... yes and no. It's ... complicated."

"What's it about?"

"Dillon, let's meet, okay?"

"No," she said. "I hate these dramatics, Dahlia. Just fuckin' tell me what it is. You have me worried now."

"I promise this is not something I want to tell you over the phone."

"Is Mom okay? Is Dad okay?"

"Of course, everyone is okay."

"Just tell me!" she yelled.

"Dillon—"

"Fuck's sake, Dahlia, if everyone is okay, whatever you have to say cannot be that bad. Just say it."

"I'm dating Michael," I blurted out.

Michael squeezed my hand and I looked up at him. He wore an expression of surprise and confusion and I shrugged helplessly.

Dillon had gone quiet.

Shit.

"Dill?"

"My Michael?"

A flare of indignation momentarily quelled my guilt. "Technically, he's my Michael. We were friends before you and he dated."

"Bitch!" she screeched, and I flinched. "You know how I feel about him!"

Just like that, my remorse flew out the window as I let go of all my hurt and suspicions. "No, you knew how I felt about him, and you asked him out anyway!"

Michael let go of my hand and fell back against the driver's seat with a groan.

"Ugh!" she growled. "Not true! I wouldn't do that!"

"Yes, you would. And you did!"

"How can you be yelling at me when you're in the wrong?" she sobbed, and my remorse came flooding back.

"Dillon—"

"No!" She was back to yelling. "Did he break up with me for you? I swear—"

Her strangled, high-pitched scream filled my ear, followed by a harsh squeal, a sickening bang like a gun going off, but louder, and then a shattering sound, like glass exploding.

Then nothing.

Deathly silence.

My heart stopped.

"Dillon?" My heart started again, racing so hard I couldn't catch my breath. "Dillon?"

"What is it?" Michael's eyes were round with worry.

My face crumpled. "She . . . something happened."

"What happened?"

"Michael, we have to go, we have to go. We have to find her. I think she was in an accident."

I could still feel the panic I'd felt when I realized Dillon was in a car crash. As I sat in Michael's apartment, feeling his gaze on my face, that memory bled into another and then another . . .

Being around Dillon almost transformed me into a kicked puppy. I hated that feeling. Guilt made me put up with it. My sister laid in her hospital bed, where she'd been in and out for eight weeks now, and stared balefully at the ceiling.

"I could bring something different to read?" I waved the historical romance paperback in the air that she'd described as unrealistic smut. "What do you want me to read?"

Her jaw clenched. "Something I can relate to. Like a girl whose sister betrays her and causes her to get into an accident that leaves her a fuckin' paraplegic?"

Hearing the bitterness, the hate, in my sister's voice hurt but I held stoic. Dillon's life had been irrevocably changed by the car accident two months ago. She wasn't a paraplegic, but she had suffered severe damage to her spinal cord, and it would take months of brutal physical therapy to get her walking again. She'd never have the strength she had before. Not to mention she'd suffered a couple of broken ribs, a fractured collarbone, and a pretty severe concussion.

I hated that I was the reason she wasn't paying attention to the road, but it wasn't my fault she was driving and talking on her phone at the same time. I didn't make her answer, and she'd pushed me to keep talking.

I did feel guilty about Michael.

I blamed myself for Dillon's subsequent depression, feeling sure if this had happened without her learning about Michael and me, her attitude would have been way better.

My sister was mad and rightly so. But it was also like she'd given up.

"When is your next therapy session?" I didn't acknowledge her last comment.

She blamed me.

I got it.

We'd get through it.

"Tomorrow." Her head turned on the pillow toward me. "You'll be there, right?"

Either because she needed me there or because she was attempting to keep me away from Michael, Dillon insisted on having me around at her beck and call as much as possible. The only time I couldn't be with her was when I had class. However, I'd assigned a ringtone to Dillon, so I'd know it was her right away. My teachers were good about letting me take calls from her at school.

Her constant demands were exhausting, but I saw them as part of my penance and hoped that eventually, once she was back on her feet, we'd get back to a good place again.

Maybe when that happened, my mom would get off my back too.

Dillon had told her everything, so Mom was blaming me as much as Dillon was. She couldn't even look at Michael. I felt terrible because it was causing problems between her and Dad, and I knew things were already strained between them over money. We had insurance, but it didn't cover all of Dillon's medical bills. Even though she was talking on her phone and not paying attention, the truck that slammed into her had run a red light. Mom and Dad were talking with a lawyer about getting damages to pay for Dillon's bills.

My brothers and sister were fine with me, thankfully. And Dermot liked Michael, so they were getting along great.

And Dad was always Dad. Supporting me. He tried to assure me none of this was my fault, but I couldn't help how I felt.

"You seeing Michael tonight?" Dillon asked.

It enraged her that her car accident hadn't caused me to break things off with Michael, even though she was sweet as pie to him when he was around.

I got all her vitriol.

But I could handle it, I reminded myself.

"Yes," I answered.

"Have you had sex yet?"

"*Dillon!*"

She glared at me. "What? You told me when you had sex with Gary."

"*You know this is different.*"

Tears shone in her eyes, and she looked away. "I'll take that as a yes, then."

I sighed. "We haven't had sex." We hadn't had time. Whenever we saw each other, we usually ended up talking in his car for hours. He hated his apartment in Southie and wouldn't let me near it. And Michael didn't want our first time to be in his car. I didn't care where we did it. I just wanted him. And tonight was the night. I'd decided. I'd even bought sexy lingerie to surprise him.

Guilt suffused me at my excitement.

Dillon was lying in a hospital bed while I planned to seduce my boyfriend.

"*Good.*" *She harrumphed.*

"*Are you mad that I'm with Michael or that I'm not in that hospital bed instead of you?*" *I dared to ask.*

"*I wouldn't wish this on my worst enemy,*" *she replied.*

I winced. "Then, it's still about Michael?"

She was silent so long, I didn't think she was going to speak. Then, "He's the first guy I ever wanted to sleep with. I don't know if I loved him ... but I wanted him." She rolled her head to look at me. "If I weren't lying here, I could be out there, making his decision to choose you harder by reminding him how awesome I am. Instead, I'm a cripple who no guy will ever want again."

There was so much in that to hate, and I had to remind myself that Dillon wasn't herself right now. "You're not a cripple. You will walk again, and it'll happen faster once you fight. Not me. Not the doctors. But fight for you." I sucked in a breath and stood up. She followed my movement. "And once you're out of here and you're walking again, I can't stop you from pursuing Michael if

*you want to. But I'll tell you something I haven't even told him ...
I love him, Dillon. Like, can't breathe without him kind of love."
Tears blurred my eyes. "You have to know that because you have
to know I would never let a guy come between us otherwise. I
met him before I knew who he was to Gary, and he and I have
had a connection ever since. He never meant to hurt you. We were
both pretty mixed up about it, and I'm sorry you got caught in
the crossfire."*

*I approached her bed as I saw her chin wobble with emotion.
"I adore you. I'm so sorry that I've hurt you and I will do almost
anything to make that up to you. But giving up Michael would be
like cutting off my arm."*

Tears rolled down her cheeks and hope filled me.

*I reached for her, and that hope deflated when she turned her
head away. "I'm tired."*

*Dropping my arm, I nodded. With a heavy heart, I slipped out
of her hospital room.*

*Hours later, the need to disappear in Michael was greater than
ever. As soon as he pulled his car to a stop in the dark, empty lot
by the woods, I jumped him.*

*He laughed against my mouth, his hands firm on my waist,
and he broke the kiss with a breathless chuckle. "No 'Hi, dahlin',
how was your day'?"*

*I shook my head, my whole body buzzing with need. Frantic,
almost. "I want you."*

*Michael groaned. "Fuck, you know I want you too, but not
in the car."*

"Your apartment, then."

*"I told you that place is a shithole. I'm not taking you there.
My lease is up soon, I'll get a nicer place, and then we're
good to go."*

I narrowed my eyes. "Do you not want me?"

His expression was incredulous. "Do you know how many cold showers I've taken these past two months? In fact, longer than that." *He lifted his right hand. "I've grown more acquainted with this hand than I ever fuckin' did as a horny, blue-balled teenager."*

I bit my lip to halt my laugh but was unsuccessful. "Then let's have sex." I peppered his face with kisses.

"Dahlia."

"Fuck me," I whispered against his mouth.

His grip on my hips turned bruising, his face dark with desire. "I don't want to fuck you the first time," he said, his voice hoarse. "I want to make love to you. And not in my car but in a nice bed in a nice place because that's what you deserve."

My God, could he be any more perfect?

I kissed him with all the love inside me that I hadn't vocalized yet. I was going to tell him tonight. After we made love in his car, I was going to whisper those three little words in his ear.

"Dahlia . . . " Michael broke the kiss. "You're driving me crazy."

I knew I was. I could feel his erection digging into my ass, and I deliberately rubbed myself against it. He hissed, his fingers biting into my waist.

Despite the pleasure, the need, saturating his features, I could still sense his resistance. There was something very hot about seducing Michael Sullivan. We kissed—slow, sexy kisses that seemed to go on forever. But it wasn't enough to break his will. Deciding to bring out the big guns, I released my hold on him, grabbed the hem of my sweater, and yanked it up over my head.

My heavy breasts bounced with the movement and Michael froze beneath me.

His hot eyes locked onto my breasts, somewhat concealed in an emerald-green satin bra that was made to tantalize way more than it was made to support.

"You like?" I whispered. *"I bought it for you."*

Michael's answer was to cup my breasts. They spilled over his hands, and he grew harder beneath me. *"I like. I love. Love your tits,"* he muttered, spellbound by them.

I grinned. *"Yeah?"*

His eyes flew to mine, and he kneaded them, making me whimper as pleasure shot straight between my legs. *"I've thought about doing a lot of dirty things to your tits."*

I covered his hands with mine and squeezed again, rolling my hips against him. *"Tell me."*

So he did. In lurid detail. Until I was burning hot and losing my mind.

"Do it," I demanded against his lips. *"Michael."*

His mouth covered mine, swallowing my pleas in his voracious, deep, wet kisses that took my skin from hot to combustible. His fingers fumbled for the buttons on my jeans.

Yes!

"Get in the back," he growled against my mouth.

No need to tell me twice.

I clambered off him, and less than gracefully fell into the back of the car. Michael was too big to get between the seats so as I scrambled out of my jeans, he got out and opened the back door. I let out a laugh of breathless excitement as he got in and slammed the door behind him.

Then I was wrapped around him, my arms, my legs, as he kissed me passionately, hungrily, his hands searching for my bra clasp. It snapped open, and we broke our kiss to pull it away. Then his mouth and tongue were on my breasts, and he pushed beneath my underwear to rub at my clit.

"Oh, God." I clawed at his T-shirt, wanting to feel his skin.

He got the message and whipped it off. Seeing his determination to torment me, I reached between us and unzipped him. *"Now,*

Michael. I'm ready. You can feel I'm ready." Pushing beneath his jeans to his boxer briefs, I slipped my hands down over his hard ass, taking the clothes with him, so his cock sprang free.

"I need you." I looked deep into his eyes. "I'm on birth control, and I'm clean. Are you?"

He swallowed hard and nodded.

"Then come inside me."

His expression was fierce with passion as he gripped my thigh in one hand. He braced himself over me with the other. He was hot and throbbing against me, and I was thrown back to that day in the darkroom. We'd been so frantic to have each other, it was a miracle we'd made it this long without doing it!

"Michael."

"God, I love it when you say my name." He pressed forward into my wet—

My cell rang, blasting the car with its loud music. We froze against each other.

It was Dillon's ringtone.

And Michael knew it.

He made a throaty noise of frustration and hung his head.

Tears filled my eyes at being thwarted once again, and when the ringing stopped only to start up immediately, I whispered, "I have to."

He lifted his head. "Does she know you're with me?"

I nodded, those tears threatening to break loose.

"Then don't you think her interruption might be deliberate?"

I nodded.

"Then maybe it's okay to let this one go."

I squeezed my eyes closed, and the tears slipped free. "I can't."
As much as I wanted to, I couldn't.

Michael's lips touched my cheek, over the wet trail of my tears.
"I know," he whispered tenderly before sitting up.

I loved him so much. "I'm sorry."

He rubbed my thigh in comfort, reassurance. "We got all the time in the world, dahlin'."

Grateful, believing he was right, I quickly righted myself and reached through to the front seat for my purse. My cell was still ringing. I answered, hoping I didn't sound too breathless.

It wasn't Dillon.

It was my mom.

That call had changed my life forever. Dillon had unexpectedly caught an infection, and I was needed at the hospital. She deteriorated so quickly, it didn't feel real. And she was too weak. Emotionally as well as physically. The infection fought her and won, and she went into organ failure.

Mom and Dad had to take her off life support a few days later.

Grief tightened its hold around my ribs and crushed me. Most days it was manageable, but lately, its viselike grip had returned.

I stared at Michael. He'd taken the armchair across from me and was waiting patiently for me to speak. After Dillon's death, after my mom attacked me, blaming me, telling me it should have been me, I pushed everyone away. Including Michael.

"I blamed you." The words tore out from the depths of buried shame. "When she died hating me, I blamed you. I blamed you for dating her. For setting off events between us."

The stricken look on his face made me feel sick.

"I know you're not to blame," I hurried to say. "I don't blame you now. But I did back then when I couldn't see clearly, and that's why I pushed you away too. You were perfect with me. I look back, and I wonder how anyone could be so lucky to have met someone like you. And I can't believe that I blamed you and pushed you away." I swiped angrily at my tears. "I don't deserve you, Michael."

He shook his head in denial. "Is that the reason why I'm here, and you're still over there? Because you think you don't *deserve* me?"

I lowered my eyes. "Not only that."

"Then what? Tell me."

I saw my sister in her room before the accident. Sitting at her vanity table putting on her makeup, laughing with me about everything and nothing. Sliding the rose brooch I'd made onto the lapel of her blazer, and throwing me a sweet smile. So young and alive. Her whole life ahead of her. One stupid phone call changed that forever.

"You are everything that makes me happy," I confessed.

"Dahlia . . . " He moved as if to come to me, and I warded him off with a wave of my hand.

"If I let myself be happy like that, then I'm afraid that everything my mom thinks, everything Dillon thought about me, was true. She cared about you, and I knew that, and I didn't care back then, Michael. I wanted you so much, nothing else mattered. I convinced myself that she'd forgive and forget and it would all be okay. Even as she lay in that hospital bed, I resented her for hating me for being with you. She made my mom hate me too. And I blamed her for that. That night in your car when we were about to make love, and I thought she was calling to interrupt, there was a moment, just a flash, when I selfishly wished she didn't exist."

"God, Dahlia—"

"She's dead. Gone. And I'm still here. But maybe if I live half a life instead of a full one, then she'll know, wherever she is, that I love her more than I love myself. Because she died never knowing that and I have to show her now somehow . . . "

He stared at me, lost, as my broken words echoed around us.

Michael rubbed a hand over his beard and hung his head.

He got it now.

He understood.

"I have never"—his head jerked up, his eyes flashing irately—"heard anything so fucked up in my entire life."

I jerked back like he'd hit me.

Michael stood, his whole body bristling. "You loved Dillon. Everybody knows you loved your sister. You were never away from her bedside. So you resented her a little? So fuckin' what? She was a great girl, she was, but Dillon had your mother's nature, and she was spoiled. She didn't love me." He pointed to himself in exasperation. "Dillon was pissed because she thought you'd stolen one of her toys, and she was angry at the world because a fuckin' asshole tore through a red light and smashed into her. No one can blame her for being angry about that, but she decided to take that anger out on you. And you took it. You took it better than most people would because you loved her. And it's okay to have felt resentment about that. It's called being human, Dahlia.

"But this," he said, gesturing between us, "giving up your chance at happiness to even some fuckin' cosmic score with Dillon is beyond screwed up!"

Anger seethed within me, and I launched to my feet. "Do you know how hard it was for me to tell you that?" I pressed a fist to my chest. "I've never told anyone that!"

"Yeah, because it's messed up!" He crossed the room and grabbed my shoulders, bending his head to mine. His voice lowered, his words desperate. "You're not only forcing yourself to live half a life here, Dahlia. You're asking me to as well."

Just like that, my anger deflated.

More guilt filled me.

Great.

"That's not fair."

"No. But it's the truth. You loved your sister, but how much do you love me?"

I was afraid of how much—that was how much I loved Michael Sullivan.

Lifting my hand in his, he placed it over his heart where I could feel it thudding wildly. "I can *exist* without you, Dahlia. But I can't *live* without you. Don't make me."

31

Dahlia

Fury hummed in my veins as I switched off the TV. Ian Devlin had given a grief-stricken statement to the news about how he believed the sheriff's department and a certain detective were not only failing in their pursuit of the criminal who had murdered his son but were daring to blame the corruption inside the sheriff's department on him.

Bastard.

It was on national news.

Deep concern for Michael suffused me. After I'd left his house that morning, unable to answer his plea to love him, I hadn't been able to get the look on his face out of my head.

For once, instead of locking that shit up tight, I'd gone to Bailey. She no longer slept at the inn but had shacked up with Vaughn in his stunning, multimillion-dollar beach house.

Vaughn had answered the door in his pajamas, the scowl of annoyance he wore disappearing at the sight of me disheveled and tearstained on his doorstep. Ushering me in as Bailey hurried downstairs in her robe, Vaughn had made us tea and then discreetly disappeared back upstairs so I could spill my guts to my best friend.

Afterward, I fell asleep on their couch.

When I woke up, it was to Bailey waving coffee under my nose. She told me Vaughn had gone to the hotel, even though it was a

Sunday and he and Bailey typically spent the day together. Bailey switched on the news while I nibbled toast and seethed over Ian Devlin.

"I called the girls. They're on their way over."

I turned my irritation to her. "Why?"

"Because I feel out of my depth here." Her features were strained. "I don't know what I can say to convince you to let go of this spiritual promise you've made to your sister, for lack of a better phrase. But I think Jessica might be able to help."

"So why not only call *her*?" I was petulant, vulnerable, now that my deepest fears were out in the world.

Bailey turned pensive. "Because you're right about Emery. Something isn't right about her situation, and I hope that if you and Jess trust her enough with your history, then maybe one day she'll trust us with hers."

"Two birds, one stone," I muttered.

"If I had a deep, dark past, you know I'd share it in a heartbeat to help her out. Fortunately, my life has been rather blessed."

I shot her a disbelieving look. "Your boyfriend of ten years cheated on you. Stu Devlin assaulted you, and then your sister tried to sell your inn out from beneath you."

Bailey waved her hand. "That's child play compared to what you and Jess have been through."

Despite my reluctance to share with Emery and Jess, I couldn't help but admit that I *was* curious about Jessica's past.

While we waited for the girls, I washed up and borrowed yoga pants and a T-shirt from Bailey. The yoga pants were a little too long and the T-shirt a little too tight across the chest, but it would have to do. Feeling marginally more human, I made my way downstairs and discovered Emery and Jessica had arrived.

They watched me with round eyes filled with curiosity and concern.

"Let's get this over with." I flopped down on an armchair with more nonchalance than I felt. "Get comfy ladies." I gestured to the enormous L-shaped couch.

Once they were settled, I pushed through my fears, my nerves, and reminded myself this was Jess and Emery. I *could* trust them. Bailey believed I could trust them too.

Now I'd opened up to Michael, I was desperate for someone to tell me they understood why I believed I owed Dillon. Michael hadn't understood. Emphatically not. Bailey didn't say it in so many words, but I had a feeling she didn't understand it either.

So I told Jess and Emery the whole story. Beginning with meeting Michael, loving him while I was with his best friend, Dillon's involvement, our betrayal, her accident, her death, my mother, my drinking, Bailey's rescue ... all of it. Thankfully, I told it without tears. It seemed I'd used them all up with Michael.

I told them about last night. My confession. My penance.

The sounds of the gulls flying above the sea outside filled the living room, along with the gentle lap of the water against the bollards that held the living room balcony up. My friends remained silent.

Emery was crying so she couldn't speak.

Sweet girl. Full of so much empathy. For some bizarre reason, I felt like *I* should comfort her.

However, the look on Jess's face arrested me. It was as if she'd seen a ghost.

"Jess?" I was concerned.

She turned to Bailey instead, her blue eyes wide with understanding. "This is why you wanted me here."

Bailey nodded. "I need someone to get through to her, and I believe only you can."

Why?

Why Jessica?

Jess straightened her shoulders as if readying for battle. "If it's okay with you, I want to tell you *my* story now."

I nodded, a strange feeling of dread filling my gut and I didn't know why.

I would understand why very soon.

"I had a little sister too," she said, her smile melancholy. "She was a ballet dancer. Her name was Julia."

My eyes moved to Emery, and I saw that this was news to her.

"She was eleven," Jess continued, "I was fourteen. Our parents were very social people, and they often put their needs above our own. They'd leave us alone a lot, and I was left in charge of Julia. My aunt Theresa would watch her for me when she could, but often, it was left to me to babysit. And I was fourteen—I wanted to be out with my friends." She grimaced and looked at her hands, pressing her fingertips nervously together. "A few years before the summer I turned fourteen, my father's little brother, Tony, moved back home. He took a lot of interest in us. I was grateful," Jess scoffed, the sound hard and ugly. "I would go out with my friends, and he would watch Julia."

When she looked at me, I shook my head, part of me not wanting to hear what I knew was coming. I saw it in the horror that still lived in the back of her eyes. "I came home early one afternoon, and they weren't around. Then I heard something down in the basement."

Emery let out a low moan, and Jess reached for her hand without breaking her gaze from mine.

"He ... he was raping her."

Nausea welled inside of me, and I covered my mouth to hold back the cry I wanted to release. That poor little girl. *Oh my God.* What Jess had seen ... I couldn't even imagine. If someone had done that to Dillon, I would've killed him.

"I flew at them," she recalled. "I was in this blind rage, and it gave me enough strength to get him off her. We tried to escape.

We were running up the stairs, but he caught Julia. I got him away from her, but he came at me at the top of the stairs. He had me on my back, punching me. My sister screamed, and then he wasn't on me anymore. It disoriented me at first, but when I got up, Tony had Julia pinned against the wall, and he was choking her." Her hands went to her throat. "And I knew. I knew he wouldn't let us out of there alive.

"So I killed him," she announced, the words hoarse, like they'd been dragged out of her.

That dread I felt wrapped itself around me.

Jessica.

"I took one of my father's golf clubs, and I hit him over the head. He fell down the stairs and broke his neck." Swiping at a tear, she continued. "Julia told my parents and the police what had happened and we learned that he'd been raping her for two years. Since she was *nine*. My parents were so caught up in their own lives, and I was such a self-involved teenager, we hadn't paid any attention to her. We hadn't seen the signs.

"Our parents put us both in therapy rather than deal with us themselves, and Julia focused on her dancing. Obsessively." Her eyes took on a faraway glaze. "When she didn't get into the school of her dreams, she hung herself in that basement. I found her. My parents blamed me. They didn't want to believe it was Tony's abuse that caused all her pain. They said it was the memory of me killing a man in front of her."

I was cold. All the way through. Because I hated that this was her story. She was so kind and warm, and she took care of people. She helped people. I *hated* that this was her story. She deserved so much better.

Emery and Bailey were both crying, and I realized that my cheeks were wet too. Our eyes locked as an unspoken connection wrapped itself around us.

"For a long time, I blamed myself. I wanted to punish myself for killing Tony, for failing Julia. I believed I didn't deserve good things. That living an empty life was my penance."

"Jess," I sobbed. It was like she was inside my head, my heart. I didn't feel alone anymore.

And then she was up and across the room. She lowered to her knees in front of me and grabbed both my hands in hers. "I put Cooper through the wringer because I was afraid to tell him what I'd done. That he would realize he deserved better than me. He made me see the truth. His love—his strength—helped me find the peace I thought I didn't deserve. But I do deserve it." She tugged my hands to her chest, her eyes pleading. "And it breaks my heart you don't think you deserve it too. You do, Dahlia. The guilt won't go away overnight, maybe not ever," Jess whispered. "Not completely. But loving Michael, letting him love you, will make it a little easier every day. Do you know what my redemption is?"

I shook my head, unable to speak past the emotions in my throat.

"Cooper. Knowing I make him as happy as I do. That he needs me. That's my redemption right there." Her expression turned fierce. "I don't believe you need to prove yourself or find redemption. But I know you think you do. So ... make Michael yours."

I slid off the chair and wrapped my arms around her, inhaling her strength, breathing it in. If Jessica Huntington-Lawson could get through such horror and come out the other side as strong as this warrior in front of me, then for God's sake, so could I.

32

Michael

Instead of going into Cooper's to question the introverted cook, Crosby, Michael wished he was going in there to drown his own sorrows. In lieu of that, he was chasing their only lead so far. Cooper had called to tell him Crosby might have seen Jackson but wasn't one hundred percent sure and didn't want to waste police time.

It wasn't a waste of Michael's time.

He was following every lead possible.

Cooper nodded to him as soon as he strode through the door. Michael could sense the bar quiet down a little and eyes were on him as Cooper lifted the bar top, came out from behind it, and gestured for him to follow into the back room.

"He's pissed I called you," Cooper said as he led Michael down a short hallway and into the kitchen.

Crosby made that clear from the moment he saw Michael. "I hate goddamn cops," he blurted, shaking a metal basket of fries in the fryer.

After baring his soul to Dahlia that morning, Michael wasn't in the mood for anyone else's shit. "Just tell me what you saw."

Crosby glared at Cooper. "I said I wasn't sure."

Michael snapped his fingers in front of Crosby's face, his own expression severe with impatience. "Answer my question."

"That's why I hate cops," Crosby grumbled. "No manners."

"That's funny coming from you, Crosby. Answer Detective Sullivan's questions or I'll send Isla in here."

Michael didn't know why the idea of sending one of the wait staff in here would bother the cook so much, but it did. He cursed under his breath and then glared at Michael like a petulant schoolboy. "I got a trailer over on Oak Meadows."

Michael nodded, knowing the area well after searching all over Hartwell for Jackson.

"This morning, before dawn, I saw someone sneaking out of Willy Nettle's old trailer."

Michael turned to Cooper.

"He died about eight months ago," Cooper explained. "His daughter lives in New York. She must not have gotten around to selling it."

Jesus. Son of a bitch. Michael had been out all over the county looking for him, they had an APB out all over the East Coast for this dirty bastard, and he'd been hiding under their fuckin' noses?

"How did I not know about this?"

Cooper grimaced at Crosby. "Please tell me you didn't know that place was lying empty and didn't say anything?"

His cook scowled. "If I had seen anything weird going on there, I would have said something. And we don't know it was Freddie Jackson I saw."

"Was the person male or female? How tall? What build?"

"It. Was. Dark," Crosby spoke condescendingly slow.

Michael tried to hold on to his patience. "But you saw someone. You also saw how big they were."

He shifted uncomfortably. "It was a man. But that's all I know."

Giving Crosby an abrupt nod, Michael turned on his heel and pulled out his cell. Jeff picked up after two rings.

"Got a lead. Pete Crosby saw a man leaving Willy Nettle's

empty trailer out on Oak Meadows just before dawn. Can't say for sure it was Jackson, but I think it's worth checking out."

"I'll send a couple deputies." Jeff sighed. "If that son of a bitch has been in town this whole time ... "

"I know." Michael shared his frustration. "I'm on my way there now."

They hung up, and Michael followed Cooper out of the kitchen.

"I'll be glad when this is over," Cooper said.

"Yeah, we don't want a killer on the loose, scaring off tourists."

Cooper glared at him as Michael rubbed the nape of his neck.

"I didn't mean that," Cooper said. The glare dissipated, replaced with concern. "You okay, Mike?"

"I've been better." Together they pushed the doors open.

Michael wished he'd stayed in the hallway.

Standing at the bar, lips pursed, his eyes dark on Bryn, one of Cooper's bartenders, was Michael's old man.

What the hell was Aengus Sullivan doing in Hartwell?

His dad jerked his head toward him.

It was like the floor fell away under his feet.

As Aengus strode around the bar to come to a stop in front of him, Michael fought the need to walk away, like always. He knew before Aengus even spoke that he was drunk. It was a goddamn miracle he'd made it all the way to Delaware in this state.

Alcohol was also the reason he'd do something so ridiculous as driving here for a son who'd made it clear he wanted nothing to do with him.

Michael hated being in the same room as his dad. Looking at him now, no one would know that he'd once been a handsome bastard. So good-looking, he'd snared Michael's mom, the prettiest girl in Southie. Michael hated that he looked like his father and was grateful for the miracle of genetics that gave him his mother's blonde hair.

Just that little difference to separate him physically from the asshole in front of him.

Of course, Aengus Sullivan wasn't what he used to be. His face was haggard from smoking, and he had a gut from drinking.

"What are you doing here?" Michael was grateful he sounded calmer than he was feeling.

His father scrunched up his face in disgust, his voice loud when he answered, "You're on the news. My fuckin' waste-of-space son is on the news. And everyone is asking me why the fuck my son is in this pissy little town pissing away that detective badge he's so fuckin' smug about."

"Jesus," Cooper muttered behind him.

Michael's neck grew hot and he bit back the urge to lash out at his father. Was he so sick in the head, he'd come all this way to berate his own son? "Lower your voice."

Aengus curled his lip. "I know why you're here."

Before Michael could respond, his evening went from bad to worse as Cooper's door flew open, and Dahlia rushed in with Bailey at her back.

Jesus Christ.

His father turned to see what had grabbed his attention as Dahlia spotted him. The look of relief on her face turned to confusion when she recognized Aengus. She stepped toward them.

"And speak of the fuckin' devil."

"Dad." Michael grabbed his arm, jerking him back around. "I'm on duty right now, so let's step outside. You can say what you came here to say, and then you'll get the fuck out of my town."

"Your town?" He guffawed loudly, and the bar went silent.

Michael pinched the bridge of his nose as if it would somehow stop his headache and make his father disappear at the same time.

"You move to this nowhere little shithole on the sea for that piece behind me—"

"Watch it," Michael warned.

Aengus smirked as Dahlia got closer, his eyes flickering to her with malice. "And your mom tells me this girl doesn't even want you. You always thought you were better than me, but you're not better. You gave up a job I could be proud of you for to chase some tail down the East Coast, only to fumble on a fuckin' murder case. I'm here to talk sense into you. Come back to Boston, Mikey. Stop making a fool of yourself and make your old man proud for once."

Before Michael could even formulate a thought, Dahlia was in Aengus's face.

"How dare you?" she spat.

He sneered, opened his mouth to say something, but she put her palm inches from his face to shut him up.

"My turn. This is *my* town. And you do not come into my town, berate and insult the man I love, a man who is working his ass off. Do you hear me? You've never known what it means to be a good man so how could you possibly recognize it in anyone else? You have no honor. And you have no right to demand anything of Michael considering the shit you've put him through. Never mind whether *you're* proud of *him* ... what have you ever done to make *him* proud of *you*?"

Still reeling from hearing her tell his father—his *father*, not him—that she loved him, Michael's reaction time was slow. His father had already grabbed Dahlia around the wrist, to spit a retaliation in her face.

One second his father was in front of him, touching Dahlia, the next his face was slammed down on the bar top and Michael was clipping him into cuffs. "You're drunk," he said loudly enough so the patrons would understand why he'd gotten phys-ical. His heart hammered with rage. "You can spend some time in county jail getting sober before you get your ass in your car and leave."

Then he leaned down to whisper darkly in Aengus's ear, "You ever touch what's mine again, and that includes Mom, I'll fuckin' end you." He pulled him up, and his dad struggled against his hold.

"Want me to hit him?" Cooper looked like he'd take great pleasure in it.

Michael smirked, but he knew it was more of a snarl. "How about just letting me put him in your office until I can get a deputy out here. I need to get to that trailer."

Cooper nodded, and Michael shuffled his dad, who fought all the way down the hall. He shoved him inside, and Cooper locked the door behind him. His dad's drunken yells followed him down the hall.

Fuck, he was shaking.

"You okay?"

"What? Him?" Michael shrugged and then lied, "I stopped letting him get to me years ago."

"No, I meant Dahlia."

He glared at the door that would lead him back out to her. "Woman fucks me up."

Cooper was sympathetic. "Been there."

Bracing himself, he walked back out into the bar and tried to ignore Dahlia's big, concerned eyes. In fact, he brushed right past her and out the door. He didn't think he could talk to her without yelling. Plus, everyone was gawking.

Everything Dahlia said to his dad was great, but she should've said it to him. Which made him question the validity of it.

Was it pity?

Did she say that all out of fuckin' pity?

"Michael!"

He kept striding down the boards. There was too much pain he needed to stay locked up right now, and Dahlia had a habit of opening the door to it.

"Michael." She grabbed his arm, and something split open inside him as he spun to face her. Her beautiful face was taut with anguish. "Talk to me."

"About what?" he bit out. "About that awful fuckin' scene in there? About you facing off with that drunken dickwad because you felt sorry for me?" He bent his head to growl his ire in her face, "I don't need your fuckin' pity."

She was aghast. "It wasn't pity. It was the truth." She grabbed at him, but he shrugged her off. A mulish expression fell over her features. "I realized today that what I said to you this morning . . . it's . . . I have to fight it. I was just tired of always feeling guilty, and I thought to be with you would mean always feeling that way, but I need to let that go. I *know* I need to let that go. Michael, it hurts more to be without you. So much more."

Everything she was saying should've meant everything to him. It was what he wanted. But his dad's voice was ringing in his head, and now the last few weeks looked different than they had yesterday. What had been a determined pursuit of the woman he loved seemed more like a dog scratching at the door for scraps.

Now he questioned everything.

Did she love him like he loved her?

Would it always be a struggle to be with her, to get her to open up to him?

Would she always make him feel like he was failing . . . like his dad made him feel?

"I have to go," he muttered. "I'm on duty."

Michael was a little woozy, a little light-headed, as he turned to walk away, but he knew she'd let him go. He knew she wouldn't fight.

"Michael."

He faltered, hesitated at the plea in his name.

"I know what he said hurts. I understand better than anyone, so when the pain of that awful scene fades away, when you can see me clearly again, I'll be here. This time forever."

The words wrapped around him, almost like she'd put her arms around him and rested her head on his back. Was it enough? Could he trust that tomorrow she wouldn't wake up and remember that she was supposed to pay some kind of screwed-up penance to Dillon?

Exhausted, weary beyond measure, Michael walked away.

He had a job to do.

A killer to catch.

That was at least something he knew he could do.

All the rest would have to wait.

For once, *she* would have to wait for *him*.

33

Dahlia

I had a tight grasp on my panic as I parked my old Mini in my parking spot and got out of the car. What a day. It seemed never-ending. Between my morning with Michael, Jessica's heartbreaking revelations and the much-needed lightning bolt of perspective they'd given me, the encounter with Aengus Sullivan, and then Michael's dejected anger, I was a mess.

After Jessica's story, I went home to shower and change. I'd paced my apartment, going back and forth on how I should approach Michael, what I should say, and eventually decided to go to him and tell him I loved him. I'd gone to the station, only to discover Michael had taken a call at Cooper's. The deputy had muttered something about Michael being popular that day, and it all made sense when I turned up at Coop's to find Aengus Sullivan berating his son.

The rage I'd felt.

Oh, man. I'd never wanted to hurt someone the way I wanted to hurt Michael's father.

How dare he! My blood was still hot from the encounter as I let myself into my apartment block.

And Michael was so mad at me. I didn't blame him. Even when I wanted to yell at him, I couldn't. Because I got it. I absolutely understood. When a parent went off like Michael's dad had, it didn't matter how old the child was. It stung, and it locked a person inside his own head for a while.

But he'd come out of it. He would.

We'd work this out.

For the first time, I had hope.

Honest.

I wasn't panicking. I wasn't—

A muffled shout from my left intruded on my thoughts as I climbed the stairs. Eyebrows drawing together, I turned my head toward Ivy's apartment and cocked my ears to listen.

A loud shatter followed by the deep baritones of a male voice from inside the apartment sent a chill down my spine.

Ivy.

Goddamn it. This day really *was* never-ending.

Slipping back down the stairs, I quickly untied the ankle strap on my shoes so I could move without being heard. I winced at the cold tiles underfoot and scurried across the hall to Ivy's. Pressing my ear to her door, I could hear the muffled voice again. The guy's words were louder but unclear. Still, there was more than a hint of agitation in his tone.

Thinking it was better to be yelled at for being nosy than to ignore the gut feeling that told me Ivy was in trouble, I tried the door handle and held my breath when it opened with a soft click. Pushing it ever so slightly, the voices came to me loud and clear.

"Stop fucking around," a male voice whined. "I know you got money. That dead boyfriend of yours must have left you a shitload too."

Horror filled me.

I knew that voice.

It was Freddie Jackson.

Ivy sounded emotionless as she responded. "Even if I had it, transferring that kind of money doesn't happen overnight. There's a ten-grand transfer limit for online banking."

"Then you must have something I can pawn. Jewelry. Anything. I need money to disappear."

For a moment, I wondered how someone who had evaded arrest and a subsequent police hunt could be this stupid? Panic and desperation turned people into morons.

The thing was, it also made them dangerous, and Freddie had already killed.

Fear crawled over me at the reminder.

Ivy was in there alone with a killer.

Pushing the door open carefully, I slipped inside the apartment. Ivy's floor was covered with deep-pile carpet that masked my steps as I slid along the wall. The apartment opened from the short hall into a living room, like mine.

I swallowed past the lump of apprehension in my throat, heart hammering. I ignored the cold sweat gathering under my arms, and forced myself to peek around the wall.

Freddie stood in the center of the room in a shirt and jeans that looked too big for him. A baseball cap was drawn down over his head.

And he was pointing his gun at Ivy.

Ivy didn't look as emotionless as she sounded. There was fear in her dark eyes as she stood before him in her sweatpants and T-shirt. Shattered glass lay along the tiled hearth of the fireplace at her back.

"You give me the money, and I'll leave. You don't give me the money, I'm going to fuckin' shoot you in the head. And I will. I got nothing to lose."

"I-I-I can call my bank manager," Ivy said, nodding slowly. "It might take a few days."

"Are you listening, you dumb bitch?" He cocked the gun. "I don't have a few days."

Instinct took over.

One second I was behind the wall, the next I was diving at Freddie Jackson without any thought but to stop him from shooting Ivy. We slammed into the ground, Freddie's expletives filling my head. The gun fell into the thick carpet.

Adrenaline crashed through me as I lunged for it, my hands colliding with Freddie's. We started to wrestle. The little shit was stronger than he looked. I screamed in rage, pouring all my strength into the fight and—

BANG!

Agonizing pain tore through my shoulder, and I slumped, curling into myself. Fire streaked up my neck and down my arm, and I couldn't catch my breath.

"Dahlia McGuire." A wet glob hit my cheek and the realization I'd been spat on cut through the pain.

Furious, I turned to look up at him, feeling something warm and wet trickle down my shoulder. Blood.

The bastard had shot me.

He straddled me, the gun pointed at my face.

"Does that make you feel like a man? Murderer," I spat back at him, teeth gritted in agony.

His face crumpled in on itself with temper. "This is what happens to—" Surprise slackened his features. His eyes rolled.

And then he slumped over me and slid onto the carpet, unconscious.

Blinking in shock, I stared up at Ivy, brandishing an Academy Award statuette.

"Did ... did you just kill him with an Oscar?"

I didn't hear Ivy's response. Black dots spread across my vision. Lots and lots of black dots ... until there was nothing but black.

*

An irritating beeping noise filled my ears, bringing me out of sleep. Consciousness was followed by unbearable pain. I groaned, pushing my eyes open to see what the hell was burning my goddamn shoulder. Michael's face, fuzzy, appeared before me.

Michael?

My eyes slammed shut without my say.

"Dahlia, you're okay. You're going to be okay," an unfamiliar voice said. "We're on our way to the hospital. Just hold on."

I forced my eyes open, wanting to tell the unfamiliar voice that someone had set fire to my shoulder and could they please do something about that. But the words couldn't make it past the pain. Michael's face appeared again. Closer.

Something squeezed my hand.

Michael?

He leaned over me. "I'm here, dahlin'. Don't let go, okay? Don't ever let go."

I wanted to mumble "okay," but the darkness pulled me back under before I could get the word out.

34

Dahlia

There was that beeping noise again. Jesus Christ, it was irritating. This time as I swam up out of unconsciousness, the pain in my shoulder wasn't so bad. Not at all.

My eyelids were heavy, and it took me a couple of tries, blinking against fluorescent lights, to get them to stay open.

When they did, the first person I saw was Michael. He sat sprawled in a seat beside me, his eyes closed, his face pale beneath his natural tan. I wondered what he was doing in my bedroom. Then I processed how high my bed was.

And the beeping.

Christ, the beeping.

Without moving my head, I took in the room around me and realized I was in a hospital bed.

A needle with a drip was stuck in my hand.

The beeping was from the monitors above my head.

What . . .

A loud bang ricocheted in my ears, and I winced.

It was a memory. Just a memory.

Freddie Jackson shot me!

Indignation caused movement, and pain blasted down my arm from my right shoulder. Son of a bitch!

Michael jerked awake. His eyes were wide and haunted as he looked at me.

"Hey," I whispered.

Then something happened I'd never witnessed before.

Michael Sullivan bowed his head over my lap and started to cry.

Distress flooded me. I reached out with my good arm and sank my fingers into his hair to soothe him. "Baby," I hushed, "I'm okay, I'm okay."

He shuddered beneath my touch, and I felt him fight to control his emotions. Then he sat up, rubbed his hands hard down his face as he gazed at me with dark eyes still shiny with tears. Then he stood, braced himself over me, and kissed me.

I could taste the salt from his tears on my tongue.

When he broke the kiss, he sounded haggard. "Don't ever do that to me again."

I reached for his face, cupping it in my hand. "I love you."

Watching as he struggled to hold back more emotion, I fell even deeper in love. How that was possible, I had no idea.

"I love you too," he replied, his voice hoarse. "So fuckin' much, I swear it's going to kill me."

I laughed and then winced as pain flared up my neck. "I got shot," I said, sounding as indignant as I felt.

Michael's face clouded over. "That little fucker will pay for it."

The memory of Ivy smacking him across the head with her Oscar came to me. "Ivy didn't kill him?"

Michael smirked despite the hum of fury I could feel vibrating off him. "That statuette weighs over eight pounds, and it gave him a nasty concussion, but it didn't kill him. Unfortunately. He is in custody now, though."

"Shouldn't you be there interrogating him?" I trailed my fingers over his mouth. He curled his hand around them.

"I'm right where I'm supposed to be. Jeff is leading the

interviews. I do need to call him—I promised I would let him know as soon as you woke up."

"How long have I been out?"

"You went straight into surgery." He glanced at the wall behind me, presumably at a clock. "It's been a couple hours." He kissed me softly again. "I need to go tell a nurse you're awake. And I'll track Bailey and the girls down. Cooper and Vaughn forced them all to go to the cafeteria because they were driving me a little crazy."

I gave him a tired smile. I could only imagine.

"I called your dad," he said. "He's on his way."

Oh God, my dad. "He'll be worried."

"Of course, he is. He's your dad." Michael kissed me. "Okay," he whispered over my lips, "I'm going." But he kissed me again.

"Michael . . . " I tried to soothe him. "I'm not going anywhere. I'll be here when you get back. I promise."

The muscle in his jaw flexed. "What I said to you on the boards . . . I didn't mean it."

"Ssh. I know. But *I* did mean it. I'll wait forever for you, Michael Sullivan."

He shook his head. "No waiting required. I've been yours since day one."

After the doctor came in to see me, I realized why Michael had been so freaked out. I'd lost a lot of blood, and they'd had to give me a transfusion. But the shot was clean through (they found the bullet in Ivy's carpet), so that was good. I'd sustained some soft tissue damage, but I was young and healthy, and he was confident I'd make a full recovery.

When the doc left, Bailey, Jess, Emery, Cooper, Vaughn, Iris, Ira, and Ivy all crowded into my room while Michael stood by my side. Not for long. The nurse appeared as my friends clucked and cooed around me and demanded most of them leave.

Iris grabbed my free hand before the nurse expelled her. "I won't ever be able to thank you for what you did for my Ivy."

"Me neither." Ira's eyes shone with tears.

"Anytime." I pretended to be cool and nonchalant about it.

Ivy, who looked way more awake and alive than I'd seen her in a long time, followed her parents out but not before thanking me too. "You saved my life."

"You saved mine," I returned. She nodded, but I called out, "Ivy."

"Yeah?"

"Don't waste it. It's precious."

Ivy gave me a shaky nod before disappearing out of the room.

"I'm not leaving," Bailey insisted.

"Only three visitors at a time," the nurse said.

"Cooper and I are leaving," Vaughn said, attempting to placate the nurse. "Can't you let the ladies stay? They're like sisters to Dahlia."

"Two of them can stay or all three if the detective leaves."

Michael tensed at my side, and I glanced up at him as he crossed his arms over his chest.

Yeah, he wasn't leaving anytime soon.

"I could leave," Emery offered.

Vaughn gave her a slight shake of his head and then turned to the nurse. "Mabel, is it?" He flashed her a rare but beautiful smile. "Surely you won't deny them their chance to visit? Their best friend was shot, and they're scared. They need some reassurance."

Mabel exhaled heavily under his potent stare. "Fine. They can stay. But keep it down. Ms. McGuire needs her rest."

Cooper clapped Vaughn on the back and then leaned over to give his wife a quick kiss. His eyes came to me. "I'll see you soon, Wonder Woman."

I rolled my eyes but nodded.

Vaughn surprised me by coming over to the bed to press a kiss to my forehead. "Glad you're okay. I don't know what she'd do without you." He nodded at Bailey.

I gave him a fond smile of thanks.

Once the men—with the exception of Michael, of course—had departed, the girls pulled up seats around my bed. Once they had reassurances from me that I was okay, they chatted about the events of the last twenty-four hours. Their voices washed over me like a soothing bubble bath, and the comfort of having all my soul mates in the same room drew me into a healing sleep.

Whispers filtered into my subconscious, tugging me upward and out of the dark until my eyelids fluttered against the light.

My vision cleared and I took in the hospital room, remembering that Freddie Jackson had shot me.

Last time I'd been awake, the girls and Michael had been in the room with me.

Now I was surrounded.

I guess Mabel had lost her battle against the force of the McGuires.

An ache flared in my shoulder, but despite it, I smiled to see my family.

Dad occupied the chair Michael had when I'd first woken up, and he was whispering across the bed to Darragh, leaning against the wall with his ankles crossed. Davina was in the seat next to Dad, curled up with her knees to her chest, her head on her hand as she slept.

Dermot was sprawled across a chair on the other side of my bed, his head hanging back, his mouth open while he snored.

"How is anyone supposed to recover from a gunshot wound around here with that kind of racket going on?" I grumbled.

"Dahlia!" Dad was louder than I knew he meant to be as he

pushed out of the chair to press his cheek to mine. "God, Bluebell, you scared me to death."

"I'm okay, Dad." I patted his back.

Awake now, Dermot and Davina took turns hugging me gingerly after Darragh let go.

"Krista's with the boys in the cafeteria," Darragh said. "They'll be right back."

"Astrid is out of town," Davina added. "But she's flying out here today."

"I, uh . . . I told Mom," Dermot hesitated to say. "She's . . . she's not coming."

Even though I wasn't surprised, it stung. My mother's desertion would always be a wound buried deep in my chest.

"And I'm fuckin' done with her," Darragh bit out.

I flinched, not wanting that. "Dar, don't."

"No, Dahlia. Your kid gets shot, you get your ass on a plane to make sure she's all right. I don't want anything to do with her anymore."

"Dar . . . " My dad shook his head. "Let Dahlia rest."

My brother heaved an exasperated sigh. "Shit, I'm sorry, kiddo."

"It's okay." The subject hurt too much. Instead, my eyes went to Dad. "Where's Michael?"

Dad pressed my hand to his cheek, and I felt as well as saw him smile. "I forced him to go home for a shower. That was ten minutes ago, so my guess is he'll be back in another ten."

It was selfish, but I was glad. I wanted him with me. "I'm sorry I scared you all."

"You did," Dad agreed. "But I can hardly be mad about it when you saved a woman's life and helped the cops apprehend a killer."

The tips of my ears grew hot. "When you say it like that, it's very cool."

They laughed, and Davina nudged my leg. "I always said you had a hero complex."

I let my family's banter wash over me. Not too long later, we had to call for a nurse because I was in pain. She allowed my family to stay, and she didn't say a word when Michael returned, adding to the numbers. He kissed me on the lips in front of everyone and didn't even seem to care that I had hospital breath.

"You hungry?" he asked.

I was. A little.

Michael fed me spoonfuls of Jell-O, and I grinned between every bite, making him chuckle. Despite the pain, it was pretty great. I didn't feel mad about the gunshot wound so much anymore.

I was alive.

I had my family with me.

I was in love.

And I felt strong, infused with the power of forgiveness and devotion.

35

Michael

Hartwell, Delaware
THREE MONTHS LATER

The soft sunlight filtered through the gauzy curtains Dahlia had hung over the bedroom window. It spilled down over their bed, and Michael rested his chin on his arm as he watched Dahlia sleep.

Her sling had come off yesterday, and it was the first time in three months he'd seen her look relaxed in her sleep. There was still some pain. She'd been lucky—there had been no bone damage—but Michael thought she wouldn't be fully healed for another few months yet.

Her long lashes fluttered in her sleep and contentment washed over him.

She was beautiful. She didn't need a scrap of makeup to be beautiful. It shone out of her. Even more so since she'd charged to Ivy Green's rescue and helped him apprehend Freddie Jackson.

Nothing could ever have prepared Michael for the almost paralyzing fear that rushed over him when he saw Dahlia being wheeled out of her apartment building on a stretcher. To sit with her in the ambulance as she lay unconscious, chalk white ...

Shot.

He knew then he'd been wrong when he said he could exist

without her, but he couldn't live without her. Michael knew he couldn't even exist in a world where she was no more.

And he didn't give a fuck if that made him weak.

He reached out and trailed the back of his knuckles down her arm. They were a pair, him and her. The halves of one whole. Neither of them made sense without the other. Living together was proof of that. Michael had moved in with her during her recovery so he could take care of her. He'd helped her shower, he'd held her when she woke up, sweating with nightmares that were typical signs of trauma in a GSW victim, and he talked her through her fears since she didn't want to go back to seeing a therapist.

The nightmares eventually stopped.

But Michael never left.

She made him promise not to go.

The easiest fuckin' promise he'd ever made.

She shifted in her sleep, and he saw her nose crinkle in a little flinch. He scowled at her shoulder. She was sleeping on it.

Gently moving her, Michael rolled her to her back, and she moaned in her sleep.

He felt that moan in his gut and cursed himself.

In spite of her wound, Dahlia insisted on feeling him up every chance she got, the goddamn vixen. Michael grinned on a groan and fell onto his back. She'd talked him into fooling around about six weeks after she'd been shot and he'd given in because she was the hardest woman on the planet to resist.

But no sex.

That had pissed her off, but it was for her own good. There was no way to do it without jarring her shoulder.

He rubbed a hand over his eyes. It wasn't easy waiting to be with her again.

Feeling the heat gather in his lower spine and cock, Michael forced his thoughts elsewhere.

He had to be up for work soon. So did Dahlia. The height of the season had kicked in now that summer was upon Hartwell, and Dahlia's shop needed to open. Michael knew it was best for her to be at work, to get on with life as normally as possible, but he'd also asked her to hire someone to help her out at the shop for a while.

A seventeen-year-old artist whose wealthy family owned a summer house in the Glades had jumped at the chance to work with Dahlia. Dahlia was enjoying teaching the girl about metalsmithing, so it was a win-win.

As for Hartwell itself, it was trying to find its feet again. Freddie Jackson couldn't make bail, so he was in jail awaiting his trial. As for the Devlins ... it looked like those fuckers might get away clean. Freddie had confessed to sharing confidential information with the Devlins and harassing certain members of the public upon Ian Devlin's request. Devlin had been arrested, but they had to let him go on the grounds of insufficient evidence.

The fuck.

There was nothing substantial to tie Freddie's story to the Devlins. He said he panicked when Michael arrived, afraid he would lose everything, and he'd gone to Stu for help. He said Stu told him it wouldn't be a problem anymore, that the cops would find Freddie's apartment filled with enough coke to put him away, so he wouldn't be around to fuck everything up for the Devlin family. When Freddie tried to reason with him, Stu kept saying he didn't know what Freddie was talking about, laughing all the time, like it was a joke.

Freddie lost his temper.

Stu came at him as if to attack him, and Freddie shot him.

The Devlins had gone quiet for now. But Michael was determined to bring Ian Devlin down. He'd find a way. It helped that the media furor that had sprung up after Freddie had shot Dahlia had died down. Ivy Green's involvement was too exciting for the media, so Hartwell had been in the news for weeks.

A breathy little moan brought Michael's head around, and he watched as Dahlia blinked against the light.

Eyes the color of bluebells, ringed by the darkest lashes, gazed sleepily into his. She gave him a cute little smile, her dimple playing peek-a-boo with him. "Hey, you."

"Hey yourself." He rolled onto his side. "How's your shoulder?"

She pushed up to sitting and grimaced. "A little sore."

"You slept on it. I had to nudge you onto your back."

Dahlia shot him a saucy look. "I'm sorry I missed that."

He groaned in frustration. "Don't start."

She turned toward him, and he recognized the mischievous glint in her expression. Oh God, save him from this fuckin' temptress.

Then God did.

Dahlia blinked, her face clouding over. "I just remembered my dream. Ugh. It was not good." She shot him a filthy look.

Michael sat up, pushing his pillow against the headboard. "I'm guessing I did not behave well in this dream."

She narrowed her eyes as they dipped down over his naked torso and back up again. "You were on the boardwalk with your ex-wife. I kept calling your name, but this little boy appeared that looked like you and you took his hand and hers and walked away."

That was a dose of heavy he had not been expecting. "Hey." He reached for her hand and pulled her gently into him. She rested her head against the headboard, her eyes on their entwined hands. Michael placed his fingers beneath her chin and nudged, forcing her to make eye contact.

"We've been through so much shit. You cannot tell me after all of that, you've got insecurities about Kiersten."

Dahlia shook her head. "I didn't think so. Maybe the dream

was more about the kid." She seemed to hedge and then took a deep breath. It sounded shaky, which made him nervous. "Do you still want kids? With me?"

Honestly, it was something he hadn't thought about in a long time. But it wasn't something he needed to deliberate over. The answer was clear. And the thought filled him with so much anticipation, he almost couldn't stand it. "I want that." His voice was thick with emotion.

Her smile was slow and a little wobbly. "I gave up on that dream a long time ago because I never wanted marriage and kids unless it was with you. I'm not saying we have to rush into it ... I just wanted to know that it's an option for us."

He kissed her hard, leaning his forehead against hers. "It's definitely an option for us."

They were silent a moment, drinking in the idea of that beautiful future.

Then she whispered, "Do you hear from her? Kiersten? Ever?"

"Nope." He answered. "When she said she wanted out, she meant completely."

"Is that not weird for you? Even a little? You did spend four years with her."

Michael thought about it, knowing his answer mattered more than he wished it did. Finally, he said, "It feels like a weird dream or another life. Nothing feels as real as you."

Dahlia

I knew my dream about Michael's ex-wife was only a stupid *dream*. After the traumas we'd been through, his ex-wife would not be another. But subconsciously, I must've worried if it was as easy for Michael to let go of that relationship as he'd let on.

Maybe it was callous of me, but I was glad he'd let Kiersten go as easily as he had. After spending three months living with him, knowing the joy of it—even when he irritated me with his neatness and healthy eating—I was possessive of this knowledge. I hated that another woman had it.

I wanted to erase her from his memory, and that was selfish and Neanderthal-like—and I didn't care one iota.

His sweet words of assurance melted through me, as did the knowledge that one day we'd have kids. That stoked a fire in me that was unexpected, but welcome. I rose over him, swinging my leg across his opposite hip to straddle him. I ignored the twinge in my shoulder.

"What are you doing?" Michael's voice was hoarse as he gripped my waist.

Schooling my expression, I lifted my T-shirt over my head and stoically avoided flinching at a bite of pain in my shoulder. I wasn't wearing a bra, so I was good to go.

Michael's hot eyes fell on my breasts, and his hands flexed against my waist. "Dahlia," he said, "fooling around only."

I shook my head, so ready to have him inside me, I couldn't even stand it. "The bases are wonderful. Phenomenal even. But I'm ready for that home run." Slipping my hands between us, I pushed at the sheets around his waist.

Michael grabbed my hands to halt me. "Your shoulder."

"Is much better." I leaned in and pressed a soft kiss to his gorgeous mouth. He'd shaved off his beard three days ago, and I couldn't decide whether I missed it or loved seeing all of his handsome face again. "I'll ride you. Gently. Slowly."

He hardened beneath my lap. "Dahlia ... "

I kissed him deeply, hungrily, and as he lost himself in the sexy kisses, I pushed down my underwear, only breaking the kiss to flick them off completely.

"We should wait," Michael murmured, his eyes devouring me.

Yeah, he didn't sound too sure about that.

Shoving down the sheets, I tugged his pajama pants down over his erection.

"Let me take them off," he grunted.

"No." I was almost drooling at the sight of him straining and hot and hard. "I can't wait." Then without preamble, I straddled him, guided him between my legs, and sank down with a pleasurable sigh.

It didn't take long.

For either of us.

We came together, wrapped tightly in each other's arms, my inner muscles pulsing in little aftershocks around Michael every time he murmured the words "I love you" against my skin.

EPILOGUE

Michael

Striding into the sheriff's department, Michael was in a good mood. Beyond good. Phenomenal. Memories of that morning kept playing over and over in his head, and he knew he was sporting a stupid-ass smile on his face.

When Bridget told him Jeff wanted to see him first thing, her expression grim, he inwardly cursed.

Something was up.

Dammit.

It was always when you were in a tremendous fuckin' mood.

Sighing, Michael nodded to his colleagues who were in the office and made his way to Jeff's. Everything between him and his boss was settled. There had been a bit of tension when Michael moved in with Dahlia, but Jeff was a solid guy. Seeing how happy Dahlia was, he let it go. Not surprisingly, he let it go enough to pursue a friendship outside of work. Michael considered Jeff a good friend now.

If he was calling him into his office first thing, that wasn't a good sign.

Before he could get there, Jeff appeared in the corridor. He nodded at Michael as he approached, his whole countenance heavy with gravity.

"What's going on?"

"I need you in Interview Room One." Jeff kept his voice lowered. "We had a walk-in this morning. A confession of murder."

Michael's lips parted in shock. "Stu Devlin?"

Jeff shook his head. "No, Freddie's confession still stands." He motioned for Michael to follow him. As they crossed to the interview room, Michael's mind raced. No murders in Hartwell in twelve years and now there were two? So much for the quiet life.

Jeff led him into the interview room, and Michael's eyes alighted on the person sitting alone at the table.

A young woman.

He and Jeff took their seats opposite her, and she looked at them with big blue-gray eyes. Her dark blond hair was cut short, skimming her narrow jawline. Michael studied her. Pretty, but much too thin. Her cheekbones were prominent, her eyes hollow. She looked like a stiff wind would blow her over.

Her expression was nothing short of haunted.

Michael felt uneasiness settle in his gut.

"Rebecca, this is Detective Michael Sullivan. He'll be sitting in on the interview."

She flicked a nervous glance at Michael and squeezed her small hands together in front of her. She nodded.

Jeff switched on a digital recorder and placed it in the middle of the table.

"Please state your name for the record," Jeff said.

She licked her dry, chapped lips. "I'm Rebecca Rosalie Devlin."

Surprise rooted Michael to the spot. *What the fuck?*

"I have advised you, Rebecca, not to do this interview without a lawyer present but you have chosen to proceed without a lawyer, is that correct?"

"Yes," she whispered.

"Please tell us in your own words why you're here, Rebecca."

Her gaze moved between Michael and Jeff, and any color that was in her cheeks drained out. "I'm here to confess to a murder that my brother, Stuart Devlin, and I covered up four years ago."

Always the professional, Michael kept his face blank but he reeled inside.

Well ... fuck, he thought, *I did not see that coming.*

Dahlia

"I think we should invite Ivy to our lady gatherings," Bailey said.

She, Emery, Jess, and I were strolling down the boards with frozen goodness in hand. It was too hot in the bookstore so we'd all closed up shop during Jess's lunch break and grabbed an ice cream together to celebrate my lack of a sling.

"I'm up for it." I nodded. "Ivy and I share a bond now."

It was true. In the three months since Freddie Jackson had attacked us, Ivy stopped by my shop every week to chat. There was something still faraway about her, like she was living in her head somewhere elsewhere the rest of us couldn't reach, but she was much better than she had been. She hated the apartment, of course, and had temporarily moved back in with her parents. She was, however, about to close on a very nice place on Johnson's Creek. She didn't want to move back to Hollywood but wouldn't tell us why, so we could only guess at the reason. But she'd started to write again, which I took as a good sign.

She and Bailey were also hanging out again, and it was pretty darn hard to be miserable around Bailey Hartwell. I knew that firsthand.

Jess shrugged. "Sure. I don't know if I'll have anything in common with a stunning Hollywood screenwriter, but I'm game."

"She's not like that," Bailey promised. "Ivy can get along with anyone."

We wandered in silence—Emery hadn't given her approval for the idea.

I shared a look with Bailey and then Jess as Emery stared ahead.

I nudged Emery. "Em, you're awfully quiet about it."

She pursed her pretty mouth. "We're not in high school. You don't need my permission to add someone to our group."

"But?"

"No buts."

"There's a but," Jess surmised.

"Definitely a but," Bailey added.

"A big one."

Emery rolled her eyes. "It's nothing."

"Oh, for the love of God, spit it out," Bailey said.

Flushing, Emery threw her a dirty look. I also saw that as a good sign. Every day she trusted us more and more to be herself. "Stop trying to embarrass me."

"Then talk." Bailey bit into her ice cream and then made a face. "Brain freeze."

Ignoring her antics, I turned to Emery. "Is there something you don't like about Ivy?"

"It's not Ivy." Emery stopped and leaned against the railing, looking out at the ocean. We followed suit, crowding around her. "You guys ... you guys feel like my family. I feel comfortable around you. I'm worried that'll change with someone else around."

I snuggled into Emery's side and pressed an affectionate kiss to her bare shoulder. She looked down at me in surprise, and I grinned. "Then we wait."

"Yeah," Bailey agreed. "It can just be us for a while."

"It's terribly selfish of me," Emery said. "Ivy probably needs good friends too."

"Ach, she's got Bailey. That's enough for anyone to handle."

"Hey!" My best friend whacked me on my shoulder.

I pretended to wince. "Gunshot wound!"

Her face paled. "Oh my God, I'm so sorry!"

I grinned. "Wrong shoulder."

"You are such a brat."

"What was that about high school?" Jess asked Emery.

Em didn't smile. "We can invite Ivy to our lady gatherings. I'm being selfish."

"Let's just see what happens," Jess offered. "Let things take their natural course."

Emery relaxed and we stood in comfortable silence, enjoying the way the sun glittered over the water, the waves lapped at the shore, the laughter of kids as they ran circles around their parents on the soft, hot sand.

Gulls cried overhead while the sounds of arcade games played somewhere in the distance.

"I've been here almost ten years," I said. "And I've never been happier than I am right now."

Bailey slid her arm around my waist and gave it a squeeze. "It feels like things are falling into place."

"Yeah," Jess said. "About that ... "

We turned to her expectantly.

Tears shone in her eyes. Happy tears. "I'm pregnant."

I was sure our squeals of delight scared the absolute crap out of anyone in our vicinity, but we didn't care. We crowded Jess, taking turns to hug her and pepper her with questions.

"Yes, of course, Cooper knows." She laughed at Bailey's query.

"How, why, when?" I blurted.

"Well, we've been trying for a while, and I was starting to

worry that I couldn't. But then it happened." She looked relieved. "Coop's hovering because he didn't know that once a woman hits thirty-five, it's considered a mature pregnancy, and there are more tests involved."

"Are you too hot?" Emery asked. "Maybe we should get in the shade."

"I'm fine," Jess assured her. "Please, don't you guys start hovering too."

"How far along are you?"

"Twenty weeks. We wanted to keep it quiet. Miscarriages are common in those early weeks."

As we strode toward Main Street, we planned our future as aunts.

"Everything *is* falling into place." Bailey sighed in contentment. "All we need now is for Emery to meet a guy."

"Yes, I'm sure I'll snag a fine eligible bachelor with my witty repartee and finely honed seduction skills."

I snorted at Em's sarcasm.

Bailey rolled her eyes. "Now, what kind of attitude is that?"

"An honest one." Her gaze turned melancholy. "Let's focus our wishes on something that might happen. Say ... " She turned to me. "You and Michael getting engaged."

I grinned not only at her using me to take the heat off her but at the thought of being Michael's fiancée.

"One day." I was confident of that.

That evening I let myself into the apartment with takeout in hand. Michael had called to let me know he was finishing up at the station and he'd agreed to Chinese food. He was a health nut, but I'd persuaded him that one treat a month would not kill him.

After I'd gotten off the phone with him, my sister called to check on me. I heard from at least one member of my family every day, but I wasn't complaining.

It was pretty freaking great.

Plus Darragh, Krista, and the boys were taking a vacation in Hartwell with Dad in two weeks. Davina, Astrid, and Dermot would stop by for one of the weekends too. I couldn't wait.

Dumping the cartons of Chinese food in the kitchen, I rolled my shoulder and winced. Michael would lecture me for carrying the food upstairs, and maybe he was right. Grumbling to myself and my impatient desperation to be fully healed, I strolled through the apartment to our bedroom to change into yoga pants and a comfy T-shirt.

As I walked toward the closet, however, something shining on the bed caught my eye.

Frowning because there hadn't been anything on it when Michael made it that morning, I walked over to it.

My pulse raced as recognition moved through me and I rounded the bed on shaky legs.

I stood, looking down at the object as goose bumps rose all over my body.

The silver rose brooch I'd made for Dillon sat perched in the middle between my pillow and Michael's. Like a bridge between the two.

The silver rose brooch I kept locked in a treasure box I was pretty sure Michael didn't even know existed was on our bed?

"Earth to Dahlia," Michael's voice broke through.

I glanced up, surprised to see him standing in the doorway.

He frowned. "You okay?"

I looked down at the brooch. "Did you put that there?"

Michael stared at it and shrugged. "No. What is it?"

Knowing he was telling the truth, the little hairs all down my arms stood on end.

Dillon.

Not answering him, I hurried to the closet, pulling the little decorative chair over that I kept in the corner of the room. The one I usually piled clothes on, driving my neat-freak boyfriend nuts. Stepping up onto it, I pushed through the shoeboxes arranged on the top shelf and felt for my treasure box.

"Dahlia, what the hell are you doing?" Michael huffed. "Watch what you're doing with your shoulder."

"I am," I grunted, pulling out the box.

It was still locked.

Jumping down off the chair, I hurried past a very confused Michael and back through the apartment to the sideboard in our living room. Opening it, I searched through until I found the trinket box I was looking for.

Pulling it out, I flipped it open. Small familiar keys sat inside.

The keys to my treasure box. Right where I'd left them.

"You want to tell me what's going on?" Michael followed me as I hurried back to the bedroom and to the treasure box. My hands shook as I opened it.

Inside were letters between me, Davina, and Dillon when we were younger. Letters from Aunt Cecilia. A movie ticket stub from the first movie Michael had taken me to, and a letter my dad had sent me when I first moved to Hartwell. No brooch, even though I'd kept it locked in that box for years. No brooch.

Because it was on our bed.

Somehow.

I shut the box and rounded the bed again to stare at the silver rose.

Dillon.

An unbelievable sense of peace moved through me. Eyes bright with tears, I looked up at Michael.

"What am I missing?"

I smiled, the tears spilling over. "It's Dillon."

Michael moved around the bed as I reached for the brooch.

Curling my hand around it, I turned to him as he wrapped his arms around me. I melted into him. "I made it for her. Years ago. It's the only thing of hers that I kept."

Michael reached for it with one hand while he kept his other tight around me. He studied the brooch. "I remember it. It's beautiful."

"I kept it locked in that treasure box, Michael."

Understanding dawned. "You've never moved it?"

I shook my head. "I haven't looked at that brooch in years. It was buried at the bottom of my treasure box. I came in here to change, and it was just ... there."

"And you think ... you think it was Dillon?" I could hear the uncertainty in his voice. Michael was a realist, not given to flights of fancy or notions about ghosts, but the circumstances were weird, and he knew it.

I didn't know if it was Dillon. I'd never believed in that kind of stuff before.

But something had settled in my soul at the idea of my little sister finding a way to send me a message. To tell me she was happy for Michael and me.

"I don't know," I whispered. Joy, so much I could burst with it, warmed me from the inside out. "But I'd like to think so."

Love blazed from Michael's eyes as he dipped his head to kiss me softly.

"I love you, Michael."

"I know." His arms tightened around me. "I love you too."

"I'm going to say it until you're tired of hearing it. I'm going to say it for all the times I left it unsaid."

"There's only one thing wrong with that plan," Michael replied, easing me gently down on the bed and covering my body with his. "I'm never going to tire of hearing it, dahlin'. Not in this lifetime, or the next."

Keep reading for the first chapter of *Fight or Flight*, Samantha
Young's standalone contemporary romance ...

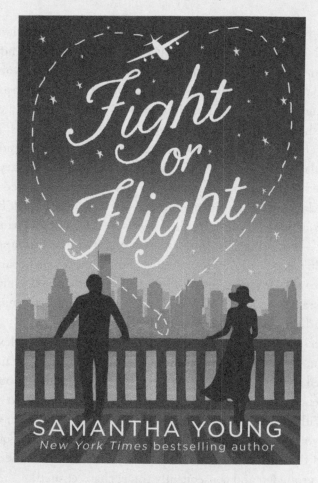

Available now from

piatkus

Food. Food and coffee. I knew those should be my priority. The grumbles in my belly were making that perfectly clear. And considering the purpose for my visit to Phoenix, it was no wonder I was marching through the terminal after having my bag searched in security, feeling like I might claw someone's face off if I didn't get a shot of caffeine in my system.

Even though I was hangry, my priority was to get upgraded to first class on my flight home to Boston. I could be hangry all I wanted in an airport. But as I was someone who suffered from mild claustrophobia, sitting in coach—with my luck stuck beside someone who would take their shoes *and* socks off during the flight—would be a million times worse than being hangry. I couldn't chance it. A pair of strange, hot, sweaty, smelly bare feet next to me for four and a half hours? No, that was a hell my current state of mind couldn't deal with. I shuddered as I marched toward the desk at my gate.

Seeing a small group of people crowded under a television screen, I faltered, wondering what had drawn them to the news. I slowed at the images of huge plumes of smoke billowing out of a tremendously large mountain, my curiosity drawing me to a halt.

Within a few seconds the news told me that an unpronounceable volcano in Iceland had erupted, creating this humungous ash cloud that was causing disruption in Europe. Flights there had been grounded and consequently travel chaos ensued.

The thought of being stuck in an airport for an indeterminate number of hours—days even—made me shudder in sympathy for my poor fellow human beings.

I couldn't imagine dealing with that on top of the week I'd just had. I liked to think I was someone who was usually cool and collected, but lately my emotions were so close to the surface I was almost afraid of them. I asked the universe to forgive me my self-absorption, thankful that I was not someone who wasn't going to make it home today, and continued on my path to the gate desk. There was no one in line, and the man behind it began to smile in welcome as I approached.

"Hi, I was wondering—*Oof!*" I winced as a laptop bag attached to a big guy whacked against my right shoulder, knocking me back on my heels. The big guy didn't even realize he'd hit me as he strode right past and cut in ahead of me.

Rude!

"I'd like tae upgrade tae first class, please," he said in a deep, loud, rumbling, very attractive accent that did nothing to soothe my annoyance with him for cutting in front of me.

"Of course, sir," the gate agent answered, in such a flirtatious tone I was sure that if I'd been tall enough to see over the big guy's shoulder I would see the agent batting his lashes at him. "Okay, flight DL180 to Boston. You're in luck, Mr. Scott. We have one seat left in first class."

Oh, hell no!

"What?" I shoved my way up next to Rude Guy, not even looking at him.

The gate agent, sensing my tone, immediately narrowed his eyes at me and thinned his lips.

"I was coming here to ask for an upgrade on this flight and he"—I gestured to my right—"cut in front of me. You saw him do it."

"Miss, I'm going to ask you to calm down and wait your turn. Although we have a very full flight today, I can put you on our list and if a first-class seat opens up, we will let you know."

Yeah, because the way my week was going, *that* was likely.

"I was first," I insisted, my skin flushing as my blood had turned so hot with anger at the unfairness. "He whacked me with his laptop bag pushing past me to cut in line."

"Can we just ignore this tiny, angry person and upgrade me now?" the deep, accented voice said somewhere above my head to my right.

His condescension finally drew my gaze to him.

And everything suddenly made sense.

A modern-day Viking towered over me, my attention drawing his from the gate agent. His eyes were the most beautiful I'd ever seen. A piercing ice blue against the rugged tan of his skin, the irises like pale blue glass bright against the sun streaming in through the airport windows. His hair was dark blond, short at the sides and longer on top. And even though he was not my type, I could admit his features were entirely masculine and attractive with his short, dark blond beard. It wasn't so much a beard as a thick growth of stubble. He had a beautiful mouth, a thinner top lip but a full, sensual lower lip that gave him a broody, boyish pout at odds with his ruggedness. Gorgeous as his mouth may be, it was currently curled upward at one corner in displeasure.

And did I mention he was built?

The offensive laptop bag was slung over a set of shoulders so broad they would have made a football coach weep with joy. I was guessing he was just a little over six feet, but his build made him look taller. I was only five foot three but I was wearing four-inch stilettos, and yet I felt like Tinkerbell next to this guy.

Tattoos I didn't take the time to study peeked out from under the rolled-up sleeve of his henley shirt. A shirt that showed off the kind of muscle a guy didn't achieve without copious visits to the gym.

A fine male specimen, indeed.

I rolled my eyes and shot the agent a knowing, annoyed look. "Really?" It was clear to me motorcycle-gang-member-Viking-dude was getting preferential treatment here.

"Miss, please don't make me call security."

My lips parted in shock. "Melodramatic much?"

"You." The belligerent rumble in the Viking's voice made me bristle.

I looked up at him.

He sneered. "Take a walk, wee yin."

Being deliberately obtuse, I retorted, "I don't understand Scandinavian."

"I'm Scottish."

"Do I care?"

He muttered something unintelligible and turned to the agent. "We done?"

The guy gave him a flirty smile and handed him his ticket and passport. "You're upgraded, Mr. Scott."

"Wait, what—?" But the Viking had already taken back his passport and ticket and was striding away.

His long legs covered more ground than mine, but I was motivated and I could run in my stilettos. So I did. With my carry-on bumping along on its wheels behind me.

"Wait a second!" I grabbed the man's arm and he swung around so fast I tottered.

Quickly, I regained balance and shrugged my suit jacket back into place as I grimaced. "You should do the right thing here and give me that seat." I didn't know why I was being so persistent. Maybe because I'd always been frustrated when I saw someone else endure an injustice. Or maybe I was just sick of being pushed around this week.

His expression was incredulous. "Are you kidding me with this?" I didn't even try not to take offense. Everything about this guy offended me.

"*You*"—I gestured to him, saying the word slowly so his tiny brain could compute—"*Stole. My. Seat.*"

"*You*"—he pointed down at me—"*Are. A. Nutjob.*"

Appalled, I gasped. "One, that is not true. I am *hangry*. There is a difference. And two, that word is completely politically incorrect."

He stared off into the distance above my head for a moment, seeming to gather himself. Or maybe just his patience. I think it was the latter because when he finally looked down at me with those startling eyes, he sighed. "Look, you would be almost funny if it weren't for the fact that you're completely unbalanced. And I'm not in the mood after having tae fly from Glasgow tae London and London tae Phoenix and Phoenix tae Boston instead of London tae Boston because my PA is a useless prat who clearly hasn't heard of international direct flights. So do us both a favor before I say or do something I'll regret . . . and walk. Away."

"You *don't* regret calling me a nutjob?"

His answer was to walk away.

I slumped in defeat, watching him stride off with the first-class ticket that should have been mine.

Deciding food and coffee could wait until I'd freshened up in the restroom—and by freshen up I meant pull myself together—I wandered off to find the closest one. Staring out of the airport window at Camelback Mountain, I wished to be as far from Phoenix as possible as quickly as possible. That was really the root of my frustration, and a little mortification began to set in as I made my way into the ladies' restroom. I'd just taken my emotional turmoil out on a Scottish stranger. Sure, the guy was terminally rude, but I'd turned it into a "situation." Normally I would have responded by calmly asking the agent when the next flight to Boston was and if there was a first-class seat available on that flight.

But I was just so desperate to go home.

After using the facilities, I washed up and stared long and hard into the mirror. I longed to splash cold water on my face, but that would mean ruining the makeup I'd painstakingly applied that morning.

Checking myself over, I teased my fingers through the waves I'd put in my long blonde hair with my straightening iron. Once I was happy with it, I turned my perusal on my outfit. The red suit was one of the nicest I owned. A double-breasted peplum jacket and a matching knee-length pencil skirt. Since the jacket looked best closed, I was only wearing a light, silk ivory camisole underneath it. I didn't even know why I'd packed the suit, but I'd been wearing black for the last few days and the red felt like an act of defiance. Or a cry for help. Or maybe more likely an act of denial.

Although I had a well-paid job within an exclusive interior design company as one of their designers, it was expensive to live in Boston. The diamond tennis bracelet on my wrist was a gift on my eighteenth birthday from an ex-boyfriend. For a while I'd stopped wearing it, but exuding an image of success to my absurdly wealthy and successful clients was important, so when I started my job I'd dug the bracelet out of storage, had it cleaned up, and it had sat on my wrist ever since.

Lately, just looking at it cut me to the quick.

Flinching, I tore my gaze from where it winked in the light on my arm, to my right wrist, where my Gucci watch sat. It was a bonus from my boss, Stella, after my first year on the job.

As for the black suede Jimmy Choos on my feet, with their sexy stiletto and cute ankle strap, they were one of many I was in credit card debt over. If I lived anywhere but Boston, I would have been able to afford as many Choos as I wanted on my six-figure salary. But my salary went into my hefty monthly rent bill.

It was a cute, six-hundred-square-foot apartment, but it was in Beacon Hill. Mount Vernon Street to be exact, a mere few minutes' walk from Boston Common. It also cost me just over four thousand dollars a month in rent. That didn't include the rest of my bills. I had enough to put some savings away after the tax man took his cut too, but I couldn't afford to indulge in the Choos I wanted.

So, yes, I'd reached the age of thirty with some credit card debt to my name.

But I guessed that made me like most of my fellow countrymen and -women, right? I stared at my immaculate reflection, ignoring the voice in my head that said some of those folks had credit card debt because of medical bills, or because they needed to feed their kids that week.

Not so they could live in a ridiculously overpriced area of Boston (no matter how much I loved it there) or wear designer shoes so their clients felt like they were dealing with someone who understood their wants better.

I bypassed the thought, not needing to mentally berate myself any more than I had since arriving back in Phoenix. I was perfectly happy with my life before I came home.

Perfectly happy with my perfect apartment, and my perfect hair, and my perfect shoes!

Perfect was good.

I straightened my jacket and grabbed hold of the handle of my carry-on.

Perfect was control.

Staring at the pretty picture I made in the mirror, I felt myself relax. If that gate agent had been into women, I *so* would have gotten that first-class seat.

"But forget it," I whispered. It was done.

I was going to go back out there and get a much-needed delicious Mediterranean-style salad and sandwich from one of my favorite food stops in Phoenix, Olive & Ivy. Feeling better at the thought, I relaxed.

Once I stopped being hangry, it would all be fine.